By Norman Collins

NOVELS

Bond Street Story
Children of the Archbishop
London Belongs to Me
Anna
Love in Our Time
"I Shall not Want"
Flames Coming Out of the Top
Trinity Town
The Three Friends
Penang Appointment
The Bat That Flits (a thriller)

FOR CHILDREN

Black Ivory

CRITICISM

The Facts of Fiction

The Governor's Lady

Norman Collins

Simon and Schuster : New York

First U.S. Printing

SBN 671–20318–5
Library of Congress Catalog Card Number: 79–79627
Designed by Irving Perkins
Manufactured in the United States of America
By American Book–Stratford Press, Inc.

for Joan and Bob

CONTENTS

FOREWORD

Look in the atlas and you won't find Amimbo there. Consult the Colonial List of the 'twenties and 'thirties and you will see nothing about Sir Gardnor Hackforth, C.V.O.; or Mr. Arthur Drawbridge, C.B.E.; or Mr. Harold Stebbs, for that matter. Debrett's contains no mention of Lady Anne; and even the telephone directory does not give a line to Sybil Prosser. African reference works are similarly unrevealing on the subject of Prince Ngono, once of Sidney Sussex, and Mr. Talefwa, B.Sc.Econ. (Lond.). Again, no legal register along the entire West Coast gives any entry for Mr. Chabundra Das, Barrister-at-law.

Nor are these omissions surprising. The place and all the characters are entirely fictitious. Some of the birds and animals are, however, taken direct from nature, and I am happy to acknowledge my debt to them.

Epilogue, Part One

A Case of Conscience

THE FAN, badly worn at its bearings through incessant use, kept up an unpleasant jarring sound in the darkness overhead. Sooner or later, the Chief Magistrate assumed, it would come down, scattering things, breaking bottles and glasses, possibly killing somebody.

In the meantime, the heat demanded it. All day the temperature had been away up in the top nineties. And so had the humidity. In consequence, everything in the room was sticky, misted over as though it had been sprayed with something. The red binding of the *Times* Book Club novel that he had finished earlier that evening had left him with a broad strawberry-colored stain right across his thumb and forefinger.

With the coming on of night, it was cooler. Much cooler. But all during the day, the wooden walls had simply been absorbing the sunlight. Devouring it. Now they were giving it out again. They were like radiators.

Even out there on the veranda, the air was still tepid, heavy and stagnant with the sour-sweet, dungheapy smell of the tropics. The whole atmosphere seemed in need of stirring. Indoors, as long as it lasted, the fan did at least achieve that. And there was always the chance that the next train from Motamba would bring the new fan that Stores had ordered. Or, if not the next train, the one after; or the one after that.

The Chief Magistrate reached out his hand automatically to thrust the yellow-labeled gin bottle in the direction of the man sitting opposite. They had been there, simply the two of them, for a long time. Ever since ten o'clock, in fact. And it was well past midnight by now.

If they needed another bottle of Gordon's, the C.M. would have to go in search of it himself. That was because quite early on, when the houseboy had come through on his bare feet, his white gown flapping sloppily around his enormous ankles, the C.M. had sent him away again; told him to go to bed and not squat at the bottom of the steps as he usually did.

The C.M. felt that the fewer people who might overhear the conversation the better. He didn't want it to go circulating all round Kubunda tomorrow; didn't want it to go circulating at all, in fact. Already he had the distinctly distasteful feeling that he, the sole listener to these confidences, had somehow been one too many.

But he could hardly be rude to the Governor. He couldn't simply refuse to listen. Not just snub him like that. He had warned him, of course, had asked rather pointedly whether it was in his private or his official capacity that the Governor, Harold Stebbs, was addressing him. And the Governor had evaded the point. He had merely said something to the effect that they had rung up from the House, hadn't they, to say that he might be coming over? Rather deliberately, it seemed, H.E. had left it in the air like that.

Not that the visit itself was so unusual. Or rather, not so unusual as it would have been even a few months ago. The fact was that the Governor had been growing increasingly restless of late. Only last night at the Club, the Financial Secretary had remarked on it. From being practically a recluse, the Governor, he observed, seemed suddenly to have developed a strong taste for human company; and it was particularly in the evenings that H.E. seemed most anxious not to find himself alone.

He had even taken to inviting people up to Government House for drinks before dinner; quite unimportant people, very often, with no influence of any kind in the whole Colony. Naturally enough they had been flattered, but left a little bewildered. The more intelligent of them had come away half suspecting that anyone else would have done as well. Some of them, taken entirely by surprise and with their wives left unexpectedly high and dry at the bungalow down below somewhere, had even been asked, almost begged, to stay on afterwards for a meal in the long blue dining room with the slanting white shutters and the bad, highly varnished portrait of the Queen, with only the very small talk of the A.D.C. to keep the conversation going.

The darkness on the veranda opened for a moment. The Governor was lighting another of the mild, meaningless Dutch cigars that he always smoked. The C.M. could see him framed in the little circle of the match light. It was certainly not a strong face that was revealed there. Ordinary, rather. Neat, regular features, with thin, graying hair and an overclipped moustache like a small white butterfly resting insecurely on his upper lip.

There was nothing in the least remarkable about his appearance, except for the black silk eye patch; and even that was worn unassumingly. His expression, too, was retiring rather than assertive. He shared it with a lot of other senior Colonial Servants —that resigned, rather withdrawn look of habitual authority: it was the price that had to be paid for a lifetime spent resisting the blandishments of colored politicians on the spot while trying to educate some distant, apparently uninterested, Assistant Secretary in Whitehall.

"So you see my position," the Governor reminded him.

His accent was as precise and overclipped as his moustache. It was a voice that had never really made itself heard in any but quite small assemblies.

The C.M. did not reply immediately. He hated unprofessional confidences. Disliked being drawn into other people's private lives. He was the jurist, not the father confessor, of the Colony.

Quite different in nature from the Governor. That was because the C.M. was a bachelor. He was entirely self-sufficient. Whereas the Governor was the marrying kind; or had been. He needed the company of women, and had been forced to deny himself ever since his wife had gone back, so soon after the wedding.

It was really the climate that was to blame, the C.M. supposed. Temperature and humidity have ruined quite as many marriages as unfaithfulness or incompatibility. The C.M. had often wondered why the Governor hadn't simply thrown his hand in long ago and returned to Worcestershire, or Salop, or wherever it was, while there was still time to enjoy their two lives together.

"I see that it's preyed on your mind if that's what you mean," he said.

He slapped his hand to his cheek as he said it. Despite the mosquito netting that ran all round the veranda, he had been bitten twice as he sat there. He would put one of the houseboys onto the job of checking things tomorrow. Probably the present lot of netting had gone rotten. There was another roll of the stuff on order. It was due to arrive any moment now. Along with the fan, possibly.

"That's scarcely surprising after more than thirty years," the Governor reminded him.

The tone irritated the C.M. It reminded him of a prisoner he had once tried in a *crime passionnel*. The man had ignored his counsel altogether and had sought—deliberately it seemed—to convict himself. It had been willful and exhibitionistic. The C.M. did not like people who tried to take the law into their own hands. He wished now that instead of making things harder for him, the Governor would finish his last drink and go home.

"I still don't see the point of raking it all up again," he told him. "It isn't even as though there's any fresh evidence."

The rattan chair in which the Governor was sitting creaked sharply.

"Oh, but there is, you know. That's why I came over."

The C.M. could hear the crackle of paper while the Governor was speaking. Then something flat, one of the Government House envelopes it looked like, was pushed toward him across the table.

The C.M. made no move. This was the very last thing he

wanted. He was determined at all costs to keep his hands off the document, whatever it was. Talk was one thing. But documents were a damn nuisance: they had an awkward way of turning up again afterwards.

"Perhaps you could put the light up," the Governor suggested.

The C.M. still did not move.

"I'll take your word for it," he said.

There was no reply for a moment. Only the faint, unmistakable, long-drawn-out sound of a sigh coming out of the darkness opposite.

"I suppose you're right," the Governor answered. "It wouldn't mean anything. Not just by itself it wouldn't. You'd have to know the people."

He paused, then went on almost as though speaking to himself.

"Him. My wife. Me; as I was then, that is. Everyone. Then you'd understand. You'd see what I'm driving at."

He leaned forward, nearly upsetting the bottle that was in front of him.

"If you could go right back to the beginning, you'd realize how it happened. It's all like yesterday to *me*."

BOOK I

The Residency

Chapter 1

EVEN BEFORE the *Ancarses* had dropped anchor, the boat was already halfway from the shore.

She came out in the clear light of the pearly dawn more like a sea bird than a boat, dipping behind the breakers one moment, skimming airborne over the crest of them at the next.

The young man with the bright English complexion who was leaning over the rail reflected that he would probably be seasick all over again—just the way he had been those first few days out of Tilbury—as soon as he had climbed down into the shore boat.

He was a very clean-looking young man. His new white ducks were spotless. And they were only a trifle too close-fitting. As soon as the sun was properly up and it got really hot, they would cling to him, go into folds like toweling. He would regret the extra inches that a better tailor would have provided. There hadn't, in fact, been any tailor; the clothes were simply an off-the-peg job. He was a pretty standard-size young man.

Ever since first light he had been up there, wedged in between the ventilator and the rail, staring out at the gradually emerging coastline. Feeding his eyes on it; gulping down Africa; knowing that his future lay there and wondering what it had in store for him.

The steward, getting worried about his tip, had already carried the young man's second cup of coffee all the way up to him on the boat deck, and was ready to go on being nice right up to the minute when he finally lost him.

The only other passenger to go ashore was a clergyman. A Presbyterian from Walthamstow. He was spectacled and rather anxious-looking, wearing an expression of dismayed surprise, if not astonishment, at finding himself at all in such surroundings.

He was on his way, he explained, to the Central United Mission at Bangu. To take charge, in fact. The Mission had fallen on evil days, it seemed. But all that would soon be over. The moment he had got things properly organized, his wife would be coming out to join him. A mixed partnership was, in his opinion, essential. That was because—here the missionary dropped his voice and spoke out of the corner of his mouth—of the peculiar initiation and other ceremonies of the natives of those parts. "Totally misguided hygiene measures" was how the missionary described them. His wife had been a nurse in Liverpool, he went on, and would be able to put things into their proper medical perspective.

The young man avoided the missionary's pale, shining eyes and wished him—and his wife too, for that matter—the very best of British luck: he had a feeling that they might be in need of it.

Conversation was impossible in the shore boat because the waves were too high. Even there in the shelter of the *Ancarses,* they were going up and down as though on a seesaw. The boat was an open one, with hot wooden seats. And there was a lot of water slopping around their feet in the bottom. The young man saw his two suitcases, very new and inexperienced-looking, swung out from the deck and placed by one of the boatmen in the center of a dark, slimy patch where somebody had been cleaning fish or oiling something. They were light-colored suitcases. Pale fawn, from the Army and Navy. And as he watched, he saw them begin to suck up the wet like lumps of sugar in a messy saucer. He would have moved them somewhere else if he had not felt so seasick. Not that it would have made any difference. They were shipping water continuously. Soon the suitcases would be wet all over.

In the meantime, the entire crew had gone down to the stern for a conference because the engine wouldn't start. There were five of them. Very black, and mechanics to a man. With bottoms up and heads down inside the small engine house, they uttered shrill screams of pain and rage as they cut themselves or touched something painful. There were the sounds of banging and hammering. And more screams. One of them got his fingers crushed in a wrench. Then the graduate of the party, one-eyed and practically naked, thought of fuel. He poured a can of kerosene into the tank. A moment later, with a belching gray thundercloud from the exhaust and a noise like machine gunning, they were on their way to the shore. In the confusion, the rest of the kerosene had gone over the missionary's holdall.

It was Sir Gardnor's idea, this ridiculous disembarkation at Kiku of all places. Less than five hundred miles farther to the south the *Ancarses* would ride into the sheltered natural harborage of Nucca, and the passengers, politely waited on by the white-uniformed staff of the Royal West African Railroad, could travel by the chocolate-and-cream *Coronation Flyer* straight through to Amimbo.

By rail, the whole journey, from quayside to terminus, took only thirty-six hours. Unless, of course, there were elephants on the track; or a bridge, weakened by the rains, had collapsed into the mud bath beneath it; or ants had eaten away too many of the ties.

Sometimes, too, the locomotive—of the 1902 class, and with as much polished brasswork as a fairground merry-go-round— would burst one of its pipes, or plow enthusiastically through the switch at the only junction. Even allowing for all reasonable hazards, however, the journey by train was still three or four days quicker than by road.

That was because the road was not really a road at all. It started off all right. With lampposts; six of them. And flower beds of poinsettia and bougainvillaea. And a glass-sided traffic-control box, complete with an umbrella over the top. This part of the road was fully paved and passed the new Post Office in one magnificent sweep. Then, when it reached the suburbs, the surface ceased abruptly. The contractor was still in prison.

The first section of the highway was Portuguese, and very unhealthy. It ran, mostly at sea level, across a mangrove swamp. And in places, it disappeared completely.

The Minister of Highways was the brother-in-law of the unhappy contractor. In consequence, the Department tried to put the best possible face on things. Whenever a fresh submergence occurred, gangs of convict laborers were detailed to put down bundles of reeds to form a new foundation. It was not an easy task. The reeds simply floated away as soon as they were laid. Heavy stones and pieces of rock had to be placed on top of them. Then more reeds were added to cover up the rocks. Then rocks again to hold down the reeds. It was a life's work, this kind of road building. The gangs toiled away day after day in the endless sunlight with nothing whatsoever to show for their labors. In sheer contentment, they chanted as they worked.

Every so often, the level of the piled-up rubbish would break the black, brackish surface of the water. Then a mammy wagon would attempt to pass. After hitting one or two of the larger concealed rocks, it would begin to settle. Soon the axles would be covered. Then the springs. There would be a scramble to unload. Finally, more boat than truck, it would be half-floated, half-towed away, with the ruined cargo carefully packed inside again.

A little farther inland, things got better. The road began to climb. It spiraled up and up through the red hills, getting cooler with every hairpin bend. Even here, however, there were difficulties. Every week or so, large portions of the sandstone, baked dry and flaky like pastry, detached themselves and went slithering down into the valley. Sometimes they carried the road with them; sometimes they merely lay across it, smothering the surface. Either way, it called for giant-size gardening to get things going again.

On the map, this portion of the road was still shown as a continuous thick black line. Thirty miles ahead, the thick black line gave way to a succession of little dots.

There things really began to grow desperate. The road builders had given up trying. Or succumbed to sunstroke. The road simply went mad. It followed river beds that flooded without warning. It tried to climb waterfalls. It nosed its way into mountain culs-de-sac. It led to the edge of precipices. It went straight as an arrow across wide plains and then turned at right angles because no one had remembered the lake on the other side. It plunged into forests. It ended. Only the larger kinds of American cars ever attempted the journey.

But Sir Gardnor insisted. It was part of his faith. He believed in that road. Even though, at some point in its course from Amimbo, the nationality of the landscape invisibly changed—this thornbush British, that one Portuguese—it was undeniably, so the Governor said, God's intended passageway toward the open sea. The Arab slave traders had used it for centuries.

The railway, on the other hand, was entirely artificial. It came thrusting through from the wrong direction. It was political, rather than natural. Only British Colonialism at its most obstinate would ever have thought of building it at all; or have succeeded.

Financially, it was a write-off. It paid no dividends; owned no assets except practically valueless land, utterly obsolete rolling stock. But it was still part of the Imperial network. It joined an inland British Colony—a mere foreign island in the middle of hostile Africa—with the remote ocean. And every ant-indented tie along its six hundred and fifty wandering miles was British too.

Even that, however, in Sir Gardnor's eyes did not excuse its elementary wrongness, its irrelevance. A glance out the train window was enough to show. Different ecology. Different tribes. Different customs. Different loyalties. Different sins. Nothing to do with his own beloved Amimbo.

That was why, with no argument at all, Sir Gardnor required all new members of his staff to make the proper approach, the one that took so much longer.

There was no denying, the young man kept reminding himself, that it was a privilege to serve under such a figurehead. Sir Gardnor Hackforth was already famous, something of a living legend in the Service.

At forty-five he was head and shoulders above anyone else, and there seemed no Proconsular heights to which he might not eventually climb. He was there at his own wish, in Amimbo, at this moment: that much was common knowledge. But when he was ready—it was understood that, by now, there had been a hint here, a word dropped in the right quarter there—he could take his choice. A really fat Governorship. A Governor-General-ship perhaps. Even Delhi possibly. Or Westminster. The Lords, of course; and his own Department.

In the meantime, Sir Gardnor was finishing his book. It was the book that had got young Harold Stebbs the job. He was scarcely the type to which an Interview Board could be expected to warm irresistibly. Altogether too self-effacing; too diffident. No presence; and too many of his sort coming forward nowadays, the Chief Establishment Officer considered.

Asked the key question of how he thought he would behave in a civil emergency if he should find himself the sole representative of British authority, he had replied, briefly but damagingly, that he had never been in such circumstances and so did not know. Pressed to amplify an answer so very disastrous, he had mumbled something about supposing that things would sort them-selves out in the end somehow because they usually did; and worst of all, he had been content to leave it at that.

It was not until the observer from Finance and Estimates asked the other key question, "Are you afraid of figures?" that the interview really came to life at all. For the answer came back as an uncompromising "No." The observer became interested and began to probe. Series, it turned out, were Harold Stebbs's speciality. Not series of anything in particular; just series. Numbers in the abstract; the very purest of pure mathematics. His last year at Cambridge, he explained, had been devoted to them.

Because the Finance Observer felt himself getting out of his depth, he switched the conversation to statistics. Was Mr. Stebbs interested in anything so ordinary as statistics? he asked. And again the answer came back promptly. "Naturally," he said. "They're the raw material." The observer felt that he had got him there. "Isn't it the *figures* that are the raw material, Mr. Stebbs?" he asked in a voice that carried with it just the right note of superiority and rebuke. "Aren't the statistics the finished product?"

And once more there came the prompt, singularly mannerless reply. "Statistics are just tables," he said. "A clerk can get out statistics. They don't necessarily mean anything. It's only when you begin to analyze them that they become interesting. It all shows up in the presentation. With figures . . ."

The Establishment Officer coughed. He did not like conversations that were conducted across the chair. "And are you interested in people as well as figures, Mr. . . . er . . . Stebbs?" he asked.

Not that people apparently mattered for the job. Sir Gardnor had made that perfectly plain in his last memorandum. "I am not looking for a leader of men, a Milner," he had written in his elegant, only mildly indecipherable longhand. "I am not searching for a District Officer, or a Chief Magistrate or even an observant Tax Collector. All that I require is an intelligent, educated assistant with a good head for figures to work beside me for the next twelve months. I have already indicated that the Chief Secretary can spare no one. If the Office is unable to provide such a clerk, possibly one of the Merchant Banks . . ."

It was because the Appointments Board, sitting there in that quiet room in Whitehall, had decided that Harold Stebbs was not a leader of men that he now found himself somewhere on the Equator, standing in the shade of the Chevrolet, scratching his ankle where he had just been bitten, and watching while the native driver and his assistant changed the wheel.

Like the boatmen, they were tremendous hammerers. The din alerted the whole countryside. A flock of white egrets mounted frantically into the air from the adjoining marsh like disembodied spirits; and soon an entire rose garden of flamingoes joined them and moved off as well. The sky became carmine, striped with black, as they passed over.

The hammering continued. When one engineer got tired, the other took over. From time to time, their attention strayed. They hammered out dents that they had just noticed in the wings. They removed deposits of rock-hard mud from under the chassis. Somewhere underneath they found a small angle bracket. They hammered that too. It broke. They threw it away. They returned to the rear axle. They hammered even harder. The hammer broke. They rested.

Because the tool kit was open, one of them tried the lug wrench. As a makeshift hammer, it was no more than second-rate. It bent. But as a lug wrench, it was perfect. They tried fitting it onto one of the nuts. Then onto all the nuts in turn. It matched. They tried turning it. The nuts loosened and came away. With cries of appreciation and delight, they tried tightening them up again. They succeeded. They forgot why they had started. They undid and redid. They lost one of the nuts altogether. They quarreled. Then they remembered the flat tire. They burst out laughing.

With a suddenness that was alarming, the sun dipped abruptly behind the distant range of blue hills. As it dipped, it appeared to be accelerating. At one moment it had been floating clear, huge and red and angry-looking. At the next, it was declining so fast that the mountains appeared to be stretching up to eat it. Soon the teeth had done their work, and a large chunk was missing. Then there was only half a sun. Then no more than a flaming rim. Then the eclipse was complete.

Harold turned toward the drivers.

"Where do we spend the night?" he asked.

The mechanics rose politely to their feet and stood at attention while he addressed them.

"Yassaar," the man in charge answered. "Spend the night. Yassaar. Bad wheel. Very bad wheel. Soon drive on now, saar. Spend the night. Yassaar."

Harold's ankle was itching badly by now. Already it had begun to swell.

The resthouses on the route proved to be well spaced rather than comfortable. They were as pleasant to leave next morning as they had been to arrive at overnight. And there was a sameness about them. The same whitewashed mud walls, and the same corrugated-iron roof. The same tin washing basin set on an enameled metal tripod, with a bucket underneath it to receive the slops. The same earth latrine. The same hospital-type bed, with its casters resting in saucers of paraffin to discourage the creepie-crawlies. And the same rearing white catafalque of mosquito net.

On his first night under one of them, Harold had learned to hate all mosquito nets. Mere heat and stickiness were one thing. Heat and stickiness plus suffocation and imprisonment were quite another. In the end, he had kicked his way out in desperation. Wriggled his feet about in the darkness. In consequence, his other ankle was now bitten and badly swollen too.

Nor had sleep for the past five nights been blissful and unbroken. There had been thunderstorms overhead; howlings and roarings through the surrounding night. And the dawn chorus, too, had proved to be uncongenially strident, like carnival music. One particular bird appeared to be following Harold about. Either it or its twin had landed on his roof each morning. A large bird with hard feet, it trampled noisily on the corrugated-iron sheeting. It whistled. It screamed. It imitated car brakes. It hooted. It made a sound like corks popping. It laughed. It evacuated.

But already the journey and the little prison-like resthouses were in the past. The Chevrolet mounted a small hill with the Government radio station on the summit. And there, on the plain below, shimmering in the heat, lay Amimbo.

Harold told the driver to stop and climbed out. He had forgotten about all his tiredness and bad nights by now. He was excited again, remembering that he was the one who had been selected.

The capital itself was not in the least like the handbook

photograph. That had been in plain black-and-white. Whereas Amimbo itself, even from a distance, was pure Kodachrome. Red roofs. Yellow-and-green banana trees. Purple, scarlet, and orange flowering shrubs. Pale lavender-tinted smoke rose vertically into the still African air. Even the sky was Kodachrome, too. A clear robin's-egg blue overhead, it changed to indigo in the distance and ended on the far horizon in a bank of battleship-gray storm clouds.

Even so, the photograph was a help. Harold could identify all the principal landmarks. The railroad station, with its nursery layout of sidings. The Anglican cathedral, looking like a village church in Kent. The gas-storage tank, recently repainted and now standing out in its new coat of screaming vermilion. The basilica of the Roman Catholic Mission. The cattle market. The mosque. The cricket ground. The barracks. The Victoria Gardens. Government House and the law courts. The hotel. The administrative offices. The hospital. The Asian section. And, half a mile or so to the west toward the river, the Residency.

The Residency was pure white. Like icing. With a confectioner's portico overlooking the main lawn. From Telegraph Hill, the sightseer could look straight down into the grounds. The drive was of bright red gravel. It kept disappearing and re-emerging, obscured in places by its own bright avenue of flame trees.

And as Harold followed it with his eyes, he felt that he had been along it before, many times. Knew what it was like, even where it dipped and hid itself behind the trees and hillocks. Knew what lay beyond. The terrace. The flower beds with their concealed sprinklers. The bungalow within the grounds.

Knew the inside of the house, too. The hallway with the Book on the polished mahogany table. The tapestry-and-gilt furniture in the drawing room. The pictures. The staircase with the big royal portrait at the top. The double doors, green-baize-covered and studded with brass nails on the nondomestic side, which led through to the Governor's official suite. Knew, too, the doorway in the West Wing—the one leading to the side of the house that the Governor, for some reason, never visited.

And as he stood there with the sweet, stale heat of the valley breathing up on him, Harold shivered. He must, he realized, be even more exhausted than he thought he was.

The rest of the ride was easier; there was nothing to it.

The dirt track down the mountainside ended sharply. Suddenly the boulders and the potholes ceased, and they were on tarmac. It was a real road again. The native driver roared along it, marveling that his gas had not run out. For him this was home again, and he was happy. Even though there was nothing in front, he sounded his horn in fierce, jubilant blasts. He thought about beer and women and his new bicycle. He remembered his small son, for whom he had bought the present of a toy watch with a brightly decorated dial. He sang. He narrowly avoided a stationary oxcart. He shouted at the occupant. He remembered to go carefully. Bent forward over the steering wheel, he concentrated. Turning his head over his shoulder, he addressed his passenger.

"Amimbo, saar," he said. "Two minutes more, saar, Amimbo."

He hit a chicken.

Chapter 2

THERE WAS no one there to meet him when Harold Stebbs finally reached the hotel. Not that this was unreasonable. By road, journeys from the coast could not be calculated to the exact hour; or even to the exact day, for that matter.

But at least the hotel was expecting him. The polite Indian clerk at the Reception Desk immediately produced from under the counter a large, important-looking envelope with the words CHIEF SECRETARY inscribed at the bottom left-hand corner.

"For you, sir. By hand this morning. And your key, sir," he said. "Please to make sure to return it to us when you next choose to leave us again."

The letter was from Mr. Frith, Assistant Chief Secretary. It was bleakly welcoming. One of the Government bungalows, it explained, would be ready by the end of the month, or shortly afterwards. For a short stay, it went on, the Royal Albert Hotel should really prove quite comfortable. And could Harold Stebbs please be over at the Assistant Secretary's office sharp at eight-thirty next morning? If, in the meantime, he wanted anything, he had only to pick up the receiver and ask for the Government switchboard.

While Harold was still reading, he was aware that the Indian clerk was watching him intently. And with good reason. No matter how closely the clerk had held the envelope up to the naked light bulb above his desk, he had not been able to make out anything but the outline of Mr. Frith's signature.

Catching Harold's eye, he smiled with a glitter of fine, white un-European teeth.

"You come this way, sir? I show you your room. Good comfortable quarters. Very pleased to have you with us. Government accommodation. First class. I will send for the iced water. Very cold indeed, sir."

Already Harold's two suitcases were being carried in. They did not look new any longer. And after the hysterical lurchings of the Chevrolet, the room seemed strangely stationary.

It was not, by resthouse standards, at all a bad room, but scarcely home. There was a sofa of sorts, as well as a bed. A dresser with a long, mistily discolored mirror. A handbasin. A chest of drawers with one of the wooden handles missing. A waste-paper basket that had been used by someone who had been eating fruit. An upright chair which remained upright as long as it was resting up against something. And a large framed repro-duction of *The Last Supper*, faded to a mere outline sketch after long years of exile in the bright African sunlight.

Harold wondered what the Government bungalow was going to be like.

In the meantime, there was his unpacking to do. He was pre-cise and methodical. First, because he was hot and he could feel the sweat running in little trickles between his shoulder blades, he stripped down to his underpants. Next, he opened up his suitcases, setting out everything in little piles upon the sofa—his shirts here, his undershirts there, his socks neatly arranged beside them.

Then he opened the bottom drawer of the dresser to begin putting his things away and found that a colony of minute white ants had moved in before him. Disturbed by the light, they now seethed over one another, trying frantically to reinsert themselves into the cracks in the woodwork.

He was still wondering where people in the tropics kept their clean laundry when there came a knock on the door.

Still in his underpants, he went over and opened it. But it was not the iced water that the Indian clerk had promised. Instead, Harold found himself confronted by a small, rather crumpled figure wearing a badly knotted Club tie. One uncertain, damp-looking hand was already raised to knock again if necessary.

"Oh, good evening. I'm Frith. Mr. Frith," the man said. "May I come in? I'm not disturbing you, am I?"

Harold Stebbs stood back. He wished now that, instead of simply stripping down to his underpants, he had changed them for a fresh pair. And the room behind him looked frankly ludicrous. It might have been the tail end of a not-too-successful jumble sale.

"You must excuse all this," he said lamely. "I . . . I've only just got here."

"Oh, don't apologize, please," Mr. Frith begged him. "It's my fault, breaking in on you like this. May I sit here?" He moved a heap of socks and handkerchiefs from the end of the sofa, and then turned nervously to Harold again. "They did give you my letter, didn't they? They don't always, you know."

"As soon as I got here," Harold told him. "You said eight-thirty in the morning. I'll be there."

Mr. Frith passed a moist, creased-up handkerchief across his forehead.

"That's the whole point," he said. "It's been changed. It's tonight, H.E. wants you. For dinner. That is, if you're not too tired, of course."

He gave a little sigh as he said it and simply sat there, looking vacantly around him. Harold noticed that he had a slight twitch, a tic, on the left side of his face. It kept bringing his lower eyelid into a humorless, unmeaningful wink.

Harold Stebbs came over to the sofa.

"I'm afraid that I can't offer you a drink," he told him. "You see, I haven't got anything."

Mr. Frith looked up.

"That's all right," he said. "Just ring. The service is terrible. But they'll come eventually. Better keep a bottle in your room. It's the only way. And soda for me. Don't touch the water. It's typhoid."

The bell pull had a china handle. As Harold tugged at it, he could hear a long scraping of wires along the corridor outside, but nothing else. Mr. Frith was listening intently too.

"Better shout," he said. "Open the door and call, 'Boy.' You'll get used to it." He gave Harold a sympathetic smile. "You know why you're here, of course," he went on. "It's the book. H.E.'s going upcountry tomorrow and wants you to get on with it. It's months behind already. H.E.'s getting in rather a state."

Mr. Frith dropped his voice a little and continued almost as though talking to himself.

"I'm afraid your predecessor made a complete mess of it. Not that it matters. H.E.'s been revising it all again. You'll have to make a fresh start anyhow." He turned to Harold accusingly. "You did ring, didn't you? Perhaps you'd better shout again."

When, at last, the bottle of Red Label was brought in, Mr. Frith revived like a flower. Slumped over sideways on the sofa at one moment, he was sitting bolt upright at the next. The first two drinks were taken very short, practically neat; and after that a little of the soda was carefully added. It might have been medicinal, the way he poured it.

But already the tic had faded and disappeared; a new, resurrected Mr. Frith was beginning to assert himself.

"When you're properly settled in, your driver can get it for you," he explained. "It's half the price that way. And keep it locked up. Everything disappears out here. They're like children. Steal anything."

He looked up in astonishment.

"You're not drinking," he said.

"I don't drink whisky," Harold replied.

"But they've got gin. Cases of it, if you want gin," Mr. Frith said severely. "And you've let the boy go away again. You won't get him back now. It's too late. In any case, I've got to be going."

Mr. Frith looked at his watch, and shook himself.

"I'll come back and pick you up," he said. "Eight-twenty sharp. H.E. doesn't like to be kept waiting. Better be in the bar. I'll meet you there." He finished his drink and began tugging at his tie. "Forgot to tell you. Black below. H.E. likes it better that way."

"Black below?"

"And a white jacket. Rule of the house, out here."

"Anything else?" Harold asked.

Mr. Frith pondered for a moment.

"Don't think so," he said. "Play it quietly. Just take the lead from me. H.E.'ll do most of the talking. He's usually a jump or two ahead of the rest of us."

Mr. Frith suddenly slapped his thigh.

"Oh, my God," he said. "Went clean out of my mind. Don't say anything about Lady Anne. That's *verboten*. H.E. can bring her up if he wants to. That's his affair. You keep off it."

"Is anything wrong?"

Mr. Frith put his forefinger up against his lips.

"Some other time," he said. "Not now. We'll be late. See you in the bar at eight-twenty."

The way to the Residency lay through the Asian quarter.

Abruptly, everything became packed and noisy. Harold was aware of Asian skins, Asian hair, Asian eyes, Asian faces, Asian souls probably. There were shops everywhere, some of them simply hollowed out alcoves in the mud walls. Others were two planks underneath a striped umbrella. One—a haberdasher's—was around the roots of a large tree, with the branches overhead taking the place of coat hangers and display cases.

Then they reached the local Bond Street. Here they were in the midst of a whole arcade of the more exclusive kind of stores, with awnings and metal shutters and signwriters' lettering—HAPPY-

NESS GROCERIES; P. CHAPANDRA LADY'S IMPORTS; MAH WONG, FOOD SUPPLIERS: DAS AND SONS, GENTLEMANLY CLOTHING . . .

But already Mr. Frith was giving good advice again. He laid his hand on Harold's knee.

"When H.E. asks you if you like the claret," he said, "have a guess at Barton. That'll please him. Leave him to tell you what year."

Mr. Frith's earlier nervousness momentarily returned to him.

"You do drink, don't you?" he asked. "I didn't notice in the bar just now."

"I'm very fond of a good claret," Harold told him.

It was quite untrue: he knew next to nothing about any kind of claret; but it sounded convincing, and he was pleased with himself for having said it.

Mr. Frith was pleased too.

"That's a relief," he said. "H.E.'s very proud of his cellar. Hell of a job getting the stuff out here."

The car was slowing down by now and there was a military feeling in the air. Two ebony sentries in ivory-white uniform came smartly to attention, and the car turned into the long drive under the jacaranda trees.

The feeling of having been there before, of somehow belonging to the place, returned to Harold more sharply than ever.

Just the way I knew it would be, he found himself thinking. Just like my dream.

Seen at close quarters, the Residency was a vast blanc-mange edifice with a lofty Colonial portico and a row of highly polished antique cannon facing nothing down the drive. The guard all wore broad scarlet sashes across their tunics and gold shoulder tabs. The sentries, two of them, standing alongside the cannon, had their bayonets fixed.

Mr. Frith strode in across the threshold. Fortified as he now was, he showed himself completely at his ease. He was beaming.

"Don't bother about the Book," he said. "That's only for outsiders."

Together they went on, under the big crystal chandelier, across the tennis-court-sized area of blue carpet, and began to mount the staircase. It was a long staircase, and the climb did not agree with Mr. Frith. He was breathing rather heavily by now, and small beads of perspiration had begun to break out along his forehead.

At the top, the A.D.C. was waiting, his charming, slightly tired smile at the ready. A slim young man with a lock of brown hair that he was constantly thrusting back from his forehead, he was undoubtedly good-looking in a smooth, orthodox sort of way. It was only on closer inspection that the features seemed somehow too regular, too standardized. It was as though if any one of them should get bent or damaged or mislaid it could be quite readily replaced—at Harrod's or Fortnum's, probably.

But already he was stepping forward.

"Mr. Stebbs?" he asked. "His Excellency's expecting you."

The introduction was marred only because Mr. Frith did not raise his right foot quite high enough to clear the top step. At one moment he was politely ushering Harold forward, and at the next he had catapulted him into the A.D.C.'s arms.

The A.D.C. appeared entirely oblivious.

"Evening, Tony," Mr. Frith said. "You well?"

The A.D.C. turned again to Harold Stebbs.

"It's not a dinner party," he explained. "It's entirely stag. You might call it a working session really—the book, you know. H.E.'s going off on tour tomorrow. That's why we're in the Library. H.E. does hope you'll excuse us."

The corridor along which they were passing was wide, high, and apparently endless. The blue carpet seemed to go on forever. A pair of tall double doors stood open on one side, revealing a big, shadowy interior. It made the whole house seem somehow emptier and more lifeless.

Mr. Frith had caught up with them by now. After pausing for a moment to inspect himself in front of the mirrors, he had recovered all his old self-possession. He was whispering.

"Not a word about Lady Anne. And don't be surprised if H.E.'s offhand: it's only his way. And try and keep the conversation going. He likes that. The claret'll be Barton, by the way. Don't let yourself be caught out."

The A.D.C. had opened the door at the far end and was standing back for Harold to go in ahead of him.

"Excellency," he said, speaking just loud enough to be heard distinctly but not so loud as to be disturbing, "Mr. Stebbs has arrived."

Harold waited. All that he could see was the high back of a red leather chair. From behind it there was a movement and a rustle of papers, and then Sir Gardnor appeared. A tall man, he gave the impression of still rising even when he was already standing. He pushed the chair back and came round, hand outstretched, smiling.

"Mr. Stebbs," he said. "How kind of you to come like this. Without warning, too. This is a bachelor household at the moment, you understand. You're not tired, are you—after the journey, I mean? You wouldn't rather be in bed?"

By now, Sir Gardnor seemed somehow to be hanging over him. But it was Mr. Frith whom Sir Gardnor was already addressing.

"Good of you to go out of your way like this to bring Mr. Stebbs here tonight," he said. "You weren't thinking of doing anything else, were you?"

While Sir Gardnor was speaking, Harold was able to observe him more closely. It was a remarkably effective smile that he had; quite enveloping, in fact. Not that Harold was unfamiliar with it: he had seen Sir Gardnor's photographs often enough in the papers. It was only that, in real life, the face, like the smile, was even more impressive.

The whole effect was rather formidable: there was the iron-gray hair; the wide forehead coming down to the dark, jutting eyebrows; the high arch to the nose; the massive, deeply divided chin. Like some bloody Roman gladiator, Harold found himself thinking.

And while he was looking, he noticed the smile again. It bore no relation to what Sir Gardnor was saying; was simply turned on and off at will, like floodlighting.

There was one other thing that Harold noticed. Sir Gardnor introduced a question into every other sentence and then turned to another topic before there was time for a reply.

"Your trip," he was now saying to Harold, "you read it up, I hope? The birds are particularly interesting. And the geology, didn't you find? The watershed explains a great deal about the Mimbo. You noticed their stature? Clearly a hill people, but living in the plains. And their language. Are you interested in native tongues? 'Mimbo' also means 'palm wine' you know. A once great people, divided by a valley and a river—and a war of conquest, of course. Have you read much African history, Mr. Stebbs? It's most rewarding. Essential, in fact, if you're to see exactly where we fit into things."

The smile had flitted in and out half a dozen times while Sir Gardnor was speaking, and around his feet the little pile of unanswered questions was steadily getting deeper.

He turned to Harold.

"You don't mind dining early, do you?" he asked. "I want to talk to you afterwards. It's about the book. You've heard I shall be away upcountry? I don't want to lose any time. While I'm on my tour, I thought you could be getting on with things. It's really the tables, you know. We can't afford to have them out of date, can we?"

Sir Gardnor had been sipping the hock without any apparent interest. Then the Mimbo butler poured the claret. He was a lined, ancient creature, the butler, with no more than isolated tufts of hair left upon his scalp. But the other servants all seemed in awe of him: Harold noticed how they stepped back for him to pass. He noticed also how attentive he was, how watchful. His head held slightly to one side, he was observing Sir Gardnor all the time.

Sir Gardnor raised the claret to his nostrils and closed his eyes as he did so. A sudden hush had come over the room, and the silence remained as Sir Gardnor slowly and very deliberately sniffed. Then he opened his eyes, and the tension was over.

He turned toward Harold; the warm, sweet glare of his smile was now full on him.

"I think you'll find that, for its age, it's traveled well," he said. "You must give us your opinion."

Harold remembered his cue, and the question came blurting out.

"Is it Barton?" he asked.

Mr. Frith gave a short, nervous cough, but Sir Gardnor ignored the question altogether.

"And what are they drinking in Cambridge these days?" he enquired. "In my time it was St. Julien, and a rather cheap Pommard mostly."

He glanced across at Mr. Frith. It was only a half-smile, this time; a mere token.

"Which bungalow is Mr. Stebbs having?" he asked. "Have you put him somewhere near you?"

Mr. Frith had been perspiring heavily ever since he had sat down. He kept running his handkerchief over his forehead. And hot as he was, he suddenly appeared hotter.

"Sorry, Excellency," he said. "There isn't a bungalow. Not till the end of the month, that is." He cleared his throat as he was speaking and gave a rather silly little laugh. "Mr. Stebbs is at the Royal Albert, sir. Nice room. You're all right where you are, aren't you, Stebbs?"

Before Harold could reply Sir Gardnor had intervened.

"But I thought that a bungalow was understood. For Mr. Stebbs's sake, you know. As well as mine. I couldn't allow my papers to be left lying about in a hotel, now could I?"

This time the pause was so long that it was obvious that, for once, he actually expected an answer.

"I suppose I could turn someone out, Excellency," Frith began.

Sir Gardnor, however, was not listening. He was addressing the A.D.C. instead.

"Our own bungalow," he said triumphantly. "The one that poor Miles had. That's free, isn't it?"

The A.D.C. winced slightly.

"No staff, sir. Not for the moment."

Sir Gardnor raised his eyebrows.

"Then they can service it from the House," he said. "We shall be away for a week. Possibly ten days. Perhaps longer. It's difficult to tell, isn't it? You can fix up permanent staff for Mr. Stebbs when we get back. And you, Mr. Frith, can dismiss it from your mind, can't you? It's all solved."

He was smiling again as he said it, but he was also drumming with his fingers on the table top.

"You do see my point, Mr. Stebbs, don't you? You'll need to work on it in the evenings. Most evenings, I'm afraid. And I'm sure you'd much rather be on your own, wouldn't you?"

Harold started to thank him, but Sir Gardnor's attention had already strayed. He was looking hard at Harold's glass.

"You approve, then?" he asked. "And what year would *you* say it was?"

Dinner was already finished when the A.D.C. got up and went over to the door. There was a whispered conversation. Then the A.D.C. came back and stood behind Sir Gardnor's chair.

"It's Major Hastings, sir," he said. "The General asked him to come over."

Sir Gardnor continued with the business of lighting his cigar.

"Well, ask him to come in," he replied. "It's no good leaving him out there, is it?"

The cigar was drawing nicely by now, and Sir Gardnor seemed in the best of spirits. He was smiling.

His really big smile, however, was reserved for Major Hastings.

"Ah, come in, Major," he said, springing to his feet, as if his whole evening had suddenly been made for him. "You haven't come across specially, have you?"

Major Hastings came respectfully to attention, at exactly the three feet six inches laid down in the textbook.

"Sorry to disturb you, Excellency," he said, "but we've just had some bad news come through."

Sir Gardnor leaned forward.

"You've dined, of course?" he asked, his face suddenly lined by anxiety. "Then sit down and have a glass of port with us. Or would you rather a whisky-and-soda?" He beckoned the A.D.C. "Tony, give the Major a glass of port."

Sir Gardnor glanced from his cigar to Major Hastings and then back to his cigar again.

"Some bad news, you were saying?" he asked.

Major Hastings sat up very straight.

"It's about your trip tomorrow, sir," he explained. "There's been another outbreak. Up at Omtala."

"Omtala," Sir Gardnor said reflectively. "That's Henderson. What's he doing about it?"

"Henderson's missing, sir."

Sir Gardnor started to drum with his fingers on the table top again.

"Missing?"

"Yes, sir. The bungalow was broken into." Major Hastings was speaking very precisely as though he were repeating a lesson that he had just learned by heart. "There was a lot of blood in the bedroom. But that was all. They killed the houseboy too, sir. His body's been found."

"What about the sentries?"

"Vanished, sir. Simply vanished. We got the message from Captain Endell. He dropped in, sir, and found the whole place deserted."

Sir Gardnor was having trouble with his cigar. For some reason, it was burning sideways. He held the match very carefully to the unsmoldering rim of leaf. Then, satisfied at last, he slowly drew in and just as slowly exhaled a long cloud of the blue smoke.

"Henderson will have to be replaced, of course," he said. "I'll see about that."

He turned to Major Hastings.

"And we must organize a proper search party. Endell's not really up to it, is he? He's only been out here six months. We must do everything we can for Henderson, mustn't we, Major?"

Major Hastings squared his shoulders and brought his chin back.

"You can take it from me, sir: Henderson was murdered last night."

Sir Gardnor looked surprised.

"Not murdered, surely," he replied. "Assassinated, possibly. But not murdered. This must be purely political. You're not telling me that there was any personal element, are you?"

Harold was watching the Major's face while Sir Gardnor was speaking. It was not a very striking face. The ginger moustache divided it neatly into two halves, without adding anything to either. At the moment, he looked resentful.

"Henderson was a friend of mine, sir," he began.

But Sir Gardnor was not listening.

"How was the houseboy killed?" he asked.

"The usual way, sir."

"And Henderson?"

"We don't know, sir. The only evidence is the blood."

"So you think it's the Leopard Men?"

"Endell's positive, sir."

"Well, we'll know tomorrow, shan't we?" Sir Gardnor observed. "I shall be passing through Omtala. I'll make some inquiries."

Major Hastings braced himself.

"That's what the General had in mind, sir. In the circumstances, he wondered . . ."

"Wondered what?"

"Wondered if you'd care to give it a miss, sir. Make a detour, as it were."

"But hasn't my tour been announced?" Sir Gardnor asked. "Aren't people expecting me?"

His tone was one of completely bewildered astonishment.

Major Hastings nodded.

"Yes, sir," he said.

"Then I must go, mustn't I?"

He looked across at the A.D.C.

"We shall have to be tented," he went on. "Perhaps you'd look after that. The police will be up at the bungalow. We don't want to disturb them. And do you think perhaps the General would like to strengthen the escort, Major? That's something we must leave to him, isn't it?"

Sir Gardnor had got up and was rocking backwards and forwards on his heels in a preoccupied, absent-minded kind of way. Major Hastings had just left them.

"You really must excuse us, Mr. Stebbs," Sir Gardnor said. "I'd no idea we should have this interruption when I asked you over. But you do understand, don't you? You've heard of the Leopard Men, of course?"

"I've heard of them, sir."

"And you know their methods?"

"I can guess."

Sir Gardnor smiled indulgently.

"We can do better than guesswork, can't we, Tony? Perhaps you'd like to show Mr. Stebbs our *objet trouvé*. It's hardly the thing to leave lying about."

The A.D.C. removed his key chain from his pocket and went over to the red-lacquer cabinet in the corner. Inside it stood a plain black-enameled safe that looked as if it had come straight out of a counting house.

Sir Gardnor turned his head toward the A.D.C.

"Give Mr. Stebbs the pouch," he said. "Let him open it himself, shall we?"

The A.D.C. was on his way back by now.

"Perhaps you'd like to sit at the table, Mr. Stebbs," he suggested. "It can be a bit awkward otherwise."

The package that he handed to Harold was surprisingly heavy, and rather unpleasantly hard even through the two layers of chamois leather in which it was wrapped. When he put it down, it landed on the table with a thud.

Sir Gardnor was watching him closely.

"Open it up, Mr. Stebbs," he said.

As Harold unwrapped the parcel, it began to jingle. He folded back the chamois leather, and there on the table was the palm of a hand made out of thick cowhide. But it was not the cowhide that was remarkable. It was what was wired onto it. Where the thumb and fingers would have been there were claws, four-inch claws, of blue polished steel.

Harold looked up for a moment and saw Sir Gardnor's eyes fixed upon him.

"Turn it over, Mr. Stebbs," he said. "Then you can see the loops the real fingers go through. I'm afraid the stains on the leather will never come out. But it's been thoroughly cleaned, I assure you."

Harold made no movement toward it. He stood there feeling suddenly sick.

"Then shall I show you?" Sir Gardnor asked. "It's really nothing. Not in our hands, at least."

He picked it up and inserted his fingers so easily that it was obvious that he had demonstrated it before. And when the glove was in position, he held out the talons toward Harold, almost as if he were shaking hands with him.

"You've noticed the quality of the steel?" he asked. "This isn't native work, of course. It's engine-turned. German, probably. They use it like this."

He went over to the blotting pad on his desk and drew the claws across it. Little tufts, and then whole chunks, of the paper began to come away. When he pressed harder, the whole of the pad attached itself and came away.

"Try it for yourself," he said. "Then you'll get the feel of it."

Harold kept his hands to his side.

"No, thank you, sir."

Sir Gardnor smiled.

"You don't fancy it?" he asked reprovingly. "But this is Africa, Mr. Stebbs," he said. "This is Africa."

Chapter 3

THE STUDY window of the bungalow looked out onto a pleasant enough corner of the grounds, with a trickle of brown water in front and the little woodland of acacia trees banked up, feathery, behind.

Spread out on the work table before him was Sir Gardnor's manuscript. The typing was triple-spaced and clear enough. But most of it had already been crossed out, and it was what was written in between the lines that kept slowing Harold up. The elegant, rather beautiful handwriting had been scribbled over and corrected too. Successive revisions in different-colored inks bulged out at the sides like toy balloons and occupied the margins.

For the moment, however, it was all out of sight, covered up by that day's issue of the *Amimbo Times*. And it was still the Omtala incident that dominated the front page. By now, the tributes were coming in. Harold learned that Alastair Henderson, the dead District Officer, had been loyal, efficient, popular, Old Haileyburian, married, the father of two children, a good all-around sportsman and ripe in every way for high promotion. He had even, it appeared, played rugger for Blackheath. "A truly memorable and distinctive wing three-quarter" was how one of the notices described him. Omtala was a long way from Blackheath, Harold reflected; and the very fact of distance made the death seem somehow sadder.

One thing at least had been established. The killing had been a quick and relatively simple one: there was only a single wound. The blow must have been delivered with great force while Henderson had been lying flat on his back.

What was concerning the police was that the intruders had started to carry away the body: they disapproved of that. The fact that the intruders had been disturbed and had dumped it had come as a considerable relief all round: decent Christian burial was a much nicer end than the opening of the whole deplorable episode had suggested possible.

Beside the *Amimbo Times* lay the native broadsheet, *Trumpet Blast,* with a Mimbo phrasebook and dictionary resting on top of it. One day—if he stayed out here long enough—Harold hoped to be able to read Mimbo; in the meantime, he had found someone in Native Affairs to translate it for him.

And it was certainly all good stuff. The Governor, it appeared, had been bewitched, and the King-Emperor himself, it said, should therefore come out and take charge of operations. For *Trumpet Blast* had repeatedly warned Sir Gardnor about forthcoming outrages and had even named the ringleader. He was a foreigner; someone from Nigeria, probably. In appearance, he was unmistakable: five feet three in height, aged fifty-four, and with a slight limp. He possessed moreover, the unusual ability of being able to turn himself at will into an owl. There were numerous, reliable witnesses to attest to the fact that after every one of the recent outrages an owl, unusually large and fierce-looking, had been seen flying away from the scene of carnage. The limp itself was attributed to a lucky shot by a loyal Mimboese as the sinister bird had soared off overhead in the direction of Lagos.

42

But bewitched or not, the Governor had somehow contrived to keep up with his ruthlessly imposed schedule. The set in the corner tuned in to Amimbo Radio was at the moment reporting the latest stage in the tour.

In addition to a big meeting with the chiefs, the announcer said, Sir Gardnor had declared open a new Methodist missionary school as well as the hospital-block extension to a Catholic leper colony. Between the crackles on the loudspeaker—there was evidently quite a big storm coming, or the Chief Engineer was having trouble with the transmitter again—Harold had been able to make out that tomorrow's arrangements included another display of ceremonial dancing by Mimbo warriors and the official reopening of a bridge that had collapsed two rainy seasons ago.

The sound of the latch on the garden door roused him.

The bungalow was quiet, very quiet by now, with the two houseboys out at the back somewhere, asleep probably. But there was certainly someone around. A moment later, he heard the little rasping noise that the screen, warped down one side, always made as the door opened.

Whoever was there was coming in, secretly and unannounced, by the door that none of his other visitors had ever yet used. Harold found himself remembering Henderson.

His study was at the far end of the bungalow. It led onto a short passageway, bounded at the other end by a curtain of brightly colored native beads that the flies for some reason regarded as impenetrable. Harold moved quietly along the strip of coconut matting that carpeted the passageway and stationed himself behind the screen.

The garden door had been left wide open, and a shaft of bright yellow light now cut the room in two. The long divan with the pile of cushions up against the wall was brilliantly lit, even though the drawn shutters left the rest of the room in semi-twilight. The shaft of light was cut suddenly by a shadow. It was the shadow of a girl. A moment later—she was moving quite silently—he saw the girl herself. She was young, somewhere in her twenties, Harold reckoned; her face hidden from him by the loose dark hair. She paused, her back toward him, to glance toward the open door as though to make sure that she had not been followed.

He noticed then that her dress was creased and that there were dust stains across it. It was the red Amimbo dust that followed you about like a cloud as soon as you got off the five miles of paved highway.

When she turned, Harold could see that she was carrying a flower. It was simply one of the magenta blooms that tried everywhere to smother the mosquito netting outside. But she was holding it as if it were precious. And as he watched, she brought it up to her lips and kissed it.

Then she went slowly over to the divan and stood there, not moving, her head bent forward. She was so still that he had the impression that she might even be praying. He waited. When at last she came away, he saw that she had left the flower lying on the piled-up cushions.

He shifted his position. As he did so, his shoulder set the bead curtain rattling. It began a little jingle that he could not stop. The girl immediately spun round. She was frightened.

"Who's there?" she asked.

Harold stepped forward, separating the hanging beads with outstretched arms like a swimmer. She was facing him now. She had one hand raised to her face and with the other was reaching out, trying to steady herself.

"You'd better sit down," he said.

She began to sway. He went over and put his arm round her. As he did so he was aware of two things: of how small she was, and of the perfume she was using—it came as a sharp, clean smell in the atmosphere of that sultry, unused room. She was still trembling as he led her across to the divan.

"And put your head down," he said when he had got her to a chair. "I'll get you a glass of water."

When he returned with the water—it was practically at blood heat because the houseboy had forgotten to put any ice in the jug—she was already sitting up again. But she was very pale. As he approached her, he was conscious simply of dark, shining eyes set in a dead-white face.

"You'll feel better in a moment," he said.

As soon as she had drunk a sip, she turned on him.

"And what the hell are you doing here?" she asked.

Her eyes were very wide open now: he was looking straight into them.

"Because I bloody well live here," he replied. "Because it's my bungalow."

"Your bungalow?"

Harold nodded.

"Who told you you could have it?"

"The Governor," Harold answered. "It's his, isn't it?"

She brought her hands up to her face as if to protect herself.

"Oh, no," she said. "He couldn't have done that. He couldn't."

She turned her head and began brushing some of the dust stains off her dress.

"I've been away, you see," she said. "I've only just got back. I didn't know."

He stood there, staring down at her.

"Would you like a drink?" he asked. "A proper drink. Like gin."

"I've been drinking whisky."

"Isn't any. Gin do?"

She nodded.

The drink he poured her was a stiff one. He shook in the pink and added only a splash of the warm water from the thermos jug. Then he poured himself a drink too. "Try this," he said. "There's no ice. It's practically all gin."

Before she even took a sip she began thrusting her hair back, first behind one ear and then behind the other. She gave her head a little shake as she did so. Then she raised the glass to her lips and looked full at him again.

"Happy days," she said.

"Happy days."

He was watching her closely now; so closely that he could see the veins of color begin to come back into her cheeks. As he looked, the whole face was suddenly alive again. She had crossed her legs and was now smiling at him.

"Have you got a cigarette?" she asked.

Harold felt in his pocket.

"It's only an ordinary Players," he said, wondering as he did so why he should seem to be apologizing.

"Light it for me, please."

He was clumsy with the match, and she put her fingers on his hand to direct the flame. They were cool, soft fingers.

"I suppose you know who I am?" she asked.

She was still looking at him as she put the question, and she had her glass raised to her lips as she asked it. The question was vague and entirely casual, as though it would be funny in an unimportant sort of way if he shouldn't know the answer.

He paused.

"Are you . . . are you Lady Anne?"

"Then you've heard of me?"

"I have."

"What have you heard?"

"Only that you were away somewhere."

She laughed.

"Well, I'm not, am I?" she said. "I'm having a drink in your bungalow. And I don't even know your name. Who are you?"

"Stebbs," he said. "Harold Stebbs."

She was still laughing at him: he could see that.

"Stebbs is a funny name," she told him. "It isn't even like a name really. I think I shall call you Harold."

"Just as you please."

He had lit his own cigarette now and, having something to play with, felt more at ease.

She put her head to one side.

"Now you're cross with me," she said. "I don't wonder. I've interrupted you. I'm sorry." She paused. "What are you doing here, anyway?"

"I'm helping Sir Gardnor," he told her. "I'm doing some work for his book."

She raised her eyes to the ceiling.

"Oh, that," she said. "But you can't just live here like a hermit. You come over to the house sometimes, don't you?"

"Sometimes," he told her.

"Then I'll send a note across. I don't mean for one of the big parties. You'll be invited to all of those anyhow. I mean for drinks. Sometime when we're both feeling bored."

She was smiling at him again. And while she was speaking, she was groping behind her on the divan for the flower that she had left there. When she found it, she crushed it up in her hand. And still with the flower held in it, she put out her other hand to say goodbye.

Not that it made much difference to the flower. In that heat, any bloom had less than an hour's life once it had been pulled off its stem.

Chapter 4

THE GOVERNOR's return to Amimbo was magnificent, simply magnificent; the great Bwana was back, and in triumph.

Mr. Frith was the first to agree that no one else could have accomplished so much. Too much, in fact. With the Chief Secretary away, it meant that Mr. Frith's staff was working late every night, starting new dossiers, typing drafts, filing reports, preparing estimates, losing things.

In consequence, Mr. Frith was in a bad way. His facial tic, in particular, had grown worse. And his drinking habits had been disturbed. Not returning to his bungalow before half-past nine or even ten, he was forced to concentrate into the few remaining hours a process which in the ordinary way would have begun at six o'clock at the latest or, on a good evening, around five-thirty.

Also, he was worried. The Governor, like some Moslem potentate, had been giving away money—Government money. There was the promise of a thousand pounds for a T.B. testing station for cattle up at Omtala; an annual sum, unspecified, for a colony for the blind which had not even been down on his itinerary; and there were the minutes of a brief and alarming conversation with Mr. Ngo Ngono, in which Sir Gardnor seemed to have committed himself to plans for some kind of technical-training school away out in the bush where they were all pastoralists, anyhow.

Everything that Mr. Ngono had ever suggested had led to trouble. There was the hydroelectric plant—fifty thousand acres of good agricultural land flooded to make the new reservoir, and then the two-year drought during which the dam itself had cracked and disintegrated. There was the village-industry program under which lathes and drills and band saws had been distributed to astonished tribesmen merely to get broken, rusted, lost, or just plain stolen; the only evidence that the machinery had ever existed were a few maimed unfortunates who hobbled round as best they could after having got themselves tangled up in sharp and moving parts that they hadn't asked for in the first place. There was the anti-pest campaign, with teams of unsuspecting natives out all day devotedly spraying their crops with a noxious chemical—someone had misread the instructions—which killed everything it touched, the crops included; there was the big grain silo—the first of a chain that was to stretch across the whole country—that had blown up through spontaneous combustion and set a whole township ablaze simply because the ventilating valves had all been turned the wrong way. And now, Mr. Ngono, thoroughly Europeanized with his double-breasted blazer and his wristwatch and his gold fountain pen and his portable gramophone and his motorcycle, had sent a letter saying that he was already on his way to Amimbo in order that he might, with the Governor, continue his respectfully above-mentioned and deeply esteemed conversation.

As for Harold, he had been working hard—flat out—on Sir Gardnor's book; putting eight or nine hours a day into it. It was the hardest that he had worked since his Finals, and he had been thoroughly enjoying himself.

Not that he was up to date, or anything like it. That was because of the typing problem. Mr. Frith had set aside one of his best clerks, practically the star performer in the whole Department. But typing was as yet scarcely his *métier*. Instructed as he had been in the Amimbo Commercial College and allowed to practice on a machine in the Y.M.C.A. in the evenings, he was still only somewhere in the high-grade amateur bracket. Enthusiastic, yes; proficient, no.

And overawed by his new responsibilities, he grew nervous. Sometimes he left out whole sentences; at other times only odd lines or key phrases. Every so often through overconcentration he just shoved the carriage back, forgetting altogether to use the line-space lever. When that happened, everything went black: words got piled up on top of other words, or filled up the little spaces in between. Then he would rub out furiously, tearing great gashes in the paper.

But still he persevered. An enormously strong young man, he hammered. And when he pulled things, bits of the typewriter came clean away in his hands. One of the corrugated knobs on the platen had been missing for weeks, and the other, which had come off only yesterday, was now resting on top of his inkwell.

Touch typing was the method in which the Commercial College specialized. Even now to glance down at the keyboard for a single moment to satisfy himself that it was still intact would have seemed tantamount to cheating. As a result, breathing heavily and with his eyes hypnotically fixed on his copy, he diligently hit one wrong key after another, bearing down on it each time like a navvy, and pausing only to wrench the little typeheads apart when two of them happened to come up together and get jammed. The flimsy trestle table at which he worked rocked and sagged and shuddered, and the floor around him looked as though it had been showered in pygmy confetti as the centers of the "o's" and the insides of the loops on the "b's" and "d's" and "p's" were cut clean out of the paper by the hammer blows.

Not that it really mattered. With so many urgent affairs of State on the Governor's mind, even the book itself seemed temporarily to have been forgotten. And with the last section of the Trade Tables finally handed over to the typist, Harold found himself suddenly with nothing to do.

There he was, nearly five thousand miles from home; scratching himself at intervals because the heat had already brought up a rash on both his forearms; slightly queasy inside from the blown-up, overripe dessert that the houseboy had just served him at dinner; and dispirited.

From his chair on the veranda, with the pot of pale, ineffectual coffee on the table beside him, he could see the lights of the Residency through the distant bank of bombax and uroko trees.

It was less than half a mile away, but somehow the distance seemed immeasurable. The lights might have been illuminations on another planet. They made him feel more isolated still. And with his legs stuck out onto the stool in front and his chin resting on his chest, he found himself thinking about Lady Anne.

He remembered those full, shining eyes set in the pale face with its frame of dark hair. He remembered the amused, almost pitying kind of smile. And he wondered if she had remembered that invitation that she was going to send him to come across to the Residency sometime when they were both feeling bored.

He gave a little shudder and shook himself. Even the bar at the Royal Albert would be better than the empty bungalow. It would give him something to do; even possibly someone to talk to.

It was not until nearly ten o'clock that Harold finally reached the Royal Albert. That was because the taxi had broken down. An ancient landaulet of immense size, it had proved to have something gravely—even mortally, Harold suspected—wrong with the engine. The driver, surrounded by a small circle of his more knowledgeable friends, had remained in the hotel court-yard, standing beside the open hood assuring everyone that it was the matter of a moment, a mere twist with a wrench, or a screwdriver or something, to eliminate those deafening back-firings.

The bar itself was empty when Harold entered. He had just ordered himself a lager that the boy had assured him was cold— very well cold, sir, like iced—when he saw someone approaching. He was a young man; a remarkably fashionable young man. Beneath the glistening black face, the pale blue shirt and the marigold-colored tie caught the eye like a challenge. He was wearing a red boutonniere, and his new plaited shoes were strikingly crisscrossed in strands of contrasting leathers.

He walked up to the bar with an easy, contemptuous swagger.

"Good evening, Charles," he said, as he perched himself on one of the high stools. "My usual."

The barman smiled back at him.

"Yassaar," he said. "Your usual. What you want to drink, sah?"

It was a gin fizz that the young man ordered. He was very knowledgeable about it and insisted that the boy make it with Booth's and Rose's. He was still discussing the merits of other gins, other fruit juices, when he suddenly became aware of Harold. He looked again. And, having looked a second time, he gaped. His glass held halfway to his lips, he was transfixed.

Then, impulsively pushing his drink away from him, he slid off the high stool and came over.

"Excuse me, sir," he said with a little bow as though he were a floorwalker. "Do I disturb private thoughts, or may I be so bold as to inquire if that is an Emma tie you are wearing? You follow me, sir? Emma—Emmanuel College of Cambridge University, England?"

Harold shifted round to face him. The young man bent forward, arching his shoulders as he did so. His politeness was overwhelming.

"Yes, it's an Emmanuel tie," Harold told him.

The young man was temporarily overcome. Then he shot out a powerful hand of welcome.

"Permit me to introduce myself," he said. "The name is Ngo Ngono. You've heard of me? I was at Cambridge University too. At Caius. Often I, also, wear my College tie. But tonight it is a flowered one, unfortunately. Permit me to give you my card. It has my name on it."

While he was speaking, he had produced an expensive-looking morocco wallet and was carefully drawing out a card from between its two little leaves of tissue paper.

"As you will well know, sir," he explained, "it is not usual to mention the name of the college. Only the University. And the degree, of course. Is this your first visit? Are you happy? Do you have any wishes? Allow me to offer you a drink, sir. A token for old good times beside the Cam. Tell me your pleasure."

"I'm drinking lager," Harold told him.

But Mr. Ngono would not hear of it.

"It must be champagne," he said. "Champagne for a celebration. Often when alone I drink champagne. It is quite my usual. I prefer it."

He clapped his hands as he said so and called to the boy at the far end of the bar.

"A bottle of champagne in a bucket with ice and two glasses. Champagne glasses of course, all double quick." Then turning to Harold, he added. "This is such great pleasure for myself bumping into you like this. Think of the talks that we shall have. There is so little conversation in Amimbo. Not deep, intellectual conversation, I mean. Not about mutual friends."

Over the champagne, Mr. Ngono became not merely convivial, but inquisitive.

"And your important employment?" he asked. "You are connected with the Government? You will be our new Resident Officer? Is it Omtala you are destined for? You have heard about the regrettable vacancy, of course. They will be most pleased to see you."

"I'm a statistician," Harold replied. "They won't be wanting me up there."

Mr. Ngono waved the point aside.

"Permit me, sir, to disagree. Emphatically, bloody-well disagree. Statisticians are needed everywhere. This is a very backward country in some respects. Omtala has not even one statistician. Not damn one. You know why I am here?"

Harold shook his head.

"Then I will tell you. In great confidence, of course. I have come to found a publishing house. To counteract the backwardness. A publishing house like Macmillan's. There is widespread illiteracy among my people. Among the women especially; it is deplorable. The books will be in the native dialects, with the corresponding pictures in color facing opposite. And all in foreign translations, at a later stage. It will be a very large publishing house. I myself as founder shall be its managing director."

"Should be interesting," Harold told him.

"Most interesting, indeed," Mr. Ngono continued. "Of course, I shall require Government backing. I shall demand it—very discreetly, but most firmly. It will not succeed unless books are made compulsory. I shall ask the Governor to declare illiteracy illegal. Ban it right out with heavy fines."

He paused, breathless for a moment, and then resumed.

"Have you met our Governor?" he asked. "Maybe I could help you with an introduction? Purely out of friendship, I mean. Because of our Cambridge bond. I am very close to the Governor. Often, I advise him. I am starting also a new technical school. The Governor will be our first Patron. I shall ask him. That is yet another reason why I am here."

The bottle of champagne was almost finished by now, and already Mr. Ngono was a little drunk.

"Our Governor is much like a good king," he was saying. "He is all-powerful and also extremely nice. Most philosophic and intelligent, and of great patience. If he should leave us, I verily believe the crops would fail. By Jove, I do really. It will be a great regret for me always that I could not have been the first to introduce you to such a man."

Mr. Ngono was leaning forward by now. His face was up close to Harold's.

"But there is one other," he said. "It is Her Excellency—the Governor's wife, you understand. She is not a personal friend, I am most sad to say. I have shaken hands, yes; but spoken, unfortunately never. She is the most extremely beautiful person I have ever seen. Like a photograph. A goddess. A veritable goddess. Everyone who has cast eyes on her agrees that."

Mr. Ngono poured out the last of the champagne.

"But"—here he drew the corners of his mouth down and dropped his voice to the merest audible whisper—"also a most naughty goddess, so I have heard tell. A most extremely naughty one."

He was leaning so far forward on his stool to impart this confidence that he accidentally slipped. He had to put both hands on Harold's shoulders to save himself.

"But I should not have spoken," he said. "If she should become your friend, I am ruined. Also my publishing house. Please altogether to forget my last remark. It is no more than idle hearsay, I don't damn well doubt. Not a single word of so-called truth from start to finish."

Chapter 5

IT WAS there ready waiting for him on the tray when he got back from seeing Mr. Frith. One of the boys from the Residency must have delivered it.

The envelope had a crown on the back, and inside was the crisply printed invitation card. It stated, formally enough, that Her Excellency, Lady Anne Hackforth, would be at home at four-thirty P.M. next Wednesday. His own name had been written at the top in a precise, impersonal kind of script. But in the bottom right-hand corner there were two words scribbled in a contrastingly bright ink: *"Do come."*

So she's remembered about me, has she? Harold asked himself. I suppose that means that she's feeling bored again. Or perhaps she thinks that I am.

He was, at it happened, not in the least bored. Sir Gardnor had found time to send him a line of thanks for the new presentation of the Trade Tables. And other people, too, in Amimbo had just caught up with the fact that he was out there with them. At breakfast that morning there had been a letter from Establishment, confirming his appointment and thoughtfully enclosing an Overseas Allowances form; a mimeographed sheet from the Milner Sports Club, requesting the sum of three guineas; and a black-rimmed card with deckle edges inviting him to the memorial service in the Anglican Cathedral for poor Major Henderson.

There was also someone else who had remembered Harold: Mr. Ngono. His letter put on record how extremely much the writer had enjoyed meeting him the other evening and proposed full dinner next time, with or without dancing just as Harold preferred. Mr. Ngono's own car could be available to call for him, the earlier the so much better; and would Harold's official position, Mr. Ngono wondered, permit him to take a prominent seat on the board of a little syndicate that Mr. Ngono was about to form for the import of American fertilizers. He was ready, Mr. Ngono stressed, to come along to the bungalow at any time for a few drinks and a most friendly chat if Harold would rather have things that way.

Harold took great pains to make himself presentable for Her Excellency's tea party.

If he was going to meet the cream of Amimbo society, he wanted to be looking at his very best. And the visit to the barber at the Royal Albert had not been entirely successful. The man had cropped, rather than merely cut; and studying the result in the mirror, Harold decided that it made him look rather younger: it was an effect that he disliked intensely. On the other hand, he had already learned the great secret of dressing in the tropics. It was simply to leave it all until as late as possible, not putting on the jacket until actually leaving the front door, so that the sweat marks between the shoulders would have less time to work though.

The only thing that was still worrying him was the emerald-green hair oil that the hotel barber had sold to him. The color vanished magically as soon as it reached the scalp, but the smell remained. And it was a peculiarly powerful and pungent kind of smell. As he crossed the Residency threshold, he was still conscious of it.

This time there was no A.D.C. waiting for him at the top of the stairs. The black servant with white jacket and the gold sash led him along the corridor toward the west wing. And even when they had reached it and turned sharply right by the last of the royal portraits, there was still that same endless expanse of blue carpet stretching ahead of them.

As he reached the doorway at the far end, Harold glanced down at his watch.

Oh, damn, he reflected. I'm punctual. I've bloody well done it again. I'm the first.

The room into which he was shown was strikingly different from the Governor's library on the other side. For a start, it was feminine: all white and chintzy. There were a lot of photographs in silver frames, and the flowers looked as though they belonged there, rather than having simply been arranged. It was like any room in a pleasant country house in Sussex.

Already there was someone coming forward across the large

white rug to meet him. It was a thin, straw-colored woman, and she was thrusting out a thin, straw-colored hand.

"Oh, Mr. Stebbs," she said. "Her Excellency will be so glad that you were able to come."

She paused for a moment, and then added in the same flat, rather high-pitched voice, "I'm Sybil Prosser."

"How d'you do?" he said. "I'm afraid I'm early."

"Not a bit," Miss Prosser assured him, looking across at the Empire clock on the mantelpiece. "You're not. Really you're not. You're exactly on time. To the very minute."

She broke off long enough to gather up some petals that had fallen onto the table from the flower vase beside her and turned toward him.

"Do sit down, won't you, Mr. Stebbs? Lady Anne ought to be here by now. She's only resting."

It occurred to Harold as he sat himself in one of the small, cushiony chairs that he had never seen anyone quite so ill at ease as Miss Prosser. Even her new-looking white dress did not fit properly. There was something wrong with the collar, and while she was talking, she kept tugging at it in an irritable, absent-minded kind of fashion. She had chosen the corner of the couch for herself, and she did not fit there either. With no natural, built-in comforts, she could find nowhere to place her left arm. In the end, she left it hanging helplessly by her side and tried crossing her legs the other way. The gesture drew attention to her rather strangely oversize feet in their pointed white suede shoes.

"Smoke if you want to," she told him. "They're beside you. I don't myself. I used to. But not any longer."

He had not yet lit the cigarette when Sybil Prosser spoke again.

"May I ask a favor?" she inquired. "A personal one, I mean."

It was the voice that did it. On her lips, it did not sound like asking for a favor at all: there was the distinct note of a threat underlying it. He finished lighting his cigarette.

"What is it?" he asked.

She leaned forward, the collar of her dress rising still further from her long neck as she did so.

"Don't stay too long," she said. "Please just have tea, and then go away again. You don't understand, but it's my responsibility.

Lady Anne isn't well, you see. She's been under great strain lately. That's why I took her away. Why I went with her, I mean. I wanted her to be away longer. But she insisted on coming back again. She'll be very glad to see you. I know she will. If only you don't stay . . ."

Harold put down his cigarette.

"Would you rather I left now?"

It was not Miss Prosser who answered him. It was Lady Anne. She was standing in the far doorway. Her hands folded and her head inclined to one side, she was smiling. There was something in her attitude that made Harold wonder whether she had been there all the time, whether she had overheard the whole conversation.

"Has Sybil been trying to get rid of you already?" she asked. "Whatever *have* you done to deserve it?"

She came forward, still smiling and walking rather slowly as though she were enjoying the situation and did not want to see it pass.

"She should have been apologizing, you know," she went on. "For dragging you up here, I mean. Because this isn't a real do. There's no one else. It's only the three of us. Do you mind?"

The smell of the emerald hair oil had just reached him again: he wondered if the others were aware of it too.

"Not a bit," he replied. "It's nicer this way, isn't it? Not so many people, I mean."

Lady Anne stopped smiling.

"Do you know why I sent you one of those invitations?" she asked. "Because you'd have refused if I'd just written to you—you know you would. But you couldn't very well if I sent you an official card. And so you're here."

She was facing him by now, and Harold was conscious again of what remarkably fine eyes she had. It was as though they were actually lit up from within and were shining outwards.

This was an entirely different woman from the one who had come over to the bungalow. She seemed somehow taller; tall, and composed and elegant. And beautiful. To his annoyance Harold found himself remembering Mr. Ngono's words, "like a photograph. A goddess. A veritable goddess."

The little, withered-up locust of a butler came in to set out the tea table. Harold noticed that he did not allow the other servants anywhere near Lady Anne; there was an invisible line, and he stood on his side of it.

"You'd better be prepared for it," Lady Anne was saying. "It's no good searching for a decent bookshop in Amimbo because there isn't one. The only thing is to write back home to *The Times*. It takes weeks, but at least you get what you ask for. Or sometimes you do. The last lot never got here at all."

Miss Prosser took her cue.

"They sent two copies of *The Green Hat*," she said. "And we never sent the second one back," she added. "So they charged us for it. It's still about here somewhere."

"Then I shall lend it to Mr. Stebbs," Lady Anne told her. "You'd like that, wouldn't you, Mr. Stebbs? It can be very dull here in the evenings if you haven't got anything to read. And when you've finished it you can bring it back, and tell me what you think of it." She took a cigarette from the box that the butler was holding out to her. "We're nearly always here, aren't we, Sybil? All that Mr. Stebbs has to do is to telephone and come over."

Miss Prosser did not answer immediately. She had been looking across at Harold. Whenever she thought that Lady Anne was not watching, she raised her sparse, straw-colored eyebrows. But this time she was observed.

"Oh yes," she said hurriedly. "Nearly always. In the evenings, that is. Almost any evening. Unless Lady Anne is doing anything, of course."

Harold could smell the hair oil again.

"It'd be very nice," he heard his own voice answering. "Very nice indeed. I should enjoy that."

"Then you shall come," Lady Anne told him. "And we shall sit in here after dinner and pretend that we're back in England again. We'll send the servants away and put the big center light out and drink highballs and just talk. If Sybil finds that she's getting sleepy she can go to bed and leave us together. We shall be able to find plenty to talk about, shan't we, Mr. Stebbs?"

"Thank you very much," he said. "I shall look forward. But I really must be getting back now. It's late. I'm afraid I've got things to do."

Lady Anne did not even look at him as she answered. She was staring right over his shoulder into space.

"It can't have been any fun for you," she said. "Not this afternoon, I mean. But there'll be plenty of other times. And Sybil is quite right. I haven't been well, you know. I'm not really well now. I get tired so quickly."

Miss Prosser had uncrossed her legs and got up. Harold noticed that she gave a little shooing motion as she approached him. He obeyed by holding out his hand to say goodbye.

Suddenly Lady Anne came to life again.

"But he can't go without seeing the photograph, can he?" she asked. "He can't go without seeing my Timothy."

She went over to her desk and came back with one of the little silver frames.

"That's my Timothy," she said. "Don't you think he's adorable?"

The face that regarded him from the frame was that of a small boy of seven or eight. It had the Governor's high forehead and her enormous eyes.

"He's jolly good-looking, isn't he?" Harold said truthfully. "When can I meet him?"

Lady Anne reached out her hand for the photograph. Because she thought that he was slow in giving it to her she almost snatched it from him.

"You can't," she said. "That's the whole point. And I can't either. He's in England, and I'm out here. Oh Timothy, Timothy darling, I do love you so. Some day, Timothy, I'll make it all come right. I promise I will."

She was still hugging the photograph up against her bosom as she was speaking and seemed temporarily to have forgotten that Harold was standing there. He was relieved when Sybil Prosser, awkward and angular as ever, went across to the bellpull to summon one of the servants to show him out.

The houseboy who opened the door of the bungalow was wearing an expression of idiotic self-importance. Harold recognized the expression immediately: it meant that someone had telephoned.

As it turned out, the telephone had rung more than once. Three times, in fact; and, each time it had been Mr. Frith who was at the other end. Harold, he said, was to ring back immediately, at once, no delay, now, straightaway, very top urgent.

More to impress the houseboy than for any other reason, Harold took his time. He went through to the bathroom, washed, combed his hair and, quite unnecessarily, changed his tie. Then he walked slowly back to the hall—sauntering deliberately when he was sure that the houseboy was still peering through the bead curtain—and picked up the receiver.

It was certainly an agitated Mr. Frith who answered.

"Where have you been?" he demanded. "They've been looking everywhere for you. The Governor wants you. Or at least, he did. It's too late now. Nothing you can do about it. But for God's sake don't let it happen again. H.E.'s furious. Wanted to get on with the book, or something . . ."

"I'm sorry, sir."

"That won't help," Mr. Frith replied. "The harm's done now."

He paused.

"Got anything on this evening?" he asked.

"Nothing in particular," Harold told him.

"Better come across to the Club. Know where it is?"

"I'll find it, sir."

"Seven o'clock, then. In the bar. Give you time to think up something for me to tell Sir Gardnor."

There was a sharp click in Harold's ear, and Mr. Frith had rung off. He was still annoyed with him, Harold gathered.

The Milner Club was a handsome one-story building with a raised roof to let the air in. It was approached by a long, dusty drive, bordered on either side by a lawn of coarse, closely cropped grass. A large notice, from which the paint was already flaking, read: STRICTLY MEMBERS ONLY.

The bar to which the steward showed him was certainly imposing. It extended the whole length of the clubhouse. And it was staffed for emergencies. Despite the fact that there were only two members lost somewhere in the distance up at the far end, there were three bartenders—all wearing clean white jackets, all standing to attention, and all staring vacantly over the mahogany counter into space. Other black faces showed from behind the service hatch.

Harold sat down and waited for Mr. Frith. He was late; really late. It was nearly seven-thirty when he arrived. And he was perspiring. There was no sign of the tic any longer: the muscles around his mouth had already sagged. It was now an overrelaxed, imprecise kind of face that he was wearing.

"Why aren't you drinking anything?" he asked. "Thought I told them to make you a member."

"I've sent my three guineas."

"Then you're a member," Mr. Frith told him.

He was signaling to the steward while he was speaking.

"What are you doing, boy?" he demanded. "Come over here. We need you."

It was not until Mr. Frith had composed himself, holding his glass in both hands in between the sips, that he seemed to remember why he had asked Harold to come over. Then he suddenly became very serious.

"You've got some explaining to do," he said. "And not just to me. To H.E. Where were you this afternoon? The whole bloody switchboard was trying to find you."

"I was about," Harold told him. "As a matter of fact, I was up there all the time. Having tea with Lady Anne."

Mr. Frith slopped most of his whisky down his shirt front.

"Don't tell me that's started up again," he said. "Not already."

"What's wrong with it?" Harold asked.

But Mr. Frith ignored him. He was wiping himself down with one hand and, with the other, trying to call the boy over. He wanted his glass refilled.

When he turned back to Harold, he had lowered his voice and drawn his stool up closer.

"You don't want to go blotting your copybook the first month out here, now do you?" he said. "You're the third of them, remember. H.E. got rid of Number One like that."

Mr. Frith attempted to snap his fingers in the air, but the effect was only mildly dramatic because it was entirely soundless.

"Slung him out," he went on, "before he'd even got his bags unpacked. Here today, gone tomorrow. H.E.'s like that."

Harold leaned back on his stool and lit a cigarette.

"What happened to the last one?" he asked.

But Mr. Frith only shook his head.

"Some other time. Not now," he said. "I've had enough for one day."

Chapter 6

THE MEMORIAL service for the unhappy Henderson was, for reasons of Government policy, designed to be a really slap-up affair.

Ever since nine o'clock that morning, Queen Victoria Avenue had been posted by the South Shropshires, already sweating heavily beneath their close-fitting dress uniform; the native militia, carrying black sashes across their white jackets, were stationed at the side roads to cut off cross traffic; and the very go-ahead Bishop of Osimkwa and Amimbo had flown in by light plane the evening before, with his chaplain and his collapsible pastoral staff. All along the route to the Cathedral, there was a brisk trade going on in Union Jacks, small celluloid dolls, Boat Race trophies, models of the Lord Mayor's coach in gilt, and various kinds of nut toffees, lemonade powders and cooked meats.

St. Stephen's Cathedral itself was scarcely large enough for the ceremony. But small as it was, it did at least look English. The Roman Catholic counterpart on the other side of the town, with its copper dome and campanile, suggested something of Italian or even Near Eastern origin and was generally regarded as looking out of place there.

Harold's own card, he found, entitled him to a pew in the eighth row. It was definitely behind the big shots, but appreciably in front of retail commerce, railway employees, postal workers, and other miscellaneous hangers-on.

As for Mr. Ngono, he was humiliatingly near the rear of the church. He had, however, managed to secure himself an aisle-side seat. In consequence there was rather a lot of waving and flapping of the printed Order of Service as he greeted mourners and friends alike as they passed by him. Harold noticed that Mr. Ngono was in a black tail coat and carrying a black topper and black gloves and was wearing a band of black crepe around his upper left arm. He also had an umbrella. Harold suddenly wondered whether the black tie with his own lounge suit was sufficient.

Despite the electric fans, the temperature inside the Cathedral was already nearing the eighty mark, and the verger was going round spraying the banks of fast-wilting flowers with a watering can. Up in the loft, the organist had a glass of water beside him and kept throwing back the loose sleeves of his surplice so that they should not cling to his wrists.

The Governor's instructions for full ceremonial had been carried out to the letter. In front of the high altar stood a symbolic coffin draped in the Union Jack: the real interment had, of course, because of the temperature, taken place at the earliest possible moment up at Omtala. And in front of the empty coffin were arranged a couple of gold armchairs, thrones almost, on a square of the distinctive Residency blue carpet. There were two more chairs for the Household, still gold but without arms.

In that heat, the organ was inevitably a trifle flat. But the organist had grown accustomed to that. Sometimes for a three P.M. Children's Service he had known the open diapason to go down by as much as a semitone, until it was just an incoherent rumble and nothing more.

Today, however, he was too intent upon keeping watch in his rear mirror to care very deeply. And a moment later, he saw what he had been waiting for. At exactly eleven o'clock, the figure of Colonel Hudson of the Shropshires appeared in the little oblong of looking glass. There was a crash of Army boots being brought down onto the hot gravel; arms came up to the Present with a rattle; and the blast of Regimental buglers signaled the arrival of the Governor.

The congregation rose. The Dean of St. Stephen's, who had been waiting at the top of the steps, descended; the Bishop of Osimkwa and Amimbo, his pastoral staff now assembled to its full height, emerged from behind a pillar; the Governor and the Governor's Lady got into position, with the A.D.C and the Hon. Sybil Prosser one full pace behind; and the procession moved forward.

As the Governor went past him, it occurred to Harold that he had never before seen anyone quite so absolutely splendid. And more than splendid: Viceregal at least.

Half a head taller than those around him, with his gold-braided uniform buttoned up to the neck in that suffocating heat and with his plumed hat stuck under his arm, he dominated. His mere presence seemed to give a grandeur to death that would otherwise have been missing.

Lady Anne, dressed in black from head to foot and with a black veil that hid her face, was almost entirely obscured by him. Harold caught a brief glimpse of her: shoulders bowed, and eyes lowered to the ground. Then the Governor's gold braid and medals and plumes got in the way and he lost sight of her again.

With the entrance of the Governor, the West Door of the Cathedral had been closed, and the temperature inside began to mount steadily. Sweat drops started to run down the Bishop's face, and Harold could see Sybil Prosser using the Order of Service as a fan.

Immediately in front of her, Lady Anne was sitting. Against the magnificence of the Governor's uniform, the black that Lady Anne was wearing seemed blacker still. She was motionless, with her head bent forward, her hands folded in her lap.

My God, doesn't she look like a widow, he suddenly found himself thinking.

He did not see Lady Anne again until the Service was over. Then she came down the aisle on the near side of the Governor. Against the blackness of her dress, her face showed paler than ever. It seemed to be quite drained of blood; of life almost. As she passed his pew, she momentarily pushed back her veil as

64

though gasping for breath in that asphyxiating air. It was a tired, pathetic gesture. If the service had gone on any longer, he doubted if she could have survived it.

Then he looked across at Sir Gardnor. He was still as upright and tightly buttoned-up as ever. The gold braid and the medals shone in the light from the West doorway, and his plumed hat was being carried at exactly the correct angle.

He had, however, been weeping: his eyes were still red and moist-looking. After all, Henderson had been one of his men. He had picked and promoted him. And it was only natural that the service should have moved the Governor deeply; so deeply, in fact, that he seemed scarcely to be aware that Lady Anne was beside him.

When she faltered for a moment and put out her hand instinctively for some support, it was Sybil Prosser who caught hold of her. Sir Gardnor was already half a pace ahead, chin up and staring out into the distance.

The final gesture of respect to the dead man—it was a volley of blanks fired into the air by the exhausted Shropshires—sent the kites that had been monotonously wheeling overhead into a sudden pattern of power dives and spirals and raised a black-and-white cloud of all the crows in Amimbo, which took off with a noise like surf and made helter-skelter for the peace and safety of the marshaling yards.

As the last echo of the volley was still dying away, Harold saw that Mr. Frith was beckoning. He seemed to be agitated, and Harold noticed that his tic had grown worse again.

"It's H.E.," Mr. Frith said as soon as Harold had managed to reach him through the dispersing crowd. "He wants you back at the House. Straightaway. And he wants me to come along, too. You'd better be ready for it. This may be your return ticket."

The tone of voice and Mr. Frith's state of nerves annoyed him. If the Governor felt like being bloody-minded, Harold was perfectly ready to be equally bloody-minded in return.

"Okay," he told him. "Let's go along together." He paused and then added, "I shouldn't think there's any particular hurry.

From the way he was looking just now, he can't be exactly ready for receiving visitors."

But Mr. Frith was not so sure.

"You don't know H.E.," he said. "Wants us round as soon as we can get there. A.D.C. said so."

Even with the flag on the front of Mr. Frith's car, it was a little difficult to get through the crowd. The path for the Residency Rolls had been kept wide open, but by now the sightseers had surged forward again. Mr. Frith kept glancing at his watch and telling the driver to hurry.

There was certainly no delay when they reached the House. The A.D.C had already miraculously changed back into his plain white and was waiting for them. He agreed with Mr. Frith that it had been a simple and beautiful Service.

"Rather good singing, I thought."

"Full turnout, too."

"Henderson was Methodist, actually."

"Really?"

And with that, they passed through into the Governor's suite. The Governor himself appeared to have been caught unprepared. Still wearing his blue dress trousers, he had removed his scarlet jacket altogether and undone the stud of his collarband. But he was at his most cordial. He was standing with his back to the empty fireplace, glass in his hand.

"Ah, come in, Mr. Frith. Come in. And you too, Mr. Stebbs. You'll join me in a drink, I hope. Very hot in the Cathedral. Very hot indeed." He looked over to the A.D.C. "Remind me to have a word with the Dean about it. It's really quite intolerable. There must be something they can do." He had swung round again. "You enjoyed the ceremony, Mr. Stebbs?"

"I thought it was very moving," Harold told him.

The Governor seemed pleased.

"It was, wasn't it," he replied. "Pity there were no relatives. And the Bishop was too long again. He knows: he saw me looking at him. You don't want a sermon on an occasion of that kind. You simply want a tribute."

"I agree," Harold said politely.

But he had spoken too soon; spoken when there had been no

need to speak at all, in fact. The Governor immediately turned on him.

"Not that a human life can be dismissed just like that," he went on, with a wave of the hand. "After all, it *is* Divine Service, and it *is* a Funeral Oration. It's not exactly in the nature of a testimonial, is it, Mr. Stebbs?"

This time, Harold knew enough not to answer; Mr. Frith could have saved himself the little damping-down motions that he was making with his hands.

"But I didn't bring you here to discuss sermons, Mr. Stebbs," the Governor told him. "I brought you here to congratulate you. And you, Mr. Frith, for finding him. The statistical pages are excellent. Quite excellent." He paused. "They'll all have to be done again, of course. But no matter."

"Done again?"

"That surprises you, Mr. Stebbs? You're entirely blameless, I assure you. It's simply that I have decided to redraft the Budget. There will be an entirely new Budget along entirely new lines."

Mr. Frith gave a sudden, little jump.

"Does Financial Secretary . . ." he began.

"Oh yes," Sir Gardnor replied. "He knows. I've just told him. I've asked him to come over, in fact. It seems he's short-handed. Is he, Mr. Frith?"

"Two down in Establishment, sir," Mr. Frith told him, "and one on extended sick leave. Financial Secretary is due to go away himself, sir, at the end of the month."

"Then that may have to be postponed, mayn't it, Mr. Frith?" Sir Gardnor continued. He was at his blandest and most smiling by now. "A new budget will naturally mean more work for all of us, won't it? And that is where our friend Mr. Stebbs can be of such assistance."

He was speaking in the encouraging manner of a School Visitor at a prize-giving.

"And you can assist me, too, Mr. Frith," he said. "Perhaps you could put Mr. Stebbs on Financial Secretary's strength. That would strengthen it, wouldn't it?" Sir Gardnor poured himself another drink while he was speaking and smiled at Harold. "I don't doubt that between us we can produce a Budget, do you, Mr. Stebbs?"

The A.D.C. had come back into the room, followed by a servant carrying Sir Gardnor's white suit on a hanger. But Sir Gardnor seemed oblivious to him.

"In primitive societies, it is only a system of indirect taxation that ever produces any revenue," he was saying. "And that means that rich and poor alike pay the same taxes. It's really most inequitable and I intend to tackle it. You are an economist, are you not, Mr. Stebbs?"

"No, sir. I'm a mathematician."

Sir Gardnor, however, was in no mood to be put off.

"Then you are exactly what is needed, aren't you?" he replied. "It's mostly figures when you come down to it, isn't it, Mr. Stebbs? Budgets are simply figures—with some imagination and a little common sense. You must forgive me for a moment while I change." He was over at the door by now. "Don't go," he called over his shoulder. "Please don't go. There is one other matter."

Mr. Frith caught Harold's eye.

"You'd have been better off with your ticket," he said. "There'll be all hell to pay if he starts monkeying about with the taxes."

Harold shrugged his shoulders.

"I don't mind having a bash at it," he said. "It's more or less my line of country."

"And it's mine when the trouble starts," Mr. Frith replied. "Things are comparatively quiet at the moment."

Sir Gardnor re-emerged while he was still dressing. The servant followed close behind him trying hard to slip the Governor's white jacket properly into place. But the man's presence annoyed Sir Gardnor. He motioned him away.

"I understand, Mr. Stebbs, that you've seen Lady Anne," he said. "When was it? Last Thursday, I believe. Tell me frankly, how did you think she was looking?"

Harold was conscious that Sir Gardnor's curiously pale blue eyes were fixed on him as he waited for the answer. There was no trace at the moment of that famous, all-embracing smile.

Harold did not reply immediately.

"I thought she looked rather pale, sir," he said at length.

"I'm afraid she does," Sir Gardnor replied. "It's the climate, you know. It's not kind to women. It doesn't suit them." Sir Gardnor paused. "But you wouldn't see the difference, of course. You hadn't met Lady Anne before, had you?" he asked.

He was no longer looking at Harold as he put the question, and his manner was casual and offhand. But for the second time, Mr. Frith gave a noticeable jump. His right eyelid began to go *tic-tic* again.

Harold's reply took even longer this time.

"Only once, sir," he said. "Over by the bungalow."

The effect on Sir Gardnor was remarkable. He at once got up and came over.

"But this is excellent news," he said. "Excellent. It means that Lady Anne's getting over it."

He turned to Mr. Frith.

"Do you know," he said, "that at first Lady Anne wouldn't go near the bungalow, not even when she was with me?"

Chapter 7

Trumpet Blast had just undergone a palace revolution.

There had been an Extraordinary General Meeting, followed by a Stockholders' Committee; a conspiracy, really. As a result, the Editor had resigned, and his Judas-like General Manager, Mr. Talefwa, had succeeded to the editorial chair, combining with it the posts of Managing Director and Chairman of the Board.

The question of where the money came from to run the paper was in everybody's mind. There were some who held that it must be Italian; the more responsible said German; and a few, looking broodingly into the future, suggested Russian. Locally, the name of Mr. Ngono was whispered; and for forty-eight hours, Mr. Ngono, neither confirming nor denying the rumors, accepted drinks and other presents from those wanting the posts of Advertisement Manager, Fashion Editor, Paris Correspondent, Chief Sub., and Circulation Director.

Mr. Talefwa himself was a rather remarkable young man. For a start, he was still on the right side of thirty; and he was a Ph.D. Not that, with his powers of application, the outcome of his University career had ever been in any doubt. He didn't drink. He didn't smoke. He didn't play games. He didn't go to the cinema. He had no girl friends; had no friends of any kind, for that matter.

Throughout his five years in London he had spent his entire time either listening to lectures or working in his back bed-sitter in Belsize Park. He had been an ideal lodger, quiet, courteous, and unexacting. The only trouble had been on weekends when the landlady, because of his unending studies, found it difficult to get into his room to tidy up.

The London School of Economics was justly proud of him; would have been delighted to have him on the teaching staff and had been genuinely sorry when he decided to return to his native Amimbo.

Now that he had control, the first of Mr. Talefwa's changes was to rename the paper *Amimbo Mirror*. The second was to print the whole of the front page in English. And it was particularly unfortunate that the first issue under his editorship should have been the one to cover the Memorial Service in St. Stephen's.

IN HONOUR OF WHAT? the headline ran across the whole front page. What made it so maddening, too, was that the editorial that followed repeated almost word for word the Governor's Reassembly Speech of six months before to the effect that it was the duty and privilege of the Colonial Service to bring their black brethren through education into political consciousness and ultimately on to self-government. Why then, the article demanded, had only the British been allowed to conduct the Service? Was there no African, after nearly sixty years of white rule, sufficiently educated even to read the Lesson?

Moreover, if the District Officer deserved a Memorial Service— and the *Amimbo Mirror* did not seek to question it—when was the Governor planning to hold a Memorial Service for the murdered houseboy? If not, why not? Was all human life sacred? Or only white human life?

Mr. Talefwa certainly had scored a hit. His assistant reported that not once but twice, a Government messenger had called on a bicycle to collect more copies: six on the first occasion and no fewer than eighteen on his second visit.

Even casual sales picked up in consequence. Forty-three copies were sold over the counter during the morning rush period. And Mr. Talefwa, with the instinct of a born journalist, decided to cut tomorrow's article by three hundred words, leaving space for a solitary single-column ad at the bottom of the final column.

Altogether, Mr. Talefwa consumed a great deal of Government time. Native Affairs first tried to shrug it off because the article was in English, then asked that it be referred back to them because the rest of the paper had an exclusively Mimbo circulation. The Chief of Police was strongly in favor of raiding the *Mirror* offices, confiscating the press, and placing an armed picket at the door to prevent re-entry. The Postmaster General, on the other hand, recommended a more subtle approach: the Obscene Publications Act of 1912 seemed to him to fit it to a T—and had the additional advantage of leaving politics out of it altogether. Mr. Frith was for ignoring the article. And the Bishop was for demanding full right of reply with equal editorial prominence.

As for the Governor, his attitude was entirely different. And at the 11 o'clock Council, he made himself embarrassingly plain. He was looking hard at Mr. Frith as he said it.

"But how can we ignore it, Acting Chief Secretary?" he asked. "Even if we decide to close our eyes to it, it is there for others to see. And it is not Mr. Talefwa who is condemning us. We are condemning ourselves. This apparently talented young man has been so grossly neglected by *us*." The "us" was so heavily accentuated that it obviously meant "you." "He is entirely ignorant of our purpose. Indeed, he has wholly misconstrued it. Perhaps Native Affairs could tell us how long he has been here."

Head of Native Affairs glanced hurriedly down at his papers. With commendable forethought he had picked them up from Immigration Control on the way over.

"Approximately six months, Excellency," he said. "As a returning national, he came in on an A.N.3."

But the Governor was not listening.

"Six months," he said, "six wasted months. By our neglect a potential friend has been converted into an enemy; possibly a very dangerous enemy."

The Governor paused: it was a long pause. He intended to keep the Council in uneasy suspense.

"I myself," he announced at last, "will see him personally. Not immediately, of course: that would indicate concern. And not indefinitely postponed: that would be misinterpreted as indifference."

He turned to his left for a moment, revealing his magnificent profile to the whole table.

"Council Secretary," he said, "would you remind my A.D.C. that I shall be inviting Mr. Talefwa to luncheon. In a fortnight's time. The Thursday, of course. We will decide later about numbers."

It had come: the letter in the handwriting that didn't look as though it had been handwritten. And along with Miss Prosser's polite little note was the promised copy of *The Green Hat*.

So far he had not had time to open it. The Financial Secretary had been keeping him busy. Harold was at his desk at eight-thirty every morning, while it was still cool enough to think properly; and in the evenings he brought a briefcase full of work back with him so that he could get on with it again out there on the veranda after the breeze had come up.

Not that the Financial Secretary was grateful. On the contrary, he resented Harold intensely. Until Harold's arrival, he had dealt direct with the Governor on everything: persuading Sir Gardnor that this or that wouldn't work, or might have undesirable side effects, or ought to be investigated before a decision was taken, or should be held in abeyance until after the next lot of estimates. As a result, over the years, he had frustrated as many new proposals as anyone in the whole of Central Africa and was held in some awe in consequence.

That was why it was so deeply irritating to have this new young man suddenly thrust upon him. Moreover, Harold appeared to have the Governor's entire confidence. And more than confidence: even a growing intimacy. H.E. kept sending for him all the time.

In the end, Mr. McDonald decided that he would tackle the Governor in person. It was the Constitutional point that he wanted to emphasize: the importance in Colonial administration of an unbroken line of communication and command going direct without intervention between the Governor and his Ministers.

But perhaps he put it badly. Or Sir Gardnor's mind may have been occupied with other matters. Whichever way round it was, the Governor entirely misunderstood.

The smile he gave was one of his bigger ones.

"Please don't thank me, Financial Secretary," he said. "Don't think of it. If you must thank anyone, thank our Acting Chief Secretary. He arranged it all. You ought to be away on leave by now. It's overdue, you know. Considerably overdue, isn't it? That's why I'm so delighted to think that you've got all the extra help we can spare. We don't want our Financial Secretary cracking up on us, do we? Not with all this extra work on hand."

It was Saturday, and Harold was glad of it.

After a full week in the Treasury Office, it was rather pleasant to put his feet up in the quiet of the bungalow, with the fan mounted on the ledge over his head and a large gin-and-tonic on the side table.

As African days go, it had all been agreeable enough in a blind, purposeless, time-consuming kind of way. Now, with nothing else better to do, he had picked up *The Green Hat* and had begun to read. From five thousand miles away, the other world of Mayfair and the Ritz seemed strange and rather improbable; what made it seem stranger still was the fact that he had never known it even when he was at home.

It was a call from the garden that roused him. And he recognized the voice of Sybil Prosser.

"Anyone at home?" she asked.

And a moment later he heard Lady Anne's voice.

"He's there, all right," she was saying. "I can see him."

Harold put his book down and got up, sending the side table rocking as he did so. The gin-and-tonic slopped over the edge of the glass, and the book was left standing in a pool of it.

Lady Anne had already opened the screen door to the veranda and stood there facing him.

"Not disturbing you, are we?" she asked. "You weren't doing anything, I mean?"

And before he could answer, she had turned to Miss Prosser.

"Oh, isn't he sweet?" she said. "He's reading the book we sent him."

Miss Prosser held her hand out.

"Good afternoon, Mr. Stebbs." She paused. "I hope you're enjoying it."

And again before he could reply, Lady Anne was speaking.

"Just look at the mess he's made of it," she said. "He's spilt his drink all over it. I shan't lend you any more books, Mr. Stebbs, if that's the way you treat them."

The last time he had seen Lady Anne had been in the Cathedral. She had looked like a sick woman. But a change had come over her. Her tiredness, her air of having had all life somehow drained out of her, had entirely vanished. Even her paleness now merely served to set off those shining eyes of hers.

"You're going to offer us a drink, aren't you?" she was saying. "It's not too early, is it? Just one drink. To show us that we're both forgiven. And then we'll leave you in peace again."

"Forgiven?" Harold asked.

Lady Anne put her finger to her lips.

"Drinks first," she said.

"A soft one for me, please," Miss Prosser told him. "A lemon or an orange. Or a tonic. I don't mind if it's just plain soda."

But Lady Anne seemed rather amused.

"He's got plenty to drink in the bungalow," she said. "I know he has. He's got gin, and he's got whisky. And he's probably got brandy too, if you asked him. I'm going to have whisky. Just straight with a lump of ice."

It was lime juice that he poured for Miss Prosser.

"And now what's all this about?" Harold said as he brought the glasses over. "Why have I got to forgive anybody?"

Lady Anne looked across at Miss Prosser.

"Shall we tell him, Sybil?" she asked. "I can't believe it, but I really think he doesn't know."

"Delicious," Miss Prosser replied, holding up her lime juice. "So cooling."

"I will tell him," Lady Anne went on. "It's not fair on him, otherwise." She turned to Harold as she was speaking. "For getting you into all that trouble," she explained.

"But I haven't been in any trouble," Harold told her.

Lady Anne smiled.

"That's what you say," she said. "But we know better, don't we, Sybil? Sir Gardnor was furious. Simply furious. And it's all our fault. We didn't put your name down on the pad when you came to tea with us. So no one knew where you were. That's why they couldn't find you."

Harold shrugged his shoulders.

"I seem to have been forgiven."

"I did my best," Lady Anne replied.

"But we didn't come over just to apologize, you know," she said. "Or, at least, I didn't. I came to say thank you."

" 'Thank you' for what?"

"For trying to protect me," she told him. "It was darling of you. But you didn't have to. Really you didn't. We can take care of ourselves, can't we, Sybil?"

Harold was aware that Miss Prosser was sitting forward in her chair, her lime juice clutched up close against her bosom. She said nothing. Lady Anne herself was leaning back, smiling at him.

"I shan't forget it," she said. "About saying that I was just walking past the bungalow, or something. Because I wasn't, was I? I came in here. I had to. I couldn't help myself. And I told him so. I think I told him why." She passed her hand across her forehead. "I think I did. But I'm not sure. I can't remember."

"Does it matter?"

She was still smiling at him.

"Only that he knows that you weren't telling him the truth about me," she said. "And he's wondering what's behind it all. I suppose it's only natural."

Chapter 8

IT WAS generally agreed that the Governor's luncheon party for Mr. Talefwa was no more than a modified success; throughout the whole ninety minutes of it, Sir Gardnor glowed rather than actually shone.

Not that it was Sir Gardnor's fault; or anybody else's, for that matter. It was purely meteorological. After the almost incandescent heat of the past month, the rains were now approaching.

In consequence, the whole climate of Amimbo was in decline. Hour by hour, it deteriorated. With the thermometer remaining in the upper nineties, the humidity slowly crept up until it was now running level. Everything became saturated, sodden. Metal objects like brass door handles and nickel-plated taps were perpetually misted over, bearing upon themselves an invisible, residual film. Prickly heat became endemic, and everyone white by birth began scratching.

As for the Mimbo, they went their own dark, secret ways, more subdued, more morose and more enigmatic than usual. Even on large public projects, the local labor force dwindled away to practically nothing; and crimes of inexplicable violence abruptly rocketed upwards.

Meanwhile, the whole landscape of the Colony had undergone a profound change. In the meaningless blue African sky, clouds appeared from nowhere; and even between the clouds, the blue faded. It was no longer purely savage. And already, in the distance, the big stuff had begun massing. Over the Alouma Hills, huge mountain ranges of steel-colored cumulus were now piling up, and at sunset everything turned crimson.

In the reflected light, the Government buildings, St. Stephen's

Cathedral, the avenues of trees, the flower beds, the lawns all changed color too. Amimbo had become a different Amimbo.

By one o'clock on the day of the luncheon, Sir Gardnor had changed his jacket three times.

It was the Bishop in particular who had provoked him and made him hotter than he need have been. First, His Grace had refused in any circumstances to meet the offensive Mr. Talefwa; then, on second thought, he had decided that, if reinvited, he would accept; and now, at the last moment, he had asked if he could sit next to the man. Sir Gardnor told the A.D.C. to re-arrange the table.

The party itself was a small one. In addition to Mr. Talefwa, there was Mr. Ngono from the African side. It had occurred to Sir Gardnor that this would be an opportunity of having Mr. Ngono to the Residency without actually having to talk to him. Accordingly, he had been placed at the far end, with only the A.D.C. and Native Affairs for company.

Next to Mr. Talefwa was the Bishop. Opposite Mr. Talefwa was Mr. Frith. And next to Mr. Frith was Harold. In the result, it worked out exactly wrong; the Africans were outnumbered by two and a half to one, and the general effect was lopsided.

In his enthusiasm, it was Mr. Ngono who arrived first. He was a good five minutes early. There was only the A.D.C. to receive him. But between two people of such good manners no problem presented itself.

"How d'you do? I'm afraid His Excellency is detained for a moment."

"No, no. The fault is entirely all mine."

"What'll you have?" The A.D.C. asked. He indicated the dumbwaiter beside him. "Gin, whisky, sherry?"

"Oh, you are more than kind. Gin, please."

"And tonic?"

"You are most kind, indeed."

"Ice?"

"With ice it is even better. Damn good, in fact."

Mr. Ngono smiled inwardly as well as outwardly. Swearing

always made him feel better. It served when talking to a white man to remind him that, despite the distance of continents and oceans, Cambridge was still close at hand and all Cambridge men were bloody well equal.

"Cigarette?"

"My own, please. Turkish, you understand. They are personally imported for my convenience. You will please try one. Most mild. Most exceptionally mild."

The A.D.C. excused himself.

"Don't use them," he said. "Light?"

The next to join them was the Bishop. All the way in the car he had been reproving himself for his earlier lack of charity toward Mr. Talefwa, and he was determined to do everything in his power to make amends. In consequence, he did not even listen to the introduction and immediately began congratulating Mr. Ngono on his outspokenness, his sense of justice, and his feeling for the underdog.

It was only the emergence through the inner door of the Governor, followed a moment later by the arrival of Mr. Talefwa himself, that saved Mr. Ngono from the humiliation of having to explain. As it was, he had merely stood there, glass in hand, smiling politely and waiting for the Bishop to go on.

The Governor immediately made Mr. Talefwa his own special target. He advanced upon him, smile extended.

"How good of you to come," he said. "I know how busy your paper must be keeping you. What will you drink? Gin, whisky . . ."

Mr. Talefwa shook his head.

"Thank you, sir, no," he said. "I do not drink alcohol. I am a Moslem."

The reply appeared to please Sir. Gardnor.

"I wish we were all as strict," he said, and to avoid giving the wrong impression, added, "I myself drink nothing during Lent."

The Bishop caught Sir Gardnor's eye and nodded understandingly. But Mr. Talefwa was still pondering.

"Christian self-strictness is the greater, sir, I assure you," he replied at last. "Abstinence during your fasts must be much harder, once there is addiction."

78

Sir Gardnor looked across at his A.D.C.

"Are we all ready?" he asked. "Shall we be seated?"

Over luncheon it was the Bishop who set himself out to charm. He mentioned the fact that among his closest friends was one who had in the past been a leader writer on the *Daily Telegraph;* he recalled a recent, laughable misprint in the *Church Times;* and he confessed that, for him, breakfast was intolerable unless he had a newspaper that he could prop up against the marmalade jar.

Mr. Talefwa appeared both impressed and surprised.

"Then you must be much interested in journalism," he said, with a little bow of his head. He turned toward Sir Gardnor. "And you, sir, do you see my paper regularly?" he asked.

Sir Gardnor resented the question: it was altogether too early in the meal for it. And in any case, he had himself intended, over coffee, to bring the conversation round to the newspapers in general and the *Amimbo Mirror* in particular. Now—thanks to the Bishop and all his silly press talk—the initiative had been snatched from him.

"Not regularly, I am afraid, Mr. Talefwa," he replied, with one of his warmer smiles. "Not regularly. But I understand that you are now printing articles in English. Do your readers appreciate the change?"

Mr. Talefwa shook his head.

"Most of them cannot read English," he said. "Only a proportion can understand. But it is not for them that the articles appear."

Sir Gardnor frowned.

"Not for your readers?" he asked.

"No," Mr. Talefwa told him. "They are intended for those who cannot read Mimbo. They are addressed, at second hand of course, to our rulers, so that they may know what are the matters that are most troubling the Mimbo mind."

"Really," said Sir Gardnor. "How interesting. How very interesting."

"Then you have not studied what they say?"

Sir Gardnor looked across the table at Native Affairs.

"You read Mr. Talefwa's paper, don't you, Mr. Walters?" he asked. "The section in English, I mean."

Mr. Walters coughed discreetly.

"I read the Mimbo parts, Excellency," he replied.

Sir Gardnor turned back to Mr. Talefwa. He was beaming again.

"There you are, Mr. Editor," he said. "You have a regular reader here at this table. And you don't even have to translate for him."

Mr. Talefwa gave a deep sigh.

"But the topics are entirely different," he explained. "My Mimbo readers are backward, uneducated, and superstitious. For them it is necessary to write of very simple and trivial affairs. The English articles are highly political. They deal with matters of national consequence and controversy. In journalistic terms, they are dynamite."

"Indeed?" Sir Gardnor had leaned forward, as though anxious not to miss a word. "Pray tell me more."

But Mr. Talefwa was, for the moment, exhausted. He had been ready for an attack on him; a polite reprimand; a sly hint of possible closure; even an official warning from the Governor himself. Like the Bishop, he had wondered whether it was wise to accept at all. And now everyone was being nice to him; being nice without caring about him in the slightest. It reminded him heartbreakingly of the attitude of his widow landlady in Belsize Park.

"Then you have not considered my solemn warning on famine?" Mr. Talefwa blurted out. "It is the writing on the wall, sir. It is nothing less."

Sir Gardnor addressed Mr. Frith.

"A famine warning?" he asked. "Has this been brought to your notice? It sounds most important. I should like to see it sometime. We certainly need all the advance information we can have, don't we, Mr. Talefwa?"

"The facts are all there," Mr. Talefwa answered. "The terrible facts."

Mr. Frith was about to answer, but Sir Gardnor stopped him.

"You were about to say something, Mr. Stebbs?" he asked.

80

"As a matter of fact, sir," Harold replied, "I was wondering where Mr. Talefwa got his facts. They've gone a bit haywire somehow. Too bad in places, and too good in others. They need to be presented differently."

"Ah." It was Sir Gardnor who had spoken. And he paused. "There, Mr. Talefwa," he said, opening the palms of his hands as he was speaking, "you see. Even at luncheon we still keep you busy. Fresh information all the time. You and Mr. Stebbs should see more of each other. I'm sure Mr. Stebbs would like to check any figures you care to send him. You would, wouldn't you, Mr. Stebbs?"

Sir Gardnor had glanced at his watch while he was speaking, and Mr. Ngono recognized that in a moment he would be too late. Stuck down at the far end of the table, he had been left out of things: had failed entirely to make his personality felt. Everyone would think that Mr. Talefwa was all-important and that he, Mr. Ngono, was nothing.

He tapped with his coffee spoon on the side of the cup.

"Before we break ourselves up, Excellency, sir," he said, "may I on Mr. Talefwa's behalf and on my own extend our sincerely happy thanks for this most glad occasion. It has all been extremely delightful, not for today's excellent repast alone, but for the opportunities it gives of other intimate follow-ups in the near future. Thank you altogether warmheartedly again, sir."

Mr. Ngono gave a deep sigh of contentment. He had got it out. He had triumphed. He had shown where, on his side of Amimbo, the social graces really lay.

Chapter 9

Toward evening, the lightning that had been playing over the Alouma Hills all day had become incessant.

The peaks and the under surface of the huge clouds were continuously illuminated. And in the flickering blue-white dazzle, jagged diamond-colored shafts, branching out at times into the pattern of inverted ferns, tore downwards, making the surrounding brightness look like night.

Within Amimbo itself, odd by-products of the seasonal discharge had already begun to manifest themselves. Power substations and transformers suddenly went down. Telephones stopped. The weather vane on St. Stephen's Cathedral flickered fitfully for a few seconds with St. Elmo's Fire. And the Radio Station closed its service, crackles and all, until the storm was over.

Because it was Tuesday, Harold was staffless. It was Amimbo's big evening, Tuesday. The Y.M.C.A. showed—free for all comers —films, in color, of the Lake District, Shakespeare's England, and the Yarmouth herring fleet; the R.C.s had their instruction classes; the Non-Coms were teaching First Aid and the Bible; and one of Mr. Ngono's business enterprises was devoting itself to a Western Style Dance Contest, with all pleasures.

Tuesday was Harold's night for the Milner Club. But tonight it was not the same Milner Club. On one side, Mr. Frith was midway through his nightly run of whiskies; two bridge fours had been arranged; and the congenial Chairman of a coffee syndicate was heavily impressing an exhausted-looking stranger.

But on the other, the serving side, things were different. The three boys, spruce and immaculate as ever, were not merely staring vacantly into space; they were waiting for something. Waiting, and listening. Every time the remote barrage of thunder intensified, they nodded secretly to themselves and exchanged glances, the whites of their eyes glinting. They had ceased altogether to be Club servants. They had reverted to pure Mimbo. They were praying.

"Think it'll rain tonight, boy?" Harold asked.

The barman detached himself from another, more private world and jerked himself back into business.

"Your usual, yassah. Your usual."

"I'm all right." Harold pointed to his glass as he said it. "I asked if it was going to rain."

The barman did not reply immediately. And with good reason. Last year, after all the right signs, nothing at all had happened. Not a single drop. The crops had perished, and womenfolk and young children had died. The barman did not doubt that foolish, ill-considered talk had been responsible. It was playing with Providence even to refer to the rains at all.

He deftly turned the conversation into less dangerous channels.

"Yassah," he said. "Tonight, sah, on the menu there is roast lamb, sah, or mudfish. With compôte of fresh fruits and ice cream." He was taking no chances and went on hurriedly. "The roast lamb is with potatoes and mint sauce, sah, or red-currant jelly. And the mudfish, sah, has a thick white sauce. The ice cream is vanilla with nuts on top."

In the headlights of the car, the bungalow looked lonely, deserted, and inhospitable.

I'll have one more drink, he told himself. One more drink, and then turn in. If the storm breaks, I'll probably sleep through it.

As he slid out of the passenger seat, an African raindrop the size of a small grape hit him on his forehead and burst there. An instant later, the sodden, uneasy sky had released itself, and the rains, the unpredictable, the long-awaited, the much-prayed-for rains, had come at last. Big, swollen drops hit bare scaly leaves and buried themselves in the loose soil below. The drops came down joined on to one another; the rain was now hosepipe and bath-water stuff. At his feet, patches of open ground became ponds, lakes, rivers.

He ran toward the bungalow, shielding his face with his hands. The weight of the water was pressing down onto his shoulders. When he opened the front door, a screen of brown spray bounced up from the step into the empty hallway.

The electric-light switch on the wall simply clicked up and down; somewhere on its way from the substation the supply had been cut off.

He started to strip off his jacket, his tie, his shirt. The rain, hammering on the iron roof, made a noise like trains passing. Inside, it was all very close and stifling and familiar. He was conscious of the hot, inhabited smell of the bungalow; the characteristic odors of the woodwork, the flowers on the table, the bowl of fruit that the boy had forgotten to put away in the icebox, even the cigarettes left open on the bookcase.

"I thought you were never coming."

He turned, and she was standing there in the doorway. All that he could see was the pale oval of her face, the whiteness of her dress.

"Anne," he said.

It was the first time that he had ever called her by her name.

He let go of the sodden shirt that he was holding and went over to her. She was already holding out her hands toward him.

"You can kiss me if you want to," she told him.

He could feel that she was trembling. But a moment later, she had pushed him away again.

"Silly boy," she said. "You don't even know how to kiss. And look at the mess you've made of me. I'm soaking."

Harold stood there facing her. He was surprised how fast his breathing had become; how he was trembling, too. And inside his mind, one thought was forming. I must play this cool, he kept telling himself. I must act experienced. That's it—cool and experienced.

"Would you like a drink?" he asked.

"I got myself one," she replied. "But it's finished."

"Then it's time for another."

He groped his way through into the dining room and poured out two whiskies. He must have drunk a little more up at the Club than he had realized, because he was clumsy; the soda came shooting up out of the glass into his face. And on his way back he bumped into the furniture.

"Coming," he said, and added pointlessly, "I can't see a thing."

"I'm over here," she told him.

He tried to kiss her again as he handed the drink to her, but she avoided him.

"Were you surprised to find me here?"

He kept his voice deliberately low and casual-sounding.

"Not really."

"Pleased?"

"Very."

"And you don't know why I came?"

"I think I do."

"That's where you're wrong," she said. "Utterly, completely wrong."

She paused.

"Have you got a cigarette?" she asked.

He managed to light it for her without revealing how unsteady his hand was.

"Quite wrong," she repeated.

"I don't care so long as you're here," he told her.

"And you can't expect me to go back out into that. Not at once, I mean. Now, can you?"

Her face was toward the shuttered window as she was speaking.

"Won't they begin looking for you?"

She turned sharply.

"Are you afraid?"

"I only wondered. About Sybil Prosser, for instance."

"You don't have to bother about Sybil." He could tell that she was smiling as she said it. "Sybil's asleep. And H.E.'s away upcountry somewhere. Nobody knows I'm over here. Not officially, that is. I just got bored with everything. So I walked across."

Harold put his glass down with a jolt.

"Why won't you let me kiss you?" he asked.

"Because I'm not ready."

"And what about me?"

She began stroking his face again.

"You are funny," she said. "Five minutes ago you didn't even know I'd be here." Then her voice hardened. "But you can't behave like that. It's no use. I'm not made that way."

She had dropped her hand and moved farther away from him.

"If you're not going to finish your drink, give it to me," she said.

"I'll get you another one."

"No. I don't like being left in the dark. Besides, you've had enough already. You'll just go off to sleep."

"I'm not a bit sleepy."

She gave a little laugh and reached out so that she could touch him.

"But you may have to stay awake for a long, long time. You can't tell, can you? You can kiss me now, if you like. That's if you really want to," she said. "Only this time you'll have to let me show you how."

The storm, which all day had been muttering around the outskirts, had now closed in on them. The noise of the thunder rose above the rain; and, through the closed shutters, the lightning flashes lit up the room in streaks and patches of pale, flickering blue.

"Hold me tighter than that," she said. "Much tighter. I'm terrified of thunder. I always have been. Ever since I was a little girl." He could feel her trembling again. "Hold me as tight as you can," she said. "Show me how tight you can hold me."

It was the sound of her crying that woke him in the night. He slid his arm under her and pulled her toward him.

"What's the matter?" he asked.

"It's nothing," she told him. "Nothing that you'd ever understand." She began kissing him. "I'm furious with myself for crying. It spoils everything. And it's not your fault, darling. You must know that. You were wonderful. You don't know how wonderful. I should be so grateful."

"Grateful?"

"Is that what I said?" she asked. Her voice sounded drowsy now, and she had stopped crying. "Well, if I said it I suppose I must have meant it. Meant every word of it."

A moment later, he could tell from her breathing that she was asleep again.

He lay there with his arms still around her. He was sober, completely sober by now.

She trusts me, he thought. Oh my God, how she trusts me.

Next morning, when the boy brought in his tea and opened up the shutters, she had gone. There was only the second pillow beside him to show that she had ever been there.

Outside, the sun was shining. It was usually like that at the beginning of the rains: a real downpour one day and perfectly fine the next.

Chapter 10

THREE DAYS later, the Governor's return—already delayed by the rains—was rendered positively ridiculous when he reached Amimbo.

That was because the King Edward VII sewer (no one except the City Surveyor even knew of its magnificent name) first overflowed and then, under increasing pressure of the deluge, burst its concrete piping and completely disintegrated. In consequence, the whole of central Amimbo was awash, and Queen Victoria Avenue was closed to traffic.

The Governor's car and the two escort vehicles had to make the big detour round the stockyards and enter the Residency grounds through the farm gate by the native compound. The last quarter of a mile was covered in total darkness on foot, trudging through the mud under umbrellas, mackintoshes, spare tarpaulins from the station wagon—anything waterproof that could be grabbed hold of.

Not that the return was by any means inauspicious. On the contrary, ever since four P.M. the telegrams from London had been pouring in. They reported that *The Times* and the *Manchester Guardian* had both, and on the same day, carried stories from their diplomatic correspondents quoting well-informed sources to the effect that Sir Gardnor was to be the next Viceroy.

Travel-stained and aching for a bath as he was, Sir Gardnor found time to read all of them. When he had finished, he turned to the A.D.C.

"Has Acting Chief Secretary had copies?"

"Yes, sir. He telephoned about half an hour ago. He said he'll be there if you want him."

"Want him?" Sir Gardnor asked. "I don't see why. There's nothing he can do about it. These things must simply be allowed to take their course." He paused. "After dinner, perhaps. We'll see. He's probably anxious. He would be, wouldn't he?"

"And the other telegrams, sir."

The A.D.C. had pushed the red box forward as he was speaking, but the Governor ignored it.

"In the morning," he said. "I've glanced through them. There's nothing there." He sat back and stared at the ceiling. "Give me another whisky, would you. I feel as though I may have a chill coming. It's quite as easy, you know, to catch a chill in a hot climate as in a cold one. One should always be careful. And pass me the text of what the *Manchester Guardian* said. I take it it's in full."

He was completely unhurried as he sat there sipping at his whisky. He appeared to be sipping at the telegram, too. Then he turned again toward his A.D.C.

"It's really most remarkable, isn't it? I've never known the *Manchester Guardian* to be so friendly toward me. They've always seemed hostile before. But they're quite right this time. India does need someone who . . ."

He broke off and fixed his tired, pale eyes on the A.D.C.

"You should have reminded me," he said. "I wanted to see Lady Anne before dinner. It may be that side of the house doesn't even know that I'm back. But it's too late now. I should have been in my bath ten minutes ago. Send a message over to Lady Anne that dinner is put back to eight-thirty in the small dining room. And get hold of Acting Chief Secretary. We can talk over the table. He's bound to be on tenterhooks. I wouldn't have been surprised if I'd found him waiting here. And when do we get the originals—the actual copies of the papers, I mean? There's bound to be further press comment."

Sir Gardnor did not have so long to wait. The further press comment was all there next morning in the *Amimbo Mirror*. And because Sir Gardnor did not himself read the paper, Mr. Frith paid a special visit to the Residency so that he could show him personally.

By then, the Governor was fully prepared. Native Affairs had already sent through a Minute saying that he was genuinely concerned about the effect upon any of the *Mirror's* African readers who happened to be bilingual; the Chief of Police stated confidently that, given the necessary authority, he and his men could ensure that all circulating copies would be immediately impounded and that no further editions would appear until the Order was lifted; and the Postmaster General still favored applying the Obscene Publications Act of 1912.

As soon as Mr. Frith arrived, the Governor had him shown in.

"Ah," he said, "how good of you to come. How very good. You're well? We didn't keep you up too late, I hope?"

Mr. Frith began fumbling with his official dispatch case, stamped with the letters G.R. on the flap.

"I've got it here, sir," he explained. "I've brought three extra copies in case . . ."

The Governor smiled. It was his best smile—quizzical, benign, and pontifical.

"*Three* extra copies? *Four* in all? Mr. Talefwa should be delighted."

"I only thought . . ."

"Quite so. Quite so." He paused. "I often wonder, Acting Chief Secretary"—Mr. Frith winced: this formality, even when they were alone, only went to show how wide the gulf between them really was, how normal human intimacy had never quite sprung up—"I often wonder how these journalists get their facts."

"By telegram, sir," Mr. Frith explained. "Mr. Talefwa would have had his last night. Along with ours, sir. Reuter's and Exchange Telegraph and that kind of thing."

Sir Gardnor looked hard at him. There was no trace of the smile this time.

"I was referring to the London newspapers," he said. "I can understand about *The Times*. There's always been a special relationship there. The Editor of *The Times* is, I believe, the only journalist ever allowed inside No. 10. It's a tradition. But the *Manchester Guardian*. Right up in the North, remember. People in office don't exactly confide in the *Manchester Guardian*. They wouldn't, would they?"

Mr. Frith, lifelong Liberal as he was—shaken a little by the mystery of Mr. Lloyd George and the Party Fund, but still loyal, still steadfast—became defensive.

"It's one of the world's great newspapers, sir."

"You see it regularly?"

"Not out here, sir. Only when I go back home."

"Ah." Sir Gardnor smiled again, less benevolently this time. "But I hear that their attitude has changed a great deal recently. For the worse, I'm afraid. Germany, you know. In fact," here Sir Gardnor dropped his voice almost to a whisper, "I'm told that at the moment they're quite—how shall I put it?—unreliable."

Mr. Frith opened up the top copy of the *Amimbo Mirror* and placed it conspicuously on Sir Gardnor's desk. Sir Gardnor ignored it.

"And if these things should come to pass, Acting Chief Secretary," he asked, "how would you feel about it? What would you say if I were to move on to Delhi?"

"I would offer you my most sincere congratulations, sir. I can't think of anyone . . ."

"How kind. How very kind. But what I really had in mind was Amimbo. My work here can hardly be said to be complete, now can it? I was wondering what a new man out here would get up to. We must think of the future, Acting Chief Secretary, mustn't we?"

Sir Gardnor broke off and temporarily became a ceiling-gazer. Then he glanced down at his desk. "Oh," he said, in a tone of surprise, almost of astonishment, "so this is it, is it? This is what our local Editor has to say. I must read it, mustn't I?"

Mr. Frith studied Sir Gardnor's face as he was reading. But there was not one particle of expression. It might have been the local bus timetable that he was holding in his hands.

Under the headline, INDIA BEWARE, it led straight into the attack. "Our Iron Governor," it ran, "under whom we have for so long been living under conditions of Martial Law and police coercion, is soon to be sitting astride the Taj Mahal, the Red Fort and the lice-infested, cholera-stricken slums of Calcutta. Hindus and Moslems, be on your guard. Famine, not arms, is the weapon by which you will be destroyed. Consider carefully the terrible facts assembled by the *Mirror* staff of truth-seekers . . ."

—Mr. Frith could see that the Governor was beginning to skip—

". . . in the memorable drought of 1917 twenty-three villages were denied all water supply upon the Governor's orders . . . the demand of empty, swollen bellies was met by an unparalleled display of military force." And finally, in the heaviest type that his compositors could muster, Mr. Talefwa delivered himself of his peroration: "Indians, free your country; spare your wives and remember your children. The Iron Governor threatens."

Mr. Frith had been following the passage of Sir Gardnor's eyes down the page. At what he judged to be the appropriate moment, he gave a little laugh.

"And to think, sir," he said, "that only last week he was lunching here at your own table. It's really quite inconceivable."

Sir Gardnor had slid back in his chair and was intent again upon the same spot on the ceiling. He remained silent and transfixed.

"Do you know," he asked at last, "whom I blame for the whole of this? One man and one man only."

"And who would that be, sir?"

"Our Bishop," Sir Gardnor told him. "The damn fellow specially asked to come, and then he wouldn't stop talking. Just like his sermons. If I'd had Mr. Talefwa to myself, this disgraceful article would never have appeared." He broke off. "We'll ignore it, of course. Ignore it completely. I don't think we tremble, do we, Acting Chief Secretary, when Mr. Talefwa speaks?"

Chapter 11

THERE WAS a message left on the pad beside the telephone to say that Miss Prosser would be coming over to the bungalow after tea. And through the rain, the wheels of her car churning up the red mud, Miss Prosser came.

"I guessed I'd find you here," she said, as she stripped off her streaming oilskin. "After all, there isn't much to do in Amimbo on a Saturday afternoon, is there? Not when it's like this, I mean."

She had brought a spare pair of shoes with her in a waterproof bag and began thrusting her overlarge feet into them while she was still talking.

"You've heard the news?" she asked. "He's been sent for. It came through just as I was leaving."

"You mean about India?"

"It looks like it. That's why I'm here."

They had gone through into the drawing room by now, and Miss Prosser sat herself down in Harold's chair. She reached out and took one of the cigarettes from the open box beside her.

"I'm sorry," Harold said, as he brought out his lighter. "I thought you didn't smoke."

"Only sometimes," she told him. "Like now, for instance."

He stood there looking at her. On any showing, she certainly was an extraordinarily unattractive woman. And today her thin, sallow neck seemed longer than ever. It seemed to rise endlessly out of the collar of her dress. Also, she didn't know what to do with the hand that wasn't holding the cigarette. She kept trying in vain to find somewhere to put it.

"Would . . . would you like a cup of tea?" he asked.

She did not reply immediately because, in an awkward, amateur kind of way, she was still sucking hard at her cigarette. Then she blew the smoke out slowly, through deliberately rounded lips, as though it were opium.

"I'd rather have a drink," she said. "I need it."

"But I thought you didn't drink, either."

"I don't. Not when she's around. It only encourages her."

Sybil Prosser made the statement quite casually, in that flat, expressionless voice of hers, and then added as an equally casual afterthought: "She drinks too much. It's not good for her."

"What'll you have?" he asked.

"Whisky," she answered. "Make it a short one."

When he came back, Sybil Prosser had settled herself. She was sitting bolt upright in the chair, and her hands were together as though she had just gathered up invisible reins.

She took the drink without even thanking him.

"I've got something on my mind," she said.

"What is it?"

"It's Anne."

"What about her?"

"We've got to stop her coming here."

"I didn't . . ." Harold started to say, but Sybil Prosser interrupted him.

"That's what makes it so difficult," she said. She sat back as though she had finished, then suddenly leaned forward again. "It's not safe, you know. Really, it isn't."

"I don't know what you mean."

Sybil Prosser ignored him.

"The houseboys," she explained. "They're always around somewhere, even when you think they aren't watching." There was another pause. "And they talk."

Harold took her glass to refill it.

"What have they got to talk about?" he asked.

He turned his back on her as he said it and walked slowly—very slowly and deliberately—across the room. He wanted time to think things out; wanted time to decide just how much she knew.

"Like the other night," she said. "I don't know if they saw her when she got here. But they certainly did when she got back. I know, because I was watching too." She was silent for a moment, and then added petulantly: "It's not fair on me, either. I didn't get one wink of sleep all through the storm. I was half dead all next day."

"Well?"

"That's why I came over. H.E.'s off on Friday. Back home, and he's not taking her with him. It's all too easy. I don't like the look of it." There was a long silence this time; so long, in fact, that Harold thought that the conversation must be over. Then Sybil Prosser resumed. "It wouldn't be the first time he's had her followed," she said.

The last remark was delivered quite quietly and without emotion. It seemed simply an observation that had happened to come into her mind.

"But how can I stop her?"

"You can't. She's made that way." She paused again. "That's why you've got to come over to us."

"And suppose I don't choose to?"

Sybil Prosser gave a little irritated wriggle.

"What's the alternative?" she asked. "If you don't come over to us, she'll go on coming over to you. Then there'll be all hell let loose."

"What's the difference?"

"The difference," Sybil Prosser said firmly, "is that our apartments are private. Yours aren't. There's nobody around once we close the door." The pause again. "I know enough to keep out of the way."

Harold got up and stood facing her.

"Aren't you taking rather a lot for granted?" he asked.

Sybil Prosser's pale, straw-colored eyes stared back at him.

"I have to," she said. "I'm her friend."

Chapter 12

THE GOVERNOR'S impending departure had thrown all Government Departments into complete disorder.

Mr. Frith's life, in particular, had been reduced to the lowest level of human misery. That was because of H.E.'s fondness for running-over-everything-once-again-shall-we? And as Mr. Frith grew daily more exhausted—his tic was appreciably worse, and kept puckering up his left eye even at breakfast time—the Governor himself seemed more than ever serene and proconsular.

"After all, Acting Chief Secretary," he had said as they had broken up their last meeting around midnight, "it isn't as if I shall be away for long—a fortnight, at the utmost. And there's always the telephone or a telegram, isn't there? You won't be completely cut off, you know. And tomorrow perhaps we could look over the Estimates. We don't want things to go wrong at this stage, do we?"

That was why it was so absolutely maddening for Mr. Frith to find that his idiotic secretary had made an appointment for him to see—of all people—Mr. Ngono. And, by the time Mr. Frith had discovered the blunder, it was too late. Already he could hear Mr. Ngono outside explaining to one of the native clerks the reason for his sudden and unwelcome visit.

"It is most extremely urgent; otherwise I would have been altogether unwilling to disturb anyone so decidedly busy. It is also most extremely delicate and confidential. Entirely private, in fact. Also, most timely. When the nature of my call is known, everyone will be exceedingly grateful and happy."

Mr. Ngono had left nothing to chance and was dressed specially for the occasion. His new silk shirt had his initials embroidered on the breast pocket, and over his arm he was carrying his blazer, carefully folded so that the badge was showing over his forearm.

Because of Mr. Frith's abruptness, he came to the point at once.

"It is the attacks upon our Governor that bring me here," he said. "The quite disloyal attacks which Mr. Talefwa makes in his newspaper. He is a remarkably proud and obstinate man, Mr. Talefwa. But he is not by any means rich. Most pressed for money, indeed."

"And you want the Governor to bribe him?"

Ngono showed his teeth in a white, glittering smile.

"An altogether different idea entirely, sir, and most engagingly attractive in every respect," Mr. Ngono assured him. "It is upon importing in the most modern sense that it depends. A Government Trading Corporation is highly sophisticated, extremely modern and right up to date to the very minute. Also highly profitable for all concerned. I would free myself completely to manage it—with a distinguished and highly influential Board, of course. It would all be most democratic."

"And Mr. Talefwa?"

Mr. Ngono bared his teeth again.

"It is in his paper that we should solely, exclusively advertise. Full and attractive pages of advertisement every day. All at the utmost top rate. Most generously paid for." Here Mr. Ngono stopped smiling. "Provided, it goes necessarily without saying, that there are no more reprehensible attacks upon our Governor.

The least hint of criticism, even a joke in poor taste, and all advertising stops like—" Mr. Ngono pursed his lips and blew rudely into the air. "You see how at once clear the present proposal all will be from the point of view and general aspect of Mr. Talefwa? It is happiness or ruin. Great financial happiness and power, or extremely sad ruin."

It was entirely Sir Gardnor's idea to hold a farewell party; and all on the spur of the moment, too.

The Governor had not so much as mentioned it to Mr. Frith when he had left the Residency at around five-thirty. But the invitation was there waiting for him—telephoned through by the A.D.C.—when he returned home shortly before seven. And that was unfortunate. Because Mr. Frith had already dropped into the Milner Club for a moment on his way back. The moment had prolonged itself. Frayed at the edges as he was after the ceaseless abrasive meetings with the Governor, he had stayed on. All that he now wanted was to go to sleep.

Harold's own invitation had reached him in good time. He was, in fact, already bathed and changed. At any moment now, the houseboy, with the broad smile of a triumphant artist, would come in on his big bare feet to announce that another uneatable dinner at last was ready. And in the meantime, Harold was standing by the window doing some quiet and serious thinking.

It can't go on like this, he was saying to himself. It just bloody well can't. It's not fair on anyone. It's not fair on Anne. It's not fair on me. And it's not fair on Sir Gardnor. I'm pulling out. That's what I'm doing: I'm pulling out.

Through the mosquito-screen on the veranda he could see the lights along the drive leading up to the Residency. The rain, during the late afternoon, had slackened. It was now no more than a dense, descending vapor. And when he turned his head for a moment, the string of lights alternately blurred and blazed up again as he saw them through the myriad lenses of the drenched netting.

They knew what the form was, he went on. And I walked right into it. Bloody well right in. But if they think I'm stopping on here, that's where they're wrong. He can get someone else to finish his damn book for him. I've had it. I'm pulling out.

The phrase "pulling out" seemed somehow strangely comforting. It had a mature, definitive ring to it that Harold liked. And it served to place things in their true perspective. Put that way, there was no fluster, no panic, not even any very acute regrets. It was just a sensible adult decision.

I'll go along tonight as invited, he concluded. And I'll take it all very quietly. At my own pace throughout. I'll wish H.E. a pleasant trip and tell him how much we are all looking forward to his safe return. I may even let fall the word "India": it's all he really cares about. And if Anne's there, I'll be on my best party manners. Nice to her. And nice to Sybil Prosser. Nice to everyone, in fact. Back home by midnight. And on Wednesday, I'll take the Coronation Flyer. No farewells. No goodbye scenes. No tears. Nothing. Just my bags on the rack, and me with my feet up on the seat opposite. I'm not funking it: I'm just doing the right thing. Pulling out, before it's all too late.

There were some twenty people already gathered under the chandeliers in the Long Drawing Room when Harold was shown into it. Some of them he had never seen before, not even in the Milner Club. He could only suppose that they were from Public Works, or the Railway, or somewhere really remote upcountry.

And there were the wives. There were unfamiliar faces there too, with a startled, just-out-of-purdah look about one or two of them. The A.D.C. was now going round from group to group explaining that it wasn't in any sense a party—just a few intimates whom Sir Gardnor would naturally wish to see before he left.

The arrival of Mr. Frith could not, even by his friends, have been regarded as other than unfortunate. During the waiting period between seven and nine P.M. he had avoided alcohol in any form. By five past nine he was all ready, and quite desolate, and solely to brace himself for the unwelcome and entirely unasked-for evening, he poured himself a drink. It was, even by his own standards, a large one. And he felt better for it. Much better. Well enough, in fact, to have another. When at last he got into his car, he was totally refreshed. He felt like Napoleon.

As a result, he entered the drawing room somewhat impetuously. While his name was still being called, he was already in there and had to queue up to shake hands behind someone from Education who was still chatting with the Governor.

But Mr. Frith had his speech fully prepared and delivered it immediately.

"Bon voyage, Excellency," he said, "and safe *Séjour*."

It was only after he had said it that he realized that it—or something like it—was what he had intended to say on departure, and not as soon as he arrived.

He hurriedly corrected himself.

"Don't give us a thought after you leave us, sir," he added reassuringly. "We shall get on all right until after you get back."

A little flushed, but relieved that he had so quickly been able to correct his mistake, the Acting Chief Secretary moved on to mingle with the other guests.

Sir Gardnor turned to greet Harold, and he seemed genuinely pleased to see him. He was at his most affable; indulgent, even.

"Not working late tonight, Mr. Stebbs?" he asked. "That's not like you, is it?"

He paused; and, during the pause, Harold watched the famous Residency smile develop. It started, Harold noticed, with the corners of the mouth. But somehow they seemed to be drawn down, not upwards.

"And it won't always be raining, I assure you," Sir Gardnor went on. "Next month the roads will be quite passable again. Slippery, but still passable. Then"—the smile itself was steadily widening, even though the pale eyes remained as cold and fixed as ever—"we must show you something of the country, mustn't we? The bush, I mean. On safari. Something of the real Africa."

The radiance of his smile had, Harold reckoned, passed progressively through the range from Simmer to Slow Roast. By now he could feel himself being scorched by it. But Sir Gardnor was not yet finished.

"It can be very dull in Amimbo, can't it?" he asked. "Damnably dull. Especially for a young man. Let's be frank about it: so few women—of the right kind, that is. And"—here Sir Gardnor gave his rather shrill little laugh—"none of the other sort at all. It's the only real famine that lasts for twelve months every year."

"As a matter of fact, I've been so busy I haven't really noticed, sir."

He was aware that Sir Gardnor's eyes were still on him. But he was not looking into them. He was thinking of the Coronation Flyer instead.

"D'you shoot?" Sir Gardnor asked.

"I've used a rifle, sir."

"Excellent," Sir Gardnor replied. "Excellent. You must join our party. Are you interested in big game?"

Harold remembered the heads of rhino and buffalo in the Governor's study; remembered particularly the great ivory-tusker with the enormous butterfly ears at the top of the staircase.

"Such as, sir?" he asked.

"Leopard," Sir Gardnor told him. "Leopard."

He had rocked back on his heels as he was speaking and thrown his chest out.

"Mankind's natural enemy," he went on. "Slinking, treacherous, deceitful—and cruel. Cruel beyond everything else in Africa. And dangerous. Highly dangerous. To destroy a leopard you have to become like him. You have to match your instincts and intelligence against his."

Sir Gardnor drew himself up to his full height, and Harold was aware that he reached up only to the black tie.

"You see the importance of it, don't you, my dear fellow?" he asked. "Every leopard that is killed makes the Leopard Men that much less feared. It's their god, and we've destroyed it. Publicly—that's the point. That's why I always have the pelt mounted. I like as many people as possible to walk over it."

Sir Gardnor bent forward, and Harold was level with his chin again.

"But I mustn't detain you," he said. "I'm sure you have a great many friends."

Harold felt rather relieved. Behind him a long queue of other guests had been forming while Sir Gardnor had been talking.

He was relieved, too, that there was still no sign of Lady Anne or Miss Prosser. It was going to be easier, much easier, if he could simply make the rounds and then slip quietly away again. He was even wondering whether anyone would notice if he left now. He felt that it might be safer.

Mr. Frith, however, was already coming over toward him. He appeared to be in what for Mr. Frith was absolutely top condition—gay, animated, possibly a trifle flushed.

"Well, young man," he asked, "what was H.E. saying to you? Offered you the Acting Governorship yet?" Mr. Frith dropped his voice a little. "I'll tell you one thing," he said. "Won't know the place when he gets back." He paused. "Probably won't know ourselves, either."

The remark struck Mr. Frith as being funny; indeed, very funny. He laughed a lot over it and spilled some of his champagne down his trouser leg. That struck him as rather funny too.

"Looks bad," he admitted. "Very bad. But it's the glass really. The shape, you know. Too shallow. Doesn't hold the stuff properly. All slops out."

While he was speaking he had caught sight of Native Affairs. He began waving. But Native Affairs pretended not to see. He walked away, and Mr. Frith began to follow.

Harold took this for his opportunity. He was near the door already. Then, as he reached the threshold, he realized suddenly that this would be the last time he would ever see the Long Drawing Room; the last time he would ever see Sir Gardnor, Mr. Frith, any of them. He was filled suddenly by an immense, irrational sadness. He turned and looked back.

As he did so, he heard a voice behind him.

"I only came down because I thought you might be here," it said.

And immediately afterwards there was Sybil Prosser's voice.

"You *knew* he was here," she said. "I told you."

When Harold faced her, he could see at once that Lady Anne had been crying. Her eyes were still red-looking. But the mascara was fresh on her lashes, and she seemed anything but miserable now; defiant, rather.

"You know why he isn't taking me?" she asked.

Harold shook his head.

"Because I might see my Timothy," she told him. "That's what he is afraid of. He knows Timothy likes me better."

"Are we going inside?" Sybil Prosser asked pointedly.

"No," Lady Anne told her. *"He's* in there. I just want to talk to Harold." She rested her hand on Harold's arm for a moment. "You can get me a glass of champagne if you like," she said. "I wouldn't mind that a bit."

When he returned, Lady Anne and Sybil Prosser were standing face to face.

"If you're going to be perfectly horrible, you can go to bed," Lady Anne was saying. "I don't want you near me. You might as well go to bed in any case. Harold and I have got plenty to talk about, haven't we?"

She turned toward him, and Harold found himself smiling back at her. Then Lady Anne remembered Sybil Prosser.

"Oh, do go to bed," she told her. "You'll only go on telling me I'm drinking too much. It's all you've said the whole evening."

"Good night then."

Harold watched the long yellow neck and loose dangling arms of Sybil Prosser as she walked away from them down the blue carpet of the corridor.

"Oh God, now I've gone and upset her," she said. "You don't know what that means. Sybil can be very spiteful."

Two late guests, a little breathless after the stairs, were being shown into the drawing room. Lady Anne laid her hand upon his arm.

"We can't just stand here," she told him. "We'd better go into the library."

As soon as they were inside, she closed the door behind her.

"Nobody'll want to come in here," she remarked. "They're all over on the other side. Besides, he thinks I'm in bed."

She was close to him, and she was stroking the lapels of his coat. It was the backs of her fingers that she used when she was stroking, he noticed.

"Dear Harold," she said.

"Dear Anne."

"Don't you want to kiss me?"

She stayed there in his arms, looking up at him.

"You're a lot more important to me than you realize."

He kissed her again.

"If it hadn't been for you, I don't think I should be here."

"It's your party."

"I didn't mean that. I mean be here at all. Anywhere. I was going to kill myself. I tried once before; didn't Sybil tell you? It's no secret. Everybody knows about it."

She was facing him as she was speaking. Her hands were raised to her face, and she was screwing on an earring.

"And it wouldn't have gone wrong this time. I know how many you have to take to finish you." She paused. "But with you here, I shan't have to now, shall I?"

Chapter 13

To GET onto the Coronation Flyer, there was a good deal more involved than merely buying a railway ticket.

For a start, there were the sleeping cars. The whole of the *wagon-lit* and *wagon-restaurant* side had been let off to a separate concessionaire with a one-story wooden office block some fifty feet down the platform from the ticket office. The two administrations were entirely separate. And both were eager for business. In consequence, travelers not infrequently found themselves with a perfectly valid ticket, but with nowhere to eat or sleep for the two and a half days of the journey; or, alternatively, with a *de luxe* single sleeper compartment, all duly booked and dated, but with no train actually running on the day in question.

In an effort to overcome the difficulty, the Royal Central African Railroad had arranged for the installation of a telephone service between the two offices. The instruments were black, shiny and securely padlocked to the iron window bars.

Harold presented himself before the R.C.A.R. ticket counter shortly after midday, an hour at which he judged the white population would be absent. He was right. But he had reckoned without the black population: they were absent too.

With some difficulty, he finally found the Station Master. No, the Station Master explained, the issue of tickets was not his responsibility; under his general supervision, of course yes, but directly no. He would, however, be delighted to find, if not the senior ticket clerk himself, at least a highly trained and qualified assistant.

Harold waited. An eager and affable young man, the stand-in booking clerk came leaping over the tracks, his striped shirttails flying. He would attend to Harold immediately, he said; at once; just as soon as he was able to locate the key.

It was the Station Master who had it. A moment later, the little doors behind the metal grille of the *guichet* were flung open, and the booking clerk was sitting there, all smiles, with his fountain pen at the ready.

"I want a First single on Wednesday for Nucca."

"Very sorry, sah. No trains today to Nucca."

"Not today. Wednesday."

"Wednesday, yassah. Coronation Flyer on Wednesday. Where to, sah?"

"Nucca."

"Yassah. What class, sah?"

"First."

"Yassah. Single or return, sah?"

"Single."

"Yassah."

The clerk turned his back on Harold and began rummaging about in various pigeonholes. In some there were tickets that he had never seen before. He took them out and studied them. He folded back the corners of old tickets that had become dog-eared. He rearranged the Third Returns. He discovered a Luggage Receipt that had been missing for weeks and weeks. Then, with a cry of triumph, he found just what he wanted—a First Class Single to Nucca. He came back to his desk with it. He dated it. He corrected the date. He used too much ink. A great black blot like a birthmark spread all over the spongy cardboard. He went back to the pigeonholes and took out another ticket.

It was just as Harold was coming away that the booking clerk remembered his full instructions.

"Sah, sah," he called after him, "you want sleeper reservations, sah? Sleeper reservations and meal vouchers?"

The booking clerk was always delighted to have a chance to use the connecting telephone. The Sleeper Manager was a friend of his, a personal friend. And on days when no trains were running, the two of them would often spend whole hours chatting together. The booking clerk kept an official railway duster specially for wiping out the mouthpiece during prolonged conversations.

But today was disappointing. He cranked and recranked the little ebony handle on the instrument, but there was no answer from the other end. What made it particularly shaming before a stranger was that he could so plainly hear the bell ringing all the time.

" 'Scuse me, sah," he said at last. "Back in no time at all."

Harold could hear, outside on the platform, the shouts of the booking clerk. Then came an answering call from somewhere behind the Goods Depot. A moment later, there was the noise of loud laughter and the sound of returning footsteps.

The booking clerk reappeared behind the grille.

"Everything is ready now, sah," he said, cranking away again at the handle. "No more delays. Your sleeper reservations will be made absolutely forthwith."

Because the conversation was in rapid Mimbo, Harold could not make out a single word of it. He even began to doubt whether they were talking about him at all. Then the booking clerk turned anxiously toward him.

"The Sleeper Manager wishes to know which Wednesday, sah."

"Next Wednesday," Harold told him. "Like my ticket."

"Yassah. Certainly, sah."

There was more Mimbo from the booking clerk; more intense listening to what the Sleeper Manager had to say.

"He is asking whether you wish full meals? No partial refreshments served at all any longer. Only full meals."

The conversation became heated again. The booking clerk

banged his fist down on the receiver. Then, covering up the mouthpiece with his pale pink palm, he referred to Harold again.

"Twenty per cent reduction if you pay for the return journey at the same time," he said. "All full first-class meals throughout. Dinner five courses."

"Single," Harold told him.

There was more Mimbo; more laughter. The booking clerk rang off.

"Everything absolutely O.K., sah," he said. "All fixed and in order. The Sleeper Manager asks if you would please be so good as to go to his office to confirm the details. It is close beside on the same platform. The very next building, in fact. Ah'll phone, sah, to say you're on your way. In fact, sah, Ah'll accompany you mahself."

The taxi was due in twenty minutes, and Harold's bags, all packed and labeled, were blocking up the little hallway of the bungalow.

So he had done it. There was no turning back. By tomorrow morning, Amimbo would simply be a township somewhere on the map, and Sir Gardnor would have to find someone else to help him with his book.

It had to be this way, he kept telling himself. There isn't any future for either of us. And it isn't fair on her. She's the one who'd have got hurt. Not me. Pulling out's the only thing. Now, before it's too late. She must see that.

He was staring out the window across the garden. Through the trunks of the acacia trees, he could see the white sun blinds of the Residency.

It was only talk. She didn't really mean it. People who talk about killing themselves never do. She'll get over it. She'll forget all about me.

He had just finished the last of the breakfast coffee and had lit a cigarette. On the table beside him stood a little pile of letters that he had sat up most of the night writing.

The one to Mr. Frith had been comparatively easy. Reading

between the lines, it would tell him all that he needed to know; all that he knew already, most likely. The one to Sir Gardnor had not proved unduly difficult either. It mentioned urgent family business at home and finished up with an apology and regrets for not having been able to see the book right through to the proof stage. It gave nothing away.

It was the letter to Lady Anne that had been written, torn up, rewritten and rewritten. Twice he had ripped the envelope open again, and each time he had decided that the letter had better go as it was.

After all, it's the truth, isn't it? he kept saying to himself. So why not be frank and face up to it? I owe her some kind of explanation: I can't simply disappear. It's kinder this way. God knows I don't want to hurt her.

He looked at his watch. The Coronation Flyer, in its cream and chocolate paintwork, would already be standing in the Terminus.

Not long now, was the one thought running through his mind. Not long, and I've made it. I'll write to her again when I get to Nucca.

The taller of the two houseboys came sidling into the room, his big hands flapping, the toes of his strong black feet wriggling with excitement. Harold recognized all the signs. It meant that the boy had just broken something; or the frying pan had been stolen; or there were ghosts round the bungalow again; or he had just seen the tail end of an enormous python gliding in behind the kitchen stove; or the cook once more had said something unpleasant about his mother.

Harold caught sight of the cook behind the bead curtain; it was the vivid white glint of his eyes that gave him away. The curtain parted and the cook came through. He was carrying something.

It was a bulging and misshapen hamper. Waddling awkwardly because of its size, he placed it proudly upon the table. It was a surprise, he said; a big surprise, planned specially for the journey. He started to undo it. The taller boy snatched it away from him. They pulled. One of the straps on the hamper came clean away in the struggle. This made things easier. Between them they began removing the contents to display them. There were two roast chickens; a ham; a tin of Fray Bentos corned beef; oranges; bananas; a Huntley and Palmer Rich Dundee Cake; a Christmas pudding with a label on the jar saying BOIL FOR FOUR HOURS; a packet of chocolate biscuits; ten cigarettes.

For between meals, they kept saying; and in case of waking up at night when the restaurant car is left in darkness.

The huge hamper made Harold's parting gift of money seem mean and ungenerous. But they were delighted. Absolutely delighted. And why not? All for free, they'd had the fun of packing a monster picnic basket. They'd had the additional fun of solemnly presenting it to the man who had already paid for it. And he had given them, in return, not merely full wages but a dowry as well. What more could they ask?

It was the sound of the taxi wheels slithering to a stop on the wet earth that interrupted them. Frantically, they began packing up the hamper again, breaking off only to shout out the window to the driver to tell him to stop honking. Because of the broken strap, they used string. The string snapped, and they found a piece of sash cord. They knotted it fiercely. They carried out the hamper between them like pallbearers. They returned for the suitcases.

With their going, the bungalow suddenly became strangely quiet and empty. He could hear the *thud-thud, thud-thud* of the pressure pump at the top of the garden.

I know I'm doing the right thing, pulling out, Harold kept repeating to himself. It's for the best in the long run. Best for Anne and for me.

The two houseboys were outside with the taxi driver. They were in the middle of a disagreement as to how the luggage should be loaded. Through the window, Harold could see that it had all come off again and was standing in the mud while they argued.

He went through into the deserted bedroom. It looked as though no one had ever slept there since the bungalow had been built. In the bathroom, there was at least one memento of him: his squeezed-out tube of toothpaste had been left out on the shelf below the little mirror. He tried the kitchen. It looked different, smelled different. There were the breakfast things all washed up on the drainboard, but the stove was full of ashes. There was nothing cooking on it.

He came back into the dining room, and there was Sybil Prosser standing in the opposite doorway. He hadn't heard her enter, didn't know how long she had been there. But she was watching him. The middle button of her blouse was undone, and her hair was escaping in all directions from the various grips and pins and slides that she always wore. Her usually sallow complexion was flushed and fiery-looking.

"And she thought she could trust you," she greeted him.

"What do you mean?"

She stood there, her flat bosom rising and falling.

"Then you don't know?"

The note of utter incredulity was obviously genuine.

"Know what?"

Sybil Prosser drew her tongue across her thin, dry lips.

"She heard you were leaving. It was all round Amimbo."

"So?"

"So," Sybil Prosser repeated. "So she took a whole bottleful of sleeping tablets. We've had the doctor up there all night. She was unconscious for hours. Simply hours. And when she came to, she began asking for you."

Sybil Prosser paused for a moment and her pale eyes lit up again.

"God knows why," she added.

"Asking for me, did you say?" Harold repeated dully.

"I can't stop her," Sybil Prosser told him.

"And she's all right again?"

"Don't ask me. All those tablets. And she'd been drinking."

"Is the doctor still there?"

"He's not leaving her."

There was a pause; a long pause. All that Harold could hear was the noise of Sybil Prosser's heavy breathing and, in his ears,

the sound of his own heart pounding. Then, abruptly, he **went**
over to the door.

The houseboys were there waiting for him.

"Take those bags off again," he said. "I'm staying."

Chapter 14

IT WAS nearly a month now since Sir Gardnor had returned.
There was still nothing definite. No word from the Prime
Minister. Sir Gardnor had merely taken up the African reins
again with the huge question mark of India tantalizingly hanging
over him.

Not that he seemed to care. He was back in his beloved
Amimbo, he kept saying; as far as he was concerned, there was a
whole lifetime of work waiting for him on his very doorstep.
Indeed, while away, Sir Gardnor appeared to have discovered a
fresh source of energy. Council had been brought forward to nine
A.M., and a new body that he had invented—the Governor's
Committee—sat with individual Ministers every afternoon at the
Residency. Amimbo, in short, was enjoying all the benefits of
zealous and enlightened modern Colonial administration.

There were difficulties, of course. Mr. Talefwa, under the
pseudonym "Truth-Teller," had started a new series entitled
"Hidden Places." Only yesterday he had warned his readers that
with the Governor's return, the hangings in Amimbo Jail would
shortly begin again. There were at the moment, he stated, three
innocent men—all victims of aggressive imperialism—ready to be
sacrificed on trumped-up charges of treason, rape, or murder.

And Native Affairs was uneasy because Mr. Talefwa had succeeded in upsetting Mr. Ngono. In a leading article, he had
referred to a certain notorious dark-skinned jackal, educated at a
foreign university and with local interests in dance halls and
importing establishments, cultivating the Governor's retinue for
immoral purposes or corrupt commercial advantage.

What made it so awkward for Mr. Ngono was that the clerk in

whom he had confided in Mr. Frith's office had since been dismissed for stealing and was now on the staff of the *Amimbo Mirror*.

In the circumstances, there was little that Mr. Ngono could do in the Courts. He had therefore arranged to have Mr. Talefwa beaten up. But he had not reckoned on Mr. Talefwa's natural built-in flair for martyrdom. Mr. Talefwa insisted that the ruffians who had attacked him were all plain-clothes policemen acting under direct Government orders; from a reliable source, he further reported that a made-to-measure coffin with his name on it was already stored in a secret room in Police Headquarters.

Nor was the rest of the Colony any calmer. In Okuro Province, typhoid epidemics had broken out in two districts nearly a hundred miles apart; a landslide had disrupted the telephone system to Omtala; a road surveyor had shot himself, or been shot, at Omurumu; tribal warfare had led to a mass killing less than three hours' drive from Amimbo; and the rains had washed away a small township on the banks of the Abatele River.

Sir Gardnor, for his part, took it all in his stride. He was imperturbable. It was always the same, he said, after every wet season; year by year, disaster followed close upon the heels of disaster. But, he pointed out, the rains were now easing. The sky in places was already blue again.

His long-projected safari, he added, would be able to take place, as planned, in four or five weeks at the outside. In the meantime, he was only sorry that Lady Anne should have gone down with another of those inexplicable illnesses of hers.

Because of the climate, he had already been forced to send his son back home to England. And if Lady Anne's health did not materially improve in the near future, he would—he openly admitted—have to make the ultimate sacrifice and ask her to leave him as well.

"But how can you possibly think I'm well enough?" she was saying. "I haven't been outside the place once since it happened."

"It'd do you good," Harold told her. "Get you out of yourself."

Lady Anne did not reply immediately. She was lying back on the long couch with the cushions all piled up behind her. In between answers, she closed her eyes and appeared to be sleeping.

"She's not asleep really," Sybil Prosser told him. "She's enjoying herself."

Harold turned to Lady Anne.

"Would you rather we left you?" Harold asked.

Lady Anne opened her eyes for a moment.

"I don't mind either way," she said. "It makes no difference to me. I'm still half dead. That's what you don't realize."

"She probably wants a drink."

It was Sybil Prosser who had spoken.

Lady Anne's eyes were closed again.

"Drinking won't help me to come to life again," she replied. "It simply makes me feel a little bit less dead."

With her hair loose over her shoulders, and in the plain white dress that she was wearing, it might have been an exhausted schoolgirl who was lying there. It was only the hands that were not a schoolgirl's hands. The blue pattern of the veins was too plainly stamped there.

"I'll give her another one," Sybil Prosser said in her flat, unraised voice from which all emotion had been drained long ago. "If I don't, I'll only have to get it for her after you've gone. I'm tired out."

Lady Anne was looking at Harold now.

"You didn't believe I'd do it, did you?" she asked. "I told you, and you didn't believe it." She reached out her hand for the drink. "But as soon as you heard you decided to stay on. That's all that matters. That's what I keep telling myself."

There was a chair beside the couch, and Sybil Prosser sat down on it. She crossed her long legs. Then she uncrossed them. Yesterday, it was her hands that had been giving her trouble: she had kept clasping and unclasping them. Today, it was her legs. She couldn't keep them folded over on the same side even for five minutes.

"Well, are you going on safari, or aren't you?" she asked abruptly. "Don't forget, I'm the one who has made all the arrangements."

"I'm too tired," Lady Anne replied. "I can't stand the journey.

Besides, there's no point in it. I don't enjoy killing things. He does. I don't."

Sybil Prosser stirred. She refolded her legs the way they had been.

"There's no point in staying here," she said. "Everyone else is going."

Lady Anne took a sip of her drink and put the glass down on the table beside her.

"Not everyone," she replied, with a little half smile. "Not me. And not Harold. I haven't given him permission to go. Not yet I haven't."

"But I've said I'll go," Harold told her. "I said I would when H.E. asked me."

"Then you may have to change your mind. I don't know yet. It's too early." She gave a little sigh. "But don't worry. There's plenty of time. We've still got a fortnight. We're bound to have heard by then."

"Heard what?"

"About India."

Lady Anne suddenly roused herself. She was sitting up on the couch now. The smile had disappeared completely.

"Are you blind, both of you?" she asked. "Why the hell should Gardie"—it was the first occasion on which Harold had heard her call Sir Gardnor by his pet name—"want Harold with him? It stands out a mile if only you could see."

She had closed her eyes as she was speaking.

"Now please go away, both of you," she said. "Go away and leave me alone. I don't want to talk to either of you. I just want to go to sleep."

Chapter 15

THE PRACTICAL arrangements for the forthcoming safari were already well in hand. An air of anticipation, almost of foreboding, hung over the whole Residency; and those, like the A.D.C., who had been through it all before knew what they were still in for.

That was because Sir Gardnor insisted on personally supervising everything. His personal tent—it was marquee-size to begin with—was having another complete section laboriously stitched into the middle of it; an electric generator unit delivered by the Royal Engineers had been rejected out of hand because it was too noisy; Army Signals, quite unnecessarily in their view, were carrying out extensive tests with lash-up aerial masts, under what Sir Gardnor referred to as "service conditions"; and another telegram—a peremptory one this time—had been sent to the gunsmiths in London demanding that the telescopic rifle sight, returned for some minor optical adjustment, be flown back out immediately.

Nor was this the only telegram that had passed. Ever since his last recall, the exchange between Amimbo and the Colonial Office had become incessant. The word "India" was never once used: Sir Gardnor was extremely strict about that. But phrases like "contingent situation," "matter we discussed," and "foreseeable changes" appeared daily; and from the Whitehall end, "nothing to report" and "no development to date" turned up in the replies with monotonous regularity.

In conversation, however, Sir Gardnor was altogether less discreet; quite lightheartedly so, in fact.

"Westminster is like that," he had just remarked. "The delays are endless. And deliberate, I fear. But they'll have to say something sometime. One can't leave India in suspense forever."

It was a small dinner party. There were only six of them, including the A.D.C. Harold had an uneasy feeling that he had been invited simply to keep up the numbers.

"I see Lord Eldred's name mentioned in *The Observer,*" Sir Gardnor continued. "I'm not surprised. You could hardly say he's been happy in Ceylon, could you? It's his manner that puts people off, I suppose. Not that he means it. His friends speak very well of him. It's only surprising that so few people seem to know him. In some circles he's quite unheard of. What do you say, Mr. Frith?"

The question was unfair because Mr. Frith was temporarily

enjoying one of his cherished moments of relaxation. He had sunk lower and lower in his chair, and his eyes were closed. He raised his head with difficulty.

"I thought it was the Earl of Delmer, sir," he said.

He had struggled upwards as he was speaking, and now that his chin was above table level, he wanted to show how acute and well informed he was.

"It was one of the Sunday papers that had it, sir," he explained. *"The Observer,* I think it was. It mentioned your name, sir, and Lord Eldred's and"—he was visibly slipping downward again—"the Earl. The one I said just now."

Sir Gardnor's smile was immediately cut off at the source.

"But Delmer's scarcely suitable, would you say? It's been a most undistinguished career throughout. Passed over every time, in fact. And Lady Delmer, let's face it, has hardly been an asset. Quite the reverse, in fact. Can you seriously imagine either of them in Delhi?"

Sir Gardnor paused and appeared to be making the supreme imaginative effort. But it proved to be too much for him. He frowned and shook his head decisively.

"Unthinkable," he said. "Quite unthinkable. It would simply make us a laughingstock. The Indians aren't savages, remember. They're a highly civilized people. They'd spot the shortcomings immediately. Besides, the poor fellow drinks too much. That's why they sent him to the Caribbean. It's not so conspicuous out there. But you could hardly offer Delhi to a drunkard, could you? India's not just another Colony to be administered. It's an entire subcontinent waiting to be governed."

He had extended his arms while he was speaking and seemed to be embracing something.

"The Viceroyship," he went on, almost as though speaking to himself, "is the supreme Imperial appointment. And it presents the ultimate test. It calls for an unusually able and dedicated man at the very height of his powers." Here he gave his nervous, rather shrill little laugh and smiled on Harold for a moment. "It is, I suppose a reflection on the age we live in that my name should even have been considered."

Harold wondered if he was expected to reply. It was Mr. Frith, however, who replied for him. He had sunk down dormouse-fashion in his chair, and his chin was resting on his black tie, crumpling it. But he managed to get the words out.

"Hear, hear," he said. "Quite agree, sir." Then he closed his eyes again.

Sir Gardnor did not appear to have noticed. He did not, in fact, appear to be noticing anything. Quite unfocused, he was staring out across the dinner table into a remote Asian world of durbars and gold turbans and Sandhurst-educated Maharajas.

Chapter 16

LADY ANNE's new Morris had at last reached Amimbo terminus.

Owing to an oversight at the dockside, the crate had been loaded onto the train upside down, and the little car had traveled the three hundred and fifty miles from the coast with its wheels in the air. The Station Master, understandably perplexed by the large wooden packing case with all the lettering the wrong way up, was still standing on his head trying to decipher it when Army Transport arrived for the unfreighting.

Its upside-down journey from the coast had left its cream paintwork practically unscratched; and standing there in the fierce African sunlight, with its bright brass radiator, the enormous rubber bulb for the horn and the Lucas battery in the gleaming black case on the running board, it shone out in all its showroom newness.

"Isn't she a darling?" Lady Anne asked. "An absolute darling, I mean. Have you ever seen anything so perfect?"

She had remained where she was in the driver's seat while she was speaking. The car itself was drawn up outside the bungalow. And it was the loud hooting of the horn that had brought Harold out to her.

"I hear you've decided," he said. "You are coming on safari after all."

"Well, you couldn't leave her behind when all the other cars were moving off, now could you?" Lady Anne replied. "It'd break her heart."

She was speaking rather fast, and her voice had just that little catch in it that Harold noticed always came when she'd been drinking.

"If you're not doing anything, get in," she said. "I'm going for a drive anyway."

He stood there with his hand on the side of the car, looking at her. He liked her best with her face framed inside the oval of a scarf. And it was the first time he had ever seen her with any color in her cheeks. It had come suddenly while she was speaking to him.

"Going to let me drive?" he asked.

She gave a little laugh.

"It's quite safe," she said. "I'm not the least bit tiddly. I only had a teeny-weeny little one—like that." She opened her fingers for a moment and then closed them again until they were about a quarter of an inch apart. "I wouldn't have dreamed of having a proper drink when I was taking her out for the first time. I'd have been far too scared."

Harold moved round to the passenger seat.

"Does Sybil approve of you going out alone like this?" he asked, after he had climbed in beside her. "It'll be dark in half an hour. Suppose I hadn't been here?"

"Oh, but I knew you were," she told him. "I could see your light. I often look over to see the light just to make sure you're in. In any case, Sybil's got one of her headaches. I told her to lie down." Again the little laugh. "As a matter of fact, I told her to have the headache."

They had already turned down the drive past the sentries and were now heading west out of Amimbo towards the foothills.

"Doesn't she run beautifully?" Lady Anne asked. "You can tell how much she's enjoying herself."

"Where are you taking me?"

"Anywhere," she told him. "Anywhere that's a long way off and right away from everyone." She broke off for a moment. "You don't know what safari's like. You haven't tried living in tents. I have. You are right on top of everybody all the time."

She bent forward and patted the shiny varnish of the dashboard.

"But this isn't really our treat," she said. "It's hers. I told her we'd take her out this evening. Just the three of us, I said. She understood perfectly. She's a very understanding little car."

The sun was already slipping down over the horizon, gathering up speed for the final plunge, when they came to the Busimo cutting.

"This'll do," she said. "Let's go to the Falls. They frighten me. I like being frightened when I'm with someone."

With the tiresome heat and dazzle of the day almost over, the bush around them was slowly coming to life again. It was time for the local night shift to take over. A pair of hyenas, carrying their shoulders high like athletes and dragging their withered rumps after them, crossed the road ahead of them.

"If Gardie was here, he'd shoot them," Lady Anne said. "He always shoots hyenas. Just to keep his eye in, he says. Not that it bothers me much. They're just too nasty to mind about."

They drove on for a while in silence. It was getting dark, really dark, by now. Lady Anne switched on the headlights.

"Any news from London?" Harold asked.

He didn't have to say what kind of news he had in mind.

"Yes, and it's no news," Lady Anne replied. "That's what's so marvelous. And there isn't going to be any. Not for weeks and weeks and weeks. Gardie had a letter this morning that said so. He's furious."

In the rainless African night, the windshield of the car began to mist over. There was the noise of thunder in the air. They turned the last of the horseshoe bends in the road, and there it was, the Busimo River—wide, muddy, and imperturbable—suddenly denied the solid ground it crawled upon and launching itself aimlessly into space.

"It's supposed to be a beauty spot," Lady Anne remarked. "But it's all wet and beastly, really. You'll like it much better where we're going."

She turned the nose of the Morris up the narrow, winding track above the Falls, and Harold watched the steering wheel joggle in her hands. Stones and pebbles from underneath the tires went flying into the bushes on either side. Then, round the last bend, they came on the smooth grass of the plateau. They had climbed higher than the mist, and the stars appeared again. Lady Anne switched off the engine.

"It's best with a full moon," she said. "But you can't have everything." She leaned back in the driver's seat and gave a little sigh. "I've been promising myself this all day. Ever since I woke up this morning."

She had taken off her scarf and was shaking out her hair.

"There's some drink in the back," she added. "I asked Sybil to see about it before we left. And we don't have to just sit here in the car. There should be a rug or something." She gave the same slightly husky little laugh. "I asked Sybil to see about that too."

Lady Anne sat watching him while he unpacked the wicker hamper with the drink. As well as the bottle of Haig and the soda, there was a metal box with ice cubes in it. The box had been carefully wrapped round with one of the Residency napkins.

"That's right," Lady Anne was saying. "We'll have a drink first. Then you can make love to me. Then we'll have lots more to drink. Then I shall feel sleepy. And you can drive back. I shan't mind by then."

She spilled some of the whisky when he passed it to her because, instead of simply taking the glass, she tried to stroke his hand.

"And there's one more thing we've got to do," she said. "I told Sybil we'd go in and say goodnight to her. She gets fussed when I'm away like this. Poor Sybil, she never gets any fun out of life herself. And she's rather a darling, really."

It was late when they got back to Amimbo. The native stalls had been packed up and put away, and the row of Indian shops were all battened down until tomorrow. Only the cafés remained open. In them was still light, music, joy.

Lady Anne was asleep beside him in the car. Her head kept falling over on his shoulder. Harold was watching the road. Ahead of them a red light was showing. It was at the grade crossing; somewhere, still miles away probably, the one night freight train of the week was slowly making for Amimbo.

As he stopped the car, Lady Anne woke up.

"What's the matter?" she asked. "Where are we? Perhaps I *should* have driven after all."

Then she went to sleep again.

It was while they were waiting that Harold heard the sound of the approaching motorcycle. It was a robust, full-throated sound, and whoever was driving kept turning the throttle up and down, evidently for the sense of sheer power that it gave him. The machine came round the corner, and the cone of the headlight lit up the Morris. With a crunch of tires in the dust road as the brakes were applied, it drew up alongside. In the saddle, goggles pulled down over his eyes, sat Mr. Ngono.

"I told myself as you passed by that it was you," he announced delightedly. "And you see that I was right. No mistake about it. Most remarkably quick thinking, too. Because I did not even recognize the car."

He had pushed his goggles up onto his forehead by now and was staring across at Lady Anne.

"My most sincere forgiveness," he said. "I had absolutely no wish of any kind to intrude. Entirely the contrary, in fact. It was the car I saw first. It is a model much advertised in all the best motoring papers. Absolutely the latest thing; 1930 to the very minute."

Lady Anne was awake now.

"Good evening, Mr. Ngono," she said.

It was her best Residency voice that she was using: quiet, rather clipped, and, to some ears, possibly even a trifle patronizing.

Mr. Ngono tried to stand up in the saddle and make a little bow.

"You remember my name from the last garden party?" he asked. "How extremely gracious and most thoughtful. With over three hundred of your high and very eminent guests, it is indeed a distinguished honor that I am by no means forgotten."

"You must come to our next one," Lady Anne told him.

"Absolutely the very moment the invitation comes," he assured her, glancing toward the car again. "And may I be permitted," he asked, "to say that this is the most sporting and up-to-date vehicle in the whole of Amimbo. It sets an altogether new and fashionable standard for these parts."

Lady Anne gave him one of her approving smiles.

"You won't be seeing it again for some time," she told him. "I'm taking it on safari tomorrow."

Mr. Ngono gave his biggest bow of all.

"Then allow me most politely to wish you a very happy and contented safari. All big success to it. And to His Excellency, of course: that goes absolutely without saying. Good killing everywhere you go. Something tells me it will be quite terrific. A killing we shall all talk about, and remember."

He broke off for a moment and seemed suddenly to have become saddened and rather wistful.

"It is difficult to see in this light," he said, "but my motorcycle is a new model also. The very latest. It is an Indian twin-cylinder. Specially imported for my own pleasure. On your return, you will graciously permit me to run races with you."

BOOK II

Death on Safari

Chapter 17

WHEN IT finally got under way, the safari caravan—all eleven vehicles—was nearly three quarters of an hour behind schedule.

That was because Lady Anne up to the very moment of departure had told no one that the new Morris was coming along too. And, small though it was, it disrupted everything.

For a start, it presented the most elementary problem of precedence. Immediately behind the Governor's Humber was where the A.D.C. recommended; but Major Mills, detailed by the G.O.C. to accompany the expedition, insisted that the truck immediately astern of Sir Gardnor's car must contain his soldiery. How else in an emergency, he asked, could he be expected to give adequate protection? And if Lady Anne was to fall in behind that, they'd need one more truck if they were to be able to protect her too. As it was, the G.O.C.'s resources had been stretched to the limit by providing a scout car to head the procession and repair truck, complete with machine-gun mounting, to follow up the rear.

In the end, a solution was found by stripping down one of the service trucks containing the tents and fixing up a makeshift seat for a corporal and private of the South Staffs to cling onto. That meant restowing the displaced canvas while the Transport Officer, head down over the Morris handbook, was trying to work out how much extra gas and oil, let alone spares, would be required for one ten-horsepower car, not yet broken in, over unpaved roads, for a journey of unspecified duration, in tropical conditions.

There was more military show of force than on previous safaris because of the sudden rise in outrages. There had been another peculiarly objectionable demonstration by the Leopard Men at a small village less than sixty miles to the south; and the season's graph of stabbings had also risen sharply.

Only last night, a report had come through that a white supervisor employed by Post and Telegraphs had been found half naked in a ditch with a six-inch wound in his back and all his personal possessions—private papers, combined volt-and-amp meter, wrist watch, money even—intact. That made it much more sinister: it looked inevitably as though murder and not clean, straightforward robbery had been the motive.

All the South Staffs men had been told to travel with their rifles at the ready.

The column came to a halt, waved down by Sybil Prosser, two hours outside Amimbo. It was an unscheduled stop. But also unavoidable. Lady Anne, much as she loved the Morris, had to admit that in that heat, that dust, that sunlight, she could go no farther. And Sybil Prosser, all swathed in white scarves like a cocoon, dismounted to ask what could be done about it.

Sir Gardnor immediately had room made in the Humber. It was where he had expected Lady Anne to ride anyway, and it was only when she had chosen to bring her own car that he had moved a lot of his own things—official boxes, binoculars, books, camera, gun case—in beside him.

But re-storing the cargo was not Major Mills's only anxiety. They had been rounding a bluff of rock when Sybil Prosser had started her gesticulations, and the scout car was already past it. Bristling with guns and all eyes front for hidden ambushes, it had gone hurtling on, oblivious of the fact that it had left its train behind it. What Major Mills, professionally trained to anticipate disaster, most wanted to avoid was a head-on collision with the Governor's Humber at the blind corner when the scout car, flat-out and bewildered, came roaring back to see what had happened.

Harold sat himself at the wheel beside Sybil Prosser and looked across at Lady Anne in the official Humber. It was a big car with a wide back seat. In one corner was Lady Anne; in the other, the Governor. So far, they did not appear to have spoken.

"Oh God," Sybil Prosser asked suddenly, "why did she have to bring the damn thing? I told her not to." Her voice was as ironed-out and expressionless as ever, but inside her white cotton gloves she kept clenching and unclenching her fingers. "I wish now she'd stayed back at the House. We're in for a packet, I can tell you. I feel it *here*." She indicated a point somewhere in the middle of her breastbone. "I'm never wrong about that kind of thing." Then she leaned over in her seat to get a better look at the Humber. "Well, anyhow, we all know where she is for once," she said cheerfully. "I suppose that's something."

The first official stop, the one for the night, had been arranged for one hour before sundown. By then they should have been on the rolling grasslands of the Tibbuta plateau. But with the late start, this was out of the question. Sir Gardnor was aware of this, and he and Major Mills went into conference.

It was a situation dear to Major Mills's heart. He was comparatively new to Africa, but had a natural flair for terrain, and contours and compass readings were his specialty. He spread out his maps by the roadside and consulted them reverently like a priest. Section by section he opened them up, using little stones to keep the corners flat, until the edge of the road looked like washing day. Then the auguries told him something. It was something to do with water, Harold gathered.

They made for it. Major Mills, compass in hand, with his map spread across his knees and the Governor's gun case catching him in the groin every time they hit a particularly violent pothole, kept alternately glancing down at his wrist watch and then lifting his head to note the height of the declining sun.

What worried him was that the contour maps belied the vegetation. The maps showed nicely wooded slopes. But already they had left the occasional shade patches behind them and were heading into arid desert. It looked like the gateway to the Kalahari.

According to Major Mills's calculations, they should have made a shallow ford crossing of one of the tributaries of the Mirabillo about five miles back and now be following the course of the great river itself. A second halt was called and the native servants closely questioned. But it was useless. To a man, they were strangers to this part of the country, and after much sniffing, one and all agreed that they could not smell water in the air—not even the faintest white trace of it, in fact.

It was Sir Gardnor who made the decision. They would laager where they were, he said; and looking hard at Major Mills, he added that they could start prospecting for rivers in the morning. He added also that they could see now why he had laid such stress on carrying adequate water tanks with them. Anything less than a full hour before sundown inevitably meant an unseemly scramble instead of a properly laid-out camping site.

Harold did not see Lady Anne again that evening. Together with Sybil Prosser, she had retired into the shelter of one of the big trucks while their tent was being erected; and alongside, dwarfing it completely, the twin poles of the Governor's marquee had been dug into the ground by Major Mills's labor corps.

Already the place was beginning to look like a small township. Smaller poles and awnings and guy ropes were going up everywhere, and in front of one of the better tents—Major Mills's, Harold reckoned—someone had deposited two white stones, one on either side of the entrance flap, to make a formal doorway.

It was the catering and hotel side that were at the moment in the lead. The field kitchens had been unloaded, their long chimneys plugged into place, and one of the orderlies had got a fire going.

Alongside, the Governor's own catering department had been opened up. And here the military were excluded. This was Residency soil, with Old Moses in command. With a white cloth tied round him, he looked more gnarled and withered-up than ever; beneath the cloth, his legs showed thin and scaly like a heron's. He was superintending the unwrapping of a side of meat from the blood-stained cheesecloth in which it had been traveling.

Beside him, one of the kitchen boys was standing. He was a new boy whom Harold had not seen before; and he was distinct from all the others. He was bronze-colored, pure bronze. He shone. He was finer-boned, too, with slender wrists and ankles. From the way he held himself, he might have been a dancer. His lips were thinner: they were like European lips. When he saw that Harold was looking at him, he didn't hump his shoulders and stare down at his feet as the other boys would have done. Head held a little to one side and baring his magnificent white teeth, he simpered.

But he was not left to himself for very long. Already Old Moses had a job for him, a butcher's job. One of the sides of beef was there to be carved, and it was beneath his dignity for Old Moses to carve it himself. Instead, with his dark, bony forefinger, he indicated the filet that he wanted. He even went twice over the outline so that his assistant would know exactly what the cut should be.

But the bronze kitchen boy was clearly quite untrained. And when he started to carve the side of beef savagely as though he were attacking someone, Old Moses snatched the knife from him. Poised like a picador, Old Moses himself thrust the blade home cleanly and firmly. Then, tiny cricket of a man though he was, he deftly cut out the slice of steak that he wanted. The whole operation was as clean and rapid as a surgeon's.

The kitchen boy gave a little laugh of sheer admiration.

Chapter 18

IT WAS a miserable spot that Sir Gardnor had chosen: more rock than sand, and more sand than soil.

But Harold had to admit that the Army certainly knew how to make the best of it. The Governor's marquee, double ceiling and all, looked as though a firm of Ascot caterers had just been putting the finishing touches to it; and on the far side of the camp, behind a polite screen of canvas, more of Major Mills's men were digging the latrines. The little mounds of freshly turned earth suggested a mass burial. Up on a little knoll behind, the Army Signals transmitter mast was braced and stayed ready to withstand a hurricane.

Sir Gardnor was already at work in his tent as Harold went past. A trestle table had been set up on a square of coconut matting, and on the table were carefully set up the tools of office. The A.D.C. had omitted nothing. There were the silver-and-crystal inkwell—Sir Gardnor always insisted on using a dip pen; the red morocco writing folder; the rocker blotter with the big gilt handle; and the long, bayonet-like paper knife. Seated in his folding chair, the Governor looked every bit as installed and comfortable as in his own study in the Residency. And every bit as imposing.

Even though it was scarcely more than dusk, the acetylene lamp over his head had already been lighted. The whole of his face was in shadow. But that served only to bring out the massive forehead, the hard ridge of the eyebrows, the boxer's shoulders that overlapped the canvas of his chair.

He looked up as Harold passed and seemed pleased at the interruption.

"Come in, come in," he said. "Pour yourself a drink if you'd like one."

He had tilted his chair back as he was speaking, and was now amusing himself with the paper knife. It was one of his favorite toys, the paper knife. He liked playing with it; balancing it like a seesaw; holding it upright, sword-fashion, and fingering the point; staring down its length as though it were a gun barrel.

"You're finding all this very dull, I'm afraid," he went on. "But things should be looking up by tomorrow. We shall be in good game country by then."

He was taking another sighting down the paper knife as he said it.

"You'll be getting your first shot, won't you?" he asked. "There's something peculiarly satisfying about a good kill. It takes your mind so entirely off everything else. Indeed, if you allowed your mind to wander you could very easily get killed yourself. You do realize there's always a strong element of danger when on safari, don't you?"

Harold started to answer, but Sir Gardnor was already speaking.

"And it is not a question of simply killing animals," he explained. "Any ruffian with a gun could do that. It is a matter of selection, and planning and forethought. This leopard I'm going after, for instance. I had the first reports of him six months ago. An unusually fine specimen, so I'm told. And a menace. I've spent hours thinking about him. Hours," here Sir Gardnor allowed himself his slow, rather quizzical smile, "when no doubt I should have been thinking of other matters. Government matters."

He replaced the paper knife and sat looking down at the official papers in front of him. Harold could see that they were all scored down the margin in his fine, flourishing handwriting.

"It's a curious business, don't you think?" Sir Gardnor asked. "We are here for the sheer pleasure, let us be frank about it, of taking life. The larger the life somehow the more pleasurable. And here"—he flipped his fingernails across the sheet in front of him—"is an appeal for clemency. A condemned murderer, you understand. One of our missionaries, I regret to say, is responsible for the petition. He's been going round collecting these pathetic crosses that he calls signatures." He paused. "I have to give my decision tonight. By radio, you understand. The execution is arranged for tomorrow."

"Suppose the radio breaks down?" Harold asked.

"Then he'll be hanged," Sir Gardnor replied. "There'll be nothing that can stop it." His smile appeared again for an instant and then vanished. "As a matter of fact, he'll be hanged in any case. I intend to reject the petition."

He sat in silence staring out into the darkness beyond his tent.

"I delayed my decision deliberately," he said. "I wanted to have more time to think about it. It's been unfortunate for the poor fellow to be kept in suspense this way, don't you think? But it's better in the long run. I'm quite sure now my decision is the right one. I was in some doubt before."

It was getting on toward midnight when Harold went for a final saunter round the camp.

And he was immediately challenged. Major Mills had posted sentries back and front of the Governor's tent, and the corporal in charge was glad enough of anything to relieve the endless starlit tedium of his vigil. There was the oddly disconcerting sound of a rifle bolt being slammed smartly home.

A moment later they were joined by Major Mills himself. He had changed into rubber-soled sneakers and, revolver in hand, was making a tour of inspection. He seemed rather to welcome it when Harold suggested that the two of them should go round together.

And on the way, he talked.

"Can't afford to take any chances," he explained. "Big responsibility, you know, having H.E. on your hands like this. Glad when it's all over. Too much knife sticking going on for my taste. Take it from me, it's the L.M.s." Major Mills always referred to the Leopard Men as though they were a kind of service corps. "When there isn't time to get their claws out, they just use a knife. In the back, usually. Shows the kind of fellows they are. Sort of thing we're up against."

His sentences were all uttered in short bursts like machine-gun fire.

"Don't know what sort of numbers, either," he went on. "That's half the trouble. Could be a company. Could be a whole battalion." There was a longer pause this time. "Could be just a few isolated fanatics, of course. No way of telling. But they're organized, all right. Make no mistake about it. From abroad, too. Found the stub of a foreign-made pencil near one of the killings. German, actually."

Major Mills dropped his voice a little before revealing the full depth of his researches.

"And don't know who they are," he said. "That's another thing. Could be your own houseboy, or the sweeper-upper. Don't exactly go around in uniform, you know. And choose their weapons where they find them." He dropped his voice still lower and was talking out of the corner of his mouth by now. "There's enough cutlery over there on the Q.M. side"—he pointed vaguely in the direction of the field kitchens—"to put 'paid' to every damn one of us. And in native hands, too. Simply inviting trouble. Asking for it." He shook his head sadly at the thoughtlessness of other people. "Just had it all counted and put away under lock and key until tomorrow. Left one of my men there to keep an eye on it. Don't want the wrong kind of steak carved up, if you get me."

He took a final look round the sleeping camp. The peak of a South Staffs cap showed in silhouette on the skyline.

"Couldn't get in from outside," he said. "That's for certain. If there's going to be any funny business, the johnny's here inside already."

He placed his hand suddenly on Harold's arm and pulled him to one side.

"Careful!" he said. "Mind your step. I've had trip wires put all round this bit. Got little bells on 'em, too."

Chapter 19

NEXT MORNING they made their start as Sir Gardnor had intended. By seven-thirty, they were packed, loaded, and under way again. Only the fresh sand on the covered-up latrines showed where His Excellency's caravan had once rested.

And by eight o'clock they had found Major Mills's river. It was exactly as the contour map had shown it. Ahead of them in the haze loomed up the outlines of the fever trees, and the cars even had patches of coarse grass to run on instead of the everlasting terraces of burnt rock.

The Morris, unprepared for anything more strenuous than the lanes of Oxfordshire, kept boiling over, cooling off, and then boiling over again; Major Mills, with his eye on the water tanks, personally administered the refills like a sacrament.

Nor was the Morris the only cause of trouble. The clouds of dust thrown up by the advancing vehicles had brought on Sybil Prosser's hay fever. And in its most severe form. When she removed her dark glasses to wipe her eyes, Harold could see that they were red-rimmed and raw-looking. Her carefully controlled sneezes sounded like suppressed sobs. Thickly veiled and with her shoulders heaving, she might have been some poor, half-demented mourner.

And all the time, in the Governor's Humber ahead of them sat Sir Gardnor and Lady Anne. They were leaning up against their separate side rests like strangers. They appeared to be oblivious of each other. Not that Sir Gardnor appeared to be the least bit put out. When the column halted for lunch, he was at his easiest and most affable.

"Well, Major?" he asked. "Which is it to be next time? Shall we divert the river, or redraw the contour map? It's entirely up to you. You're in charge round here, you know."

And to Harold he was warmly avuncular.

"Been studying the handbook I lent you?" he asked. "Remember it's a rifle, not an air gun; it wasn't designed for shooting rabbits. The recoil, you know. It can easily break your shoulder if you don't hold it properly."

He shaded his eyes for a moment and inspected the surrounding bush.

"He may even be able to get in a few practice shots this afternoon," he remarked. "Thanks to Major Mills, we've made excellent time this morning. You could spare us an hour or so, couldn't you, Major, now that you've pinpointed us?"

But Major Mills was scarcely listening, even though it was the Governor who was speaking to him. His keen soldierly eye had detected something. It was figures moving. There were four or five of them, shimmering in the haze. Black, naked savages, armed with long spears.

He slapped his hand instinctively onto his revolver butt.

"I think we have visitors, sir," he said. "Better send out a party." There came the habitual short break. "See what they want, sir," he explained.

Ever since they had left the rock desert and come down alongside Major Mills's river, they had been among habitations. They had passed beside a village of beehive huts. The residents, most of whom had never seen even one car before, had come out in their numbers, awe-struck and incredulous, to watch the vast entourage rumble past them. Only the presence of the native cooks, unshackled and grinning, served to reassure them that they were not being borne down upon by slavers.

"A good man, the Major," Sir Gardnor observed, not addressing Harold directly but rather as though he were dictating some invisible testimonial. "I think he'll make an excellent soldier. If only he were a little more at his ease. Damn rude really, breaking off in the middle of a conversation like that. He could perfectly well have sent a messenger."

Major Mills, however, was leaving nothing to chance. Left to himself he would have had the five tribesmen placed under close arrest, interrogated and, even though they were naked, searched thoroughly. As it was, he stood alongside the Governor's Humber carefully observing through his binoculars and wondering about covering fire in case of trouble.

He returned ten minutes later, a trifle tense, but pleased with the comprehensiveness of his report.

"Beef, sir," he announced. "Big beef. Down there beyond the swamp. Say they're native hunters, sir. Look the genuine article. But can't be too careful. I'm still having them vetted, sir."

Sir Gardnor gave his most expansive smile.

"I don't question the beef," he said. "I merely query the *big* beef. Everything's big to them, even if it's only a duiker. They always lie like children, just to get taken on." He shifted the smile temporarily in Major Mills's direction. "Even so, Major, with your permission, I think after lunch we might give our friend here his first taste of the real thing. So don't let them go away again. And don't give them too much to eat. After a good meal they only get sleepy. They're simply not used to it."

They were joined at luncheon by the doctor, the A.D.C., the O.C. Signals, and the Transport Officer. Lady Anne and Sybil Prosser ate alone under an awning strung between two baggage trucks. It was at Sybil Prosser's request: the attack of hay fever had taken it out of her rather, and she didn't feel up to general conversation.

"One of the most delightful things—don't you think?—about being on safari is the uncertainty of it," Sir Gardnor asked as he sat back, gingerly prodding about with the slim gold toothpick that he always carried. "Like last night, for instance. Or this afternoon, for that matter. Who would have thought an hour or so ago that we should actually be out after something, instead of simply traveling." He turned to Major Mills. "You're sure you can spare us that long, Major, and still keep up with the map? I say spare us because I'm afraid we shall have to leave you behind to take care of the ladies."

He turned to the A.D.C.

"Well, if the guns are ready, we might as well be moving off. I take it you've arranged for bearers? It's bound to be heavy going once we reach the swamp."

The native guides were still resting when the Governor's party came upon them. In the shade cast by one of the larger trucks, they were sitting in a row with their knees drawn up to their chins like dysentery patients. But they appeared to be comfortable enough. All five were sleeping soundly, oblivious of the cloud of flies that was swishing round them.

It was not so much the men themselves, Harold discovered, as their anointment that acted as a fly attractor. Before setting out, they had crowned themselves with pancakes of fresh cow dung.

Sir Gardnor and the A.D.C. knew enough to keep to windward of them.

"Not that it hasn't got its uses," Sir Gardnor observed when Harold had caught up with him. "It kills the human scent, you understand. It's strange, isn't it, that animals"—a particularly pungent blast from the leader had just been wafted across to them—"should prefer that to the smell of you and me?"

It was a good mile to the swamp that they were making for. Seen through the heat haze, it had looked nearer: a mere two hundred yards or so. And head held high and shoulders back, Sir Gardnor was striding out. He was nearly a foot taller than the A.D.C.; in shorts and bush shirt, he looked like the Chief Scout surrogate.

It occurred to Harold as he followed up the rear how magnificently Sir Gardnor always fitted any part: in full ceremonial dress with the plumed hat and tassels on his sword, perfect; in Council, dressed in a white suit that somehow or other never got a stain or a smudge upon it, perfect again; in faded khaki and a shapeless canvas hat, equally perfect.

Sir Gardnor turned his head for a moment.

"We'll have to decide what rifle to give you," he said. "You can take your choice, really. There's the Purdey—but, frankly, I think it's a bit too good for you. There's the Holland and Holland, but you may find it rather long. I generally use it myself. And then there's the Winchester. You ought to get along all right with that. It's a good piece. What do you say, Tony?"

The A.D.C. agreed politely: he left the impression that if he had been measuring up Harold for the safari, he would have fitted him up with the Winchester every time.

"And you will be using your Italian one, I suppose," Sir Gardnor remarked. "If it suits you, you're quite right to stick to it, of course. I've never really liked any Italian gunsmith. Opera, yes; but I've always felt that the Italians could afford to leave firearms to other people."

But by now they had reached the first of the pools, and the guides were beginning to fan out into a shallow crescent. There was no one in charge, no command spoken. It was simply that they knew. Inside the swamp there was something living, and it was their business to see that it got itself killed. The size of their tip depended on it.

And they had speeded up now. The crouched-up invalids beside the lorry had suddenly become hunters. On their long legs, and with their spears trailing after them, they covered the rough ground as though it had been a race track. When they came to an obstacle they cleared it, keeping low like hurdlers.

Down by the swamp, the ground was soft like sponge cake. Every step broke the surface, and the hollow that remained filled itself immediately with thick rust-colored water.

Sir Gardnor looked down at Harold's shoes.

"You're wearing the wrong kind of footgear," he said disapprovingly. "Someone should have warned you."

They were up to their ankles by now, and every moment they were going in deeper. The A.D.C. was already in it up to his knees. Sir Gardnor, however, appeared hardly to have noticed. He might have lived his whole life half waterlogged, he was enjoying himself so much. Chin thrust out, he moved purposefully forward, not forgetting that it was an instruction course as well as an expedition.

"Remember to keep it up," he told Harold over his shoulder. "A wet gun's always a dangerous gun. And if you get any leeches on your legs, don't start trying to pull them off; you'll only tear yourself. Salt's the thing. We'll send for the cook when we get back."

They were passing along an avenue between the reed beds. Ahead of them lay a small island where the rushes were trampled underfoot and matted. Sir Gardnor made for it.

"This," he announced, "is where we take up our positions. If there's anything there, those fellows will drive it out this way. They looked quite reliable to me. Rather good types, in fact. Not the slightest trace of yaws."

Sir Gardnor inspected Harold's rifle, as though expecting to find fault with it, and then passed it as satisfactory.

"Well, there you are," he said. "It's entirely up to you now. You won't do anything foolish, will you?"

He turned to the A.D.C.

"We might as well split up, I suppose. I think I can safely leave you to take care of yourself, can't I? If you move over and cover that lagoon, we'll see to this one."

He let the A.D.C wade in until the water was above his knees again and then addresssed his final advice to him.

"You'll keep a look out for wounded animals, won't you?" he said. "I'm letting our friend here have the first shot. You may be needed later."

It was hot down there in the swamp; hotter than Harold had ever known. And airless. What he was breathing was the original odors of ancestral reed beds, all one by one long since rotted into slime. Round him, bubble-gum balloons of marsh gas rose slowly to the surface, floated there for a few seconds, and then burst with a faint *plop*. The smell of eggs was everywhere.

Harold slapped at the flies and waited. Beside him, Sir Gardnor waited too, but he was motionless. Facing the steaming surface of the lagoon, he listened. And from his intentness, it was obvious that he had heard something.

Then Harold heard it, too: a sound like water at a weir. It grew louder. It was moving, changing its direction as it came. The separate splashes were distinct now, and there were other noises mingled with it: snortings, and the sticky, kissing sound of large feet being dragged out of the clinging mud.

The reeds opposite parted and the forequarters of a bull buffalo appeared. It stood there, massive and unperturbed, gleaming like black shoe leather. Then it lurched forward into the water, its flanks half covered, and started drinking. It was a leisurely animal; placid, even mild-looking. And thirsty. Every mouthful was accompanied by an immense sucking noise like the last seconds of escaping bath water.

A moment later, another pair of the same wide, curving horns appeared in the opening, and the whole reed bed began moving. There were buffalo everywhere, the noise of thick bodies bumping. The quiet lagoon, with the bubbles bursting on it, became a rodeo, a cattle market. Soon there was an entire herd wallowing there, all drinking. The noise of bath water multiplied.

Harold started to finger his rifle, but Sir Gardnor frowned at him. To be immobile: that was what was being taught. To be as stationary as a dead tree; unmoving even while the flies were biting. And even when the herd, belching and grunting, began to move off out of sight, Sir Gardnor still made no movement. He merely stood there, watching the crushed reeds and waiting.

Then, after a long interval, she came. Out of the same torn gap, a solitary cow emerged. She was slow, slower even than the others. Ancient, too, and drooping. She was the great-grandmother of the herd, long since gone sour and unsociable. She did not mix with the others any longer, but still hung onto the herd in vague, uninterested fashion, from sheer lifetime habit.

It was the island she was making for; her island. It was her hoofs that had matted up the reeds, her weight that had left it flattened like a mattress. There, most afternoons, alone and undisturbed, unbothered by the calves, she sank down to chew her cud. It was siesta time now.

She was more than halfway across the pool when she saw Harold. Only her neck and rump showing above the surface, she stood still and stared. And still she could not be sure. Her eyesight was failing, and she was face to face with the sun. She came nearer. She stared again. She tried to catch his scent. She grew curious. Raising her head, she bellowed. She waited. Then, as if she had forgotten all about him, she lowered her head once more and sloshed on, unsuspicious and uncaring.

It was when she was three-quarters out of the water that she paused and looked again. This time there could be no mistake. It was a man, all right. The mere number of his legs served to give him away. And he was on her piece of island.

For a second time, she raised her head, and bellowed. But it was no use. He still didn't move. And more to scare him than anything else, she made a little rush, churning up the shallows with her hoofs and keeping her horns high so that she appeared to be looking down on him. When she stopped, she was less than fifty feet away, and she began staring again. It was the blank, uncomprehending stare of utter incredulity.

And even if she does come on, why should I kill her? Harold found himself thinking. She looks harmless enough to me. It isn't even as though I particularly disliked her. I don't. I'm just interested to see if I can do it. Not the act of killing: that's not what is bothering me. I mean shooting straight: not making a fool of myself in front of the Governor.

Then the cow saw the outline of Sir Gardnor, too: she had not been sure about him before. But now she could see that he had two legs like the other one. And she realized that she was in danger. They were waiting for her.

There was still time for her to turn back, still room out there in the swamp to get beyond their reach: that was the way that reason lay. But she had her buffalo nature to contend with. And old and tired and swollen up with grass ends as she was, her temper exploded. She became young again. Dilating her nostrils, she drew in a long wheezy breath and charged.

The slime beneath gave her no foothold. The cow stumbled, her rear hoofs kicking up the spray and sending dollops of mud flying out behind her. Harold thought for a moment that she was going right down. Then she found firmer ground beneath. Suddenly, she was up again, and coming forward. She was near now; very near. Harold could see the shape of her horns clear cut against the skyline of the opposing reed bed.

"Yours," Sir Gardnor told him. He said it quite quietly, casually almost, as though he had arranged it all. "Take your time. There's no hurry."

Harold felt his stomach go cold. His hands were trembling. And his knees. He could feel little jerkings all over him. Inside his head, he could hear the sound of his own heartbeats. But he remembered Sir Gardnor's words: he wasn't going to do anything foolish. Wasn't going to let him down in front of the A.D.C.

And as the sight of the rifle came level with the bare bone of the cow's forehead, he pulled the trigger. It was like firing a cannon. He knew now what Sir Gardnor had meant about the recoil and about holding the rifle well into the shoulder. The whole of his right arm had been knocked numb and useless by the discharge.

But buffalo always drop their heads when the charge is almost over: they carry their armament too high to be effective otherwise. When it comes to the kill, they go right down, on their knees almost.

Harold's shot passed clean over the cow. He saw the top of one of her horns disintegrate. But that was all. And she had reached the island by now. There was something solid for her hoofs to grip into. It was suddenly all noise and thunder like a cavalry charge. In another moment she would be on top of him.

And, to his surprise, Harold found that all sense of fear had left him. Even the trembling had ceased. He was perfectly calm and reconciled, simply standing there, his useless gun in his hand held slantwise across his body as if for protection. His mind was clear, too: clear and functioning very rationally.

Well, this is it, he told himself. You've made a complete mess of things. You fired too high, and now you've had it. You can't get out of this one, Harold Stebbs. You're done for.

He didn't remember afterwards even hearing the sound of Sir Gardnor's rifle. But he could distinctly recall the flash; the barrel had been only a couple of yards from his face when Sir Gardnor fired. The cow, the top of her head blasted clean off by the charge, scarcely faltered. There was nearly a ton of her, and she had been gathering momentum all the time. She was unstoppable. Death, though untimely, had not really interfered.

Harold felt himself lifted up, carried along, deposited, and then buried alive. It was the front legs of the buffalo that had been the first to stop working, and the hindquarters had just made their final heave. Like a derailed freight car upending, the cow had stood on her horns, hung motionless for an instant, and then overturned.

Mission accomplished, she was no longer caring.

Chapter 20

"HE's COMING round. Definitely coming round. You'd say he was a better color, wouldn't you?"

The voice was Sir Gardnor's, but the first thing that Harold saw was the face of the A.D.C.

At first he scarcely recognized it. That was not so much because of the mud stains as because of the expression. The polite social look had vanished, and there was genuine concern there. It was the first time that it had ever occurred to Harold that the young man could really care about anything. What he didn't know was that while he had been unconscious, the A.D.C., flat on his stomach, had been burrowing about under the dead cow trying to find him.

"I don't think any bones are broken, sir. But it's hard to be sure. He's in such an awful mess."

While he was speaking, the A.D.C. was still prodding him. Harold could feel his hands going over his shoulders, ribs, thighs.

"He's probably all right, wouldn't you say?" Sir Gardnor's voice said from somewhere behind him. "It was really very soft where he landed."

Then, not liking the exploring hands any longer, Harold suddenly sat up.

"I'm fine, sir," he said. "Absolutely fine."

But it was different when he tried to stand. He struggled up onto his knees, clutched hold of the A.D.C., and sank back again.

"Keep your head down until you're feeling better," Sir Gardnor told him. "We're in no hurry." He turned to the A.D.C. "You can tell them to keep the meat," he said. "They'll be able to have a feast day. The head's quite useless, of course. I've blown too much of it away."

When, at last, they got Harold to his feet they had to support him, one on either side, as if he were drunk. And the going wasn't easy. They stumbled over submerged roots, went up to their waists in potholes, sank into the underlying slime.

"I must say I'd have thought the Major would have sent a party out by now," Sir Gardnor remarked, rather petulantly. "Presumably he's posted someone to keep us under observation. Surely he can see there's something amiss."

The arrival back at the camp caused more than ordinary consternation. For a start, there was blood on Sir Gardnor's khaki shirt and Old Moses imagined that it was the Governor who had been wounded; gored probably.

"Doctor *baas* quick!" he began shouting. "Doctor *baas* for the Excellency!"

But he need not have bothered: Major Mills had everything in hand. Captain Webber, the Medical Officer—a little late, in Sir Gardnor's opinion—had been there to meet them on the foreshore, complete with stretchers, first-aid kit, and blankets. Harold, on one of the stretchers, with Captain Webber beside him, was bringing up the rear of the procession. The Governor and the A.D.C. were both stepping it out in front, not even, somewhat to Captain Webber's disappointment, classifiable as walking wounded.

Sir Gardnor looked hard at the A.D.C.

"I'm going to take a shower," he said shortly and solemnly, as though it were an important public announcement that he was making. "And no doubt you will want to do the same. By all means use mine if yours isn't working. I think"—with a wave of the hand he indicated Harold, lying under the regulations blanket—"we had better leave him to Captain Webber. He's his property, you know."

With complete disregard for all human feeling, the stretcher bearers marched straight past the tent that had been set aside for the ladies. It was cooler now, much cooler, and Lady Anne and Sybil Prosser were sitting outside their tent in the comfort of folding canvas chairs with striped canopies. They might have been at Henley. Sybil Prosser was drinking what looked like orange juice, and Lady Anne had a glass of whisky in front of her.

At the sight of Harold, she gave a sudden little cry and jumped up. Harold saw the glass go over and Sybil Prosser's hand reach out instinctively to save it.

Lady Anne ran toward the stretcher.

"What's happened?" she was saying. "Is he badly hurt?"

She began pulling at the blanket, dragging it down from underneath his chin to see how much Harold had been injured.

He smiled up at her.

"Don't worry," he said. "I'm all right. It's nothing. As a matter of fact, H.E. saved my life."

Lady Anne was silent for a moment. Then she burst out laughing.

"That's funny," she said. "Really funny."

She turned because Sybil Prosser had caught up with her.

"He doesn't know quite how funny, does he, Sybil?"

And having started to laugh, Lady Anne could not stop. Sybil Prosser kept trying to quiet her, making discreet *shhh-shhhing* noises as she did so. But it was no use. She went on laughing.

As the stretcher bearers moved forward, Harold inclined his head. Lady Anne, with Sybil Prosser's arm round her shoulders, was being led back toward the tent. She was still either laughing or crying. He could not make out which.

Behind them, Harold could see Sir Gardnor. He was standing in the doorway of his own marquee, his eyes shaded against the slanting sun. Throughout, he had been watching the whole scene very closely; it was almost as though he had anticipated that something of the sort might happen.

Then, as soon as Sybil Prosser had got Lady Anne safely back to her tent again, he turned and went inside to take his shower.

Chapter 21

AT BREAKFAST next day, Sir Gardnor was in excellent form.

"Most extraordinary. Really quite extraordinary, wouldn't you say?" he remarked to Major Mills and Captain Webber as they sat facing him across the trestle-table top, with the coffeepot and the milk jug and the marmalade jar between them. "I'd read about it, naturally. But I'd never actually encountered it at first hand, had you? Simply waiting there to be killed. Like a dummy. 'Frozen' is the word you might use."

Captain Webber pushed his plate to one side and leaned forward.

"Paralyzed by fear, sir?" he suggested.

Sir Gardnor paused and regarded Captain Webber for a moment. The impression was distasteful: Sir Gardnor disliked young-looking doctors.

"I always hesitate," he said, "to impute motives. So far as I could see, he was absolutely calm. Cool and collected throughout, wouldn't you say?" He had shifted round in his seat and was speaking to the A.D.C. "Did you see any signs of panic? I confess I didn't."

"Not a trace, sir," the A.D.C. replied. "He just fired too high."

"Well, there you are." Sir Gardnor allowed himself his expansive smile. This time it was directed straight at Captain Webber. "You see how wrong laymen can be. But as a medical man, you detected it at once. I must confess that I would never have thought of Mr. Stebbs as the panic-stricken type."

Captain Webber leaned forward even farther.

"What I meant, sir," he said, "was that . . ."

But this time it was Sir Gardnor who interrupted him.

"You will excuse me, won't you?"

The bearer from Signals had come over to the table, and Sir Gardnor was in touch with Amimbo once more. He read the typed sheets slowly and carefully, his face revealing nothing. Then he folded up the paper and stuffed it under the corner of his plate.

"It seems that our native newspaper is angry with me," he said. "It calls me a bloodthirsty Governor because a murderer has been executed. It's not, I must admit, a point of view that I understand. And there have been more outrages. Two, in fact. One native, and one white." He caught Major Mills's eye. "Perhaps I shouldn't have taken you away like this. You'll be needed back there, wouldn't you say? I'm afraid our Acting Chief Secretary must be having a hard time of it."

Major Mills very nearly made the mistake of replying. But already Sir Gardnor was speaking again.

"And I gather that at home, India is still very much in the news," he said. "The press simply won't let things alone. It's poor Eldred. Apparently he's allowed himself to be interviewed. By the *Morning Post,* too. That must surely be a mistake, mustn't it? I mean, one can't exactly canvass for Viceroyship, can one? It's always been the tradition . . ."

Major Mills glanced down at his watch for a moment. It was a discreet, furtive gesture; but, even so, Sir Gardnor detected it. He broke off in the middle of his sentence.

"Am I detaining you?" he asked.

Major Mills hurriedly thrust his cuff down over his wrist again.

"Oh no, sir," he said. "Not at all. It's simply that I was wondering about . . ."

"About moving on?"

"Precisely, sir." He paused. "Before the sun gets too high, you know, sir."

Sir Gardnor gave his half-smile.

"I'm ready, Major, whenever you are. We are *all* ready. We don't want to stay here all day, do we? But"—here he turned the same half-smile on Captain Webber—"it's your pigeon, isn't it? I mean, we can't get under way until you say it's safe for our invalid to travel. He did have rather a shaking-up yesterday, didn't he?"

Captain Webber pushed his chair back.

"Then if you'll excuse me, sir," he said.

"But of course," Sir Gardnor told him. "You're on duty, aren't you? You have your rounds to make. Tell him I'll come over myself a little later on. I have one or two things to attend to."

Major Mills and Captain Webber left the tent together. As soon as they had gone a safe speaking distance, Captain Webber leaned over a little toward his companion.

"Bit tetchy this morning, isn't he?" he asked. "Did I say anything to upset him?"

Major Mills did not answer directly.

"Got a lot on his mind, remember," he said. "Never really gets away from it, you know. All those radio cables and things."

They were now twenty-five yards from the tent, and there was no possibility of their being overheard. Even so, Captain Webber kept his voice discreetly low.

"Don't think it's anything else, do you?" he suggested. "Something a bit nearer home, I mean."

But he had put his question to the wrong man. Major Mills was a serving officer, and Sir Gardnor was his Commander-in-Chief.

"Don't know what you're talking about," he replied. "Afraid I can't help you."

And rather than risk getting himself caught up in a conversation that he did not want to pursue, Major Mills made off at right angles: it was time for his morning conference with O.C. Transport, he explained.

Captain Webber continued his own way alone toward the sick bay. It was early; not yet six o'clock, in fact. And there was still a breeze. Later on, when it was needed, the breeze would die down, leaving the same furious hot stillness everywhere. Already the swampland down below them was steaming.

Captain Webber was a great believer in going round the wards as soon after dawn as possible: it helped to keep the hospital staff on their toes. But he was not to be his patient's first visitor that day. As he drew near, he could hear the sound of voices.

"But you understand." It was Lady Anne who was speaking. "It's all right for you. You're out there with *him*"—she emphasized the word ever so slightly—"killing things, and I'm left all alone here with Sybil while all those radio messages keep coming through. I just want to know what they say."

Captain Webber could not hear Harold's reply. From the sound of it, he judged that Harold was still lying down flat in bed. But Lady Anne's response was plain enough.

"He'd never agree," she said. "He'd think it was just silly and interfering if I asked him. And in any case, you know I *wouldn't* ask. Major Mills isn't any use, and Tony is on Gardie's side anyhow. It's got to be the Signals man. He's the only one who can help."

There was another mutter that probably came from the pillow. What was said was obviously unsatisfactory, because this time Lady Anne's voice was raised again.

"You don't care," she said. "That's it: you just don't care. Well, if you won't do anything, I won't either. I won't bother to see you again. I only came along for your sake."

Captain Webber gave a little cough. The voice stopped immediately. A moment later, Lady Anne appeared in the doorway. She looked cool and unconcerned, even rather elegant. Sybil Prosser must have taken care of all the arrangements. Lady Anne's dress was freshly pressed, and her white shoes were spotless.

She seemed pleased to see Captain Webber.

"Oh come in, doctor," she said. "He's much better. He wants to get up. I was just telling him not to until you'd seen him again. I've sent off the orderly to get him some breakfast."

Harold was quite well enough to be moved, Captain Webber announced. There were definitely no bones broken, and what he had feared might be a small rupture was simply where the buckle of his belt had been driven into him. If they laid out a mattress in one of the transport trucks, the patient could make the journey quite comfortably, Captain Webber reckoned.

They camped that night in hill country. And it was a different Africa. The fifteen hundred feet that they had climbed had left the stale air of the plains behind them, and they could breathe again. Major Mills made the round of his caravan site rubbing his hands together and predicting that they would need a blanket on the bed before morning.

The hills, too, had their customary effect. Everyone suddenly became relaxed and peaceful. Up there in all that stillness, senses became keener. Drinks tasted better. The smell of something roasting in one of the field kitchens was delicious, and the sound of the boys singing as they humped the portables out of the service truck reached them in faint snatches, restful rather than discordant. In case they would like some real music later on, Major Mills remarked, he'd brought his gramophone along with him.

As for Harold, he was being pampered. Sir Gardnor had insisted that one of the camp beds be moved out for him so that he could recline there, Roman fashion, among the others. And Sir Gardnor himself was in the best of high spirits.

"I take it you know where we are this time, Major?" he was saying. "No river off course, or anything like that? We should rendezvous tomorrow. The reports are excellent. My leopard is in fine condition, so I am told. We must arrange an appointment, must we not?"

He turned to Harold.

"Everything well with you?" he asked. "No aftereffects? Not regretting your decision to come along with us?"

Sir Gardnor was at his most paternal: he wanted everyone

around him to be as contented as he was himself. It was only the one empty chair that displeased him.

"Tony," he said, "do go and find that Signals fellow. It's no use fiddling about with the buzzer any longer. It won't work up here: that's pretty obvious. Tomorrow when we skirt that"—he indicated the deep-indigo outline of the mountain range to the west of them—"we shall be in touch again. And in the meantime, we must get along as best we can, mustn't we?" He produced one of his little smiles as he said it. "And the rest of the world must learn to get along without us."

He got up and allowed his hands to rest for a moment on the canvas chair back.

"Really," he said, "I suppose we should all be grateful. The complete rest, you know. And the leisure. But I must be off now. My papers, you understand. We mustn't forget that we've all got work to do, must we?"

Except for the brightness of the stars, it would have been dark, pitch dark, by now. Every detail of the camp stood out clearly. With no moon, there were no shadows. There was simply a vague, milky light that turned the khaki of the canvas into clay and made a pale-silver canal of the pathway that the trucks had flattened out.

One by one the kerosene lamps had been extinguished. Only the Signals tent was still illuminated: propped up on a chair inside and with the headphones worn round his neck like a doctor's stethoscope, a corporal was on all-night vigil in case, with nightfall, cracklings of some kind began to get through.

Because he still ached all over, Harold got up to stretch himself. He knew enough of Major Mills's sentry postings not to risk going outside the camp: there was no point in being halted, challenged, made to advance and be recognized when all that he wanted was a quiet, uninterrupted stroll. And in any case, the camp itself was large enough. He lit a cigarette and turned in the direction of the Quartermaster's side.

It was all very peaceful. The sleep of others surrounded him. There was no movement; not even, up there in the hills, any of

146

the usual nightly hootings and catcalls of the bush. Everything was entirely silent. He felt as though he had the whole planet to himself.

Then, as he rounded one of the trucks, he heard something. It was a voice, deliberately kept low, he thought: scarcely more than a whisper. And he heard something else. This time it was a little laugh; kept low, too, like the voice.

Harold put his cigarette behind his back and waited. Behind the end truck he could make out two figures. One was lying on the grass and the other seemed to be kneeling beside him. It was the one on the grass who had given that little laugh. And then Harold remembered where he had heard it before: It had come from the bronze kitchen boy when Old Moses had snatched the knife from him.

A moment later the other figure got up and straightened himself. He raised one hand to thrust back a lock of hair from his forehead. It was a gesture with which anyone who had ever known the A.D.C. would be familiar.

Chapter 22

SIR GARDNOR was extremely pleased with Major Mills. His map reading had worked perfectly. They were not merely on the spot: they were on time, too. And expected. In the shade of the acacia grove, the two native hunters were already waiting.

Nature, too, was for once promising to behave every bit as satisfactorily as Major Mills. Despite the lateness of the rains, the grass was waist-high and still growing. The river bed was neither barren nor overflowing: its ocher-red torrent might have been made to measure for easy crossing. Startled by the approach of the scout car, a herd of impala had just exploded into the air and gone aerily bouncing away as though the hard ground beneath their hoofs were an acrobats' trampoline.

Sir Gardnor, however, was not to be distracted: he declined to go after anything. It was to be a long safari, and he had all the time in the world in front of him. In any case, it was leopard, not antelope, that he was after.

Because they were going to be camped there for three or four days—or even a week, possibly—Major Mills laid everything out with the thoroughness of a town surveyor. And now that the one-night stands were over, the extra section of Sir Gardnor's marquee was hauled out of the truck and fitted on.

When fully erected, it was fairground-sized. Under one canopy there were an anteroom for the A.D.C., Sir Gardnor's own study and sleeping quarters, and a lean-to out at the back for Old Moses. At the side, connected by a hedge of khaki screens, all neatly cleated and strung, were the adjoining tents for Lady Anne and Sybil Prosser. There, even the lavatories were built in.

The whole strategic arrangement suited Major Mills admirably. It ensured that once the ladies had fastened down the front tent flap, they were entirely protected from the outside world. The only access from the camp was past the A.D.C.'s anteroom, and even here Major Mills had taken every precaution. More than once he had reminded the young man that with the L.M.s around, safari was nothing short of active service, and he had extracted the promise that the A.D.C. would sleep with his revolver on the pillow beside him.

The place was, in fact, a khaki fortress, and coupled with two sentries posted at either end of the camp and two more on patrol on the perimeter, it made things well-nigh impregnable.

Just as well, too, Major Mills reflected. Less than a mile away lay the beehive village of Kitu. It was quite famous in its way, Kitu. Only last year, his predecessor had raided the settlement and come away with a collection of rough-sharpened pangas and a set of steel claws all ready for mounting.

Sir Gardnor lost no time about it.

Leopard was what he had come for, and leopard was what he intended to have. By dawn on this first morning, he and Major Mills were interrogating the two native hunters. Patiently and without protest, they had spent the night in the adjoining grove.

This time, however, Major Mills was not doing so well. His

African languages were limited to Mimbo, and out here by Kitu it was no use to him.

"But I thought you knew," Sir Gardnor was saying. "Mimbo stops the other side of those mountains. These people aren't Mimbo at all. These are pure Kiburru. Look at their noses." He turned to Harold. "There's a job for you, if you care to stay out here long enough—a Kiburru Dictionary and Grammar. No one's written one yet. You'll find some oddities, too. Most of it's Swahili. But some of the roots are pure Hati."

Sir Gardnor was speaking as though he were in a lecture hall, or in a private tutorial at least. It suited him, the effortless showing-off of knowledge that no one else around him could possibly question.

"But we must get down to business, mustn't we?" he asked. "I'll have a word with them myself."

They were not by any standards particularly prepossessing, these Kiburru tribesmen; and the *ichi* marks carved into their foreheads did nothing to improve them. The row of jagged scars running up from the eyebrows and over the cheekbones made them look as though they had been lucky to come safely through some nasty road accident. Their color, too, was against them. They weren't bronze like the kitchen boy or gleaming, recently polished ebony like the Mimbo. They were blue-black; blue-black and ugly.

But they knew their stuff. Moreover, they were excellent actors. With their flexible black hands they were drawing leopards in the air, describing every contour of them. They ceased to be a couple of half-naked savages waving their arms about. Instead, they became two inky magicians, with one of the great cats, lying, standing, skulking, sitting there, leaping into the air in front of them.

Sir Gardnor came away entirely satisfied.

"They're exaggerating the size, of course," he said. "These fellows always do. But there's a pair of leopard here all right, wouldn't you say? One of them rather distinguished by all accounts."

He paused, not because he had finished but because he hadn't finished: he wanted someone to invite him to continue. Major

Mills, however, simply did not know the form. It was Harold who stepped in.

"Distinguished in what way, sir?" he asked.

Sir Gardnor smiled.

"It seems," he said, "that the male is by no means purely animal. He is a departed human spirit, returned in animal form. And from a hostile tribe, too. That makes him particularly dangerous and antisocial." Sir Gardnor gave a little laugh. "Nor, I'm afraid, is that the end of it." He was really enjoying himself by now: his smile was at its widest and most patronizing. "I'm told that such leopards take their revenge on those who attack them. Even a shot between the eyes, I gather, will not deter them. Because being spirits, they can still revenge themselves after death."

Major Mills caught Sir Gardnor's eye for a moment and tried to smile back understandingly.

"Folklore, sir," he suggested.

Sir Gardnor smiled and shrugged his shoulders.

"Well, we shall soon know, shan't we?" he asked. He paused. "Of course, it's entirely up to you two gentlemen whether you decide to come with me. From the point of view of the leopard, we're all in it together: all equally guilty if he wants to punish us."

They were walking back into the camp by now, and after the quiet and solitude of the acacia grove, everything around them was all bustle and activity. And it was no longer African air that they were smelling; it was the air of England. Coming from the kitchen was the reassuring odor of coffee and fried bacon.

"I suppose," Sir Gardnor was saying, "it may have been a spirit buffalo that came down on top of our friend here. Perhaps he's had punishment enough already." There was the smile again, the little laugh. "This time it'll be you and me, Major, that the spirits are after."

Major Mills cocked his head a little.

"I'm ready to take my chance, sir," he said.

Sir Gardnor looked at him approvingly.

"Out here one has to, doesn't one?" he asked. "But those fellows believe their story, all right. Apparently, you can detect a human leopard by the way it kills. It uses its claws rather than its teeth. Handling the victim, you might say. One of the hunters has actually watched it at work. Really quite remarkable."

They had reached the breakfast table by now, and Sir Gardnor sat himself down at the head.

"There appears to be one other sign," he added. "It's something to do with the spoor. A spirit spoor, you understand. Turns up in the most unexpected places." He looked across at his A.D.C., who had just joined them. "Remind me to bring Native Affairs along with us next time, will you?" he asked. "After all, he really speaks these languages. I'm afraid I've forgotten half my Kiburru."

The place of sacrifice had already been selected. It was a clearing some fifty yards across, surrounded by a backcloth of bushes and with a particularly fine baobab tree, left center. The hunters pointed to a gap on the far side and became very excited. It was no ordinary gap, they declared: it was more a porch, a gateway. From it, practically nightly, the leopards emerged—sometimes singly, sometimes as a pair. The baobab tree, in fact, stood slap across their favorite catwalk.

"It's a point on which I've always insisted," Sir Gardnor told them. "I refuse to hunt the other way. No sportsman would ever dream of shooting a leopard up a tree in India, so why attempt it here? The proper place for the hunter is on a raised platform. So that he can see what he's doing. I don't want to risk hurting the animal."

It was in the fork of the main branch, Sir Gardnor explained, that he wanted the platform to be built. The specifications were lavish and exact. The platform was to hold three at least, and in comfort. The ladder leading up to it could be a simple rope one, he conceded. There was to be ample room for guns, supplies, and ammunition; and above all, they were to take special care with the mosquito netting. Sir Gardnor did not want to be eaten up alive, he said, while they were still waiting.

It was already obvious that Sir Gardnor was preparing for a long and exacting vigil up there in his little Wendy house. And as the project grew—Sir Gardnor had only just remembered the necessity for a stout three-foot handrail—Major Mills kept adding in his mind to the size of the task force that he would have to detail for such an operation.

Then, like a fast bowler pacing out his run, Sir Gardnor slowly and deliberately took fifty steps from the tree trunk. He looked back over his shoulder to the point where the branch forked and shifted across a little to his right. He took one more step forward and looked back again. This time he seemed satisfied. With his heel, he hacked out a divot.

"Here, exactly here," he announced, "is where we will have the stake."

The Kiburru hunters looked on admiringly: it was all gibberish to them, but they were enjoying it just the same.

Sir Gardnor beckoned to Major Mills.

"You'll want to make a good job of it, I'm sure," he said. "Shall we say Monday night, then? Your men won't mind working right through, will they? I understand the kid can be available at any time."

Lady Anne had been quite right: private conversations were impossible on safari. She and Sybil Prosser came to the long table for meals; they sat around on the camp chairs afterwards, listening to Major Mills's gramophone; and they took part in Major Mills's makeshift religious service on Sunday morning. Harold and Lady Anne had been within speaking distance a dozen times or more, but so, also, had too many other people. It was not until sundown on Monday, when the party was actually setting off for the baobab tree, that Lady Anne spoke directly to him; and even then they were not entirely alone.

The procession was quite a large one. Sir Gardnor and the A.D.C. were in front. They were followed by the bearers, with the guns and the ammunition. Then came Harold and Major Mills, with two kitchen boys carrying the picnic supper that Old Moses had prepared. Behind them, the camp carpenter had brought along his assistant in case any last minute touches were needed. And in the rear came a solitary Kiburru huntsman: his companion, it was understood, was down in Kitu arranging the final details about the kid.

They were almost past the entrance to Lady Anne's tent when she saw them. And she ran out immediately. The carpenter from the South Staffs had to step back so that she could pass him.

She stood in front of Harold and put her hand on his arm.

"Do be careful," she said. "Very, very careful." She paused, and Harold thought for a moment that he had detected that familiar telltale catch in her voice. He was sure of it when she suddenly added, "Just for my sake."

Major Mills had not moved. He stood there, eyes front, looking after the retreating figures of Sir Gardnor and his A.D.C. It was not his affair, he told himself, and he was not going to get mixed up in it.

Lady Anne, however, seemed determined to involve him.

"You'll look after him, won't you, Major?" she asked. "You won't let anything happen?"

Then she ran the back of her hand across her forehead as though she were trying to brush something away.

"Oh, I was forgetting," she said. "You won't even be there, will you? You'll be back here protecting all of us."

While she was speaking, Sybil Prosser had come hurrying across to them, her lean arms flapping. Lady Anne turned to see her standing there.

"Oh, you needn't worry about me, Sybil," she told her. "I haven't said anything. I'm not the least bit tiddly. I was just wishing the boys goodbye."

Chapter 23

THE PREPARATIONS for the kill were proceeding with all the marks of really first-class staff work.

The picnic supper, now finished, had been excellent; Major Mills's mosquito netting fitted perfectly—though, as Sir Gardnor pointed out, no one had given a thought to the gaps between the planking that they were squatting on. And the rope ladder—advertised in Chandra's European Bazaar back in Amimbo as an indispensable fire accessory for all two-story buildings—had at last been hauled up and stowed away.

It seemed to Harold that they might just as well have eaten their meal in the comfort of their canvas chairs back in camp.

But Sir Gardnor must have read his mind. "You're finding the wait rather tedious?" he asked. "I'm afraid it's unavoidable." He paused and seemed to be searching for an illustration sufficiently simple for Harold to be able to understand. "You see," he said at last, "the jungle is like a pool. When we white men enter, we disturb it. We cause ripples. Break the calm, as it were. It's simply a matter of allowing the surface to become placid again."

He pointed in the direction of the clearing on the far side.

"*That* kind of thing doesn't count. It's all part of the place. It doesn't affect the tranquillity."

Above the low bushes, Harold could see the head and shoulders of a native herdsman. His flock of lean and sinewy goats was following, urged on by two boys with long sticks. There was a ceaseless *whack-whack* as the sticks fell. The goats, however, were thoroughly used to it. Moving off in twos and threes to snatch mouthfuls of the ragged grass that grew beside the pathway, they lingered, waiting for the blow to fall, before beginning to move on again.

Then Harold saw that the native herdsman was carrying something. It was a kid, held nestling in his arms. He was a large man, the herdsman, and the whiteness of the kid showed up against the broad black expanse of his bosom.

The Kiburru hunter got up off his haunches and went over to meet the herdsman. They were joined a moment later by the second hunter, who was leading a goat of his own. It was a lively animal, dun-colored like the rest, and kept putting its head down when anyone approached. This seemed to provoke the herdsman. He lifted the kid from his bosom and set it down on its four feet to show that it could stand. Not satisfied that the demonstration had been conclusive, he kicked it over a couple of times to show that it could even get up again. Then, so as not to tire it, he took the kid back to his bosom again, and the bargaining began.

Sir Gardnor smiled indulgently.

"It's always the same," he said. "Always this everlasting haggling. I can't imagine where that other goat came from. It must be some kind of private transaction, wouldn't you say?"

In the end it was the bleating of the kid that decided them. It was shrill, incessant, and irresistible. Even the private trader admitted that his young he-goat could not compete. The herdsman was paid off. The Kiburru hunter unwound half a dozen yards of twine that he had been wearing round his middle and tied one end round the kid's neck. The kid, straining at the cord, looked back at its mother for the last time.

Sir Gardnor turned to the A.D.C.

"I didn't see a pole," he said. "I hope somebody remembered to bring one. If we do get a leopard we can hardly be expected to carry it back across our shoulders, can we?"

It was already dusk when the kid, still bleating, was finally secured to the stake. The Kiburru, not wanting to risk any last-minute mishap, tested the attachment by catching hold of the animal's hind legs and pulling. For a moment, all bleating stopped. Then, when the pressure was relaxed, it started up again.

The Kiburru came away, apparently satisfied. They looked up at the fast-fading sky; they sniffed to see if there was any wind worth smelling; they pressed their bare feet into the ground; they listened appreciatively to the abandoned kid. Then, single file, they took the trail back to their village.

The dusk became darkness, and the darkness became night. Somewhere out in front of them the miserable bleating continued. Harold felt personally guilty about it: forgetting the leopard altogether, he could think only of the kid.

Sir Gardnor looked down at the luminous figures on his wrist watch.

"In less than five minutes," he remarked, "the moon should be rising."

There was just a suggestion in his voice that if for any reason there should be a hold-up, he would expect, if not an apology, at least a full explanation.

The bleating continued. Harold wanted to go down and release the kid, take it back to its mother. He began to shift uneasily. But again Sir Gardnor anticipated him.

"Don't give it a thought," he said. "They're all Moslems round here. They treat their animals abominably. It'll be a far quicker death this way than by ritual throat cutting. Bleeding can be a very slow process."

And by now the bleats were being overlaid by other noises. Over in the bushes, there was a sudden howling that stopped just as suddenly as it had begun and was replaced by a scream from somewhere close behind. The scream was repeated and started up a whole chorus of grunts and snortings below them. There was the sound of small, desperately hurrying feet; a miniature stampede. Then more screaming; and whistles—long, low whistles that ended in a rattling, throaty laugh.

There were other disturbances as well. A shape, large and agile, released itself from one of the upper branches, used the end plank of their platform as a springboard, and took off into space again. Somewhere in the forest, a tree was being strenuously uprooted. Then, near at hand, a colony of insect impersonators started up. It must have been a band saw they were imitating. They screamed, they whirred, they squeaked like unoiled machinery, they let off steam whistles, they broke down. When they were silent, the bleating of the kid could be heard again.

Sir Gardnor turned his head for a moment.

"There," he said, pointing.

Over the screen of trees that flanked the clearing, an arc of moon was already showing. It was large and melon-colored. Sir Gardnor looked at his watch again.

"And from now on," he said serenely, "there must be no talking. Not a word from anyone."

Harold nodded; it seemed hardly worth pointing out that during the past ten minutes the only person who had spoken had been Sir Gardnor. It was past midnight.

The moon had already cleared the trees and was riding high.

It was a full African moon that blotted out the surrounding stars, and down below, the clearing shone back at it. The shadow of the baobab tree had swung past them as though they were revolving on their own axis, and the moonlight was now falling on the side screen of the mosquito netting. It made it perfectly opaque, like frosted glass. Harold found his head nodding forward as he looked at it. Bracing himself, he turned and concentrated on the lonely figure of the kid. Still at the extreme end of its tether, it was lying down. It appeared to be sleeping. A moment later Harold was asleep himself.

When he woke, it was not because he was rested but because he was alert. He could feel that beside him, Sir Gardnor was tense and rigid, too. He was leaning forward, and through a gap in the mosquito netting the barrel of his rifle was now pointing. Harold raised himself and pressed his face against the bars.

And there it was at last—the cat that they had come so far to kill. Across the clearing, standing half in shadow in its own porchway, it was unhurriedly savoring the night air. Confident that it would meet nothing more powerful or savage than itself, it was totally unconcerned. As Harold looked, he saw it extend its long neck and yawn. Then, its tail drooping, it took three paces into the open and sat down to wash itself.

A moment later, the kid woke up and resumed its bleating. The leopard immediately went flat. It vanished in the grass. The bleating continued. The leopard advanced a couple of yards and disappeared again. The kid continued to call for its mother. The leopard, stomach to the ground, moved toward it. Ever so gently, Sir Gardnor edged the muzzle of his rifle forward.

Then, suddenly, the kid smelled the cat. Instantly it sprang to its feet, only to fall down again. When it had recovered itself, it stood there for a moment trembling. Then it tried to escape. The cord hindered it. It could move only in circles. But it was desperate by now: the smell of cat was all round it. Hope lay in running. Bounding, scrambling, falling over, getting entangled in the cord, it wound itself up tightly to its own stake and could go no farther. The leopard lifted its head and squatted there regarding it.

Still Sir Gardnor refused to be rushed. The position and the angle were both entirely wrong. If the beast were to drop its head suddenly, his bullet would almost certainly shatter the skull; and even if it kept its neck extended, the breastbone would splinter and fill the skin with puncture marks.

Besides, there was no hurry. The leopard wasn't going to move away again: he was sure of that. It had seen that the kid was tethered, and like Sir Gardnor, it intended to take its time. Also, it was enjoying itself. There would be a whole further series of little playful bounds and rushes before it made the final pounce. Sir Gardnor waited.

Then the leopard, unable to postpone its mealtime any longer, prepared to spring. At one moment, it was there, but invisible, flattened to the ground in the long grass; and, at the next, gaudy and brilliant in the moonlight, it was sailing triumphantly through the air, its forepaws extended like the hands of a diver. There was one last bleat, but even that was cut short. The leopard already had its teeth in the kid's neck, and the body was held down by the protruding claws. Harold could see that the white coat of the kid had suddenly been stained scarlet.

At that instant, the posture being exactly right, Sir Gardnor fired.

The shot woke up the surrounding jungle, and screams and shriekings started on all sides. The leopard, knocked flat by the bullet, recovered itself. It clambered to its feet. Then, slowly, its back began to arch. Caterpillar-like, it dragged its hind legs forward until its whole body was humped. It stood there, rocking. A second later, it collapsed. Straightening itself out to its full length, it rolled over as though resting and lay there, its pale stomach showing and its paws half-folded in repose.

"Good shot, sir."

The remark might equally well have been made on a tennis court. But Sir Gardnor seemed pleased by it.

"I think we shall find it was through the heart," he said. "The way the beast arched its back, you know."

Harold began reaching out toward the rolled-up rope ladder.

"Do we go down now, sir?" he asked.

Sir Gardnor turned his head: he was annoyed with Harold because he hadn't thought to congratulate him.

"Hardly just yet," he replied. "It may only be wounded. Then it could prove dangerous. After all, it *is* a leopard, you know."

The native hunters returned and advanced upon the leopard, their spears pointing. Sir Gardnor was their hero, their savior, their new witch doctor. Nor was it only the divine evidence of the single fatal shot that had impressed them. They were in awe, too, of his greater magic: the leopard curse apparently meant nothing to him.

The leading hunter, however, was taking no chances. He was already addressing the leopard, speaking confidentially to its spirit, assuring it that for his part he had meant it no harm and had, indeed, been absent at the time of the unfortunate accident. Behind him, his companion, as loudly as he could, was jingling a bracelet of teeth and leopard claws in order to deceive the dead leopard into believing that he was not a Kiburru at all, but a genuine family mourner.

Neither of the hunters moved in close until Sir Gardnor arrived. He was holding his rifle in front of him, ready to fire again if necessary.

The sight seemed to reassure the two Kiburru. They surged forward, keeping carefully out of the dead animal's vision, and stood there jabbering. They were admiring its weight, the firmness of its coat, the neat hole that the bullet had made, the size of its testicles. Undoubtedly a man-eater, they agreed; on the fingers of both hands they began to add up its victims.

Sir Gardnor stood over the dead leopard. It was safe now to lower his rifle, and he was relaxed. His expression was one almost of pity.

"It is sad, don't you think?" he asked, "that one should have to kill anything so superbly beautiful? Whatever its habits, you'd agree, wouldn't you, that it stands as one of God's supreme achievements? Man is puny by comparison."

He paused.

"Mounted," he added, "it will look magnificent."

He had been prodding the body with his foot while he was speaking. The carcass was limp and unresisting. Then, as he took

159

his foot away, the leopard slid over toward him. One of the forelegs unfolded itself and flailed downwards. The pad was the size of a large breakfast cup, and under it the toe cap of Sir Gardnor's boot lay imprisoned. When he pulled his foot away there were scratch marks right across the leather.

The significance of the incident did not escape the Kiburru hunters. They withdrew trembling. The one with the tooth bracelet began waving his arm frantically up and down again. And his friend panicked. Dropping his voice still lower, he betrayed Sir Gardnor and told the dead leopard everything.

Dawn was already breaking as they approached the camp. In the half-light the sentry challenged them, only to come abruptly to attention and present arms as the figure of Sir Gardnor suddenly loomed up before him.

But only half his attention was on Sir Gardnor. Out of the corner of his eye he was observing the two Kiburru. They had not forgotten the carrying pole. It was now resting on their shoulders, and slung beneath it was the dead leopard. They had made the best job that they could of their porterage, carefully leaving the head hanging downwards so that the beast could not see where it was being taken, and tucking the long tail in neatly round the loins to avoid treading on it.

Sir Gardnor told them to put the leopard down in front of his tent where he could see it and announced loudly that he was hungry. Bacon-and-eggs washed down by champagne, if the A.D.C. had remembered it, was, he declared, the only food that could be eaten at four o'clock in the morning; and tired and happy as he was, he began to reminisce about past soirées and dances long ago.

His mouth still full of fried bread, he addressed his A.D.C.

"I take it there's someone who knows how to skin it," he said. "Properly, I mean. I don't want it carved up and butchered."

He paused for a moment and yawned out of sheer weariness, not bothering even to cover his mouth with his hand.

"You might just see if any messages have reached me," he told him. "And then I think I shall turn in. You can tell them to take the leopard away now. Better get Major Mills to put it in the shade somewhere, don't you think? And tell him to place a guard over it. We don't want to find it gone in the morning, do we?"

Chapter 24

BECAUSE OF the broken nature of the night, it was at luncheon rather than at breakfast that everybody said good morning to each other.

The table—a long one—had been set out under its own striped awning; and, as at the Residency, the meal was served punctually at 1.30. The party seemed complete when, a few minutes later, Lady Anne and Sybil Prosser came to join them. Everything, in fact, would have passed off smoothly, even happily, if it had not been for Sybil Prosser.

Not that the blame was entirely hers. She was in considerable discomfort, if not actual pain. She had been bitten on the forearm by an insect of some kind, and already the swelling had extended down as far as her wrist. In consequence, she was tense and irritable. Her long neck rising endlessly from the low collar of her cotton dress, she sat there, mute and scowling, and scratching.

Out of sheer goodness of heart, Sir Gardnor tried to draw her into the conversation and make her one of them. He smiled across at her.

"And what," he asked, leaning across Lady Anne as he was speaking, "do you think of my leopard?"

"I haven't seen it," Sybil Prosser told him.

Sir Gardnor raised his eyebrows.

"Not seen it?" he said. "But how's that?"

"I don't like dead animals," she replied.

The smile flickered temporarily and was then relit.

"But we all like them, don't we, when they're on the floor in the form of rugs?" he asked.

Sybil Prosser's answer was prompt and disconcerting.

"I don't," she said. "They still remind me of dead animals."

Sir Gardnor paused. Only the corners of his mouth were smiling now.

"I can understand," he said, "people not liking mounted heads. It's something to do with the eyes, wouldn't you say? Too lifelike, I suppose."

"Heads are worse," Sybil Prosser agreed with him.

Sir Gardnor leaned forward. His smile entirely absent, he addressed her directly.

"Is it the killing that worries you?" he asked.

"Not particularly," she told him. "I just don't like animals."

It was the arrival of a Corporal from Signals that interrupted the conversation. Rather self-consciously, because there were ladies present and he was aware that he was unpleasantly soaked through with sweat from the heat of the radio van, he sidled up, saturated, thrust his envelope toward the A.D.C., and then hurriedly withdrew. Sir Gardnor, Harold noticed, almost snatched the note when it was handed to him.

They sat back in silence, watching Sir Gardnor while he read. It was a lengthy message, running to nearly four pages, all laboriously typed out in capital letters as though it might have been a very young child that was expected to read it. Sir Gardnor did not attempt to hurry. Conscious that he was being observed, he deliberately took his time, even turning back once or twice to compare the contents of the pages. Then, with a little sigh, he folded up the sheets and tucked them neatly under the corner of his salad plate.

"All the names are entirely misspelled, of course," he said. "Some of them are scarcely recognizable."

Enjoying himself because he knew that he was keeping them in suspense, Sir Gardnor sat back and folded his arms.

"All the same, it's really quite remarkable, isn't it?" he asked. "I mean the way it's got here. From Delhi to London, from London to Amimbo, and now to that little wireless aerial over there. It's been at least halfway round the world already."

Because it was obvious that Sir Gardnor was building up to the moment of his disclosure, no one cared to interrupt him. Sybil Prosser was the first to speak. She stopped scratching her wrist, which by now had come up red and puffy, and began fingering the collar of her dress.

"Was it worth cabling about?" she asked, and then went on scratching again.

The A.D.C. kept his eyes down to his plate. But Sir Gardnor did not appear to have been offended. He gave the impression rather of being amused to think that, of all impossible women, this should have been the one whom his wife had selected to bring out all the way to Africa.

"Shall we say that someone else thought it was?" he replied. "The Delhi papers are full of it. This summary shows that they are talking of nothing else."

While Sir Gardnor was speaking, Lady Anne had placed the palms of her hands on the table. She was pressing down on it, as if to steady herself.

Sir Gardnor detected it immediately: the sight seemed somehow to amuse him.

"Of course," he added, with a little shrug almost of apology, "the reports are based purely on speculation. As yet, there's been no actual announcement, has there? It's simply that the rumors are all one way."

"Which way?"

Again it was Sybil Prosser who had spoken. She had, for the time being, given up tugging at her collar and was now pushing down her watch strap, which had become tight and sticky in the heat. What annoyed Sir Gardnor was that she had not even looked up as she had put the question.

He bent forward and tried to catch her eye. But it was useless. The clasp had stuck. Head down, Sybil Prosser was still fiddling with it.

"Not Lord Eldred's, I'm afraid," he told her. "He is, in fact, simply not mentioned."

He had risen while he was speaking and was now stuffing the typed pages into his side pocket. It gave him an advantage to stand at his full height while the others were still seated, and he availed himself of it.

"It will be amusing, will it not," he remarked, "to see if they're right? I set no store by bazaar gossip myself. Most Indian journalists succeed in getting even quite straightforward things confused. They are notorious for it."

He waited for a moment for someone to put matters in a better light; and then, disappointed, he excused himself. He had work to do, he told them. The A.D.C. thrust back his lock of hair and followed.

Lady Anne sat watching them as they went toward the marquee together. As soon as Sir Gardnor had turned in under the canopy, she beckoned Harold over to her.

"Just sit here and behave as though we're talking about nothing in particular," she told him. "Gardie's probably watching us. He only read out that telegram to see how I'd take it. He knew it would upset me."

"Why should it? It didn't say anything."

"But it's getting near. It must be. If he does hear something—something definite, I mean—you'll tell me at once, won't you?"

Harold began spooning up the sugar from the bottom of his coffee cup.

"He isn't always exactly forthcoming, you know."

"That's why you should have asked Signals."

"He wouldn't have told me." He paused. "Why not try Tony?"

Lady Anne frowned and shook her head.

"You can't trust him. He's on the other side."

Harold put the spoon back in the saucer.

"Why's it so desperately important . . .?" he began.

But he got no further. It was Sybil Prosser who interrupted him.

"Damn," she said. "And I haven't brought another one."

She threw her watch strap down on the table in front of them; in dragging at the clasp she had broken it.

Then she turned to Lady Anne.

"And it's your siesta time," she told her. "You know what you're like if you miss it. Harold's all right: he was asleep all the morning. I'm half dead. My arm's hurting."

Chapter 25

Sɪʀ Gᴀʀᴅɴᴏʀ did not attempt to conceal his impatience. He was anxious to begin forthwith the long homeward journey to Amimbo.

Indeed, with the leopard nicely skinned, and with the pelt packed like a Swiss Roll round layers of salt that Old Moses had provided, there seemed nothing further to detain them. Nothing, that is, apart from Sybil Prosser.

But in her state, the return trip was unthinkable. The insect that had bitten her must have been packed full of venom. There was now a swelling in her left armpit, and her temperature had gone soaring.

Captain Webber spoke confidently of a new drug that he had brought with him, but said that he could promise nothing for at least seventy-two hours. A full three days, with the formidable pink tablets being taken at intervals right round the clock, was what the directions said; and with a human life at stake, Captain Webber felt in no mood to defy the manufacturers.

The effect on Lady Anne surprised everyone. Her anxieties seemed to vanish. She put Sir Gardnor, Harold, even the radio messages, out of her mind entirely. The rest of the camp saw nothing of her. She had her bed moved in alongside Sybil Prosser's, and day and night, she was on sick-nurse duty.

On the second day, Captain Webber admitted that he was beginning to get anxious about Lady Anne too. She flatly refused, he said, to take so much as a cat nap in case Sybil Prosser needed anything; and even though the meal trays were regularly carried across, he found Lady Anne's left untouched whenever he went over.

As for Sir Gardnor, he could not hide his restlessness. He cross-examined Captain Webber before and after every visit and kept the A.D.C. going back and forth between the marquee and the radio van to see if anything fresh had been received from Amimbo.

Finally, in the absence of all news, either medical or political, he brooded. For as much as an hour at a stretch he would sit in front of the trestle table with the silver inkwell and the long paper knife on it, staring down at the empty blotter before him.

Once, from the canvas chair outside his own tent, Harold saw Sir Gardnor take his pen, dip it, hold it for a moment over a sheet of Government House notepaper with the Royal Arms on it, and then wearily put the pen down again—as though he had only just realized the sheer futility of being both his own scribe and postman.

When Harold looked again, he saw that Sir Gardnor had picked up the paper knife and was playing with it. This time it was as a miniature billiard cue that he was using it.

Harold was already turning in for the night when the A.D.C. came over to his tent.

"Not asleep yet, are you?" he asked. "Not disturbing you, I mean?"

He was at his most charming as he stood there in the doorway, one hand in his pocket and the other up by his forehead.

"It's H.E.," he explained. "He's gone all spiky. Wants to go out after leopard again."

"Isn't one enough?" Harold asked, remembering that final plaintive bleat that had, so suddenly, been cut so short.

The A.D.C. became defensive.

"You can't really expect H.E. just to sit around doing nothing," he said. "He isn't made that way. Besides, there's a good chance of a double. Those two Kiburru have been round again. They say that the leopardess is on the prowl this time. Looking for her mate, I suppose."

Harold paused.

"Does this mean another night up that tree?" he asked.

The A.D.C. shook his head, and the lock of hair flopped forward again.

"This is the real stuff," he said. "On foot. *We* go after *her*. We don't wait for *her* to come to *us*. It's got the Major all worried."

Harold reached out for his jacket and began buttoning it up again. Anything would be better than simply lying there with a service pillow under his head, staring up at the canvas of the ceiling and wondering when Lady Anne was going to show herself again.

"When do we start?" he asked.

Lifting his cuff, the A.D.C. looked down for a moment at his watch. It was still his drawing-room watch that he was wearing, Harold noticed. It looked thin and expensive and out-of-place worn with rather dirty khaki.

"Oh, you've still got about six hours," he told him. "Or say a good five and a half. H.E. wants to be on the move by first light. And remember about the shoes, this time. It's bound to be rough going. She lives some distance from here. They're charging us extra for the journey."

It was still dark, with the moon by now hidden somewhere behind the Marabwe range, when Harold went across to Sir Gardnor's tent. Sir Gardnor was fully dressed and waiting. He gave the impression of someone who had already been waiting for a long time; of someone, even, who had been sitting up all night.

He pointed across at the coffeepot as Harold entered.

"Pour yourself out a cup," he said. "There'll be some sausages very shortly. Better make a good breakfast. We don't know when we shall be sitting down to food again, do we?"

As he drank, Harold was aware that Sir Gardnor was watching him. It was a quizzical, half-amused sort of expression that he was wearing.

"I rather gathered," Sir Gardnor told him, "that you didn't quite approve of the way I got my last leopard. You probably felt that it was unsporting. And so it was. But I couldn't afford to come back empty-handed, could I? Leopard outwits Governor—that would never have done, now would it?"

He sat back and patted the toe cap where the claws had scratched it.

"This time," he said, "you'll find that the chances are about equal. It could be the leopardess. Or, again, it could be one of us."

Harold had finished his coffee, and across the night air, the delicious smell of frying sausages had just reached him.

167

"I'll take my chance, sir," he said.

Sir Gardnor was still smiling.

"I thought that would be what you'd say," he replied. "But it was clearly my duty to warn you." His smile widened. "After that first time it's not surprising that we're all a bit anxious."

The A.D.C., when he arrived, looked sleepy and rather jaded. Harold wondered whether he had been visiting his friend the bronze kitchen boy again. But he was as polite and attentive as ever, concerned only with Sir Gardnor's well-being.

"Do you want the telescopic sight clipped on, sir?" he asked. "It's in its little case at the moment."

Sir Gardnor brightened.

"Ah, the telescopic sight," he said. "I may have an opportunity of using it. The gunsmiths tell me it's in perfect working order. I shall be able to find out for myself, shan't I?" He drew his breath in sharply. "That is, if we see anything."

He looked across at the traveling clock on his work table.

"The sausages are a little late, are they not?" he remarked. "We have exactly nine minutes in which to finish our breakfast and get going."

The Kiburru had been right to bargain for extra payment. Apart altogether from the element of danger money, the trek that they were leading was long, difficult, and in the last part, stony.

Less than a mile from the camp, they left the green shade of the forest and came face to face with the sun on the open grasslands. It was a low sun, only just risen: not yet at full heat, but still blinding. They shaded their eyes with their hands as they walked. Then the grasses grew shorter and more meager. Soon the little tufts and patches died out altogether, and it was loose red sand that they were crossing. In places, under the fury of the sun by day, the sand had formed itself into flat sheets like mica. With the morning glare coming back off them, they looked like pools of water, but they cracked like ice as soon as a foot in shoe leather touched them. The bare feet of the Kiburru, Harold noticed, passed over as though skating.

The sand gave place to scree, and soon the scree became

shingle. They had come up against the bluff on a sheer, blood-red escarpment; and, where it had crumbled and gone crashing, great boulders were now littered. They were piled one upon another like earthquake-ruins. And somewhere in this scene of desolation, the Kiburru asserted, the leopardess, now widowed, was still living.

Sir Gardnor beckoned his A.D.C. to him.

"I take it they know they get paid on results," he said. "We look like being here all day if it's purely speculation."

But the Kiburru were unshakable. The lair was in there, they said, pointing to the biggest of the rock mounds in front of them. The slanting crevice that ran beside it—that was the entrance to her homestead. Down below, on some unthinkable mezzanine, was where she had mated, littered, suckled, and slept off her overeating. At this hour in the morning, she had probably only just turned in.

There was the matter of the smell to vindicate them. Dilating their flat nostrils still further, they sniffed approvingly. It was strong, very strong, they agreed. The odor of cat was everywhere. It must, in all that sunlight, have been only minutes, they said, since the leopardess had passed by, reeking.

It was at this point that Sir Gardnor intervened. More military than Major Mills, he laid down the battle plan with quiet precision.

"If they do flush her," he said, "she'll bolt in this direction. Accordingly, we'll take up our positions *there*,"—he indicated a large boulder, half buried on the left—"*here* where I'm standing, and"—he screwed his eyes up and inspected the rockfall on his right—"over *there* by the cliff face. And aim carefully, remember: we don't want any dead Kiburru on our hands."

He seemed very much in command as he stood there, his hands resting upon his hips. He was rocking backwards and forwards, as though savouring the moment. When he turned toward Harold, he was smiling again.

"You know all about rifles, don't you, by now?" he asked. "The recoil, I mean. And taking care of yourself if anything goes wrong." He slapped at the back of his neck where something had just stung him. "As regards firing order, you may have first shot.

You deserve it. Then Tony. I shall come last—that is, if I'm needed at all, of course."

He had unclipped the telescopic sight while he was speaking and handed it back to the A.D.C.

"At this sort of range," he said reprovingly, as though the A.D.C. should have thought of it first, "I shall hardly be needing it, shall I?"

The two Kiburru were busy with their own preparations. They were going round gathering up strands of dry elephant grass that the wind had blown into the gully, withered flowers, dead leaves. If they had been keepers in a Royal Park they could not have been more thorough. And as soon as they had a handful, they deftly twisted it into a little skein and began collecting more to weave into it. It was a torch that each one was making.

When they had finished, they came up pleading for matches. At the sight of the full box which Harold handed them, they temporarily forgot about leopards. All that they could think of was matches. They planned how to steal them. One of them succeeded. Not that Harold would have been particularly anxious to have the box returned to him: it was up the brief sash of his loincloth that the leading hunter had stuffed the Swan Vestas.

Sir Gardnor gave a little cough.

"Are we ready?" he asked.

He glanced round for a moment and continued without waiting for the answer. "You will raise your hands when you've taken up your places," he said. "And I will give the order to smoke her out."

The Kiburru had their bundles of rubbish all ready. They had clambered up onto the terraces of the rock temple dragging their fire machines after them. And they were taking no chances. While the thief who had stolen the matches was securing one of the grass torches to the handle of his spear, the other stood over him like a sculptor's model, knees flexed and spear lifted.

The A.D.C. and Harold both raised their hands. Sir Gardnor acknowledged them and tried to attract the attention of the Kiburru. But they were preoccupied. Unused to Swan Vestas, the fire raiser was stroking the match gently along the side of the box as if afraid of harming it. Minutes passed, broken only by the gentle scraping sound.

"Come along. Come along, man. Get on with it," Sir Gardnor shouted.

But the Kiburru had lost his temper. He used all his strength and tried deliberately to hurt the match. In revenge, the match blazed up and burned him. He dropped it hurriedly onto the bundle at his feet, and the mass ignited. As soon as it was well aflame, he thrust it home into the crevice.

By now a thin spiral of blue smoke was rising into the air above the grotto as if the rocks themselves were on fire. But still nothing happened. The Kiburru were disappointed. They shouted. Picking up large stones, they hammered on the bare rock to cause a nuisance. Lying flat on their stomachs, they thrust their heads through the smoke screen and called the leopardess names—vile, unmentionable names that even a leopardess could not tolerate.

Then they jumped down rather shamefacedly and admitted that she wasn't there.

But it was only a matter of time, patience, and numbers, they contended. Especially numbers. In the ordinary way, a whole team of at least a dozen hunters would have been engaged for such an operation. As it was, there were only two. They would both, therefore, have to work six times as hard. And unprotected, there was the added danger: the peril to each of them of being pounced on from behind. In the circumstances, an entirely new fee—payable, if necessary, to the survivor—would have to be negotiated.

Sir Gardnor told the A.D.C. to agree to the fee. Nevertheless, he remained entirely unconvinced.

"I should be more ready to believe them," he said, "if there were any vultures around. They are like shadows. They follow leopards everywhere. And you can see for yourself, the rocks are deserted."

He indicated the vultureless landscape as he was speaking.

"All the same," he told them, "I suppose we had better deploy ourselves. If they do find her, she could be anywhere. And at all costs, we must avoid crossfire. We must therefore get ourselves a bit further back."

He resurveyed the rock hillocks behind him.

"I myself," he announced, "will be somewhere up there," and pointed to the blood-red face of the escarpment.

The Kiburru were delighted. Like this it could go on all day. "Bang, bang. Bang, bang," they cried jubilantly.

Sir Gardnor turned to the A.D.C.

"And for this," he said, "I *shall* require the telescopic sight. You might clip it on for me, would you?"

Again, there was the slight hint in his voice not so much of reproof as of surprise that the A.D.C. should not have anticipated him.

"I intend to go some distance up," he said. "The higher the better. And I shall wave my handkerchief when I'm ready. You will please do the same. And then, of course, we will none of us move. You are hardly likely to hit me, but if I can, I want to avoid shooting one of you, don't I?"

The climb up the face of the escarpment was a stiff one. What seemed to be solid, living rock crumbled away into red dust when Sir Gardnor grasped hold of it, and ledges that looked as if civil engineers had cut them there disappeared in powder. Small avalanches started. Twice it looked as if Sir Gardnor would be carried down on the crest of them. But despite his size, he was certainly agile. Each time, he merely flattened his back against the wall behind him, waited for the cascade of rubble to subside, and then mounted higher.

He paused to glance momentarily over his shoulder; then, reassured that he was being observed, he climbed even faster. He was making for a depression in the cliff face where some earlier and forgotten landslide had scooped out an alcove. When he reached it, he disappeared from sight for a moment, re-emerged at the brim, and raised his hand.

The A.D.C. was the first to choose his position. In full view of Sir Gardnor, he stationed himself beside a natural firing platform in the rock and, removing the sweatband from his wrist, waved it in the air. Sir Gardnor waved back.

For Harold, it was not so easy. He chose the other side of the gully. This meant that there was a buttress of sandstone, shoulder-high, between him and Sir Gardnor. He selected the exact spot. Then, taking off his sun hat, he stood up to his full height and signaled to Sir Gardnor. The reply came back immediately. Apparently Sir Gardnor had been keeping his eye on him throughout. Harold squatted down on his heels and waited.

The Kiburru had no intention of being hurried. They executed a little war dance. They speared imaginary leopards. They recited spells. They relieved themselves. From the cliff above them, they heard Sir Gardnor shout something. The exact words escaped them, but the tone sounded angry. Glancing understandingly at each other, they decided that they must at least do something.

And in action, they were beautiful. They ran up to the tall rocks and took them in their stride. Clinging only with their finger tips, they scaled pillars. Goatlike, they bounded from crag to crag. They rattled their spears against the sides of caverns. They shouted. They threw stones into canyons which they could not reach themselves.

And raising nothing, they were all the time retreating farther and farther up the gully, vanishing behind the rocks at times, still in search of fresh hiding places where a tired leopardess might linger.

Out of the corner of his eye, Harold could see the A.D.C. His rifle ready, and his elbow on the rock in front of him, he was following every movement of the two Kiburru. His stance, too, was perfect. At once alert and relaxed, he was an example that any big-game hunter might have copied. Resting his back up against the rock, Harold decided to make himself comfortable too.

Then, from somewhere in front, came a shout. The Kiburru had found something, and they were calling. Harold saw the A.D.C. raise his rifle. The shouting continued. A moment later, one of the hunters sprang suddenly into view. He was astride a boulder, and pointing. One hand had the forefinger outstretched, and the other was cupped like a megaphone against his mouth. Harold edged cautiously along the rock in the direction of that pointing forefinger.

He could still see nothing. But the Kiburru could see, all right. What they had rustled out was a solitary dog baboon. It was old and mangy and hollow-stomached. When it opened its mouth to snarl at them, it showed them that one of its canine teeth was missing. Without a struggle, they could have killed it with their spears. Not that it was really worth killing: it would so soon be dead anyway.

It could still move, however. Rump up and bare bottom showing, it lolloped along the gully, stopping every few yards to see if it was being followed. The shouting meant nothing to it; it had already been stone-deaf by the time it had left the troop. At the sight of the advancing Kiburru, it broke into a short, rheumatic scamper.

For an instant, Harold saw a glimpse of tawny fur through a gap between the boulders. Then it was gone again. But it was still coming his way. He crawled farther along the rock face. Then, his rifle ready, he raised his head and stood there.

The next moment, something hit the loose stones in front of him and exploded in his face. He dropped his rifle and lifted his left hand to his eye. His cheek was soft and sticky.

Somewhere above and behind him he could hear Sir Gardnor shouting.

"The damn fool," Sir Gardnor was saying. "We should never have brought him. I marked his exact spot, and he moved away from it. That's where he signaled from. Over there, I tell you." Evidently, Sir Gardnor was pointing. "Where he showed up was a good twenty feet away."

"Perhaps we'd better be getting back, sir," the A.D.C. suggested.

"And you can put the sight away," Sir Gardnor told him. "I didn't use it after all."

"Pretty unlucky he's been, hasn't he?" Harold heard the A.D.C. remark in his polite, conversational way. "First that bit of trouble in the swamp, and now this. Doesn't look as if he's really cut out for this kind of thing."

Harold was sitting some distance away from them. He had wrapped his handkerchief across his face, and he had his head down on his knees, resting. Sir Gardnor's back was turned toward him. The words came only faintly.

"Unlucky? The fellow's a Jonah, if you ask me. I shan't be sorry when this safari's over."

They made the journey back to the camp in good order, but slowly. With only one eye on the job, Harold kept stumbling. Each time it was the A.D.C. who saved him. Sir Gardnor was in no position to do so: still angry and disgusted by the whole affair, he was way out in front with the two Kiburru. And sensing that he was displeased by something, they led him back by a slightly longer route so that he would at least feel that he had been getting his money's worth.

It was not until Sir Gardnor had reached the sentry posted outside the camp that he seemed even to be aware of the rest of his party. He waited for them to catch up.

"I should get your eye seen to," he said.

It was his first remark to Harold since the shooting; and he did not add to it. He turned immediately to the A.D.C.

"The fact that it was a baboon," he told him, "makes the whole thing even more preposterous. Baboon is the staple diet of the leopard. No baboon would ever have gone near the place if it had been a lair."

They were inside the camp by now, and Sir Gardnor was intercepted by the Corporal from Signals. The man gave the appearance of having been standing around for some time waiting for him.

And once more, Sir Gardnor seemed eager for the message. Handing his rifle to the A.D.C., he ripped open the envelope. He stood there, for a moment, quite still—unnaturally still, Harold thought—while he was reading. Then, suddenly, he came to life again. He crushed the sheet up in his hand and without speaking—without even looking back again—went over to his tent.

The crumpled corners of the buff Signals form were still sticking out of his closed fist as he walked away.

Even though the hunting party was back, the camp still seemed deserted.

Captain Webber's enormous pink tablets had only just begun to have any effect, and Lady Anne remained in her tent all day alongside Sybil Prosser. Nor did Sir Gardnor appear. His A.D.C., rather subdued-looking and with his lock of hair more frequently out of place than usual, emerged shortly after one o'clock to say that H.E. was lunching inside and would the others please start the meal without him. Then the A.D.C. went back inside to Sir Gardnor again.

In the result, it was only Major Mills and the Signals Officer who sat down together. There was next to no conversation between them. Major Mills always suffered a mild stomach upset when there had been any misuse of firearms, and the Signals Officer was singularly silent. He had, Major Mills decided, got something on his mind.

Harold himself was flat out on his folding bed. Captain Webber had taken a good look at the bad eye and pronounced that the cornea was punctured. There was, he said frankly, nothing that he could do about it in camp conditions. He merely put on a proper bandage and gave Harold a couple of pills to kill the pain; the other tablets were against infection, he said. If the pain got worse, he added rather meaninglessly, Harold had only to call him.

The pills had been of double strength. One was the standard dose. But with Sybil Prosser on his hands, Captain Webber wanted to make sure. Two invalids at a time were more than he felt he could manage.

In consequence, it was not until after dark that Harold was about again. The fiercest of the shooting pains had gone from his eye—there was now only a dull ache that might have gone with any ordinary black eye—and he was feeling hungry.

He went over to the doorway of the tent and looked out. But it was too late; the dinner table had been cleared away and the chairs were all folded and stacked up against each other. Even the native end of the camp was silent. The only sound was the *hu-hu-hu-hu*ing of an eagle owl that had come from nowhere and was now hanging about in the adjacent trees.

The light over Sir Gardnor's desk was still burning. It lit up the whole marquee like a Chinese lantern. Evidently it was one of his late sessions.

Harold went inside again. Hungry as he was, there was nothing for it but to wait for breakfast time.

Chapter 26

THE SCREAM that woke him in the night seemed loud and very close at hand while he was still asleep, and faint, remote, and unplaceable as soon as he was roused.

But he could not mistake it. That was why, still dazed with sleep, he had slung his legs over the side of the bed and was groping his way past the tripod washstand for the door. It had been a woman's scream. And, his head all swathed round as it was with Captain Webber's crepe bandaging, he started to run toward the tent where Lady Anne had shut herself away with Sybil Prosser.

The tent flap that faced him, however, was closed tight, and the tent itself was in darkness. The only light still burning anywhere in the camp was in Sir Gardnor's marquee. The flap there had not been fastened down; it was laced loosely together on the outside as though someone had just gone out and had tied the cords behind him to keep the canvas from flapping.

Harold undid the knots and thrust his way inside. The light from the pressure lamp dazzled him, and he raised his hand to shield his good eye from the glare. Sir Gardnor was there, all right. He was seated at his desk; presiding over it, as it were. His eyes were open. But his jaw had fallen. Down one side of his face there was a great slicing cut that had pared off a sliver of the flesh. His throat, his shoulder and his shirt front were all soaked in fresh, wet blood.

And standing behind him was Old Moses. His hand was resting on something up by Sir Gardnor's collar band. He was straining at it. And then Harold saw what it was. Only the handle was showing. The rest of the long paper knife was hidden: pegged down somewhere inside.

As Harold made for him, Old Moses turned. It was not the Old Moses that Harold knew. This one was mad, quite mad. His lips were drawn back from his yellow, stumpy teeth, and his eyes were staring. He kept his black hand clasped firmly round the handle of the knife.

He was strong, too; stronger than Harold would have believed possible. Ancient as he was, he fought back. When Harold grappled with him, the thin, claw-like fist closed tighter. As they struggled, the cutting edges seesawed back and forth, opening up the wound.

Then Harold looked up. In the far corner of the marquee he saw that Lady Anne was standing.

A moment later, the entrance flap was jerked aside and Major Mills arrived. He had been making one of his surprise patrols when he heard the scream, and the whole length of the camp had been between them. In running for it, he had fallen over one of his own trip wires. Late and therefore ashamed of himself, he was breathless and gasping as he burst in.

But he was still able to sum things up. Also, he knew how to deal with natives. He already had his revolver in his hand; and spinning it in the air like a juggler, he caught it by the barrel and brought the butt end down on the bare, leather-looking skull in front of him.

The whole action was neat, speedy, and efficient. Old Moses collapsed instantly. But Major Mills was not yet finished. Taking off his tie, he turned Old Moses face downwards and, kneeling on his buttocks, bound his hands together behind his back, straining at the knots so that no amount of struggling would undo them. That completed, Major Mills removed his belt and strapped it tightly round the spiny ankles.

Then, because he was a humane man who had only been doing his duty, he thrust out his foot and rolled Old Moses over onto his side, so that he should not suffocate.

But he was too late to save Sir Gardnor. He had already

slumped over sideways. Quite slowly, his head fell forward and he collapsed onto his desk, his outstretched arm upsetting the crystal-and-silver inkwell, the pen tray, the holder with all the paper clips.

Across the marquee, Harold saw that Sybil Prosser, her wispy hair disheveled into a halo and wearing a grotesque magenta bed jacket that didn't button up properly, was standing over by Lady Anne. She had her arm round her and was trying to lead her away. But Lady Anne did not move. She stood where she was, her hands covering her face.

After that first scream, she had been entirely silent.

Captain Webber, neatly turned out for that time of night, had now joined them. He had his professional-looking medical bag with him. Stepping rather self-consciously over the bound body of Old Moses, he went straight across to the desk in brisk, bedside fashion and reached for the pulse in the outstretched wrist that had upset the inkwell.

Harold and Major Mills stood watching him. After a few seconds they saw him frown and, bending forward, thrust his hand under Sir Gardnor's shirt, feeling for his heart. When he had withdrawn his hand, he stood back for a moment. He might have been getting ready simply to take the patient's temperature. Instead, he began gingerly fingering round the wound where the knife had entered. Then, pressing down hard on Sir Gardnor's shoulder with his left hand, he removed the dagger, like an experienced wine steward drawing a stiff cork. The pattern of engraving on the blade showed up bright and scarlet.

"Better get him on the floor," he said. "Perhaps you'd give me a hand, would you?"

It was not easy. In life, Sir Gardnor had been a heavy man, and in death he was clumsy. He bumped rather than was laid upon the ground. But immediately Captain Webber was professionally at work again. This time it was his ear that he placed up against Sir Gardnor's chest. He stayed there motionless for some time, listening.

And this was the moment when Lady Anne opened her eyes

again. She dropped her hands and stood there, staring at the empty desk. It seemed, at first, that she could not understand. Then she saw Sir Gardnor's body sprawled out on the rug, and Captain Webber crouching over him.

"What have you done to him?" she began asking.

Captain Webber placed his two hands stiffly in the small of his back and got up. He went over to his bag and took out a hypodermic syringe. Something had told him that, if it was Lady Anne who had screamed, he might be needing it.

Very deliberately, he filled the syringe up to the two c.c. mark and went over to her.

It was Sybil Prosser whom he addressed.

"Would you mind holding the sleeve back?" he said.

Then he beckoned to Harold.

"We'll carry her through," he said. "And be careful to keep her head up. Miss Prosser had better sit with her. She'll be out for quite some time. Better that way."

When they got back to the Governor's quarters, the A.D.C. was there.

Naked to the waist and in his pajama trousers, he was standing over Sir Gardnor's body.

Not that he was of much use to anyone. All that he was doing was looking down and saying, "Oh, my God, my God." His distress was genuine, all right: he was crying.

Harold noticed, too, how unkempt he was. Everyone's hair gets mussed up and tangled in the night, but the A.D.C.'s was disgraceful. It had bits of grass and sand in it as though he had been sleeping in the open. And his bare chest had scratch marks all down it as though he had been playing with a kitten.

Major Mills did not seem to be particularly impressed by the crying.

"Where were you when it happened?" he asked.

The A.D.C. rounded on him.

"What the hell *did* happen?" he demanded.

"You ought to know," Major Mills told him. "You were his A.D.C., weren't you?"

The A.D.C. looked down at the big body lying sprawled there and said, "Oh, my God," again.

"I asked you a question," Major Mills reminded him.

The A.D.C. was breathing in very deeply. That wasn't like him either. He was in perfect physical condition, and he was behaving like an old man who had just been running upstairs.

"Where were you?" Major Mills repeated.

The A.D.C. turned round and faced him.

"I don't have to tell you," he said. "You're not a policeman."

It was a most extraordinary reply, and Major Mills took note of it. He went red in the face, redder even than his natural color.

"As the officer responsible for security," he said, realizing as he uttered them how singularly empty the words sounded, "I could have you arrested."

But that was too much. The A.D.C. found Major Mills's manner insufferable. He wasn't going to have any overpromoted infantryman addressing him in that fashion.

"You can do what you bloody well like," he replied. "It's too late now, anyhow."

He turned his back on Major Mills as he said it. Then he knelt down and took Sir Gardnor's hand in his. When he got up, he pushed his lock of hair into place, brushed the back of his hand across his cheek where the tears were showing, and walked away without another word, simply leaving them there.

Major Mills raised his eyebrows.

"I'm going after him," he said. "He's still got his revolver. Or should have. He'd be better without it."

Captain Webber looked down at the body.

"We've got to get him up onto the bed," he said. "He can't stay there all night."

He paused.

"And we'll need help," he added. "We nearly dropped him last time, remember."

It was a little unnerving when they reached the bed. Sir Gardnor sank onto it so naturally, and the bed creaked so convincingly, that they might have been helping him into it when drunk.

When they left him, Sir Gardnor was simply a large, vague

shape under one of the Residency sheets. His face was entirely covered.

Captain Webber paused for a moment.

"Was he a religious man?" he asked. "It's quite usual to leave a Bible lying on top, you know. That is, if you've got one handy."

Chapter 27

OUTSIDE THE marquee, the Signals Officer was hanging round trying to attract Harold's attention.

"You'll be wanting to get through to base, won't you?" he asked. "You give me the message and I'll do what I can. I'm not promising anything, mind you. They aren't usually receiving at this hour."

He glanced down at his watch as he was speaking. It showed ten minutes past three.

"Where's Major Mills?" he asked.

The Signals Officer winked back at him.

"Directing operations. State of siege," he said.

It was then that it occurred to Harold that, with Sir Gardnor dead and the A.D.C. in disgrace, he was the senior civilian member of the party. He found himself rather enjoying the sensation. And when the Signals Officer handed him a pad of blank forms, he accepted it.

The opening of the message was easy. In Roman capitals, he wrote ACTING CHIEF SECRETARY TOP PRIORITY IMMEDIATE. But that was where be began to run into difficulties. He had never sent a Service telegram before. But he didn't want to keep the Signals Officer waiting, didn't want to reveal what an amateur he was. He lettered on. PAINFUL DUTY INFORM YOU HIS EXCELLENCY GOVERNOR DIED REPEAT DIED SUDDENLY 0300 HOURS THIS MORNING STOP CAUSE OF DEATH STAB WOUNDS STOP PERSONAL SERVANT QUOTE OLD MOSES UNQUOTE UNDER CLOSE ARREST STOP INVESTIGATIONS

CONTINUING STOP LADY ANNE UNDER TREATMENT FOR SHOCK STOP RETURNING IMMEDIATELY SIGNED HAROLD STEBBS.

It was only when he had finished it that he wondered whether, with Service telegrams, it was really necessary to save money by cutting down the wording.

But the Signals Officer read it out approvingly.

"That's the ticket," he said. "We're trying to get through to them now. Won't be easy because they're not expecting us. Probably all shut down by now."

It came as sweet relief to get back into bed again and, in the darkness, to ease off the strapping of the bandage. Captain Webber had bound it round too tight: he could feel the wad of lint pressing right down into his eyeball.

He had just arranged the pillow under his good cheek when he heard Major Mills calling him. The voice sounded eager and excited.

"You awake?" Major Mills was asking. "Got some news for you."

Harold switched on the battery lamp beside his bed.

"Come in," he said.

There was a bottle of whisky and a jug of water on the folding table.

Major Mills helped himself to a drink. The very fact that he didn't blurt out his piece of news immediately showed that it was something big, something that would be worth waiting for.

"Aaah," he said as he put his glass down. "I think I've earned that."

Under his left arm he was carrying a bundle wrapped round in a hand towel. The royal G.R. showed up in reverse at one corner. He was hugging the bundle to him.

"What's that you've got there?" he asked.

Major Mills tapped it with his forefinger.

"That's what Old Moses was using," he said. "Key piece of evidence. Have to come up at the trial. Just going over to get the doctor to identify it. He's the one who pulled it out, you know."

He paused.

"Probably got his fingerprints all over it," he added in a lunatic flash of sudden insight.

Harold still felt sure that this was not the piece of news that had brought Major Mills to his bedside: he could see that the Major was now squaring himself up to deliver it.

"Just as well I had that roll call," he announced. "There's a man missing."

"One of yours?" Harold asked him.

Major Mills shook his head.

"Not exactly," he said. "Household. One of the kitchen boys. No sign of him. Must have slipped out past the sentries. Don't like the look of it."

Harold raised himself up higher in his bed.

"Which one?" he asked.

"New boy," Major Mills replied. "Wasn't in the lot I vetted. Last-minute arrangement. Never seen him before this trip. Tall, coffee-colored fellow."

Harold leaned back again against the pillow. He had just remembered those scratch marks down the A.D.C.'s chest.

"Pretty big kitten," he said.

"What's that?"

"Nothing," Harold told him. "Just something that crossed my mind."

Major Mills looked worried for a moment, wondering if Harold was all right. But the other piece of news was too big to be kept back any longer. Lightheaded or not, Harold was going to hear.

"And there's something else you don't know," he said. "Something I've only just found out."

"Such as?"

"It was Old Moses who signed him on," Major Mills replied. "Said he was one short. None of the others had ever met him before. Or at least, that's what they say."

"And you think the two of them were in it together?"

Major Mills nodded.

"Looks like it," he said. "Damn suspicious making a run for it."

184

He broke off to pour himself another drink and smacked his lips over it.

"Old Moses could tell you what's behind it all," he went on. "That's for certain. Only he won't talk. Gone silent, or something."

"What have you done with him?" Harold asked.

Major Mills allowed himself a little smile of self-congratulation.

"Under lock and key," he said. "In one of the trucks. Posted an armed guard round it. For all we know—" here Major Mills dropped his voice to a whisper—"there may be more of 'em in it. Not taking any chances."

He readjusted the bundle under his arm.

"Got a patrol out looking for the other fellow," he added. "Shouldn't be far away."

Chapter 28

BECAUSE NO one had really been able to get to sleep again, they were all tense, irritable, and on top of each other when they met next morning. And with Old Moses locked up and the kitchen boy gone a.w.o.l., even breakfast itself was in confusion.

Major Mills was the first at the table and Harold sat down beside him. It was by then a few minutes after five, and already the sun was up and in full fury. Because it was still early, the striped awning provided no protection. Uninterrupted, the heat and the glare came slanting in underneath it.

MajorMills shifted his chair back a little.

"My God, it's going to be a hot one," he said.

They were joined almost immediately by Captain Webber. He came out of the marquee, opposite, thoroughly hang-dog and despondent-looking.

At the sight of Major Mills, he seemed relieved.

"I say," he said, "I've just been in there."

He jerked his thumb over his shoulder as he was speaking.

"It's like an oven. Won't be nice later. Can you lay on a burial party?"

Major Mills finished the cup of lukewarm coffee he was drinking. "Give me time to get my patrols back first," he said.

His mouth was full of grounds, and he ran his tongue backwards and forward across his teeth to clean them.

"Shouldn't be long now. Probably picked him up already. Better see if they've sent a runner."

Still licking his teeth, Major Mills got up and left them.

Captain Webber leaned forward.

"I'm not too keen on moving Lady Anne," he said. "Not in her condition. Ought to keep her absolutely quiet. She's my responsibility, you know."

"Is she worse?"

Captain Webber was playing with his spoon, balancing it lengthwise across the rim of his cup.

"She's still under sedation," he said, "and I'm going to keep her that way. If she came to, she might do anything."

"Can't Sybil Prosser look after her?"

"She can so long as I keep her under. I don't know after that."

He jabbed his finger down on the end of the handle as he said it and caught the spoon as it cartwheeled up into the air.

"Out of her mind when she came to just now," he finished up. "Simply wasn't with us."

"Will she be all right?"

Captain Webber wiped away a brown stain that the spoon had made on his jacket.

"Not my department," he replied. "Hospital case, really."

"Then hadn't we better get her there?"

"It's fifty-fifty," Captain Webber told him. "I can't give her proper attention out here. On the other hand, the journey may be too much for her. Might just as well toss up for it."

He pursed his lips and seemed to be considering.

"There's still H.E.," he added. "Can't take him with us. Not in this heat. Mustn't go upsetting the driver."

Harold shook his head.

"He'd be furious if he thought we were just leaving him here," he said. "Simply furious. He'd feel it was lacking in respect or something."

This time Captain Webber merely shrugged his shoulders.

"I'm not in charge of transport," he replied. "It's up to the Major. But if you really want to move him, you'd better be quick about it. It's not too pleasant even now, over there in that marquee."

He broke off for a moment because the Signals Officer was bearing down on them. He had one of his own message envelopes in his hand.

"Just come in," he said. "I couldn't raise anybody earlier. But they came back quick enough. It's their reply."

Harold held out his hand for it, but the Signals Officer kept the envelope from him.

"It's addressed to the A.D.C.," he said. "Marked 'Personal and Immediate.'"

"Well?"

"I've tried him," the Signals Officer replied. "And he won't take it. Says he's not up to it, or something. Sounded pretty low to me."

"Okay," said Harold. "Give it to me."

He ripped the envelope open rather officiously. It was all quite absurd, of course. The envelope had been stuck down only a few minutes before, less than twenty-five yards away from where he was sitting. And in any case, the Signals Officer knew exactly what the message contained.

It was a snub; a Top Priority official snub. URGENTEST FROM THE ACTING CHIEF SECRETARY, it read. CONFIRM INSTANTLY SUBSTANCE TELEGRAM SIGNED QUOTE STEBBS UNQUOTE STOP ESSENTIAL RECEIVE CONFIRMATION BY PROPER CHANNEL STOP AWAITING IMMEDIATE REPEAT IMMEDIATE REPLY. It was signed FRITH.

Captain Webber got up and pushed his chair back neatly against the table.

"Think I'd better go across to see him," he said. "Bad business if you're an A.D.C. and this sort of things happens."

He was entirely unhurried.

"Then I'll have a look at that eye of yours. Needs rebandaging."

Chapter 29

"I'D RATHER have burned the whole lot. They'll only be fighting over it when we've gone. There's practically nothing of value in any of these villages."

Major Mills was standing in front of the heap of camp stores while he was speaking. It made a quite considerable pyramid. There were chairs, tables, spare bedding, tins of food, cooking utensils. It represented a substantial write-off of sound Government equipment.

But it was inevitable. With one thirty-hundred weight truck converted into an ambulance for Lady Anne, and the other brought into commission as a hearse, there was now a critical shortage of transport. Even Old Moses, under armed escort, was taking up valuable space in the South Staff's own regimental vehicle.

It was not the best of journeys. And they could not speed it up because of Lady Anne. Before they left Amimbo the rear springs of the thirty-hundredweight truck had been fitted with another leaf to strengthen them for the extra load; and now, lightened as the truck was, it bounced about like a Ping-Pong ball at anything much above twelve miles an hour. Making up time on the flatter stretches was out of the question. And because they were always behind schedule, there was no midday break when the sun was really at its worst. They simply drew up for a moment, changed drivers, and got going again.

With nightfall, any thought of further travel was impossible. Captain Webber was insistent, too, that Lady Anne could not stand any more of it. Or Sybil Prosser for that matter: only thirty-six hours earlier it was she who had been the camp invalid.

When she climbed down out of the truck, she seemed ready to collapse on top of them.

Harold went up to her.

"How is she?" he asked.

Sybil Prosser was still straightening up her back: she was a tall woman, and for the past eight hours she had been sitting folded and upright on a two-foot medicine case in the ambulance truck.

"We'll be lucky if she makes it," she said. "Captain Webber tells me it's all your idea."

There was no particular bitterness in the remark: it was just an observation that she was making.

"Can I see her?"

Sybil Prosser shook her head.

"It wouldn't do any good," she replied. "They're not letting her come round. And I don't wonder. I only hope her heart stands up to it. She's not strong, you know. She never has been."

Her voice was as flat and expressionless as ever. It might have been a stranger they were discussing.

"And she's been in a fever, I can tell you. There's no proper laundry. I've burned most of her things; I had to."

"Damn rotten business," the Signals Officer had just observed. "Finding that you haven't got the job, I mean, and then having this happen to you."

It was the second day of the journey, and with darkness, real darkness, on them any moment now, they had decided to laager where they were.

The differential of the two-tonner, which had been giving trouble ever since they had started up, was now in pieces on the ground, and Transport was conducting its own closed conference among the debris. Captain Webber had just emerged from the ambulance truck, thoughtful-looking and announcing that there was no change. And Major Mills and the Signals Officer, rather nervously double-checking each other, had got off the evening message to Amimbo, pinpointing their position.

There was nothing, for the time being, but to sit around

drinking, and wait—and go on waiting—for the substitute cooks to get the meal ready.

It was the second whisky that the Signals Officer had poured himself, and after his spell of practically unbroken duty, it had relaxed him.

"You don't know the number he sent off," the Signals Officer went on. "Didn't let up for a single moment. Not even out here on safari. He was on edge, all right, I can tell you. Wouldn't believe it when the news did come through. Made me go back twice for confirmation."

He took another sip of his whisky.

"Don't really know, though," he added. "May be a blessing in disguise, that stabbing. He'd have been brokenhearted if he'd lived. India was all he wanted."

The Signals Officer wasn't really very much above the level of a village postmistress who gossips about telephone calls, Harold decided. He tried to shift the way the talk was going, make it less personal somehow.

"Who *did* get it?" he asked.

But it was the wrong question: it set the man going again.

"The one he didn't like," he said. "Lord Eldred. Hadn't got any use for him at all. You should have seen some of the things he said. All *en clair*, too, so that the clerks could read it."

Dinner ended up as a quiet sort of meal because the Signals Officer left them before the coffee. He went back over to his radio van, saying rather importantly that he thought it might be better if he were standing by.

Harold stretched himself, felt stiffer for doing so, and said that he'd take a stroll. It was one of those moments when Africa had subdued itself and become peaceful. Even the ground had cooled off, and the breeze that came lapping over the little crest in front of him was no more than lukewarm. He walked on slowly, savoring the quiet, the moonlight, the brush of air against his face. And it was then that he came upon the A.D.C.

The young man was sitting by himself, sprawled out in a hollow, staring out apparently at nothing. He had not heard

Harold approach him. When he looked up and saw who it was, he did not seem to resent him. Or to be pleased either, for that matter. He gave the impression of not caring very much either way.

"Didn't see you at dinner," Harold remarked.

"Wasn't there," he replied. "Didn't want any."

"But you've got to eat . . ." Harold began, before the A.D.C. interrupted him.

"Oh, for Christ's sake," he said.

Harold took a chance on it and squatted down on the grass beside him.

"Cigarette?" he asked.

The A.D.C. shook his head and shifted over onto one elbow.

"I suppose you realize that I've had it," he said. "Really had it, I mean. I'm finished."

He was prodding with his heel at the tuft of grass. It was an obstinate tuft, firm and well rooted. When he had finally managed to dislodge it, he bent down and threw it away from him. Then he started speaking again.

"I suppose it means a court-martial," he added. "Looks like it, anyway."

Harold wasn't quite sure what kind of reply was expected.

"They'll give you someone to defend you, won't they?"

It was the best, in the circumstances, that Harold could manage. And when he heard it, the A.D.C. tilted his head on one side and gave his rather charming social smile again.

"I'd rather be the one to prosecute," he said.

It was certainly what all the others had been saying. But the young man was too obviously disconsolate for Harold simply to agree with him.

"You don't know yet," he replied. "I'd stop worrying."

The A.D.C. was sitting bolt upright now.

"It's not me I'm worried about," he said. "It's Rikki."

"Rikki?"

"That's his name," the A.D.C. told him, as though it explained everything.

Harold was not impressed.

"Oh, him," he said. "But he's made a break for it, hasn't he?"

The A.D.C. screwed up his hand and rubbed the back of his fist across his forehead as if he were trying to polish it.

"You don't understand," he said. "He's just an innocent. A poor, frightened innocent. And they're hunting him. He'll be terrified. Absolutely terrified. He may try to kill himself."

The A.D.C. turned and faced him.

"Look at it your way," he said. "Think how you'd be feeling if it was some girl they were after."

Harold rather liked the A.D.C. for saying that. At least it showed that he was being honest with himself; being honest with both of them, in fact.

"He'll be all right," he told him, not very convincingly. "After all, he's at home here. It's his country."

"Would you do something for me?" the A.D.C. asked suddenly.

"What is it?"

"If they do arrest him," he said, "and I'm not around"—it was characteristic of the A.D.C. that he should put his own predicament so delicately—"would you look after him for me? See that he's properly represented, and all that?"

Harold did not reply directly.

"They'll never catch him," was all he said.

"Oh, but they will," he replied. "They're bound to. After all, it was the *Governor,* you know. They can't just let it drop. They'll get the Army out. And when they get him, he's so simple he'll say whatever they tell him to. He's such a child he wouldn't know what was happening to him. That's his whole trouble. He trusts people."

Because Harold did not say anything, the A.D.C. repeated his question.

"You will do it, won't you?" he said. "You're the only one I can ask."

Again, Harold kept him waiting for his reply.

"Oh, all right. I'll see that he isn't persecuted, if that's what you want."

The A.D.C. seemed to relax a little.

"Because it's so frightfully important," he explained. "For him, I mean. He's only eighteen, and terribly impressionable. If he took a wrong turning now, he could so easily go to the bad. I'm the only real friend he's got."

Harold did not attempt to prolong the conversation. And as the A.D.C. showed no signs of wanting to return—seemed, in fact, to prefer simply sitting there gazing out at nothingness—Harold got up and left him.

"Well, if that isn't bloody well marvelous," he kept telling himself as he went back toward the trucks. "And to think that I walked right into it. Of all things, I've got a teen-age queer for a godson: a six-foot, coffee-colored queer. As though I hadn't got enough on my hands without that one."

It was Captain Webber who interrupted his thoughts. The man had his sleeves rolled up and was carrying his medical bag. He was already halfway inside his tent when he saw Harold.

"I'd like to take another look at that eye of yours," he called across to him. "Just let me get cleaned up first."

Harold did not like the look of the rolled sleeves and the medical bag. They had the air of an emergency about them.

"Nothing's gone wrong, has it?" he asked. "She's not worse or anything?"

Captain Webber dropped the toweling and pushed it away from him with his foot.

"I'll tell you if there's any change," he said.

He paused.

"And I'll tell you something else," he added. "It was your plan, remember? About the Governor, I mean. Had to get him back to Amimbo at all costs, you said. Well, I'm a doctor, not an undertaker. I've got Lady Anne to consider."

He glanced up for a moment at Harold's bandaged eye.

"Try not to rub it," he said. "Only makes it worse."

Chapter 30

CONSIDERING THE nature of the track and the reinforced springs in the converted ambulance, they had kept up a remarkably good average over the whole journey: 11.9 miles per hour was what

Major Mills made it, and in the circumstances, he regarded it as nothing less than a keen personal triumph.

By starting at first light and cutting down the meal breaks to a strict twenty minutes, including brewing-up time, they had, in fact, lopped one complete day off the return trip.

If Major Mills was pleased with himself, the Signals Officer was nothing less than delighted. It was the outward journey that had been torment. While Sir Gardnor and the rest had just taken him for granted, he had been battling professionally with fading, surge, static, heterodyne whistles, cracked accumulator plates, the lot.

Every night, too, it had got worse. By the time they reached Kitu, even the Amimbo call sign had come through so faintly that the ticking of the big second hand on the chronometer in the radio van had been enough to drown it.

Whereas now it was pure apprentice stuff. Last night, for instance, they hadn't even bothered to erect the full aerial: with their wire slung across to the nearest tree, Amimbo had come roaring in, loud and clear, and the Signals Officer had enjoyed one of the few entirely carefree evenings in his whole Service career.

The messages had mostly been about funeral arrangements and mental specialists. The grave in the cathedral cemetery was all ready, a return signal had said; there was a later one, too, that informed them that the Bishop and sexton were standing by on all-night duty at the cathedral and that they could call in there first if that would be better.

The replies about the mental specialist were less satisfactory. Apparently, Captain Webber's first choice, a Dr. Colin Alexander, who sounded reliable enough, was away on boat leave in England, but a Professor Jesús Fernandez had at last been run to earth in a convent asylum in Nucca and was at this very moment on the Coronation Flyer somewhere on his way to Amimbo. His exact time of arrival, naturally, was uncertain. The detachment of two senior nurses from the Royal Victoria Hospital, Amimbo, however, had—the telegram advised—all been safely taken care of.

It was significant that, for the last leg of the journey, Major Mills invited Harold to move in and share his truck with him.

Nor was it for the company alone. The fact was that the Major was painfully in need of reassurance. And the nearer he got to Amimbo the more he needed it. He did not look forward to explaining things to his C.O.

To keep his mind off the thoughts that were troubling him, Major Mills talked mainly about his prisoner. Old Moses was his key exhibit, and he knew it.

"Just as well I acted promptly," he remarked, "otherwise he'd have disappeared like the butcher boy. Very cunning lot, the Mimbo. Very. Never tell what's going on inside their heads. That's why I nailed him."

It was, with only minor variations, what Major Mills had been saying more or less continuously ever since Harold had joined him. And there was more of it, the sentences coming up each time in slightly different order, like the phrases in a musical composition.

"If I hadn't grabbed him, he'd have been off too," he went on. "Probably got his getaway all nicely planned. No good looking into their eyes to see what they're thinking. Can't tell. They're Mimbo, remember."

The moment had come to introduce a fresh theme, and Major Mills was off and away again.

"Knows what he's up to, of course, keeping his mouth shut. Doesn't want to incriminate himself. Isn't speaking a word to anyone. Just sitting there in the truck saying nothing. Got it all worked out. Mark my words, he's cooking up something."

The Major was cut short because the driver drew his breath in sharply and then let it out again in a long, grateful sigh. There, in front of them, was the highway. They were over the last foothill, and they could see the track stretching endlessly away, like a dried-up river bed. Down the whole length of it, the dust devils rose like elongated feather dusters and twirled away into the distance.

Even though there was still loose sand and shingle beneath the wheels, the driver promptly put his foot down. Harold turned and looked back at the other trucks as they topped the summit. One by one, they had spurted up. The ambulance, sensing better times ahead, came over the crest, its rear wheels spinning.

It was Major Mills who flagged them down. They were on the dot, and he was sticking to his timetable. At the prescribed twelve miles per hour, which was hardly enough to blow a breeze into their faces, they toiled on toward Amimbo.

Perhaps because he was tired, perhaps because his eye was still hurting, Harold seemed, for the moment, to be detached from the rest of the party, entirely separate from everyone around him. And the feeling, absurd but inescapable, came over him that he had been on this journey before, had known precisely what it felt like to be there at that exact point in space and time, with Lady Anne being tossed about unconscious in the ambulance behind him and with the dead body of Sir Gardnor, covered up in the Residency sheets, lying in state in the fourth truck in line.

At the same instant—and it was all in the span of a single flash that it occurred—he remembered how, for no reason and despite the heat, he had shivered when he had first looked down on the cake-icing architecture of Amimbo. It seemed now that he had known all this then.

Then the flash faded, and there was simply ordinary African sunshine all round him. He reached out toward the canvas bag that Major Mills had hung over the wiper knob below the windshield.

"Anything left in the bottle?" he asked.

But Major Mills was preoccupied. The whole saucer of the plain was spread out before them—flat, brown, and featureless. And he was peering at something. It was four or five miles away—distances were impossible to judge in the overhanging heat haze—and it was merely another cloud of dust. But it was not ordinary dust. It was approaching dust. A tight little cocoon of the stuff was advancing toward them, leaving a trail of its own unraveling in its rear like the smoke plume of a steam locomotive.

Major Mills looked down at his watch and then out at the dust cloud again.

"They're a bit late," he said. "We're bang on my E.T.A."

Twenty minutes later, when the cocoon had finally resolved

itself, they could see that it consisted of two cars—an open tourer with a flag on the front and the dark-blue Amimbo Police wagon. The two convoys drove on as though oblivious of each other, and when the leading drivers drew up, they were almost radiator to radiator.

Amimbo's head policeman was the first to get out. He jumped down from the tourer and came over to them, brushing the sand from his uniform as he walked forward. Compared with Major Mills and Harold in their khaki with the dark brown sweat stains between the shoulder blades, the man looked disturbingly smart, even dapper.

He made straight for Major Mills, and saluted.

"Well, Major," he said, "I believe you've got a prisoner for me. Like me to take him off your hands, I expect."

Major Mills took the salute while he was still seated.

"All yours," he replied. "Last truck but one. Have to ask you to sign for him, of course."

Then he turned to Harold.

"Strange lot these policemen," he said. "Only think of one thing. Didn't even inquire about Lady Anne." He paused. "Surprised the C.O. didn't send out a gun carriage. Been a nice touch. Made more of it, you know."

BOOK III

The Trial

Chapter 31

IT WAS now three weeks that they had been back in Amimbo, and the weeks had been busy ones.

Sir Gardnor's obsequies—including the memorial service, which necessarily had somewhat post-dated the interment—were over, and traffic arrangements down Queen Victoria Avenue had returned to normal. Old Moses had come up before the Chief Magistrate and been committed for trial in the High Court—October the third was the day set aside for the opening. The C.O. had expressed incredulity that Major Mills had not insisted on posting a day-and-night guard outside the Governor's marquee, and the Major had, in consequence, been temporarily relieved of his more warlike duties. He was, at the moment, doing an indefinite spell as Station Adjutant.

The A.D.C., for his part, had not visibly been disciplined; indeed, no one knew exactly what to do, except not to be seen mixing with him. The young man, in a state of official limbo, lived a solitary, cloistered life inside the Residency, reading back numbers of *The Sphere* and *Country Life* and waiting for his arrest, reprimand, replacement, or whatever it was the authorities had in mind for him.

One thing, at least, had been settled: Mr. Frith was now confirmed in the post of Chief Secretary; but his other and cherished secret dream—the one that he confessed to no one—had been abruptly shattered by the announcement that a new Governor, name still to be announced, would be coming by the end of the month.

There was one unexpected turn of events. Mr. Talefwa, in his paper, recently renamed *War Drum*, had accused British secret agents of having arranged the murder of Sir Gardnor because of his well-known sympathies for the exploited and overtoiling natives and was demanding a Royal Commission. Also, on Harold's desk there was a whole trayful of letters, telegrams, postcards, and telephone messages from Mr. Ngono requesting an instantaneous appointment on a private matter of the most delicate urgency.

As for Harold himself, he had been round to the Methodist Hospital, where they had given him eye drops to use night and morning, the address of an excellent oculist three hundred miles away, and a celluloid eye patch to wear in place of all that clumsy bandaging.

He had seen Lady Anne; it was Sybil Prosser who had arranged it.

She phoned Harold at his desk, asking if he could leave at once and come over. When he inquired if it was Lady Anne who had asked to see him, Sybil Prosser replied simply that Lady Anne was too ill to ask for anything and hung up.

Over at the Residency it was a muffled and twilit sickroom that Harold was shown into. Drugget had been laid over the parquet flooring, and the curtains as well as the shutters were across the windows.

But even in the half-light, he could see enough. Lady Anne was lying there, quite still and apparently unconscious. It was only after he had watched for a moment that he could see that she was still breathing. It was fast and very shallow—so shallow that it did not even disturb the line of the sheet drawn up below her chin. Her hand which lay outside the bedclothes looked dead already.

Her face was almost unrecognizable, because they had dragged her hair flat back from her forehead, tying it indifferently in tight bunches on either side. Her mouth, too, was different: the lips were cracked and broken, and they had been smeared with grease, which had begun to cake already at the corners. Across her forehead, little droplets of perspiration glistened.

While he stood by the bedside, one of the nurses began dabbing at her with a swab of absorbent cotton.

Then Sybil Prosser touched him on the arm.

"Well, there she is," she said. "You'd better go now. You can't do any good here. It's just that I thought she might have liked it."

All that was before Professor—or Papa, as he preferred to be called—Fernandez arrived. The Coronation Flyer, with a badly leaking cylinder, had broken down on the way. In consequence, Papa Fernandez was a full thirty-six hours late.

And eagerly awaited as he was, no one took very kindly to him at first sight. That was because he was so squat and, after the long journey, so disheveled. He plopped, rather than got out, onto the platform. There were other drawbacks. Not the least was language: he could be precise only in Portuguese. And to make things harder, his voice, naturally low and husky, was rendered practically inaudible by the long, wet panatella that he carried dangling from his lips. He was practically never without one.

When he went into the sickroom, he left it still burning in the ashtray on the table outside; and on his return to the corridor, he would examine it carefully, brushing off the ash at one end and smelling at the other, the chewed one, to see if any of it was still smokable.

His diagnosis, too, was elementary: he uttered the single phrase "brain fever" and left it at that. His recommended treatment was equally elementary. He advocated ice packs, bleeding, and a herbal concoction unknown to the Western pharmacopoeia and obtainable only in the native quarter. He was also a great believer in the qualities of burning sulphur and advised a saucer of it on either side of the bed.

His two British colleagues—Dr. Alexander's junior partner and a Dr. Simmons, now retired—were frankly dubious; even suspicious of him. But his self-confidence was enormous. In his quiet, laryngitic whisper, he assured them that it was a perfectly familiar type of case which he had treated by the hundred back in his own convent asylum in Nucca.

"Widow's Madness," he explained, was what it was sometimes called, and he was a trifle surprised that two qualified medical men should not immediately have recognized it as such.

Turning philosophical, he added that it struck down lowborn and highborn alike and that the treatment was the same for both.

Even though it was Sir Gardnor who had always invented the work—new surveys, forecasts, three-year plans, reorganizations, and so forth—it had always been on Mr. Frith that the resultant paper work had eventually descended; and Sir Gardnor had been at his most fertile just before he had left Amimbo. In consequence, Mr. Frith had never had so many unread papers in his in tray. His new office, large as it was, looked more like Central Registry than the Chief Secretary's.

Mr. Frith, too, was under considerable personal strain. During the first few days of Sir Gardnor's absence, he had naturally eased up a bit, allowing himself two late nights in succession at the Milner Club; and he had been only halfway through his second ease-up when Harold's telegram about Sir Gardnor's death reached him.

The tragedy had, in fact, come at an awkward moment for him. Mr. Frith was nearing his fifty-seventh birthday, and the timing was critical. With retirement little more than three years away, he was just too old for anything really nice to happen to him and too young to allow himself to go entirely to pieces. The middle course—the one which he saw so clearly he would have to follow—seemed singularly without attractions.

He had been particularly nice to Harold about his handling of things, telling him more than once what a pleasure it was to find someone who wasn't afraid to accept responsibility. The whole episode, he said, had been fully reported back to London; it was on his file there, and that was all that really mattered.

Harold had just left Mr. Frith when he found Mr. Ngono waiting for him at the bungalow. His motorcycle was propped up against the gatepost, and Mr. Ngono, a broad black mourning band around the short sleeve of his flowered shirt, was beside it.

Mr. Ngono came forward, hesitated, stopped, and came forward again. And then, when he was within arm's reach of Harold, he suddenly shot out his hand.

"You will most absolutely forgive my intrusion?" he asked. "You will not detest me for it?"

It was a slithering, indecisive kind of handshake. But it more than contented Mr. Ngono. He reveled in the embrace, seeking to cling to Harold's finger tips as they slid past him.

"So there is no offense caused?" he continued. "Just extremely renewed feelings on both sides?"

He paused and gave a rather embarrassed little giggle.

"You will mock me for it when I tell you, but twice or more times I nearly turned back. I was afraid of disturbing your esteem. And now everything is on the bloody old cheerio basis again. That is undeniably so, is it not?"

"Come in and have a drink," Harold told him.

But Mr. Ngono was not to be rushed.

"First, I must say my sentiments about our late Governor." Mr. Ngono dropped his head reverently at the mention of the word. "A man positively without equal in our lifetimes. Kind but stern—like a great Emperor. No argument about it: just damn well so. I have kept the Order of Service and the newspaper cuttings so that my children after me can honor his historical memory."

He had removed his handkerchief while he was speaking, and he blew his nose loudly. Then he glanced up.

"And his notable successor, our new Governor?" he asked.

"Are you permitted to mention his distinguished name yet—in the extremest confidence, of course?"

"I don't even know it myself," Harold told him.

Mr. Ngono did not believe him. But he was suddenly afraid that he might have gone too far, have overstepped the mark in a way that might invite a snub. Mr. Ngono was terrified of snubs.

He turned the conversation into safer social channels.

"And you thought the memorial service was a success?" he inquired. "Personally, I thought it was the most absolutely successful I have ever known. Those around me were full of the warmest congratulations. Nothing but top enthusiasm."

He paused.

"Once again I was in the last row but one," he said. "And behind a pillar this time. A disappointingly inferior seat altogether. But I am no longer thinking about the slight. I have forgotten it already."

They were going up the stone-bordered pathway toward the front door while they were talking; and as they approached, one of the houseboys came forward to open it for them. Mr. Ngono remembered with disappointment that, coming as he had on his motorcycle, he had nothing to hand to the boy as he went in: no hat, no umbrella, no brief case, nothing.

It was pleasant, all the same, to have his drink brought to him on one of the electroplated salvers that were on the inventory of the bungalow. And he was feeling better already.

"Chin, chin," he said as he held the whisky-and-soda up in front of him. "Very happy days. Many more safaris."

He took a sip and then remembered his manners again.

"And Her Ladyship?" he asked. "We have all been praying for her recovery most fervently. She is like a mascot to us."

Mr. Ngono was enjoying himself. He felt suddenly enlarged and carefree, like an undergraduate again.

Harold wondered how much to tell him.

"Lady Anne is much better," he said.

"Then you have seen her?" Mr. Ngono asked.

"Only for a moment," Harold replied. "She isn't well enough for visitors."

Mr. Ngono brought his hands together in delight.

"But she made an exception for you," Mr. Ngono reminded him. "Isn't that absolutely top-hole? Altogether the most gracious kind of compliment any sick invalid can possibly think of."

Mr. Ngono was indeed pleased to hear the news. By itself, it had made his visit to the bungalow worthwhile. Apart from the Residency household, Mr. Ngono was now the only man in the whole of Amimbo to know positively that the affair was still going on.

"And there is another matter also," Mr. Ngono went on. "Upon Her Ladyship's complete recovery, which is a foregone conclusion, her friends deeply and earnestly hope that she will continue to live here in Amimbo among them. It would be a most popular gesture, also of the utmost democracy."

"Is that what you have been wanting to see me about?" Harold asked him.

But Mr. Ngono was still playing for time.

"It was to request an interview with Mr. Frith, our new Chief Secretary no less," he said, glancing over his shoulder. "I wrote to him extending cordial and happy congratulations from all my staffs—those at the bar, at the dance hall, at my import business, and at the other various enterprises with which I am connected. Also on behalf of my father's tribe and his numerous villages. Very proud and well deserved, I told him. He will most undoubtedly be Sir Frith before one can say Jack Robinson. But I have received only a most formal reply."

"But why do you want to see him?"

"To pay those same profound compliments by word of mouth in person," Mr. Ngono replied. "Why else should I want to bother anyone so extremely overbusy and fussed with affairs as our Chief Secretary? It was my father's express wish, you get it?"

The houseboy had come in with more ice and then withdrawn again. He was somewhere behind the bead curtain—still listening, Mr. Ngono did not doubt; that was, if the boy was not back already in the kitchen repeating what he had just overheard.

Mr. Ngono could afford to take no chances, and he acted brilliantly.

"Your gramophone," he said. "Manufactured, I see, by no

other than His Master's Voice. I am exceedingly closely interested—with a view to securing the exclusive agency, of course.
Either that or Columbia. If I might be permitted to hear the
tone for the purposes of comparison. Something loud and jazzy to
be preferred. I shall represent the catalogue of all new records
too, most naturally."

It was the Signals Officer, in an effort to keep up the friendly
atmosphere of safari, who had insisted on lending the gramophone. Harold had not used it once since it had been left there.
Mr. Ngono turned the machine at right angles so that the full
blast of the music would be directed toward the bead curtain.

Then he came over and put his mouth down close to Harold's
ear.

"It is urgently essential, real life-and-death in fact, that we
speak where no one can hear us. The simultaneous moment the
record stops it will be too late. I shall return to my chair and we
will again loudly discuss the bloody weather."

"Then what do you want me to do?"

"Invite me, I beg, to walk in your garden without being
followed. Take a constitutional stroll with me, in fact. Shake up
the jolly old liver before dinner. Then I will most certainly tell
you all the dirt. Full dirt, and most alarming."

It was pleasant enough outside. The sun was getting low by
now, and the bank of flame trees beside the red gravel path was
lit up only on the farther side. Shoulder to shoulder, Harold and
Mr. Ngono walked across the zebra pattern of yellow sunlight
and thick shadow.

"It is always most extremely unsafe to speak before the houseboys," Mr. Ngono said reprovingly. "They repeat everything.
Diabolical mimics, some of them, too. They take off everybody—
you, me, the whole damn lot of us."

They were twenty-five yards from the bungalow by now, and
Mr. Ngono felt safer.

"Exclusively, it is about the trial that I wish to speak to you.
Already there are plots and counterplots of immense wickedness
being cooked up. They are saying that Old Moses is entirely
innocent. They will seek to prove it so."

"Well, isn't that for the judge to decide?" Harold asked him.

Mr. Ngono shook his head.

"By then it will be too late. Every single goddam witness will have been bribed. In terms of great profitability, too. And certain most distinguished people, absolute top rung in all respects, will have been exposed to the very common gaze."

"You always get rumors before a big trial," Harold told him.

This time Mr. Ngono had kept his voice quiet and level, but Harold could see that his hands were trembling.

"These are not rumors and inventions," he said. "Damn well they're not. They are the most severe and practical facts. There is one wicked and evil man, entirely without conscience, working night and day making them come true. I am here at the most considerable bodily danger to give you warning."

"And where would I find this man?" Harold asked.

"In the offices of *War Drum,*" Mr. Ngono replied. "Seated in the editorial chair itself. He is the one in charge of all arrangements—extremely ingenious arrangements, some of them. A most violent press campaign has been planned. And he has large sums of money. More than enough for all purposes. Entirely in notes, too."

"How do you know all this?"

Mr. Ngono hung his head for a moment.

"He told me," he said simply. "You see, we were friends. Most intense personal friends. But unfortunately, for entirely other reasons we have quarreled. Everything I am now saying to you was confided under a vow of the closest sworn secrecy. Vows and everything. Absolutely sacred, in fact."

"You realize that I shall have to report this?" Harold asked.

"But most naturally," Mr. Ngono replied. "It is precisely to the very bloody letter what I have been trying to fix up for some time. Then Mr. Talefwa will undoubtedly be arrested and most severely punished, and he will regret very much having quarreled with me."

They had reached the end of the path, and Harold held out his hand to say goodbye.

"Thank you for coming," was all he said. "I'll think very carefully about what you've told me."

But Mr. Ngono was reluctant to leave.

"There is one other matter," he explained. "Also of the greatest delicacy. And of the very highest importance."

"Well, what is it?"

"It is the jury," Mr. Ngono told him. "For a trial of such great importance, there will be a jury, you bet. It is the jury by law that has to say that Old Moses is the murderer. I desire most earnestly to be a member of that jury. How otherwise can we be damn well sure of the verdict?"

When Harold did not reply, Mr. Ngono looked up anxiously. Had he once again, he wondered, gone too far? He saw now that it might have been better to take things more slowly: to have revealed the danger and then, some other time, over a drink perhaps as an Englishman would have done, to have raised the matter of jury service.

So again he switched the conversation.

"I am still most unhappily worried about your poor eye," he said. "It is weeping again. I can see that tears are coming out from beneath the eye patch. It is boracic powder that is needed. One small pinch in warm water at every bedtime, and also on rising. It is what the missionaries use."

Chapter 32

IT WAS inadvisable, Papa Fernandez said, for Lady Anne to remain where she was. The climate of Amimbo was apparently notorious for its ill effects on mental cases. The soil, too, and the water were both highly suspect. Nucca was where Papa Fernandez recommended: a complete rest in agreeable surroundings until she was well enough to face the long voyage home.

It was certainly undeniable that, so far, Papa Fernandez had been proved right. The ice packs and the bleeding had brought down the temperature. The native concoction that he had prescribed had helped with the headaches. And the burning sulphur had fumigated an entire wing of the Residency. A colony of minute white ants, which previously had been swarming up and down the walls like vapor, gave up and moved over into what had been Sir Gardnor's quarters. Lady Anne, meanwhile, continued to get better.

That was why Sybil Prosser, yellower and more gaunt-looking than ever, had called in to see Harold. She sat opposite to him on one of the hard-backed chairs, wiping her upper lip where the office tea had left a thick brown stain across it.

"She's been asking for you," she said, "otherwise I wouldn't have come. I suppose it's all right. But don't let her talk too much. And don't believe everything she tells you. She's still all mixed-up inside. I know: I've had to listen to her."

"Six o'clock, then?" Harold asked.

"Better make it six-thirty," Sybil Prosser told him. "The doctor wants her to sleep all she can. And don't expect too much. I'm warning you."

The curtains were still drawn across the windows, but the drugget had been taken up, and the place looked like a bedroom again. There were flowers where the sulphur saucers had been set.

And Lady Anne herself was sitting up. Her eyes were closed, but the pillows were piled up behind her as if she had been reading. The paleness was not surprising considering all the blood that Papa Fernandez had been draining away from her. But she was recognizably Lady Anne again.

"Well, I've brought him," Sybil Prosser announced. "And I'm staying here while you talk to him. If I don't, you'll only overdo it."

She sat herself down as she said it and began to ease her shoes off.

"He's only got ten minutes," she added. "Then I'm putting him out again."

Lady Anne opened her eyes—rather slowly and deliberately, it seemed, as though she had been awake all the time. But it was not at Harold that she was looking. It was at the nurse who had been sitting over by the window.

"Oh, she can go if you want her to," Sybil Prosser said. "I told you: I'm staying."

Lady Anne waited until the nurse had left the room. Then she turned to Harold.

"Sybil got you here, didn't she?" she asked.

She was not looking at him as she spoke; had not looked at him since he had entered the room, in fact. She was simply staring down at the smooth white sheet that the nurse had tugged at automatically as she passed the bed.

"She just told me you were well enough," Harold replied.

Lady Anne shrugged her shoulders.

"Am I?" she asked. "How should I know?"

"She's a lot better," Sybil Prosser observed firmly. "You can see she is."

Lady Anne closed her eyes. She seemed to be living in a remote, separate world of her own.

"I didn't want to see you," she said. "I didn't want to see anyone."

She was addressing Harold now: speaking to him, but still not looking at him.

"Yes, you did," Sybil Prosser contradicted her. "You said so."

"Then I don't remember. I can't remember anything now."

There was just the smallest movement of her shoulders again. It made her merge more completely into the pillows.

Sybil Prosser got up and came over to where Harold was sitting. Because she was such a tall woman, she had to bend over to speak to him. It was necessary to get low. She was whispering.

"Can you see her being able to attend the trial?" she asked. "How could she be the slightest use to them?"

Before Harold could reply, Lady Anne had already spoken. She still had her eyes closed.

"I'll be all right if someone reminds me when it is," she said. "I don't even know the date or anything."

Sybil Prosser gave the bed a little pat.

"Not to worry," she said. "Not to worry."

But Lady Anne refused to be put off so easily.

"Will you be there?" she asked.

She was speaking to Harold again.

"I suppose so."

"Then I've got to be there too."

Lady Anne had opened her eyes, and she turned her head so that she could watch Harold's face.

"What are you going to say?" she asked him.

"Just tell them what I saw."

"What did you see?"

She was staring hard at him now.

"I saw Old Moses. I was the first one to get there. I tried to stop him."

Lady Anne seemed to be pondering.

"Was I there?" she asked.

"You were facing me."

"Was I?"

"Yes, over on the far side."

"Over on the far side," she repeated the words slowly. "But what was I doing? I must have been doing something. I just can't remember."

"You were looking at Sir Gardnor."

"Was . . . was he dead by then?"

"I think so."

Lady Anne started crying.

"Poor Gardie," she said. "Poor Gardie."

Sybil Prosser's hand came down on Harold's arm.

"That's all," she told him. "You've had your ten minutes."

It was Mr. Frith who suggested that Harold should dine with him up at the Milner Club; they both needed something to take them out of themselves, he reckoned.

Even so, Mr. Frith was not at his most responsive. Still off the bottle, he had been in the bar since before seven drinking nothing but ginger ale. And the stuff did not agree with him, he kept telling himself. He had undone the two bottom hooks on his cummerbund by the time Harold joined him.

"My God," he greeted him, "what a day. Didn't get a stroke of work done. Just been going over the arrangements."

Ever since the date of the trial had been fixed, no one in

Government Service had been talking about anything other than the arrangements.

Quite suddenly, Amimbo had become the center of the world, and people were getting ready to pour into it. There was not just Government accommodation to be considered: there were the hotels as well. The telegraph facilities—notoriously inadequate even when there was nothing happening—were being given a thorough going-over. And the Railway Company, taken entirely by surprise, had been warned that the Coronation Flyer would have to pull extra rolling stock as soon as the invasion started.

"It's not simply the press," Mr. Frith continued. "They're bad enough. There's an American broadcasting company, too. Says it wants to send a team over. God knows where we're going to put them all, or how long they'll be here. Have to see that the hard liquor doesn't run out."

After all, it was a *political* murder trial; and it would have seemed nothing less than unfaithful to Sir Gardnor's memory to allow the international corps to go away again with the impression that the capital city of Amimbo was simply some sort of colonial shanty town.

"It's about the trial that I wanted to have a word with you," Harold told him.

Mr. Frith did not lift his eyes from the glass with the silly bubbles bursting aimlessly on top.

"What about it?" he asked.

"It's Lady Anne."

"Well, what about *her?*"

Mr. Frith's manner was noticeably stiffening. He wanted to forget the trial, not talk about it. Also, he detested junior members of the Service getting themselves mixed up in matters outside their own department.

"It's the state she's in," Harold explained. "She's been really frightfully ill, remember. If she had to go into the witness box, the strain would be just too much for her. I don't like to think what would happen."

Mr. Frith tried hard to be bland and noncommittal.

"Oh, I think we can leave the C.J.'s office to look after all that, don't you?" he asked.

The gin-and-tonic that Mr. Frith had given him had made

Harold feel better. But it had also made him inclined to be argumentative. He was now in a mood where he couldn't bear to see other people allowing things to go wrong.

"As a matter of fact, sir, that's just what I don't think," he said. "It's merely so much legal routine for them. Naturally, they want her in Court so that they can get the whole case over. They don't know what she's been through already. I do."

Mr. Frith was scrutinizing Harold closely. He seemed to be unusually emphatic, even emotional, this evening. It occurred to Mr. Frith that perhaps the young man had been drinking, and he decided that he had better keep his eye on him.

"She's got her doctor," he replied. "It's entirely up to him. If she isn't well enough, they'll have to postpone. That's what's worrying 'em."

"Then they've got plenty to worry about," Harold replied. "I've just been up to the Residency. I've seen her."

Mr. Frith was very careful to keep his temper under control. It was not easy. All the rubbishy ginger ale inside him had left him feeling irritable and snappy. And the mention of the Residency had been the last straw. He had always resented the fact that in Sir Gardnor's day he had remained a visitor; an outsider who was brought in only when the A.D.C. wanted to make up the numbers.

But he remembered his manners. He hadn't brought Harold out to the Club to have a row with him.

He looked very deliberately at the big library clock with the name BENSON's written in bold lettering across the dial and got up from his chair.

"Shall we go through and dine?" he asked.

It was as they sat down that Mr. Frith realized that he couldn't eat anything. The ginger ale had destroyed his appetite, washed it away completely. And because he couldn't simply sit there at the table doing nothing, he ordered himself a whisky.

It was his first whisky that week, and he savored it. Also, he could feel it doing him good. The sick headache that had been hanging over him all day abruptly left him, and his nervous tic disappeared. By the time the boy had been over to his table for the third time, Mr. Frith had begun to blossom. He remembered that he was the man who had just been promoted to Chief Secretary, and he temporarily forgot the intrigues both in Amimbo and in Whitehall that had prevented him from going even higher. He felt benign and began congratulating Harold anew for taking charge of things on safari, predicting a great future for him.

That was why it was such a pity that Harold should have had to mention the name of Mr. Ngono. Ever since the tragedy, Mr. Ngono had taken to waiting disconsolately for hours on end, perched on the wooden bench in the front hall, hoping to catch Mr. Frith as he passed by; and in the end, Mr. Frith had been compelled to give orders to have him removed.

"What the hell difference does it make that he was there when you got back?" he demanded. "You could have sent him away again, couldn't you?"

"If I had," Harold replied, "I shouldn't have picked up one or two rather interesting pieces of information."

Mr. Frith drew down the corners of his mouth.

"From him?" he asked. "He was just bamboozling you. Ngono's never spoken a word of truth so long as I've known him."

"I know, sir, but . . ."

"Come on. Out with it," Mr. Frith told him. "What was it? He wouldn't have been there if he didn't want something."

Harold steadied himself.

"As a matter of fact, he wants to serve on the jury," he replied. "He thinks the others may have been got at."

Mr. Frith drained his whisky.

"There you are," he said. "So that's his game. Might have guessed it."

Mr. Frith had swung round in his chair to see where the table boy had got to. When he had located him, he pointed down toward his empty glass.

"Anyhow, he's wasting his time. It was decided last week. There's going to be an all-white jury. Too much at stake to take any risks."

"But that's not all," Harold said. "Mr. Talefwa's organizing a campaign. He's bribing the witnesses."

Mr. Frith pushed his chair back from the table.

"When you've been out here as long as I have," he replied, "you'll expect the witnesses to be bribed. I've never known a big trial where they haven't been. That's why it's an all-white jury."

He ran his handkerchief across his forehead as he was speaking.

"Let's have our drinks out on the terrace," he added. "Cooler there."

The new surroundings seemed to agree with him. He undid his jacket and put his feet up on the chair opposite.

"Funny, isn't it?" he remarked. "You outlasting the Governor like this. Never thought you would. Wanted me to find a replacement for you when he got back. Told me it was urgent."

Chapter 33

So FAR, Harold had been proved right.

War Drum, in its biggest type, opened up the attack the very next morning. AN AFRICAN CHILLON was how the headline ran, and Mr. Talefwa spared nobody. "The eyes of blind Justice," he wrote, "are running tears of blood. Her cheeks bright crimson from her weeping. Her screams stifled by Authority."

Old Moses, he pointed out, had now been held in custody for the better part of a month "on charges fabricated by certain persons in high places anxious to conceal the true identity of the murderers," and he asked the simple question: Did, or did not, the writ of *Habeas Corpus* run south of the equator?

Then came the big climax, the battle call to "all men of good will, regardless of race, color, religion, nationality, sex, calling, occupation, address or other barrier."

In short, *War Drum* was opening a fighting fund for the defense of Old Moses. To be known as "Save a Brother," it invited subscriptions as much from "the affluent European business community with their American cars" as from "the toiling Africans who may have to snatch bread from open hungry mouths of children to spare even a copper coin with which to fight the police and their false informers."

"Leading international lawyers, High Court judges, learned counsel, and humble magistrates throughout the entire civilized world will," he finished up, "be keeping their eyes, skinned like hawks, on the attempted crucifixion in Amimbo."

Mr. Frith was asking for Harold as soon as he arrived at the office. But it was not about *War Drum:* Mr. Frith was far too preoccupied to think about that.

"You're the man I want," he said, without even glancing up. "Got something for you."

He had a telegram in his hands, and he was still reading. When he had finished, he went back to the beginning and started all over again.

Then he looked across at Harold.

"Well, that's it," he told him. "We've got a new Governor coming out."

"Who's it to be, sir?"

Mr. Frith passed the telegram over to him.

"Read it yourself," he said. "It's Top Secret, mind."

Not that there could really be much point about secrecy by now. The Whitehall release date for the Gazette was tomorrow. A news leak, via Amimbo, for the evening papers seemed the sort of risk that even the most cautious public servant might occasionally have to take.

Harold read the telegram carefully. It was simple, formal, and straightforward. Also, final; not by any means the sort of telegram that you could argue about. He tried, therefore, to make the best of it.

"It's not quite so bad as it might be, sir," he said. "It gives us nearly three weeks to get ready."

Mr. Frith was gazing out of the window at the spire of St. Stephen's Cathedral.

"And do you imagine Lady Anne'll be well enough to be moved by then?" he asked.

Harold remembered the look of the sickroom, with the nurse over by the window and Sybil Prosser with her eyes fastened on the bed.

"Not a hope, sir," he said. "Just not a hope."

"Then where the hell are we going to put him?"

The question was addressed to the open window.

"What about my bungalow, sir?" Harold suggested. "After all, it's just alongside."

Mr. Frith gave a sudden little start and became Chief Secretary again.

"Dammit, man," he said, swiveling round, "he *is* the Governor, you know. If he has got to go anywhere, he'll have to have my place. That is, if there isn't room for both of them."

"And where will you go?"

"Crown Cottage, I suppose," Mr. Frith replied. "There's nowhere else."

It was the grace-and-favor house of Amimbo, Crown Cottage. Originally built for Government hospitality to important visitors, it had, over the years, been allowed to deteriorate because so few important visitors ever came. The lattice of white woodwork in front sagged in places as though it had been cut out of cardboard, and the green roof of corrugated iron had not been repainted since last year's rains.

"I'm afraid you won't find that very comfortable," Harold told him.

But Mr. Frith was past consolation.

"Don't worry about me," he said bitterly. "I don't count for anything. I'm only the Chief Secretary."

There was a knock at the door, and the native clerk announced that the Prison Commissioner was waiting. Mr. Frith jerked himself back into efficiency again.

"Well, get something drafted, and let me see it," he said. "Remember it's high level. Don't refer to accommodation."

It was about Old Moses that the Commissioner had come.

"Not a word from him, so far," he said. "Evidently made his mind up. Isn't going to speak."

"Any good trying to get him to sign something?" Mr. Frith suggested.

The Commissioner shook his head.

"Can't read," he said simply.

"Well, what do you want me to do?" Mr. Frith demanded. "I can't make him talk."

"Only make sure there isn't any postponement," the Commissioner told him. "That's all. He should just about be able to make it on the third. After that, I wouldn't like to say."

"How's he eating?"

The Commissioner shook his head again. He was a heavy, loosely built man, and every time he denied anything his cheeks wobbled.

"Nothing at all," he said. "Hasn't eaten a proper meal since we had him."

"Still drinking his milk?"

"Two or three cups a day. Doesn't seem to mind that."

Mr. Frith half-turned away and fixed his eyes on the top of the spire again. Just when the Commissioner thought that it was the end of the conversation, Mr. Frith's good idea came to him.

"Don't forget," he said, "he's been up at the Residency for years. Probably doesn't eat native food any longer. Give him what he's got used to."

The cheeks wobbled again.

"Tried it," the Commissioner replied. "Simply pushes it away from him."

"What's the doctor say?"

"Wants us to keep on with the pills. Vitamins, you know. Six a day. They're crushed up and put into the milk before he gets it."

This time it really was the end of the conversation. Mr. Frith got up out of his chair.

"Well, if there's any change, let me know," he said. Remembering Mr. Talefwa, he paused. "I don't want anything to happen to him."

The rest of Mr. Frith's appointments were as routine, and all as frustrating. The Chief of Police wanted to raid the offices of *War Drum* because a secret informer, who turned out to be Mr. Ngono, had secured an advance proof of tomorrow's leader, which openly accused the Police Department of corruption. The Government granary at Omtala had accidentally been burnt to the ground. Somewhere down to the south, raiders had driven off three hundred head of cattle, and there were rumors of blazing villages and murdered herdsmen. Cholera cases were increasing around Aktu Junction. And overnight, one of the ornamental lampposts had been impudently stolen from Victoria Square.

When twelve o'clock came round, Mr. Frith remembered that he had not seen the draft reply to the telegram. He merely nodded when Harold gave it to him and instinctively picked up his pen to make the necessary alterations. After crossing out the last sentence, he brooded over it for a moment and then wrote it in again, inking over the letters to make them stand out properly.

"Well, better get it off," he said. "Nothing we can do about it."

He had finished his morning's work and went over and unlocked the liquor cabinet.

"Care to join me?" he asked.

Harold saw his opportunity.

"What's he like, the new Governor?" he asked.

Glass in hand, Mr. Frith felt better. He was now quite prepared to talk about it; earlier, he wouldn't have been ready to face up to the subject at all.

"He's forty-eight, that's what he's like," he said. "Just the right age for top promotion. Twelve full years of being H.E. before the pension."

He paused.

"And he'll get my knighthood," he added, bitterly. "Bound to. It's a full Governorship."

Mr. Frith broke off and went across to the liquor cabinet for the other half of the drink that had just revived him.

"You said last night something about Sir Gardnor wanting to get me replaced. Did he tell you why, sir?"

Mr. Frith paused with the glass halfway up to his lips.

"Gathered it was something personal," he replied. "Said you'd understand."

Chapter 34

THERE IT WAS—Lady Anne's Morris Cowley—parked outside the European Drug Emporium.

Harold walked over and waited. A moment later, Sybil Prosser came out. She looked hot and bad-tempered. She was carrying a paper parcel that had come undone already, and she was scattering things—tooth paste, facecloths, nail polish.

He picked up the bits, and Sybil Prosser forgot to say thank you. Instead, she stood there staring hard at his eye patch.

"How much longer are you going to wear that thing?" she asked. "It can't be good for it."

"It's just that it goes misty if I take it off," Harold replied.

He half-turned away as he was speaking so that only his good eye was facing her.

By now Sybil Prosser had dumped her parcel down on the passenger seat of the Morris. That meant that her hands were free.

"Here, let me see," she said to him. "You can't afford to take chances. Not with eyes you can't."

Always abrupt in her movements, she was aggressively quick and jerky. Taking hold of Harold by the shoulders, she turned him sharply round and lifted up the eye patch. But even that did not satisfy her, because he was in the shadow of the shop front. With a tug, she pulled him out farther onto the pavement, where the light was better. A moment later, she let go of the shade, and the elastic headband brought the celluloid flap down smartly on his cheekbone.

"*Looks* all right," she said. "A bit watery. But it would be, covered up like that. You ought to see a specialist."

"I shall as soon as the trial's over."

Sybil Prosser had her head on one side, regarding him.

"And when will that be?" she asked.

"That's what I was going to talk about," he told her. "How is she?"

"Just the same." She paused. "I wouldn't say any better."

"Can I see her?"

It was significant that Sybil Prosser's permission had to be asked: up at the Residency, Sybil Prosser was now in sole command.

"It didn't do much good last time, did it?" she asked.

"That wasn't my fault. She just began remembering things."

Sybil Prosser slapped hard at a fly that had landed on her forearm.

"I didn't say it was your fault," she replied. "It's only that I don't want her going on being reminded."

It was crowded out there, on the pavement in front of the Drug Emporium. People were passing by the whole time, and they had to move over almost into the roadway to avoid being run down by a barrow loaded with live chickens, tied together by their legs, that were being delivered to the general store next door.

"Isn't there somewhere else we can go and talk?" Harold asked.

Sybil Prosser already had her hand on the door of the Morris.

"What about?"

"About Anne."

"I've told you. I want her left alone."

Sybil Prosser was at her worst, Harold decided.

"I don't want to do anything to upset her," he began to explain. "I just want to see her. It seems so rotten somehow, shut away up there."

"She isn't shut away."

"Well, not seeing anyone, I mean."

"She sees me, doesn't she?"

It was not Sybil Prosser who broke off the conversation. It was Harold. His eye was hurting him. Lifting up the eye patch in all that sunlight hadn't done it any good, and it was watering freely by now. He could feel the tears trickling down underneath the celluloid as he stood there.

It was only with his good eye that he could see Sybil Prosser. Her chin was tilted up on her long neck, and the corners of her mouth were drawn down into a pattern of wrinkles that he hadn't noticed before.

His eye gave one of its sudden jabs.

"Oh go to hell," he said, under his breath; and turning his back on her, he walked straight past her into the European Drug Emporium trying to think of what he could buy.

Mr. Talefwa's Fighting Fund, "Save a Brother," had, so the paper announced, already assumed "epic and gigantic proportions." Promises of international aid were, it said, "pouring in by telegraph and other means," unspecified, "from Calcutta, Hong Kong, Moscow, Philadelphia U.S.A., London England, Freetown, Jamaica, Boston Mass.," and "other centers of Imperial oppression of colored workers." A perfectly genuine ten-shilling postal order had, moreover, appeared from nowhere in the *War Drum's* G.P.O. mailbox and been promptly cashed at the adjoining counter.

What was even more important was that Mr. Talefwa had a new recruit—Mr. Ngono. And it was all because, between them, Harold and Mr. Frith had failed entirely to do anything.

After that stroll on the lawn beside Harold's bungalow, Mr. Ngono had come away thoroughly heartened and fairly burning with loyalty. He had simply been waiting for the moment when the raiding party would descend on the *War Drum's* offices. In his mind's eye, he had already seen it all—Mr. Talefwa being led off in handcuffs; police vans outside laden with seditious matter; and in the lean-to shed at the rear, strong men with crowbars smashing up the printing press itself.

Whereas, in point of fact, absolutely nothing had happened. He had not been called for jury service, and no one had even inquired to see if he was likely to be free.

As a result, Mr. Ngono felt lonely and rejected; even humiliated. In a flash he realized how wrong he had been to join the wrong camp, to pretend that he was what he wasn't. Despite his College tie and his handmade shoes and his Indian motorcycle, he was still an African: his future lay with other Africans.

And he went straight round to tell Mr. Talefwa so.

"You are only too entirely right," Mr. Ngono confided. "Every one of your accusations will be bloody well self-justified. And your suspicions, too."

His arm was on the back of Mr. Talefwa's chair—his editorial chair—as he was speaking.

"Then I shall put your name at the top of the column of subscribers to 'Save a Brother,' " Mr. Talefwa promised him, "and you can pay me afterwards."

Mr. Ngono removed his arm, and came round to the front of the desk.

"For purely commercial reasons associated with certain important European contracts in the offing it would be impossible for my close identity with the Fund to be immediately revealed," he explained. "But behind the scenes and under cover, like hell absolutely."

A happy thought came into Mr. Ngono's mind, and he broke into the most dazzling of his smiles.

"I will even," he said, "contribute most generously in big money, but anonymously, of course. You may, in fact, have the complete and confidential list of all bad debts from my various business enterprises, both retail and wholesale. If they do not settle up immediately, right on the bloody nail in fact, you can threaten to publish their names as people who should be made bankrupt or otherwise suitably disgraced in public. That, and other strong-arm methods, should produce a veritable small avalanche."

Mr. Talefwa remained dubious.

"And you are prepared to swear that you saw Mr. Stebbs and Lady Anne alone together in their motor car near the railway siding after midnight?" he asked.

Mr. Ngono responded enthusiastically.

"Beyond all confusion of doubt," he said. "I could, with my eyes shut, repeat the whole damn conversation *ad lib* and *verbatim*. I recall most distinctly wishing them both a most happy safari and a big killing. My very words to the last letter. Ironically prophetic, too, did they not prove?"

But Mr. Talefwa was not interested in irony.

"And were there other occasions?" he asked.

Mr. Ngono gripped the front of the desk to steady himself.

"You can take it from me, bloody well yes," he replied. "Enough to fill a bookful. Quite continuous in fact, and all entirely shameless."

"And you saw these things yourself?" Mr. Talefwa persisted.

Mr. Ngono covered his eyes with his hand for a moment.

"Not always personally and at immediately first hand, of course," he replied. "Not with my other business affairs pressing down on me. But my informants are all exceedingly trustworthy and reliable persons."

Mr. Talefwa was, by nature, disinclined to believe in either trustworthiness or reliability.

"Who are they?" he asked.

"The houseboys at the bungalow," Mr. Ngono told him. "Our own people. Why should they lie to me? Day-and-night watch, in fact. And rewarded for their revelations. Small payments for petty incidents and larger emoluments for more startling disclosures."

"And could you get the houseboys to come forward?"

Mr. Ngono shook his head and spread his hands wide open.

"I would not for a king's ransom recommend any such course of action," he said. "After all, who are they? Simply ignorant, uneducated peasants of the most humble kind. Such liars, too, both of them. I should feel highly uncomfortable the whole time they were in the witness box. How could we ever be sure that someone else had not bribed them?"

Mr. Talefwa was silent: he was thinking. Then he glanced up.

"Are there any letters?" he asked.

Mr. Ngono spread his hand, palms outwards, toward Mr. Talefwa to show how empty they were.

"It is known, though, that he frequently wrote to her, and received her most eager replies," he answered. "But the waste-paper baskets, combed through backwards and forwards with extreme care, were always most disappointing."

"A pity," was all that Mr. Talefwa said.

He looked Mr. Ngono full in the face.

"And you will be ready to tell everything you know to our Counsel when he is decided upon?" he asked. "In Court, you will be on oath, remember."

"With the utmost delight and the most extreme eagerness," Mr. Ngono replied. "As for the oath, it does not in any way worry me. I am entirely unsuperstitious. It is my European education, you understand."

Mr. Talefwa understood perfectly.

"And now if you will excuse me," he said, "it is time for me to close the office. I would be obliged if you would leave some minutes before me. For the time being it would be unwise for us to be seen together in public places. In our separate ways we are both marked men already. After the trial begins, it will be even more so."

Chapter 35

It was more than three days now since Harold had met Sybil Prosser outside the Drug Emporium, and during the whole of that time there had been complete silence from the Residency. Mr. Frith had, in fact, made a mental note to send someone round to see how the A.D.C. was getting on.

Then Sybil Prosser phoned.

"How's your eye?" she started straight in. "Got that thing off yet?"

He began to tell her. But it was too late: Sybil Prosser was already speaking again.

"I don't know what you're doing," she said. "But if you'd like to come over, you can see her now. It's the best time."

"But how is she?" Harold asked. "Is she better?"

"Judge for yourself," Sybil Prosser told him. "I've said you can see her."

"You mean straightaway?" he asked.

But he was too late: Sybil Prosser had already rung off.

The streets outside were deserted: it was still too early, and too hot, for strollers. And there was a strange empty look to the drive as he turned into the Residency grounds. With no flag flying from the masthead, a deep hush seemed to have descended on everything. The crunch of boots on gravel as the pair of sentries stamped themselves, Guards' fashion, to attention seemed like an echo left over from Sir Gardnor's day.

At the house, Dr. Fernandez was just leaving. Coming down the wide staircase, he looked more squat and toadlike than ever. He sagged from side to side on each step as he descended. At the sight of Harold he stopped and remained on the bottom step, his pleated shirt front quivering.

"When the visitors start arriving," he said, speaking slowly as though reciting some well-known Portuguese proverb, "then the doctor knows it is time for him to pack his bag."

"Then she really is better?"

Dr. Fernandez tapped the side of his nose with his forefinger.

"As I said," he told him. "Widow's Madness. It is all over. There are no complications. I speak with authority. I am a specialist in women."

The forefinger was raised for a moment admonishingly, and then the tapping started up again.

"But no excitement, please. No arguments. Just love-making. And to agree with everything she says. Then you will find how reasonable she is. How calm. Otherwise . . ."

He spread his hands as he said it to indicate that, even with his unique specialist's knowledge of the sex, there were still some extreme conditions that he could not yet control.

When Harold reached the west wing, it was Sybil Prosser who opened the door of Lady Anne's apartment; and it might have been her own front door from the way she stood there. There was no sign of any staff; not even the familiar figures of the nurses. Sybil Prosser herself was wearing one of their white coveralls. It was too short for her and left the whole length of her thin wrists showing.

"You're early," she said. "We didn't expect you yet. She's not ready for you."

She stood deliberately blocking the doorway.

"Don't be a pig, Sybil. Let him in at once. Of course I'm ready."

The voice was Lady Anne's. Sybil Prosser drew the corners of her mouth down and shrugged her shoulders.

"As you please," she said.

It was not into the bedroom that she led Harold, but into the white, countryish-looking sitting room into which Lady Anne had first invited him. An easy chair had been drawn over to the window, and Lady Anne was sitting back in it, her legs stretched out on the cretonne-covered footstool in front of her.

"I can't get up," she said. "I still go all shaky. But you can see how much better I am, can't you?"

She turned herself toward him as she was speaking. It was like the action of a child. She was waiting to be congratulated.

"Better. But not well," Sybil Prosser reminded her.

"I think you look marvelous," Harold told her.

Lady Anne was pleased. She nodded.

"Don't take any notice of Sybil," she said. "She's been perfectly horrible all day. I don't know what's the matter with her. I think she's jealous, or something."

"Jealous of him?" Sybil Prosser suddenly stuck her chin out on the end of that ridiculous long neck of hers. "Why should I be?"

"I don't know," Lady Anne replied. "But first you wouldn't phone him, and the way you didn't want to let him come in. It's obvious."

She turned to Harold again.

"But we mustn't be nasty to her," she said. "She's been wonderful. An absolute angel. I wouldn't be alive now if it hadn't been for her."

She looked over to where Sybil Prosser was standing.

"Well, I wouldn't, would I?" she asked. "You told me yourself I wouldn't."

Sybil Prosser ignored the remark and turned to Harold.

"I'm going to have a drink," she said. "D'you want one?"

"What about me?" Lady Anne tapped on the arm of her chair as she said it.

But Sybil Prosser continued to ignore her.

"It's no use," she said. "She's only allowed wine, and she won't drink that. So what can you do about her?"

"Wine's silly between meals," Lady Anne said. "And you can't drink it at tea time. It's dipso."

Sybil Prosser went over to the side table where the bottles were, and Lady Anne sat staring out the window.

"I did think everything was going to be so nice here today," she said. "Just the three of us. That's why I had everyone else sent away. I wanted it to be just like old times."

The hiss of the soda-water syphon stopped suddenly.

"It can't be," Sybil Prosser said. "Not after what happened."

She came over and sat down on the only high chair in the room. She had her drink in her right hand. It was her left hand that she didn't know what to do with. In the end, she let it simply hang down. No color came into it, but the veins began to swell.

"Tell him what we agreed," she said.

Lady Anne looked up for a moment.

"Oh for God's sake, take that awful apron thing off, can't you?" she asked. "It makes you look like a cook or something."

Sybil Prosser did not move.

"Go on," she told her.

"Which bit?"

"Everything."

Lady Anne did not look at anyone while she was speaking. She kept her eyes down on the pattern of faded red roses and pale green leaves on the cretonne cover.

"You see, I didn't really know what was happening," she began. "Nobody told me anything. The doctor wouldn't let them. I didn't even know about the new Governor."

She was speaking very slowly and carefully, almost as though she had learned it all by heart and was trying to remember.

"What difference does that make?" Harold asked.

"Oh, I can't possibly stay here," Lady Anne told him. "Not after he arrives. It just wouldn't be right." She paused. "Gardie wouldn't have wanted it," she added.

"Then what are you going to do?"

"Move into Crown Cottage," Lady Anne replied. "It's quite big enough just for the two of us."

Harold got up and poured himself the drink that Sybil Prosser had not given him.

"You don't have to bother," he said. "Mr. Frith says he'll move in there."

"Oh, no he won't. That's where we're going. We're decided." It was Sybil Prosser who had spoken. The corners of her mouth came sharply down as she said it. "After what she's been through, she's entitled to *some* consideration," she added.

Lady Anne interrupted her.

"It'll be just right for the trial," she explained. "The Courthouse is so near. And it isn't long now. When d'you say it is, Sybil?"

"On the third. Four weeks exactly."

"And you mean you're going to *be* there?" Harold asked. "D'you think you'll be strong enough?"

"I shall be by then," Lady Anne told him. "I'm getting so much better every day: Sybil says so. And in any case, I've got to go. I can't bear to think of Old Moses being kept there in prison until I feel well enough. It's just not fair to him."

"Does Mr. Frith know?"

"Mr. Frith doesn't know anything. Not about the trial or about Crown Cottage. Nobody knows. You're the first person we've told."

"We thought you'd like it better that way," Sybil Prosser observed from somewhere behind him.

Lady Anne gave a little sigh.

"I feel so terrible about Old Moses."

"After what he did?"

She shrugged her shoulders.

"He must have been mad at the time. That's obvious. They do go mad quite often, these natives, you know. Gardie used to say it was witchcraft. It must have been something, because Old Moses never used to be like that. He simply adored Gardie."

She broke off and began staring down at the cretonne roses again.

"They won't hang him, will they?" she asked.

Sybil Prosser got up to put her glass down.

"How can Harold possibly know what they'll do?" she asked. "It's not his business. Or ours, for that matter."

Chapter 36

In addition to his editorials, Mr. Talefwa had his "Save a Brother" campaign to run.

Right from the first moment when he sensed how sensational the trial was likely to be, he had set his heart on getting someone to come out from England. During his stay there, Mr. Talefwa had spent quite a lot of his time hanging round the Law Courts, and he had come away with a deep respect for English justice—its politeness, its decorum, the high damages that were sometimes awarded against even quite important companies; but above all, for the way in which the obviously guilty got off just as often as the innocent. Mr. Talefwa would have gone for an English King's Counsel every time.

There was certainly no one at the Amimbo bar: they were all too frightened, and ordinary. Besides, the significance of the fact that *War Drum* had been forced to look outside for its champion would not be lost on the people. But where to find him? There was Nigeria, of course. People were always going to law in Nigeria. But Mr. Talefwa didn't like Nigerians; he would have felt ashamed to turn to Nigeria when it was Amimbo itself that was in trouble. Or Uganda. They were altogether nicer people in Uganda, more advanced in every way and well on their own road to independence some day. But was it likely that one of their acknowledged leaders from Entebbe would be ready to risk his own career in a great free Uganda for the sake of an eighty-year-old murderer, with no tribal connections, in a little tucked-away place like Amimbo?

It looked, therefore, as though it would have to be Mr. Chabandra Das, from the Gold Coast. His record was distinctly promising: he was young, he was a fighter, and he was as Europeanized as Mr. Talefwa himself. The only trouble was that Mr. Talefwa didn't like Indians, really. They came into Africa with their superior education and a credit account at one of the Asian banks, and before you knew what was happening they were running the place.

Mr. Talefwa decided, however, to put racial prejudice to one side and invite him. He was even now writing out the telegram. Not that he liked telegrams. Too many other eyes always saw them. And for the moment, it was essential that he give nothing away.

He therefore drafted it in terms that even the most inquisitive would find baffling: REQUEST YOUR ADVICE GRAVE LEGAL DIFFI-CULTIES IMPORTANT MATTER STOP PERSONAL ATTENDANCE AMIMBO ESSENTIAL STOP SEAT BOOKED YOUR NAME CORONATION FLYER

SEVENTEENTH INSTANT STOP PAYMENT GUARANTEED STOP PLEASE CONFIRM PREPAID.

The fact that he signed it NGONO made everything quite safe. Mr. Ngono was always engaged in important matters, and he loved sending telegrams. No one in G.P.O., Amimbo, would be in the least surprised to learn that in the course of one of them he had run into grave legal difficulties.

Mr. Talefwa even took the precaution of sending the form round to the Post Office by one of Amimbo's entirely nondescript messengers. There were plenty of them, these private-enterprise common carriers. They sat about on the pavements all day, waiting for someone to hire them to take something somewhere to someone else. The messenger that Mr. Talefwa chose quite often ran errands for Mr. Ngono. Because he was quite illiterate, the discrepancy of the signature could hardly bother him; and because the Post Office building was exactly opposite, Mr. Talefwa from his front window could keep an eye on the messenger, and the money, all the way.

Even then, however, Mr. Talefwa could not afford to relax. He had other inquiries to make; and because they were confidential, he preferred to make them himself.

It was Sunday, and the booking clerk was wearing his best shirt. White like the others, this one had small, shiny stars woven into it. It had come from far off—all the way from Hong Kong, in fact—and the booking clerk was very proud of it.

He was almost asleep, gazing out across the empty platform onto the deserted track, when Mr. Talefwa arrived. And naturally, he was pleased to see him. Mr. Talefwa was a much pointed-out figure; a person of some importance—though dangerous and not to be seen with out of office hours, of course. The booking clerk assumed that things in Amimbo had temporarily got too hot for him and that he was intent on getting out of the place.

Mr. Talefwa's request for a booking *to* Amimbo therefore floored him. Not only did it shatter his theory about Mr. Talefwa's use of the railway as an escape route, but he didn't know how to issue such a ticket. In all his six years' experience, he had done nothing but issue outgoing tickets—all three classes, half-price for children, special excursion rates; returns many of them, but always *leaving* Amimbo in the first instance.

The last thing the booking clerk wanted was to give Mr. Talefwa the impression that he was foolish and ignorant and then, when the whole incident was over, find a funny paragraph about him appearing in the *War Drum*'s influential gossip columns.

He therefore went into the operation professionally, as he had seen busy clerks do in banks and post offices and other places where people wait. He did a lot of writing down on pads and tearing out of carbon counterfoils, vigorously stamping things with the Company's stamp as he went along. Caught up in the excitement of it all, he began improvising. He invented fresh routines, new procedures. He wrote out the name of the railway company every time in full. He initialed the counterfoils. He wetly inserted the date in red.

Mr. Talefwa leaned amiably on the little counter in front of the grille.

"And are there already great preparations in hand for the reception of our new Governor?" he asked.

The booking clerk thrust his green eye shade up onto his forehead; he relaxed.

"The area in which you are now standing," he said, "will be completely roped off. The Station Master has been told so. It will become official. Also, the center of the platform from the parcels office to the lavatories. Even the main exit will be closed. Ordinary passengers arriving by the same train will have to cross the tracks and make their way out through the freight yard."

"Altogether quite an occasion," Mr. Talefwa remarked.

"But still inconvenient and undignified," the booking clerk observed, because it was the kind of anti-Establishment remark that he thought Mr. Talefwa would find pleasing. "For those not holding Government passes it will be quite a scramble."

Mr. Talefwa merely shrugged his shoulders.

"New Governors do not arrive three hundred and sixty-five days in the year," he remarked. "I take it that Number Two Platform will remain open?"

The booking clerk marveled at Mr. Talefwa's self-control, his moderation.

"That is reserved for friends of the Station Master's wife," he said. "It is not official, but still strictly private. And only the top end of the platform, of course. Further down would be useless, because the train itself would be in the way. Our new Governor would be entirely obscured."

Mr. Talefwa gathered up the inky duplicates that the booking clerk had thrust through to him.

"You have been most helpful," he said. "Let us only hope for the reputation of Amimbo that everything goes off according to plan."

Mr. Das's reply was immediate. He liked railway journeys, and he saw a bright new future opening up ahead of him as he zigzagged across the Continent at other people's expense giving urgent professional advice to unknown businessmen in grave legal difficulties. Alone in his bed-sitter in Accra he spent long, useless hours wondering who on earth could possibly have recommended him.

And Mr. Ngono, for his part, was equally puzzled. Out of the blue, from someone he had never heard of, he had received an overnight telegram which read: HAPPY TO BE OF GOOD ADVICE STOP ADMIT NOTHING STOP ENDEAVOUR RECOVER ALL DOCUMENTS BEARING YOUR SIGNATURE STOP MAKE NO FURTHER PAYMENTS STOP DO NOT RETURN GOODS ALREADY IN YOUR POSSESSION STOP LOOK FORWARD MEETING YOU PERSONALLY STOP DAS.

The advice certainly seemed sound enough: but Mr. Ngono could not for the life of him imagine why this mysterious stranger should suddenly have taken his interests so closely to heart.

When Mr. Talefwa explained it all, Mr. Ngono was first very angry, then distinctly flattered. He was also secretly rather pleased. There were, as it happened, several little matters which, on the side, he would be delighted to discuss with any lawyer who showed such a sound grasp of legal principles.

"Then it is quite clearly understood that I shall be the one who steps forward personally to meet the eminent Mr. Das when he arrives at our terminus?" Mr. Ngono inquired. "No bloody jostling from behind, I mean, to get in the first big handshake."

"No one is going to greet Mr. Das personally," Mr. Talefwa replied. "As he steps down onto the platform, there will be a stampede. It will be seen by the amazed authorities merely as a great rush of bodies, a human avalanche that is quite irresistible. I shall, of course, arrange to have my staff photographer present."

The possibility of a photographer as well only made Mr. Ngono even more unhappy.

"And even with my name on the telegram—a damn illegal forgery, by the way, carrying extremely enormous damages if I should choose to complain—I am still not to appear with special prominence anywhere in the whole picture?" he demanded.

"It would be most unjudicious," Mr. Talefwa told him. "The police would immediately become suspicious."

He took Mr. Ngono's hand while he was speaking and pressed it hard.

"Remember that you are to be the surprise witness," he reminded him, "the key figure in the whole trial. Who else is there on whom we could rely for your scandalous revelations?"

Mr. Ngono withdrew his hand and sat there, head bowed, looking downwards. He was sulking.

"Considering the occasion, and the exceptionally large number of keenly interested spectators, it is still a most keen anguish," he said at last. "People not knowing the truth will look at me and say: 'There is that idle, sight-seeing Mr. Ngono again, come here merely for the spectacle. He is no different in importance from all the rest of us.' "

This time, Mr. Talefwa put his arm right round Mr. Ngono's shoulder.

"That is what people may say at the time," he replied. "But what will they be saying later when all the facts come out into the open? Then those same people will point to you and say: 'There goes the clever Mr. Ngono, the deep one, the man who knew everything and said nothing until the right moment!' "

Mr. Talefwa paused.

"It will even be as 'Mr. Ngono, the truth teller' that I shall refer to you in all editorial articles," he added.

Mr. Ngono was silent for so long that Mr. Talefwa became worried. He began to wonder what new arguments he could use.

"I have not yet told you," he said, "that I have booked the ticket for Mr. Das to arrive on the same train as the new Governor. I shall give both items equal space in my newspaper."

But Mr. Ngono interrupted him. He had jumped up and was smiling again.

"I have," he said, "already most fundamentally improved upon the whole idea. In my new plan, everyone on the platform will carry an extremely large banner. The banners will say 'Welcome' and 'Amimbo greets you,' and 'Happy stay among us'—that kind of thing. The official party will think the banners are in honor of the new Governor and will allow us to approach very closely, quite intimately, in fact. But in plain truth the banners will bloody well be for Mr. Das."

Mr. Talefwa held out his hand.

"It shall be so," he said.

"But the banners?" Mr. Ngono asked. "Is not that a damn marvelous idea?"

"Brilliant," Mr. Talefwa replied. "Absolutely brilliant."

Having been paid his compliment, Mr. Ngono was prepared to shrug it off.

"It is nothing," he said. "Simply the extremely remarkable quickness of my mind. Improvements occur to me with the utmost frequency. It is a sort of knack."

Chapter 37

PURELY THROUGH the exchange of telegrams, Mr. Frith felt that he was getting to know the character of the new Governor pretty well. And it was obvious that Amimbo was in for something of a change.

The keynote of the messages was restraint. Because of the impending trial, ceremony was to be cut down to a minimum, they said. The Regimental Band was out; and the Reception Party at the Residency was to be postponed indefinitely. Reading between the lines, Mr. Frith formed the impression that Mr. Anthony Drawbridge, C.B.E., late of Kuala Lumpur, would probably have preferred things that way even if there had been no crisis.

It was easier, however, for Whitehall to advocate restraint than it was for the Superintendent of Police in Amimbo to enforce it.

The Coronation Flyer, with Mr. Drawbridge on board, was due to pull into the terminus at eight-fifteen P.M.; and by six o'clock, the scale of the demonstration had already become alarming. At the sight of organized groups of people, all chattering excitedly and carrying long bamboo poles with slogans wrapped round them, the Superintendent began to wish that he had ignored the order to keep things normal and had called for the usual riot barriers to be erected.

As a last-minute precaution, therefore, and acting solely upon his own initiative, he closed the station approach and instructed the Station Master to keep the main door shut.

Meanwhile, the Station Master's wife's party at the top of Platform Two had been getting nicely under way. The Station Master had got two of the porters to place the family settee and two easy chairs up alongside the ticket collector's booth; a trestle table with cakes and tea and iced drinks had been arranged conveniently in the middle; and around a large crate marked PERISHABLE IMMEDIATE the Station Master's wife and three of her friends were now seated.

Their numerous children, all in their best clothes and heartily fed up with waiting, were either swarming over the coal bunkers or sitting disconsolately on the switches, casting dice among the railway ties.

And all the time, through the marshaling yards, the demonstrators with their banners had been pouring in. What at seven-fifteen had been no more than a desultory sprinkling had by seven-thirty become a host. The bottom end of Platform Two was packed solid, and as the latecomers arrived, those in front were irresistibly thrust forward onto the track.

In the melee, some of the poles became entangled; some snapped; and those of the banners left with only one support had to be waved aloft like flags.

By seven forty-five, the suspense was becoming intolerable. The Station Master had removed the crate and asked for the switches to be cleared. His wife's friends and their children were arranged in a prim double row as though they were having their photograph taken, and the Station Master himself had moved over to the reception side.

When Mr. Frith arrived at ten minutes to eight just to make sure that everything was in order, he was hysterically and tumultuously cheered.

He had, in point of fact, only just been able to get there at all. That was because the Superintendent—preoccupied by his immediate problem of cordoning off the station—had omitted to tell Mr. Frith's chauffeur. In consequence, the poor man found himself confronted by a palisade of park benches and litter bins placed across the roadway, and when he had cleared a channel for the car, he was astonished to find the waiting room and ticket office, where the reception party was to assemble, barred and bolted against him.

The next moment of excitement came precisely at eight o'clock when the Station Master, looking vaguely apprehensive, walked down the platform to the Signal Box. The crowd all turned to watch. They saw the Station Master mount the steps, enter the little glass box, and go into close conference with the signalman.

A moment later, both men came out onto the observation platform and, shading their eyes with their hands, stood there staring out along the single track that dwindled away into the distance.

So far, the reason for the inspection was a secret shared only between the two of them. But the Station Master did not see how it could remain so for much longer. The plain truth was that they had lost the train. And what was worse, they had no means of finding it.

When everything was working smoothly, three pings on the electric telegraph in the signal box indicated that Amimbo-bound rolling stock had just passed Ketebebe inspection point and was in the twenty-five-mile home stretch. The gradient was gentle and downhill all the way, and forty to forty-five minutes was usually all that was needed for the train to complete the journey.

This evening, however, there had been no pings. Either the train had not yet reached Ketebebe, or the duty officer had forgotten to report it. The Station Master—by now to the shouts of encouragement of the spectators—hurried back to his own office. Afraid that it might be taken as somehow reflecting on his own efficiency, he did not immediately break the news to Mr. Frith. He simply sat, helplessly staring at his watch, wondering how long it would take to get steam up on the shunting engine so that he could go out in search of the missing express.

On the platform opposite, Mr. Ngono was going round to make sure that everyone understood the night's battle orders.

"First, you will raise your banners above your heads, all shouting out most loudly 'Welcome' or 'God bless' or simply 'Hurrah.' That will be as the train draws in. Then I will fire my starting pistol, which gives off an extremely loud report. That will be after the train has stopped. At the signal, you will immediately rush pell-mell onto the platform, still calling out your greetings in shrill voices, and tear past the Governor, not even pausing to glance once in his unimportant direction. It is Mr. Das who is the hero, remember, not this new man."

Mr. Ngono paused because he was breathless.

"And have no unwholesome fears whatsoever about the consequences," he added. "Throughout the whole stampede from start to finish, I shall be standing right at the very back directing everything. Like a good general in his headquarters I shall be there, leading you from behind."

While Mr. Ngono was still addressing his supporters, the Coronation Flyer, in a cocoon of escaping steam, was standing motionless, six miles on the other side of Ketebebe.

Although it had kept close to schedule all the way from Nucca, the extra weight of the Governor's coach had at last proved too much for it. With a noise like a bomb explosion, six feet of copper tubing had suddenly burst open, sending nuts, bolts, splinters, and rivets flying off into the gloom of the surrounding jungle.

Heads were now thrust out of every carriage window, and the guard was going down the entire length of the train patiently explaining that it was nothing. No one, of course, believed him, but it was nice all the same to find someone who behaved as if he cared.

And the guard did more than merely reassure. He brought the whole of the Company's emergency drill into operation. This meant climbing the nearest telegraph pole so that he could tap the wires. The passengers watched fascinated as the guard—a large, brightly uniformed man—re-emerged on the track carrying crampons, lengths of wire, a canvas seat belt to support his weight once he was up there, insulators, pliers, bulldog clips and a hand telephone complete with earphones.

And as the guard mounted slowly, inserting his footholds one by one before him as he went, the passengers gazed admiringly. Somewhere above them, invisible in all that steam, were the wires. It was like being spectators at the Indian rope trick, seeing their companion disappearing into the darkness above.

Nor, in the ordinary way, would there have been any special cause for anxiety. The guard had, many times, done it all before: indeed, he rather enjoyed the moment when at last the distant voice answered and, having got his breath back, he was able to begin his rigmarole with the words: "Guard Boku, Number Thirty-seven, here. I have the honor to report a breakdown at . . ."

But on this occasion it was different.

The telegraph pole was already slanting inwards slightly, like a palm tree bending over a lagoon. Also, despite the creosote, the white ants had been at work upon it; they had fed, penetrated, and feasted there: a six-inch cavity on the far side might have been carved out of a bath sponge. Also, since his recent promotion, the guard had been putting on weight; he was appreciably heavier than at the time of his last ascent, and not so nimble.

At first, everything in the exercise went well. The pole sagged a little as he mounted it, but as he was suitably slow and cautious, there seemed no cause for alarm. It was not, indeed, until, still buttoned up in his railway uniform, he had reached the very summit that he was conscious of how far the pole was already tilting over. It was like the escape ladder on a fire engine. And as he thrust out his hand to grasp the wire, his center of gravity shifted. The pole could stand no more of him. With a wrenching sound like that of cloth tearing, it snapped off about three feet from the ground. That was when the equipment failed in the signal box and Ketebebe was cut off from the Amimbo Terminus.

Now, nearly three hours later, things were looking brighter. The guard had been recovered from the bushes on the far side, dusted down, consoled and made comfortable on a mattress of mailbags and the softer kind of parcels piled up in a corner of his van. The engine driver had hammered down and sealed off the steam pipe connected to the starboard cylinder, and his fireman was now stoking up the engine again to see if anything else had been shattered in the explosion.

At twelve-fifteen A.M., the Coronation Flyer got moving on one cylinder, and feebly assisted by its own traction power, it freewheeled into Amimbo.

By then the platforms were deserted. The Station Master's wife's party had broken up early because of the children; and by midnight the last of Mr. Ngono's supporters had thrown down their banners and gone away in search of what bars and night spots might still be open.

Mr. Drawbridge, grateful for the extra hours of sleep on the train, arrived thoroughly fresh and rested. He apologized to Mr. Frith for having kept him waiting and added that it was all just the way he had hoped it would be—no fuss, no formality, no native demonstrations, nothing.

He got straight into the Governor's car and was driven off to the Residency.

Only Mr. Talefwa remained behind to welcome Mr. Das. The two of them looked sadly isolated standing there in the lamplight at the end of the already empty platform. Mr. Talefwa presented the naturally disheveled appearance of any man who has been taking his night's rest in twenty-minute snatches on a single plank bench with the initials of the railway company carved into it.

Nor was Mr. Das looking his best. Only on arrival at Nucca had he discovered that his reservation was third class, and he had traveled through two nights with eight other people and a live chicken in the same compartment. Mr. Das's own luggage was simple. It consisted merely of a wicker holdall, tied round with string, and a pair of shiny, new-looking shoes that he was carrying under his left arm.

By then it was three o'clock in the morning. The city was entirely still. With dawn just upon them, even the owls had ceased their hooting, and the police had all gone to bed.

Suddenly there was a loud report, a bang that brought faces to windows and set the local babies screaming. It was Mr. Ngono who was responsible. He had been quietly on his way home with a friend when his companion, slightly drunk, had chosen to speak disparagingly of the night's arrangements. He had even suggested that Mr. Ngono's chosen position by the exit was so far back that even if he had still been there at the time to give the word of command, no one in front could possibly have heard him.

Mr. Ngono, slightly drunk himself, was in no mood to take that kind of talk. Then and there, to show how it would have sounded if the Coronation Flyer had been even reasonably on time, he had raised his right arm and fired off his starting pistol.

Chapter 38

THERE WAS now less than a week to go before the trial, and every bit of accommodation in Amimbo was booked solid. The special correspondents, reporters, radio men, and observers were all there; and the Supervisor at the G.P.O.'s telegram counter had accepted tips, bribes, and prepayments from everyone who came to him, promising them all exclusive day-and-night priority facilities on Amimbo's solitary outgoing line.

The other line had been commandeered outright by the Government.

As for Mr. Drawbridge—though still, in Mr. Frith's eyes, distinctly on probation—he had been accepted.

An ordinary, easygoing sort of human being in many ways, he had on his second day announced that he preferred working at ground level and had told his A.D.C. to get the large desk, Sir Gardnor's desk, carried down into the east wing.

It was an unheard-of departure from practice: the desk had been up in the Library ever since the Residency had been opened. But it was immediately recognized that there was the stamp of greatness about such a decision. At all levels, people were relieved to think that at last Amimbo really had a Governor again.

Also, he had done all the right things. He had been nice to the discarded A.D.C., whom he had found hanging, ghostlike, around the Residency, and told him that he looked forward to seeing him at mealtimes. He had called on Lady Anne and Sybil Prosser at Crown Cottage, staying on for tea in the neglected garden, overlooked by the windows of the Portuguese Consulate. He had visited Old Moses in the prison hospital and arranged for a daily delivery of fresh Jersey milk from the Residency farm.

And now, with the trial right on top of them, he had just closed his final session with the law officers. The four men had moved through into the anteroom where the drinks were standing, and Mr. Drawbridge had relit his pipe.

"It's not for me to say," he told them. "It's your side of the house. Just make everything so much easier if the fellow would agree."

The Attorney General did not reply immediately. He was the one that Mr. Drawbridge had been looking at, and he was the one who, earlier, had shown himself most frankly dubious about the whole proposal. Gentlemen's agreements were delicate plants by nature, and in his experience, the atmosphere of Central Africa was usually too humid for them.

"Great mistake to let them suspect any weaknesses on our side," he said.

"Exactly," Mr. Drawbridge told him. "That's why you are the only person who could handle it. We agreed on that in there."

His pipe was not drawing properly, and he broke off to see what another match would do. When he spoke again, he kept interrupting himself as he sucked at the mouthpiece.

"It's entirely . . . up to you," he said. "Let's leave it, shall we. . . . If you should run into him . . . and the time seems ripe . . . you can touch on it. . . . Otherwise we go ahead as we are. . . . Let's see what happens."

The next morning, the Attorney General was still feeling apprehensive, but Mr. Drawbridge had got the better of him. That was why, against his better judgment, he was now on his way down from his own quiet chambers, where the fans were always turning, to the hot, airless common room where counsel read over their briefs and sent their clerks out for little cardboard cups of iced water. It was Mr. Das he was looking for.

And, as the Attorney General had feared, there he was. Sitting at the wretched little table that was all that the Courts provided, he was bent over his document like a watchmaker. He was so deeply absorbed in what he was reading that at first he did not hear the Attorney General when he addressed him.

The Attorney General addressed him a second time.

"May I introduce myself?" he asked, a trifle louder. "My name is Ramsden, David Ramsden. I'm the Attorney General."

Mr. Das looked up without speaking. It was a summons for nonpayment of something back in Lagos that he had been reading, and he was endeavoring to conceal it by spreading his out-stretched hands flat over it.

"I shall be appearing against you tomorrow," the Attorney General went on pleasantly, "so I thought it would be as well if we met first."

This time the pause was so long that the Attorney General became puzzled.

"You are Mr. Das, are you not?" he asked.

Mr. Das inclined his head ever so slightly: it was in the manner of a rather formal bow.

"Then, if you have time, perhaps we could have a few words together."

While he had been sitting there, Mr. Das had not been idle. He had been scooping round with his foot under the table trying to locate his brief case. With a sudden swift movement like a conjurer he grabbed at it, slammed it down on the table top, and thrust his other papers away safely and out of sight inside. They had reached him only that morning, redirected from Freetown, and they made rather depressing reading: they were all bills, demands, dunning letters, urgent requests for loans from close friends, bad tidings from his family in Madras, mourning notices.

He jumped up and shook hands.

"You are more than kind," he said. "It is a great honor."

Because there was a managing clerk, his arms full of ledgers and file boxes, waiting to use the same table, the Attorney General suggested that they should go outside. He had considered proposing his own office and then had thought better of it because it savored too much of intrigue. Together he and Mr. Das walked as far as the front steps. The heat there was roasting.

"Shall we talk here?" he asked. "It's more pleasant. Because of the breeze, you know."

"Wherever you say," Mr. Das replied, shading his eyes against the glare.

"And how is your client?"

Mr. Das gave his usual polite bow.

"Well, thank you," he replied.

"But off his food, I hear."

"That is so."

The Attorney General had, for a moment, caught Mr. Das's glance. The dark, heavily lidded eyes had been turned full on him. Not that he had been able to make out anything of what was going on behind them: they seemed, indeed, to be singularly uncommunicative sort of eyes.

"And there's some trouble with his speech, isn't there?"

"It is affected," Mr. Das told him.

"Not permanently, I trust."

Mr. Das gave the same little bow.

"I cannot say. I am not a doctor."

The Attorney General took out his case and offered Mr. Das a cigarette. Mr. Das declined.

"I do not smoke," he said.

It was not true: Mr. Das was a heavy smoker. He would have liked one very much. But the Attorney General had caught him at a bad moment. His best shirt was being saved up for tomorrow. The last thing that he wanted was to thrust out a badly frayed shirt cuff. If he had known that he would be seeing the Attorney General, he would have worn his other white jacket.

The Attorney General kept tapping away at his cigarette instead of lighting it.

"I've just been looking over the affidavits," he said, as though he had found himself with time on his hands and had simply been filling in the odd moments. "I see that you're pleading Not Guilty.

"That is correct."

"May be quite a long case, then."

Again there was that little bow.

"I have made myself entirely free," he replied.

"Great strain on your client, of course."

"It is inevitable."

"And at his age."

Mr. Das caught the Attorney General's eye again.

"I cannot make him any younger," he said.

"But you think he will be well enough to appear?"

Mr. Das paused.

"I must decide that tomorrow," he replied.

The Attorney General had lit his cigarette by now. He blew the smoke out slowly before speaking.

"Great strain on the jury, too," he said. "Juries don't like finding against old people. They can't bear hearing the sentence, you know. Particularly in murder cases."

Mr. Das remained silent.

"It's keeping the defendant there in court for days on end that they find so painful," the Attorney General went on. "But they still have to do their duty: that's something no jury can avoid. It always comes as a great relief to them if the plea is one of insanity. But only when the defendant is elderly, of course. Otherwise, they tend to be suspicious."

Mr. Das appeared to be pondering the point.

"Quite so," he replied.

The Attorney General glanced down at his watch.

"Well, I mustn't detain you," he said. "I'm sure you want to get back to your papers. Until tomorrow morning, then. I just wanted to make your acquaintance."

"The pleasure has been all mine," Mr. Das replied.

Chapter 39

THE QUEUE for the public gallery began forming overnight. Mr. Das had, in fact, seen the beginnings of it—the cushions, baskets of food, beer bottles, and things all spread out on the sidewalk— as he had walked back home from the courthouse.

By eight A.M. there was already a brisk market in reservations. Places near the front were changing hands around the fifteen-shilling mark; and even for seats right at the back, under the ventilator cowling, there were still buyers at half a crown and two shillings. The queue by now numbered over eighty; the capacity of the public gallery was twenty-four.

At nine forty-five, when the door was unlocked, the rush began. The two policemen stationed inside had to keep hitting out with their fly whisks so that they could count properly.

One spare place was to be left, the Chief Usher had said. But the crowd could count too, and when the doors were closed again after only twenty-three had gone through, the clamoring began. There were shouts, catcalls, hammerings on the door, kickings.

It was not until close upon the hour that the mystery of the missing seat was finally cleared up. Then—beautifully dressed and smiling, but somewhat tense and self-conscious looking—Mr. Ngono arrived and, walking very fast, went straight through the door marked COURT OFFICIALS.

It had all been arranged beforehand. The Head Usher, for a consideration, had agreed to keep vacant the last seat beside the aisle in the front row.

Because he had been called away by the Chief, his father, Mr. Ngono had not seen Mr. Das before. It was only by reputation that he knew him.

And once inside, Mr. Ngono began looking round the Court. There, right in front of him, was an Indian with a wig on. He knew at once that it must be Mr. Das. The sight thrilled him. He began thinking how impressed Mr. Das would be when—tonight, possibly—the two of them met and Mr. Das came to learn at first hand of Mr. Ngono's star-witness revelations.

It was the first time that Mr. Ngono had seen a court assemble, and he was fascinated. He had not, in fact, been so much moved by anything since Sir Gardnor's memorial service. And when the Judge, deep-wigged and in full scarlet, appeared before them, Mr. Ngono could have applauded. It was unbelievable because, in everyday life, the Chief Justice was really rather short and quite ordinary: Mr. Ngono had seen him frequently on Saturdays in open-necked shirt and khaki shorts, even going round Amimbo on a bicycle.

The swearing in of the jury was another thing that Mr. Ngono found most impressive. Indeed, he had never before watched so many important Europeans being treated so casually. There were the District Superintendent of the Railway, a retired Inspector of Native Schools, the chief cashier of one of the overseas banks, and a big cocoa man, all crammed into the jury box like steerage. And all behaving with such meekness and humility, too. When his friend, who had reserved him his seat, handed them the Bible, one by one, they seemed nervous and afraid of him.

The sense of absolute authority, enshrined somewhere inside the pageant, came as a revelation to Mr. Ngono; he found himself wishing that instead of a life of commerce he had taken up the law as his profession.

There were evidently going to be some pretty dramatic surprises, too. In answer to the simple question as to whether there was an objection to any of the jurors, Mr. Das was on his feet immediately, jack-in-the-box fashion: it was evident that it was exactly the lead for which he had been waiting.

"I object to all the jurors, m'lud," he replied.

He spoke in a soft, polite-sounding voice as though this part were the merest formality, and he was saying simply what the Chief Justice had been expecting him to say.

The Chief Justice, however, was quite unprepared. He had been warned that Mr. Das was erratic in cross-examination and quite likely to overstep the limits. He had not, however, expected any difficulties so early. Indeed, he could not help feeling that it was rather unsubtle of Mr. Das to have antagonized the Court before the trial had even properly begun.

"Mr. Das," he said severely, "you are not answering the question. The question was quite specific: it asked whether there was objection to *any* of the jurors."

Mr. Das bowed back.

"There is an objection, m'lud. It is to each one of them. The objection is collective, not individual. But if Your Lordship chooses, I will object individually."

"On what grounds, pray?"

"On the grounds that they are all European and that my client is an African, m'lud."

The Chief Justice became even more severe.

"Let it be clearly understood," he said, "that this is a court of law. It is not a parliament, and therefore it is not a forum for political speeches. The case that I shall be judging is one of murder. Evidence has nothing to do with racial origins. And it is purely upon the evidence which they hear—evidence, Mr. Das, to the total of which you will yourself contribute—that the jurors will reach their verdict. The objection is overruled."

Mr. Das rose again.

"I am relieved, m'lud, to hear Your Lordship refer to the case specifically as one of murder. If it is murder there can, in my submission, be no reason for discrimination against Africans as jurors. If, on the other hand, the jury is exclusively European, then my client may suffer because the crime could be misconstrued as one of political assassination, m'lud. Like Your Lordship, I am most anxious to avoid even the slightest introduction of politics."

This time, the Chief Justice was more than severe: he was stern.

"The imputation of motive is purely one for the prosecution to decide."

This time Mr. Das bowed a little lower.

"I am most grateful to Your Lordship for having accepted my submission," he said.

This time, the Chief Justice recognized the danger signal: Mr. Das had succeeded in getting him annoyed. He was therefore deliberately very calm and restrained when he delivered his rebuke.

"It is my duty to warn you, Mr. Das . . ." he began.

But he was interrupted. There was a sudden disturbance in the jury box, and leaning forward, the Chief Justice could see that the retired Inspector of Native Schools had collapsed onto the rail in front of him. Then, before anyone could catch him, he had slid down out of sight among the feet of his fellow jurors.

It was not easy in the already ridiculously overcrowded courtroom to make way for the passage of a sagging and unconscious body, and the Chief Justice adjourned the court until the commotion was over. He went back into his chambers and, removing his robes, stretched himself out on the settee, using a folded-up copy of the day's Order Paper for a fan.

The problem of a twelfth juryman now presented itself. Nor was the solution going to be easy. There were plenty of other white men in Amimbo—fair-minded, responsible people; submanagers and company representatives and so forth—who would have suited the case admirably, had it not been for the house-holding qualification.

The Chief Justice closed his eyes and mentally ran through the names of all the respectable residents he could think of.

It was already after eleven when the court resumed. And by then, the Chief Justice and the Clerk of the Court had revised their entire stratagem for the handling of the case.

"Mr. Das, would you rise, please," he said.

Mr. Das's bow was most respectful.

"Before the court resumed," the Chief Justice went on, "it became incumbent on me to administer a most severe rebuke for certain improper observations which you had seen fit to make upon the composition of the duly appointed jury. Unfortunately, through illness, one member of that jury has suddenly been withdrawn from us. Emergency papers have accordingly been served on another gentleman who is present in this court at this moment. Moreover, without the due notice to which he is en-titled, he has agreed to serve. Would you stand, please, Mr. Ngono?"

From the time he was a boy, Mr. Ngono had wanted to be right at the very center of things with everyone looking at him. Possibly it was because he was only his father's favorite son and not the lawful heir that the desire was so strong in him. But now that it had actually happened, he found that he simply hated it. The whites of his eyes were showing conspicuously, and he did not know what to do with his hands. He behaved as if he were wringing something.

"Thank you, m'lud. Your Lordship has been most accommo-dating," Mr. Das replied, and sat down again.

The Chief Justice ignored Mr. Das altogether. He addressed himself to Mr. Ngono.

"Would you please follow the Usher and be sworn in, Mr. Ngono?" he asked.

As he passed the press table, Mr. Ngono avoided Mr. Talefwa's eye. Earlier, he had been trying to catch it. But when the Clerk of the Court had sent for him, and Mr. Ngono had desperately needed someone, a friend, to help him and give him good advice, Mr. Talefwa had ignored him completely. Head down, and apparently oblivious to what was going on around him, he had simply continued with his writing. Mr. Ngono had a most uneasy feeling that somehow he had been betrayed.

Only that morning Mr. Talefwa had come out with a fine leading article entitled "White Juries and Black Justice," and Mr. Ngono felt that the least he was entitled to was a smile, or a cheer, or even a wave of the hand.

And now, there he was, with the Bible in his right hand and wondering what to do with his left. Because he was nervous, he had repeated the words of the oath very loud and rather brusquely as though ordering something.

Mr. Das rose again.

"As this is now a new jury, m'lud," he said in his softest, most bubbling of voices, "may I submit to Your Lordship that all the jurors should now be asked to take the oath again. It is most irregular that . . ."

Chapter 40

"SUMMON THE prisoner."

There was a murmur that became a gasp when Old Moses was brought in.

He was so small, so withered-up and husklike, that the policemen on either side of him seemed to be there solely for his own support. They were like nurses: they walked very slowly and watchfully, making sure that he did not stumble. And when they came to the step leading up into the dock, they put a hand each into his armpits and lifted him up, like a child being helped over a high curb.

The Chief Justice was a humane man.

"Let the prisoner be seated," he said gently.

And as the policemen deposited him, Old Moses, wrapped

round mummy-fashion in his white Amimbo blanket, disappeared from the onlookers behind the high, varnished woodwork of the dock.

The charge of indictment was read out, and Mr. Ngono found himself thinking how bleak and terrible the words sounded: they were like something out of the Old Testament. They scared him.

But already the Chief Justice was speaking, and Mr. Ngono resumed his concentration.

"How do you plead? Guilty or not guilty?"

Mr. Das bobbed up rather than rose.

"Not guilty, m'lud."

The Chief Justice inclined his head toward him.

"And you are satisfied that your client is able to understand these proceedings?" he asked.

"Quite satisfied, m'lud."

"And that in a trial of this nature—a trial upon a capital charge, that is—he is fully aware of the possible consequences of such a plea?"

"I have explained everything most carefully, m'lud."

"Do you speak Mimbo, Mr. Das?"

"No, m'lud."

"Then how do you communicate with your client?"

"Partly in English, and partly through an interpreter, m'lud."

"Is the interpreter here today?"

"Yes, m'lud."

"Where, pray? I do not see him."

Mr. Das hesitated, but only for a moment. Then he was quick to give his little bow. He gave it so politely as to convey the impression that he had been just about to provide the information when the Chief Justice had interrupted him.

"He is seated at the press table, m'lud."

"At the press table!"

The Chief Justice repeated the words as though he suspected that he must have misheard them. Lowering his glasses, he peered incredulously over the edge of his rostrum onto the floor of the court beneath him.

"And what is the name of your interpreter, pray?" he asked.

There was that same momentary hesitation, that same quick recovery.

"It is Mr. Talefwa, m'lud," Mr. Das replied. "Mr. Oni Talefwa."

If he had been in his chambers, the Chief Justice would have raised his eyebrows when he heard the name. But here, in court and in his robes, it was different: he might never have heard the name before. He allowed no emotions whatsoever. Only a probing and professional curiosity.

"Would you please rise and face me, Mr. Talefwa?" he asked.

In putting the question, he had emphasized the "Mr." ever so slightly.

"In what capacity are you present in this Court?" he went on.

"I am representing my paper, *War Drum*, m'lud," Mr. Talefwa replied.

"Then you are here in a double capacity, are you not?"

"In what way, m'lud?"

This time the Chief Justice allowed his surprise to be seen by everyone.

"Did you not hear Mr. Das tell me that you are also acting as the interpreter between counsel and client?"

Mr. Das rose hurriedly.

"Mr. Talefwa's services as interpreter are not any longer required," he replied. "The fullest possible use has already been made of them. My client is in no further need of explanation."

"But he *may* be, Mr. Das. He *may* be. The prisoner is Mimbospeaking, remember," the Chief Justice reminded him. "The fact that he has a working knowledge of everyday household English is neither here nor there. It may not be sufficient. Things may be said that the prisoner does not fully comprehend. You do not speak his tongue: you have just said so. It is therefore essential that the full-time, not part-time, services of an interpreter should be retained. I will not allow this case to continue without one."

"As you so rule, m'lud."

The Chief Justice turned back to Mr. Talefwa, who had remained standing.

"I am sorry if this should interfere with your reporting activities for *War Drum*," he said. "But you cannot have it both ways, you know. The choice is entirely yours and Mr. Das's. The Court will adjourn again for five minutes while you come to a decision."

When the Chief Justice returned, he tried, by sheer pressure, to settle himself more comfortably onto the hard leather cushion decorated with the deep-sunken buttons. It was, his instinct told him, going to be a long trial.

"And what conclusions have you arrived at, Mr. Das?" he asked.

Mr. Das bowed extra low this time.

"In the interest of justice, Mr. Talefwa is prepared to give his service exclusively to my client."

"Thank you."

The Chief Justice looked down at his empty pad and then up at the Office of Works clock opposite. Dealing with Mr. Das had wasted half an hour of the Court's time already.

Then, just when he was ready to begin, he noticed that Mr. Das was still standing.

"Yes?" he asked.

"M'lud," Mr. Das began, "there is a matter which I wish to draw to your Lordship's attention. Already there has been an approach—I regret to have to say a most improper approach—from an exceedingly high quarter to try to influence me in the nature of my plea. Naturally, I resisted the approach. The promises, if they can be called promises, meant nothing to me. They did not deceive me. My client is not guilty, and I am so pleading, m'lud."

The Attorney General drew down the corners of his mouth.

Well, there's a thoroughgoing bastard for you, he said to himself. Try to help one of those fellows and that's all the thanks you get for it.

He was not, however, surprised. Even in quite trivial matters, certainly in important ones, he had always preferred Africans to Asians: they were, for some reason, so much warmer-hearted.

The Chief Justice himself had no racial prejudices: he merely disliked Mr. Das. That was why this time he was so careful to conceal his feelings.

254

"If during the course of this trial," he said, "anything is done, whether by an interested party or by a stranger, which is calculated to impede the course of justice, then the Court must be informed immediately so that suitable action can be taken."

He paused.

"I have no knowledge," he went on, "of the alleged incident, and I have no wish to have knowledge. Clearly, before entering this Court you had already dismissed it from your mind as being of no significance. Otherwise it would have been your duty to inform me in chambers before the trial had opened. As it is, you have entered your plea, and that is sufficient."

He paused again and looked downward toward the Clerk.

"Those last remarks of Counsel will," he said, "be entirely struck out."

It made Mr. Ngono feel uncomfortable to see the clever Mr. Das rebuffed in that way. But he could not help admiring the Chief Justice. It must be rather nice, too, having the last word about everything: Mr. Ngono thought that he was splendid.

That was why, when the Attorney General rose to open for the prosecution, Mr. Ngono found himself strangely disappointed. Neither grand and lofty like the Chief Justice nor subtle and faultfinding like Mr. Das, Mr. Ramsden seemed by comparison altogether too ordinary and straightforward. For a trial of this magnitude, Mr. Ngono would have thought that they could find someone more impressive.

It was not until the Attorney General got round to telling them all exactly what had happened that Mr. Ngono could tell why they had chosen him. Then it was immediately apparent. He put it all so simply. And he was such a good storyteller, too. From the way he described things, Mr. Ngono might have been there on safari with Sir Gardnor and the others, right up to that last fatal moment in the big marquee.

He could picture it all just as the Attorney General had described it. There was Sir Gardnor bent over his papers, working late into the night on urgent Government business. Beyond him, in the tent that was really an annex of the same marquee, lay Lady Anne, exhausted by the day's traveling; and beside her, on a truckle bed in the same tent, Miss Prosser, stretched out unconscious. A good deal older than Lady Anne—"of more mature years" as the Attorney General had referred to her—and drugged with Dr. Webber's pills, Miss Prosser would naturally have been the heavier sleeper of the two: she would have heard nothing.

There was no one else, except for the A.D.C. and Old Moses. It was a pity, of course, that the A.D.C.—at that of all times—should have had to step outside for personal reasons. But, as the Attorney General had explained to them, the A.D.C.'s absence didn't really complicate matters at all; if anything, it made them even clearer. No one, he said—and Mr. Ngono agreed with him—would conceivably tie up the tent flap on the *outside* if he had just gone *inside;* and still less would a murderer, fleeing from the scene of his crime, have hung about long enough to tie up anything. It was, Mr. Ngono reflected, so clever to think of putting it that way; and once put, it was so convincing.

In fact, beyond the peradventure of a doubt—Mr. Ngono's estimation of the Attorney General was increasing every moment with phrases like that coming out—the murderer must have been there inside the marquee before the A.D.C. had gone out. And the only person that could have been was Old Moses. Mr. Ngono did not see how even the ingenious Mr. Das could possibly hope to get round that one.

By now, the Attorney General had called on Captain Webber. He was asking him to describe the exact nature of Sir Gardnor's wounds. There was a hush hanging over the whole court as Captain Webber began the medical evidence.

To Mr. Ngono's surprise, Captain Webber was nervous. Even though he stood rock-still and bolt upright, military fashion, his Adam's apple kept rising and falling as if he were trying to swallow something.

"You have just told us that the space in which a weapon could enter is quite small," the Attorney General was saying. "Would you now tell us exactly how small?"

Captain Webber spread out his thumb and forefinger.

"It is a triangular cavity," he replied. "The sides of the cavity are some four inches long."

"In other words, you couldn't simply stab anywhere in that part of the body—up by the shoulder, remember—and expect to reach the heart?"

"No. A few inches either way and the blade would be deflected. It would encounter bone—the sternum, for instance."

"Then a knowledge of anatomy would be necessary?"

"That is so."

"Even quite elementary anatomy?"

"It would help."

"The kind of anatomy that a butcher might pick up by working in an abattoir?"

Captain Webber hesitated. All his training had been in hard medical facts: he didn't know where he was when it came to speculation.

"I suppose so," he said cautiously.

The Attorney General leaned forward a little.

"But come, Captain Webber," he asked, "isn't that cavity that you have been describing the very place where every bullfighter thrusts in his sword? That is surely very elementary anatomy. A butcher would be bound to know at least that much, wouldn't he?"

"Yes."

"Thank you, Captain Webber."

As the Attorney General sat down, Mr. Ngono gave a little gasp. He had only just realized what the Attorney General had been up to. All this talk hadn't been about anatomy at all, really: it had been about Old Moses. Because, quite early on, the Attorney General had made a great point of reminding the jury that Old Moses had begun life as a kitchen boy. The fact seemed so telling that Mr. Ngono wondered why the Chief Justice didn't close the trial then and there.

But there was no time for wondering. Mr. Das was already up on his feet; and from the way he tilted his wig forward over his forehead, Mr. Ngono could tell that they were in for something. It was evident that Captain Webber could tell, too. He was very close and guarded in his answers.

"You are a doctor, Captain Webber?"

"Correct."

"And a soldier?"

"Correct."

"Have you ever seen active service, Captain Webber?"

"No."

"Then you have had no experience of wounds actually received in the field?"

"Correct."

"But I take it that, in the course of your duties, you have dressed wounds?"

"Correct."

"Knife wounds?"

"Not specifically knife wounds."

"But wounds deliberately inflicted?"

"Correct."

"Were any of the wounds serious?"

"One or two."

"Was there an instrument used in any of them?"

"It was fists mostly."

"I wasn't asking what was mostly used, Captain Webber. I asked if an instrument was used in any of them."

"There was a rifle butt."

"And what did this rifle butt do?"

"It nearly killed a man."

"How did it nearly kill him?"

"It ruptured his spleen."

"Was the assailant an expert anatomist?"

"No."

"Did he have any knowledge of elementary anatomy—butcher's anatomy, as my learned friend chooses to call it?"

"Not so far as I am aware."

"But he nearly killed someone, didn't he?"

"Correct."

"And is the spleen difficult to locate?"

"Not by a doctor."

"But the assailant wasn't a doctor, was he? You have just said he had no knowledge of anatomy."

Captain Webber did not reply.

"In other words, it was by pure chance that the spleen was ruptured?"

"It may have been."

"But don't you think so yourself? A few inches either way and the spleen would have been saved, would it not, Captain Webber?"

"Correct."

"And this wound up by the collarbone—if someone had been stabbing downwards, it could have been pure chance, could it not, that the blade hit that particular spot?"

"It could have been."

"Thank you."

Captain Webber had already turned, and was preparing to leave the box, when Mr. Das raised his finger.

"One moment, Captain Webber. There was another wound, was there not? Would you describe it, please?"

"There was a vertical incision from a sharp knife. It was approximately three inches long, running from the left cheekbone to the jaw."

"And did it require any degree whatsoever of anatomical knowledge to slice the cheek open in this manner?"

"None whatsoever."

"And would the point of the blade have been deflected by such a wound?"

"To some extent."

"You are satisfied that both wounds were caused by the same blow?"

"I am."

"Then the second wound, the fatal wound, must have been inflicted where the point just happened to land, not where it was aimed, if it was aimed at all, must it not?"

Captain Webber was silent, and Mr. Das left him standing there. He waited so long, in fact, that the Chief Justice turned, first toward him and then to Mr. Das. As soon as Mr. Das caught the Chief Justice's eye, he bowed.

"Thank you, m'lud," he said. "That is all. I am quite satisfied."

Chapter 41

THAT HAD been the first day of the trial. Day two was now beginning.

It was Major Mills's turn. Or rather, it had been Major Mills's turn while the Attorney General was taking him quietly and patiently through his evidence, showing what a thorough, highly trained and conscientious sort of soldier he was.

The Attorney General kept coming back to the impressive security measures—the twenty-four-hour sentry watch, Major Mills's own surprise patrols, the trip wires, everything. And all with one object: to show the jury that no intruder could possibly have entered the camp and that once Sir Gardnor's marquee had closed down for the night, the murderer had already been *inside*.

Mr. Das rose slowly and smilingly. He coughed politely into his hand before speaking.

"You were in charge of all arrangements for the safety of the party, Major?"

"I was."

"And you took extraordinary precautions, did you not?"

"Just what was necessary."

"Were they greater or less than was usual on safari?"

"Greater. Much greater."

"Why?"

"Because of the recent outbreaks of violence—the L.M.s, you know."

Mr. Das leaned forward.

"I know nothing, Major," he said. "You are telling me. What are L.M.s?"

"Leopard Men. Native terrorist groups. Organize their own murder parties. Army slang. Always call 'em L.M.s for short."

"Did you particularly fear these L.M.s?"

"I did."

"And were you in any way troubled by terrorist groups while on this safari?"

Major Mills gave the quick sideways jerk of his head that was always an indication that he was sure of something.

"No trouble at all."

"Then if you had no trouble, have you any evidence that these terrorist groups even existed?"

Major Mills was having none of that. He gave the same head jerk and faced Mr. Das more squarely.

"They were there, all right," he said. "Under cover. All round us."

Mr. Das ignored Major Mills for a moment. He was glancing down at his papers.

"On the night of the crime, Major, what was the weather like?" he asked.

"Fine clear night. Always is, this time of year. Nothing wrong with the weather."

"And visibility?"

"Perfect."

"Was there a moon?"

"A full moon. Almost like day."

"So if anyone had approached the camp your sentries would have seen him?"

"Bound to. Spotted him at once. Clear arc of vision. Three-sixty degrees. No cover of any kind."

Mr. Das kept Major Mills waiting while he consulted his papers again.

"Including Sir Gardnor and his lady," he asked, "what was the total strength of your party when you set out?"

"Total strength? Forty-four persons."

"And with Sir Gardnor dead, that made forty-three?"

"Naturally."

"And what was the total strength of your party when you returned?"

"Forty-two."

"So someone was missing?"

"That is so."

"Who was it, please?"

"One of the kitchen boys."

"Where did he go?"

"Slipped out into the jungle. Still hiding there, most prob-bly."

"And how did he get there?"

Major Mills's chin came back.

"On his own two legs, I suppose. Skedaddled."

"Which of your sentries reported it?"

"Nothing to do with the sentries. Made a special roll call myself. After the murder, that is. Wasn't there, so I posted him."

"But did none of the sentries see him go?"

The note of surprise in Mr. Das's voice floated round the courtroom like a soap bubble.

Major Mills's chin was drawn back farther than ever now.

"Just slipped past them in the confusion."

"What confusion?"

"Screams. That kind of thing. General turnout. Everyone moving around. Bound to have distracted them."

"When was the previous roll call?"

"Sundown. Nineteen hundred hours."

"And at what time was Sir Gardnor killed?"

"O three hundred hours. Approx."

"And had you kept the kitchen boy under constant observa-tion since the last roll call?"

"Under observation? Course not. No reason to."

"But he escaped, didn't he?"

"I've just said so."

"Under the very noses of your sentries?"

"He got past them," Major Mills replied.

"And you don't know *when*, do you? No one saw him go, so you can't say. It could have been before the murder, couldn't it, Major?"

Major Mills did not reply, and Mr. Das went on without him.

"Or *after* the murder, but *before* the alarm?"

Major Mills was still silent.

"In other words," Mr. Das continued, "you haven't the slightest idea of when he ran away. All that you know is that he went. And you haven't the slightest idea because your sentries weren't looking. That is so, isn't it, Major?"

Major Mills kept his chin down and said nothing.

It was the pause for which Mr. Das had been waiting. And he made the most of it.

"I put it to you," he said at last, "that your sentries were idle. On duty, but completely idle. It was a clear, starlit night—almost like daylight: you have just said so—with the entire circumference of the camp open to inspection—no cover, remember—and this man simply walked past them."

"Ran, more likely."

"Walked or ran, it makes no difference, Major. Not one of the sentries even so much as caught a glimpse of him. That is so, isn't it?"

"Do you want me to go on telling you?"

"No, Major. I want you to tell me something else. If this man could get out so easily—not invisible, but still totally unobserved—anyone else could have got in just as easily, could he not?"

"No, he couldn't. The sentries would have spotted him."

Major Mills checked himself hurriedly: he realized now that he had been shouting.

"But the sentries weren't spotting anything that night, were they? Your camp was wide open to the whole world. You didn't think so then, but you aren't in any doubt about it now, are you, Major?"

The Chief Justice looked up at the court clock and coughed. It was a loud cough, and Mr. Das recognized it as an official signal.

"I have no more questions, m'lud," he said.

The Chief Justice folded the two wings of his blotter over onto the blank pages of writing paper beneath; he had gathered up his notes as he sat there.

"The Court is adjourned," he said.

It had been a good morning's work, and he was looking forward to his luncheon tray. A light snack—mango and a slice of cold chicken—was all he ever allowed himself while a case was actually in session.

The waiting room for the witnesses was small and boxlike. Although it was solid brick and plaster on three sides, the fourth was of temporary boarding, through which the voices of the messengers in the corridor outside penetrated as though there had been nothing in between.

The wooden chairs were all of plain regulation pattern. There were six of them. The one on which Harold was sitting was tilted back so that he could put his feet up against the table top. Because of the heat, he had unlaced his shoes all the way down, leaving the tongues hanging.

The only other person left in the waiting room was the A.D.C He had hardly sat down at all. From the moment he arrived, he had been walking up and down: four paces in one direction, which was as far as he could go; and then another four paces back again. Whenever he passed behind Harold's chair, he brushed against it. It had been annoying at first, but by now Harold no longer minded. He had got his eyes shut and was pretending to be asleep. Because the pink celluloid was so clammy, he had pushed his eye patch up onto his forehead.

The A.D.C. paused at the window for a moment, staring out into the courtyard.

"Well, I shouldn't keep them long," he muttered. "I'm only here to describe the layout of the place. You'd have thought a sketch would do."

The slats of the Venetian blind were bent permanently downwards at the center where others before him had tried to make the time go faster by peering out into the scorching expanse of red gravel where the cars were parked.

"Calling Mr. Anthony Henley. Calling Mr. Anthony Henley."

The voice was getting louder as the messenger approached them down the corridor. It stopped outside. Then the door was pushed open. The khaki uniform with the shorts and the rolled shirt sleeves looked very smart against the surrounding shabbiness of the waiting room.

"Mr. Henley, saah. All ready for you."

The A.D.C. buttoned up his jacket and straightened himself.

"Can't say they've exactly hurried themselves," he remarked.

Harold tilted his chair farther backwards; it was now as far over as it was safe to go.

"Good luck," he said. "Don't forget: remind them I'm still here."

He hadn't even opened his eyes while he was speaking.

The big center fan in the ceiling of the courtroom gave out a harsh, juddering note and stopped revolving. There was nothing really wrong with it, nothing broken. It was simply that the motor, the bearings, everything, had become overheated: when they had cooled down a bit it would start going round again.

The Attorney General paused. Because everyone was gazing upwards to see in what position the blades had stuck, he had for the moment lost the Court's attention.

"Mr. Henley, you have just told the Court that you had to slip out for a few moments," he resumed.

He made the observation as though, in that heat, he appreciated that the jury could hardly be expected to remember such things unless they were repeated for them.

"And how long would you say you were absent?"

"About five minutes."

"About five minutes. Did anybody see you go?"

"Not that I'm aware of, sir."

"Sir Gardnor, for instance? Could he have seen you?"

"No sir. He was at his desk. Facing the other way. I didn't have to go past him."

"And was there anyone else in the main tent at the time? I'm not referring to the ladies; you have said their quarters were separate. In the main tent, remember."

"Only . . . only Old Moses, sir."

The A.D.C. said the name as though he were reluctant to mention it; he kept his eyes carefully away from the dock while he was speaking.

"And was Old Moses, as you call him, awake?"

"Yes, sir."

"How do you know? Did you see him?"

"No, sir. It was just that I could hear him moving about."

"At three o'clock in the morning?"

"He was always around, sir, in case Sir Gardnor needed anything. He never turned in until after Sir Gardnor had gone to bed."

"And you are *certain* you heard him?"

"Quite certain, sir. Sir Gardnor called out to him; I think he wanted a drink, or something."

"And did you hear Old Moses reply?"

The A.D.C. paused.

"Not exactly reply, sir. There was the sound of a soda-water bottle being opened up. And then I heard a glass or something being put down."

"Was that all?"

"I heard Sir Gardnor say, 'Thank you.'"

"So Old Moses was at the desk right beside him, was he?"

"He must have been."

"And when you left, there was no one else there?"

"No, sir."

"Just Sir Gardnor and Old Moses?"

The Attorney General paused.

"Sir Gardnor, and Old Moses at the desk close beside him?" he repeated slowly.

"Yes, sir."

"Thank you. That is all."

The A.D.C. took out his handkerchief and passed it across his forehead. Then he ran his finger around the back of his neck inside the collar. He hadn't liked what the Attorney General had made him say. So far as he was concerned, Old Moses had been part of the household, a fixture: the Residency, in his day, couldn't have got on without him.

But Mr. Das was already on his feet. He had made his usual little bow and was now smiling engagingly in the direction of the A.D.C.

"How long did you know Sir Gardnor?" he asked.

"About six years. I had the honor to serve him for three."

"Three happy years?"

"Very."

"Throughout the whole time?"

"Throughout."

"No disagreements?"

"None whatsoever."

"Then you were looking forward to future service with him?"

"I was."

"Did Sir Gardnor ever mention the probability of his Delhi appointment to you?"

"He did."

"And were you to accompany him?"

"I don't know. We never discussed it."

"That's rather strange, isn't it?"

Mr. Das's smile had disappeared. He was now frowning as though completely mystified.

"Three years together," he continued. "Three happy years. No disagreements of any kind. And not a word about remaining with him. Now, why was that?"

The Chief Justice thrust his spectacles down to the end of his nose and looked across at Mr. Das. The gesture was a slight one. But it was sufficient. Mr. Das faced immediately toward him.

"M'lud?" he asked.

The Chief Justice's finger was raised in the air while he was speaking.

"Mr. Das," he told him. "I have been listening very carefully to your questions, and I am not happy about them. They are leading nowhere but into conjecture. And that I shall not allow. Mr. Henley cannot possibly tell you why Sir Gardnor did or did not mention this or that subject to him. The answer to your question is not to be discovered anywhere in this courtroom, Mr. Das. What you are seeking can be found only in the grave."

The Chief Justice paused long enough for the severity of his rebuke to be appreciated. Then he pushed his glasses back up his nose again as though nothing had happened.

"You may proceed," he said.

Apart from his bow, Mr. Das gave no indication of being aware that he had just been interrupted.

"Mr. Henley," he said, as though the idea had been in his mind all the time, "I would like you to detach your mind entirely from Sir Gardnor and consider only yourself."

Because no direct question had been asked, the A.D.C. ignored him. Right from the start, he had made it perfectly clear that he was going to keep his answers to Mr. Das down to the strictest minimum.

"You told the Court, did you not," Mr. Das continued, "that you 'slipped out of the tent for a few moments'—I think those were the words. Now, at what time would that have been?"

"About three A.M. I didn't actually look at my watch."

"And so far as you were aware, nobody saw you go?"

"That is so."

"So there is no witness as to the exact time?"

"None that I know of."

"Did you leave hurriedly?"

"No."

"Why did you leave at all?"

The A.D.C. lifted his chin a little and drew down the corners of his mouth out of utter contempt for the man.

"To go to the lavatory," he said.

Mr. Ngono found himself admiring the A.D.C. for the sheer straightforwardness of his answer. It must have been very embarrassing to have had to admit publicly that he had been taken short in the night like a child. Indeed, Mr. Ngono was rather surprised that Mr. Das should have thought of putting the question at all: the explanation was so perfectly obvious.

"But was there no lavatory accommodation inside the tent?" Mr. Das inquired, with just the right note of incredulity creeping into his voice. "Are you telling me that Sir Gardnor had to leave by his own front door whenever he wanted to go to the lavatory?"

"I am not telling you that."

"Then there was a lavatory inside the tent?"

"There was."

"Didn't Sir Gardnor allow you to use it?"

The Attorney General gave a quick glance in Mr. Das's direction. Up to that point, he had been quietly drawing on the back of a long envelope that had contained his brief. It was bridges that he drew mostly, while in Court listening to Defense Counsel; he had two arches already neatly finished—brickwork, headstone and all—and he was beginning to sketch in the outline of the long center span. Now, pencil point posed above the thick manila paper, he waited; something told him that at any moment, things would begin getting rougher.

"The lavatory was for Sir Gardnor *and* his staff."

"And did you ever avail yourself of it?"

The corners of the A.D.C's mouth were drawn farther down than ever by now; he was clearly disgusted by the whole line of Mr. Das's questioning.

"Of course."

"Then why did you not use it on this occasion?"

"I didn't want to disturb anyone."

"Very commendable, I'm sure."

Mr. Das's head was cocked a little to one side as he said it, and he was smiling. By now, it was a superior, slightly patronizing kind of smile. The Attorney General recognized it as all part of the reducing-a-witness process.

"And which lavatory *did* you use?" Mr. Das went on.

"One of the outside ones."

"But which one? The officers'?"

"No."

"Then was it the one for the other ranks?"

"No."

Mr. Das tilted his wig forward on his forehead again. The gesture was like a punctuation mark: it showed that he had come to the end of a whole paragraph in his inquiry. He cleared his throat quite unnecessarily before putting his next question.

"There was only one other lavatory in the whole camp, Mr. Henley. That was the latrine for African servants. Was it the African latrine that you went to?"

Mr. Ngono, in his excitement, was leaning so far forward that the juror next to him had to tap him on the shoulder so that he would sit back a bit and let them all get a look.

"It was."

The voice in which the A.D.C. answered was so low as to be almost inaudible.

"But that latrine was right on the other side of the camp, wasn't it?"

The A.D.C. merely nodded.

"About two hundred yards away, would you say?"

"About that."

"And when you reached it, how long did you stay there?"

"I don't remember."

Mr. Das was delighted. It was what he had been waiting for. "Don't remember" was always a sure sign that the witness was concealing something. He decided to press on.

"Then I will try to help you. Would it have been, shall we say, five minutes?"

"Possibly."

"Or even longer? Ten minutes, perhaps?"

"It could have been."

"Quarter of an hour, then?"

"I don't know, I tell you. I wasn't well. I was suffering from dysentery."

Mr. Das went back onto his heels for a moment. He was rocking reflectively to and fro throughout the whole of his next question.

"You tell me that in the small hours of the morning you had an attack of dysentery," he said. "With dysentery, when these attacks occur, you have to go to the lavatory immediately, do you not, Mr. Henley? It is not in the nature of the ailment to be able to hang about. Even so, you chose to go right past two nearby lavatories, both open and available to you, and walk across the entire width of the camp to the African latrine. Why did you do that, Mr. Henley?"

"I didn't want to run into anyone."

"And did you run into anyone?"

"No."

"You didn't encounter a soul in the whole course of your long walk?"

"No."

"Or after you had got there?"

"No."

"Are you sure, Mr. Henley?"

"Quite sure."

Mr. Das had been holding a bundle of papers in his hand while he was speaking. Now he suddenly threw the papers down on the table top in front of him. It was something that, more than once, he had seen other Counsel do. And it had never been known to fail. The whole Court had gone absolutely silent.

"I put it to you that you *did* want to run into someone, Mr. Henley," he said. "Who was it that you went to meet?"

The A.D.C. was sweating again. He had gone damp and sticky all over. There was a signet ring on his left hand, and he kept twisting it nervously round between his right thumb and forefinger.

Mr. Das took that for another good sign.

"I didn't go to meet anyone."

Mr. Das paused.

"Was the kitchen boy a friend of yours, Mr. Henley?" he asked.

"He was about the camp. I'd spoken to him."

"And was that as far as the friendship went?"

The A.D.C. drew down the corners of his mouth. He was staring straight at Mr. Das, looking him full in the eyes, and not answering. It was obvious that he did not intend to answer.

But this did not matter in the slightest. Mr. Das had been waiting, preparing, for this moment all the way along. And now that it had come, he was ready for it.

Still with the same fixed smile upon his face, he started to address the A.D.C. again.

"Mr. Henley," he said, "I put it to you that everything that you have said in this Court has been lies. All lies, and nothing but lies. It wasn't an attack of dysentery that drove you from the tent, because you never had dysentery, did you? You left the tent because you wished to see someone. That someone was the kitchen boy. It was by prior arrangement that you met him, wasn't it? And you chose the African latrine because it was so close to his quarters, so convenient for him. All that is correct, is it not, Mr. Henley?"

The sweat that had been forming on the A.D.C.'s face had begun to trickle. Even from where Mr. Ngono was sitting, he could see little rivulets running down. While Mr. Ngono watched, he saw the A.D.C. pass the back of his hand across his forehead; it came away glistening.

"It is not correct."

Mr. Das looked perfectly cool; he wasn't even sweating.

"I put it to you, Mr. Henley, that you were there to meet your accomplice. The accomplice was the kitchen boy. You had got it all worked out, hadn't you?"

"We'd got nothing worked out."

The A.D.C. had interrupted at last. It did not, however, sound in the least like his own voice. Usually he was rather quiet-spoken.

Mr. Das was not disconcerted. Eyes shut, he was reconstructing the whole affair.

"Sir Gardnor had dropped you, hadn't he?" he went on, in the same musical voice that had annoyed the Chief Justice when he first heard it. "He was going to leave you behind, wasn't he? And I put it to you that you had decided to get your own revenge. You had decided to kill him, hadn't you?"

The Chief Justice raised his forefinger.

"Do what to him, Mr. Das?" he asked.

"Kill him, m'lud."

The Chief Justice lowered his hand again.

"Thank you," he said. "I did not hear you. You may proceed."

Mr. Das's eyes were open by now.

"And when you had killed him, stabbed him with his own paperknife, you put the rest of your plan into operation. You had already bribed the kitchen boy, paid him money, hadn't you, Mr. Henley? And for one reason and for one reason only—to put suspicion on himself by running away. You knew that he'd never be found again, not out there in all that jungle. That was why you met him in the latrine that night, wasn't it? To tell him that you'd done your bit."

The A.D.C. had gone very pale.

"No," was all he said.

"Then why did you meet him there?" Mr. Das demanded.

At that moment, the ceiling fan gave a shudder that set the blades vibrating. The rattle made everyone look upwards. But there was nothing to see. The fan had started to revolve quite normally again.

Chapter 42

DINNER WAS now over, and Mr. Frith sat facing Mr. Drawbridge across the width of the small table at the end of the long dining room.

It had been a short, simple sort of meal: in Sir Gardnor's day there would have been two, possibly three, more courses. Also, the small table would never have been used at all. Whenever Mr. Frith had dined alone with Sir Gardnor, they had always been separated by an immense distance of mahogany, with the candlesticks and the silver pheasants and the big rose bowl cutting them off almost entirely from each other.

As it was, the smoke from the pipe that Mr. Drawbridge was lighting kept drifting into Mr. Frith's face. It was an old pipe, charred round the rim and burnt down on one side where the match always went. Lighting a pipe in the dining room was another thing that would never have happened in Sir Gardnor's day.

"Did the right thing, of course," Mr. Drawbridge remarked. "Sent a note down asking us to excuse him. Said he would be staying in his room this evening."

Mr. Frith roused himself. The day had been an exhausting one, just sitting there in Court listening. Now that it was finished, moments of sleepiness kept coming over him.

"Don't wonder," he replied. "Can't see how he can live it down. Not after all that native-latrine stuff."

Mr. Drawbridge nodded.

"Too bad, really," he said. "I'm told everyone knew he was that way. But you don't have to make a thing of it. Very dirty of Counsel to play it up like that."

"Dirty sort of Counsel," Mr. Frith observed. "That's why they got him out here."

"All Talefwa's doing, I suppose."

Mr. Frith leaned forward as though he were afraid of eavesdroppers.

"Hand in glove," he replied. "Anyhow, the C.J. spotted it. Cuts him down to size, doesn't it, just being interpreter?"

"How did the jury take it—the bit about the A.D.C., I mean?"

"Oh, they got the message, all right. Probably all new to some of them. Weren't all regular Residency types, you know."

"And did they resent it—coming from an Indian, I mean?"

"Slit his throat tomorrow if they got the chance. All twelve of them. All eleven, I should say. Don't know about young Ngono. He's like a kid at his first circus."

Mr. Drawbridge had passed the port bottle back in Mr. Frith's direction. Frith filled his glass again. It wasn't really his drink, port. But it would do for now; do until they got round to the whisky later. Whisky, he knew, was the only thing that would really revive him, put him back on his form again.

"Think they'll fall for the idea of the kitchen boy being mixed up in the murder?" Mr. Drawbridge asked. "Clever of Das to bring it up in that way. Bound to leave a doubt in their minds."

"Oh, he's clever, all right. Grant you that much."

Mr. Frith had spilt some of the port down his shirt front and had to start mopping at it with his napkin. Mr. Drawbridge sat watching him.

"Then how'd you think it's all going?"

"Difficult to say. Very difficult. Getting it all their own way at the moment." He paused. "Wish our A.G. had got a bit more guts in him," he added. "Taking it all too quietly for my liking. No—*whoosh!*"

Mr. Frith still had his port glass in his hand as he pronounced the word. It was careless. And too emphatic. Mr. Drawbridge had to begin dabbing at the tablecloth as well.

"Really? Only seen the transcript, myself," he told him. "Read all right to me."

But Mr. Frith had become despondent.

"Don't like to think of Lady Anne in the box," he said. "Not with the other fellow firing the questions. Might say anything, you know."

Mr. Drawbridge only smiled.

"I don't think there'll be any trouble with her," he replied.

"Never does to go for a woman. He wouldn't want to put the jury's backs up."

His pipe had gone out, and he was at work lighting it again.

"It's Stebbs tomorrow, isn't it?" he asked. "He ought to be all right. Seems steady enough to me."

"Oh, yes. I'm not worried about him. Damn it all, he *saw* it."

Tomorrow had come; and so far, things in the courtroom were moving quite smoothly.

"And what did you do, Mr. Stebbs, when you heard Lady Anne scream?"

The Attorney General asked the question in that quiet, conversational tone of his that Mr. Frith found so unconvincing.

"I jumped out of bed and ran over."

"Immediately?"

"Immediately."

"No hanging about to get some clothes on?"

"No."

"How were you dressed then?"

"I was in my pajamas."

"And how far was your tent from Sir Gardnor's?"

"About twenty yards."

"Was it a clear run, or were there any obstructions?"

"Perfectly clear."

"And could you see where you were going?"

"No difficulty at all."

"Then it can't have taken you very long, can it? How long, in fact, did elapse between hearing the scream and reaching Sir Gardnor's tent? A minute?"

"Much less."

"Half a minute, then?"

"Less."

"Less? A quarter of a minute, perhaps?"

"Not more. I got there as quickly as I could."

"So in a quarter of a minute you had reached the doorway. Was the flap open?"

"No. It was closed."

"How was it closed?"

"Only loosely. The cords had been looped together on the outside."

"You did say on the *outside?*"

"I did."

"And 'looped,' you said. Do you mean 'looped' or 'knotted'?"

"You could call it a sort of knot, I suppose. But it wasn't tied tight, or anything like that."

"Then you had no difficulty in undoing it?"

"None whatever. The ends just came apart."

"So it didn't hold you up in any way?"

"Not at all. I went straight in."

"How far did you, in fact, go?"

"There was a sort of little passageway inside the tent. I had to get to the end of it before I could see what was going on."

"And what was going on?"

"Sir Gardnor was at his desk, sir. Dead."

"Was he alone at the time?"

"No, sir."

"Who was with him?"

Harold shifted his position slightly. From where he was standing he could just see the white corner of the Mimbo blanket over the edge of the dock rail.

"Old Moses," he said.

"What exactly was Old Moses doing? Tell the Court in your own words, please."

It was the same low, almost casual, voice that the Attorney General was using. But it was not without its effect. The Court was suddenly as silent as it had been when Mr. Das had so dramatically thrown his papers down.

"He was bent over the back of Sir Gardnor's chair. He was stabbing him. There was blood everywhere."

In the quiet of the courtroom, Harold became uncomfortably aware of the sound of his own voice; he seemed to be listening to himself.

"Could you see clearly?"

"Absolutely clearly."

"No possibility of your being mistaken?"

"None whatever."

"And where was the wound that was being inflicted?"

"Right up on the shoulder. Where it joins the neck."

He raised his hand instinctively and touched the spot with his finger.

"And could you actually see the weapon?"

"Only the handle. The blade was inside."

"You mean it was just sticking there? Was no one touching it?"

Harold lowered his eyes for a moment: he found this bit distasteful.

"Old Moses was."

"And was his hand merely resting on it?"

"No, sir. He was grasping it."

Harold raised his arm as he was speaking and involuntarily clenched his fist.

The Attorney General looked at him closely.

"Would you turn, please, so that His Lordship and the jury can both see."

Harold turned. The same uncomfortable feeling had come over him; he seemed to be watching himself as well as listening now.

But already the A.G. was speaking again: in the same curiously detached voice, he was ambling on.

" 'Grasping', I think you said. Was it a good, firm grip?"

"It was."

"Considerable muscular power behind it?"

"Considerable."

"How do you know?"

"Because I tried to pull his hand away."

"And what did Old Moses do?"

"He struggled. He wouldn't let go of it."

The Attorney General pursed up his lips and nodded as though he were savoring the reply.

"He wouldn't let go of it," he repeated slowly. Then, just when Mr. Ngono thought that the Attorney General had finished, he apparently remembered something.

"Were you alone all this time?" he asked.

"No, sir."

"Who else was there?"

"Lady Anne."

"And was Lady Anne anywhere near Sir Gardnor?"

"No, sir. She was right over on the other side."

"On the other side of the desk?"

"No, sir. On the other side of the marquee. Where the ladies' quarters joined on."

The Attorney General bent down and picked up a large folded sheet.

"I have here a scale plan of the marquee," he said. "It shows the position of the desk and of the ladies' quarters. That would mean that Lady Anne was some thirty feet away, would it not?"

"About that, sir."

"And was Lady Anne simply standing there?"

"Yes, sir."

"She didn't come forward to help you in any way?"

"She didn't move, sir. She had her hands up to her face. She was covering up her eyes."

"And it was Lady Anne you heard scream?"

"Yes, sir."

"You are certain about that?"

"Positive."

"Thank you. I have no more questions."

He looked across at the jury as he said it. Then, with a little shrug, he hitched up his trousers and sat down. Once seated, he closed his eyes as if he had lost all interest in the case.

It was Mr. Das who brought things to life. He was as polite as ever. The whole bowing business started up again.

"Mr. Stebbs," he said, "I see that you've injured your eye."

"That is so."

"Is it a recent affliction?"

"About ten weeks."

"And I notice you keep raising your hand to the eye patch. Does that mean it still troubles you?"

"At times."

"Is it troubling you now?"

"A little."

"Had you hurt it by the time of Sir Gardnor's death?"

"Yes. It happened earlier on safari."

"And did you receive medical attention?"

"Captain Webber dressed it."

"Was that all he did?"

"It was all he could do."

"But didn't it hurt?"

"Naturally."

"And did Captain Webber not give you anything to ease the pain?"

"Yes, he gave me some pills."

"Were they sleeping pills?"

"Some of them were. There were two sorts."

"And you took both of them?"

"I did."

"Did you take any on the night of the death?"

"Yes."

"Including the sleeping pills?"

"Including the sleeping pills."

"At what time?"

"About eleven."

"And how long did the effects of the sleeping pills usually last?"

"I don't know. About five or six hours, I suppose. I just went off to sleep. I didn't time them."

"And at what hour did you hear the scream?"

"About three."

"And you had taken the pills around eleven?"

"I've already told you so."

Mr. Das's smile became even more polite.

"I know. I was making sure that I had understood you."

He broke off for a moment and stood there, still smiling.

"Were you wearing an eye patch on the night of the murder?"

"No. I was wearing a bandage."

"A thick bandage?"

"Thick enough."

"And did it cover up one eye completely?"

"It did."

"No vision there at all?"

"None at all."

"Was there a light in Sir Gardnor's tent?"

"Yes."

"A powerful light, or a dim light?"

"A powerful light."

Mr. Das tilted his wig forward again.

"And you are telling the Court that having taken two sorts of drugs—one a sleeping pill of which the effects were only half worn off—and having run, not walked, mark you, all the way from your sleeping tent, you went straight out of the night into a brightly lit room and with one eye covered up by a thick bandage you could still see clearly enough with the other one to condemn a man?"

The Chief Justice picked up his pencil and tapped with it as if it were a conductor's baton.

"Surely you do not mean 'condemn,' do you, Mr. Das?" he asked. "It is entirely outside the province of a witness to condemn anybody. Do you not mean 'identify'?"

"I stand corrected, m'lud."

The Chief Justice put the pencil down again.

"You were inquiring about the witness's eyesight," he said. "You may continue."

"Thank you, m'lud."

Mr. Das turned back toward the witness box.

"Do you remember my question?"

"I do."

"And what is your answer?"

"I could see clearly enough to identify him. And I could see exactly what he was doing. I've told the Court."

It was Harold's round, and Mr. Das let him have it. But he did not appear unduly concerned: the game was not yet over. He was still smiling.

"You engaged in a piece of play-acting just now," he said. "You showed the Court how the knife was being held. Would you show the Court again, please?"

"Show them again?"

"Can you not recall what you did before?"

"I can."

"Then do it, please."

He's making a fool of me, Harold told himself; he wants me to look ridiculous in front of all those jurors.

"Face the Court, please," Mr. Das was asking. "*I* know what it looks like. I want to be quite sure that the jury knows too."

Harold turned, and Mr. Das let him stand there. Mr. Ngono, who had never guessed that there would be a second time, was enthralled. Overcome by the drama of it, he kept closing his pink-palmed hand round an invisible dagger of his own.

"Thank you," Mr. Das said at length. "Now face me again, please." He paused. "So that was how the knife was held, was it, while you say it was being stabbed downwards into Sir Gardnor's shoulder?"

"It was."

"And now, *without moving your arm*, would you please show me how you would have held the knife if you had been trying to draw it out. Draw it out, I said, not thrust it in."

Harold stood there, not moving. Mr. Das observed him closely, shifting his head from side to side so that he could study every detail.

"Thank you," he said at last. "I can see no difference. But turn round once more, please, and face the Court. Perhaps the jury can see a difference."

Harold turned. Again Mr. Das was in no hurry.

"That will do," he said finally. "You may unclench your fist."

Mr. Das eased himself back onto his heels.

"I congratulate you on your powers of observation," he said. "But I put it to you that you have drawn the entirely wrong conclusion. If Sir Gardnor had already been stabbed when Old Moses came upon him, wouldn't the first thing that Old Moses would have done be to try to remove the weapon? Wouldn't it, Mr. Stebbs?"

But the Chief Justice was having none of that.

"Mr. Das," he said. "I have spoken to you before about inviting answers that can be no more than mere conjecture. And because they are conjecture they are of no interest to this Court."

He bent over toward the Clerk. "The whole of that last question will be struck out."

"I am sorry, m'lud."

"You may continue."

Mr. Das gave his politest bow.

"Thank you, m'lud. I am not yet finished."

Chapter 43

BECAUSE THE bearings had really seized up this time, the fan in the center of the ceiling had stopped revolving. The temperature inside the courtroom had risen steadily into the nineties, and the Chief Justice had just announced an adjournment of twenty minutes so that everyone could cool down a bit.

Harold returned to the makeshift waiting room. While he had been in the witness box, the sun had moved round. It now cleared the roof of the Administration block and fell full on the single window. The slats of the Venetian blind inside were lit up along the top edges as if they were on fire.

There was a knock on the door, and the Attorney General joined him.

"Everything all right?" he asked. "Like a cold drink, or something?"

Harold shook his head. There was still an empty carton on the table in front of him. It had contained lemonade—stale, warm, and cardboardy-tasting. There was a dead fly in it.

"I'm afraid I'm making an awful mess of things," he said. "He keeps on trying to catch me."

The Attorney General looked surprised.

"You're doing awfully well," he told him. "The jury obviously believes you."

Harold threw the empty carton over his shoulder into the metal bin behind him. Because the bin was already half full of other crumpled cartons, it hardly made a sound as it landed there.

"They bloody well ought to," he said. "It's the truth."

"There you are," the Attorney General agreed with him. "Just stick to the truth and he can't do a thing to you. He's damn good, really. I've been admiring him. I think he'd spot it if you were trying to conceal anything."

Harold caught his eye.

"Don't worry," he said. "I'm not."

Outside, there was some kind of panic among the messengers. They were all talking at the tops of their voices.

The Court was due to resume in two minutes, it appeared, and one of them had been sent to look for the Attorney General.

Mr. Das's smile, when he faced Harold, was a particularly friendly one. It was the sort of smile that friend gives friend after involuntary separation.

"Mr. Stebbs," he said, "I want you to cast your mind back again to the night of the tragedy."

There was a pause.

"Are you quite sure that there was no one else there when you entered Sir Gardnor's tent—just you and Lady Anne and Old Moses?"

Harold was grateful for the adjournment; his mind was clearer.

"Except for Sir Gardnor, of course."

"Of course."

Mr. Das paused.

"And he may have been dead already, may he not?"

"He may have been. I'm not an expert on such things."

"You don't have to be an expert, Mr. Stebbs. You are merely an eyewitness. In your opinion, was Sir Gardnor dead when you entered?"

"He may have been."

"And if Sir Gardnor was dead when you entered, he may have been dead some time before you got there. That is so, is it not, Mr. Stebbs? Say five minutes before, for instance."

"Possibly."

"Quarter of an hour, then?"

So Mr. Das was back to the A.D.C. again. "Quarter of an hour, then?" were the very words that he had used when he was cross-examining him. Harold determined that he wasn't going to be drawn into that one.

"All I know is that the body was still warm when I touched it," he said.

"But it was a warm night, wasn't it?"

"It was."

"And you have said that you are no expert. The heat of the body would prove nothing—except to an expert, that is—now, would it, Mr. Stebbs?"

"I've only told you what I noticed."

"And was there anything else you noticed—Lady Anne, for instance?"

"No. She was right over on the other side of the tent."

Mr. Das was no longer smiling at Harold. Head back, he was staring vacantly at the ceiling, where the fan kept giving a half turn or two and then stopping short again.

"Are you and Lady Anne what might be called independent witnesses?" he asked.

The Chief Justice stirred himself and pushed his glasses farther up his nose: he found that he always heard better when he was wearing his glasses properly.

"I don't understand you."

"There was no arrangement between you?"

"None whatsoever."

"No special understanding?"

"I have told you. None."

Mr. Das's eyes had returned to him now.

"But you are friends, are you not?"

"Yes. We are friends."

"Close friends?"

"I suppose you could call it that."

"I don't call it anything, Mr. Stebbs. I want you to tell me what your relations were."

He paused.

"Were they intimate?"

Mr. Ngono was suddenly leaning so far forward that he was

284

blotting out everything. The chief cashier, whose view he was totally blocking, touched him on the shoulder again. But this time Mr. Ngono did not move. In his excitement, he did not even notice.

"We didn't see a great deal of each other, if that's what you mean."

"It is not in the least what I mean," Mr. Das replied. "I was using the word in its more specific legal sense."

Mr. Ngono drew in his breath sharply. Mr. Das's question must mean that Mr. Talefwa had told him everything, simply stolen his confidences and used them for his own purposes. Mr. Ngono hated Mr. Talefwa.

"Do you understand my meaning now?" Mr. Das asked.

The familiar smile was there when he put the question. It was still there while he waited for the reply. The Court had gone very quiet again.

"I do."

Harold could feel his heart bumping as he said the words.

"And what is your answer?"

"No. It is not true."

Mr. Das's smile changed somewhat. It now seemed somehow toothier.

"I want to avoid any possibility of misunderstanding on this point," he said. "I will therefore rephrase my question."

He halted deliberately.

"Were you and Lady Anne lovers?" he asked.

Harold could not remember afterwards whether he had actually denied it. He had been ready to do so: that much was certain. There were some things that Mr. Das would never be able to drag out of him.

But at that moment, there was an interruption.

It came from inside the dock itself. His white cloth slipping off him, Old Moses struggled up from his chair. Now that he was upright, he looked more gaunt and scarecrowlike than ever. Pursing up his withered, crinkled lips, he spat on the floor at Mr. Das's feet.

Chapter 44

HAROLD AND the Attorney General were cool at last. Bathed and changed, they were out on the veranda of the Milner Club, and the breeze that had come up had just begun to set the corners of the tablecloths flapping. The air usually got moving in this way after dusk, when it was too late to be of real use to anybody.

"Pity the C.J. isn't here," the Attorney General remarked reflectively. "But he's awfully strict about it. No mixing while the case is on."

Over in the lighted doorway of the clubhouse, one of the bar boys was standing. While he was still speaking, the Attorney General made a circular, signaling movement with his hand to indicate that another round was needed.

"Well, I can tell you one thing," Harold said. "If he hadn't spat at him, I think I'd have done it myself."

The Attorney General shook his head.

"You did very well," he told him. "Just the right note of indignation. Keep it up that way."

"Dirty little swine."

"Oh, I don't know about that," he replied. "Only doing his job. Trying to establish conspiracy. Not a bad idea. Lots of juries fall for it."

"He didn't have to bring *her* into it—not like that, he didn't."

The Attorney General was playing with the sugar bowl. It was one of the new kind, with telescopic tongs fitted into the electroplated lid. He was selecting especially inaccessible lumps and endeavoring to capture them.

"Been expecting it," he replied. "Got to make everything at the top seem as rotten as possible. It's just African politics."

"Well, it won't work."

The Attorney General paused.

"I'd rather have had an all-white jury," he said.

Harold was silent for a moment.

"How long'll it go on?" he asked.

"A couple of days. May run into next week. All depends on him. It could be finished tomorrow."

"Think Lady Anne'll be all right?"

"Don't see why she shouldn't be. It's not like the A.D.C. She isn't trying to cover anything up."

"Not exactly nice for her, though."

"Said she wanted to be called. Told me so herself. Probably been looking forward to it. Pure revenge, of course. Women are like that."

"She isn't," Harold told him. "She can't bear people getting hurt."

But the Attorney General wasn't listening.

"Got it," he said.

And to prove what he was claiming, he showed Harold a particularly small, wedge-shaped lump nipped in the end of the new patent sugar tongs.

The arrangements for getting Lady Anne to the Court had all been worked out with Sybil Prosser.

A car was to be waiting at Crown Cottage from nine forty-five onwards, and when Lady Anne reached the courthouse, she was to be taken straight up to the Chief Justice's anteroom; it had been set aside for her for as long as she should be inside the precincts. The Chief Justice himself had volunteered to use his other door, straight out into the corridor.

It was only now, with the Usher calling everyone to order, that the Chief Justice realized what his gesture had cost him: it meant that he was entirely cut off from his own private washroom.

Punctually at ten o'clock, he addressed the Court.

"It is not possible to prescribe an exact timetable for any trial," he said. "Nor would it be my wish to do so. Events must be unfolded as the discretion of Counsel dictates. A short trial, a hurried trial, a trial in which examination is skimmed over or, worse still, avoided altogether will always be a bad trial. It is the absolute privilege of the defense to advance all arguments and elicit all available facts, so that the accused may be given a fair hearing and proper representations be made on his behalf."

The Chief Justice paused, as much for breath as to emphasize what he had just uttered. He had already rehearsed the piece that morning while he was shaving, and he had the whole thing word-perfect.

"Nevertheless," he went on, "I must remind Counsel of the condition of the next witness that the Crown will call. She is a lady recently widowed. She has suffered profound shock from the very circumstances which bring her here. Her health, I am advised, is still precarious. I will therefore ask Counsel on both sides to show every consideration and not detain the lady any longer in the witness box than the pursuit of strictly relevant information may require."

The Attorney General's eyes had been half-closed while the Chief Justice was speaking. Now they were open again. The Chief Justice had given no warning of the address; the Attorney General had, indeed, been rather surprised when the little lecture had begun. But it had certainly finished up all right. That bit about "the pursuit of strictly relevant information" had clearly been aimed at Mr. Das; and very well aimed, too.

The Attorney General bowed toward the bench.

"I am most grateful to you, m'lud, for having spoken," he said. "The delicate state of the health of the witness had, of course, been in the very forefront of my mind when deliberating on whether or not to call her. I will do my utmost to ensure that Your Lordship's wishes are in every respect complied with."

The Chief Justice bowed back in turn, and it was Mr. Das's chance to catch his eye.

"With Your Lordship's approval, I shall endeavor to be brief," he said. "Very brief indeed, m'lud."

For that, he got his own return bow from the Chief Justice. It was not much of one, however; more of a nod than a bow, really.

"Call Lady Anne Hackforth."

It was the moment for which everyone had been waiting.

With the blinds drawn at all the windows, the light in the courtroom was placid and subdued. Then, at the side, a door opened. Behind it was the bare corridor, sunlit and white-painted. And into the frame of the doorway came Lady Anne.

Mr. Ngono thought that he had never seen anything so beautiful. Lady Anne was veiled, and all in black. The white handkerchief that she was carrying made the blackness seem blacker still.

And beneath the dark lacework of the veiling, her face showed white like the handkerchief. She was walking slowly, her head bent forward, hands clasped in front of her.

The Court now had gone entirely silent. It was the presence of widowhood, of bereavement, that had subdued it. There was a hush over everything, and even Mr. Das's smile had disappeared.

Harold leaned forward.

Oh, God, he was thinking. They shouldn't have let her come. She'll never stand it. Not on top of everything else. It'll kill her.

The door through which Lady Anne had just entered was already closing when it was pushed violently open again, and Sybil Prosser appeared. Somewhere, pinned behind it, was the Court Usher: he was protesting. But Sybil Prosser ignored him. She went over to Lady Anne and put her arm around her. The Usher opened the door of the witness box.

"Please be seated, Lady Anne." It was the Chief Justice who was speaking. "The Court has been told that you have not been well."

Lady Anne did not move. She stood there, her hands resting on the rail in front of her, swaying slightly. The Chief Justice noticed that she had not raised her head since she had come in; all that he could see was the pale forehead and the veil covering it. He began to wonder if she had even heard him.

He was just about to address her again when he saw that her lips were moving.

"Thank you," she said, "but I am quite strong enough to stand."

Her voice was so low, so faint, that the Chief Justice found himself leaning forward so that he could hear her.

"Very well," he replied. "But if, at any time, you should become fatigued, you are to tell me. I have already expressed my wish that, in every way possible, you are to be spared all unnecessary strain."

He caught the Attorney General's eye as he was speaking. The Attorney General half-rose from his seat and obediently bowed back.

"You may proceed," the Chief Justice told him.

The Attorney General was gentle, very gentle. He might have been a kind teacher coaxing a nervous pupil. It was obvious that he was there simply to help her. And bit by bit, her story pieced together.

She had been asleep. It must have been somewhere toward three in the morning, because she had given Sybil Prosser her medicine at two-thirty. Then she had gone back to bed again. But tired as she was, she had wakened suddenly. Whatever it was that had disturbed her, she had felt frightened. It was like something being knocked over, she said, or something heavy bumping against Sir Gardnor's desk. She had even wondered if it might be a wild animal that had got into the tent. She had never liked the shooting of any game, she told them, and the thought had crossed her mind that it might be the mate of the leopard that Sir Gardnor had just killed.

No, she had not heard anything spoken; there hadn't been voices of any kind. It was simply because she was aware that someone, or something, was moving about that she had got up. In the ordinary way, she would have called out to ask if Sir Gardnor was all right; she couldn't do that, however, because she had Sybil Prosser asleep in the bed alongside hers. It had not worried her in the least that at three A.M. Sir Gardnor should still be working: she had known him many times to sit up at his desk practically all night. It was just that this time it had been different: she had *felt* that there was something wrong. That was why she had left her own sleeping tent and had gone through into the main marquee.

"And what did you see when you got there?"

The Attorney General waited, but there was no reply. Lady Anne had her handkerchief pressed up against her eyes.

"I am sorry that this should be so painful," the Attorney General assured her. "Please take your time. Take your time, and then tell me in your own words."

Lady Anne was sobbing quite audibly by now, and the Chief Justice was becoming concerned for her.

"Are you sure you are all right, Lady Anne?" he asked. "I can adjourn the Court if you so wish."

But Lady Anne only shook her head.

"I can go on now," she said.

"Then will you please tell me what you saw?" the Attorney General asked in the same quiet, almost wheedling, tone of voice.

Lady Anne brought her hand down from her face and took hold of the rail to steady herself. She was looking out into the Court now; it was the first time since she had entered the witness box that she had raised her head.

"I saw my husband," she said. "He was in his usual chair, where he had been sitting when I said good night to him. Only he wasn't moving. And there was . . . there was . . . there was blood all over him."

She was crying again by now, and the Attorney General waited patiently for her to recover sufficiently to continue.

"Was anyone with your husband?" he asked.

Lady Anne nodded.

"Yes."

"Who was that person?"

The pause was a long one this time. It was as though Lady Anne could not bring herself to utter the name.

"Old Moses."

The Chief Justice was leaning right forward again. He was anxious to miss nothing, and Lady Anne's last answer seemed to have been breathed rather than actually spoken.

"And what was Old Moses doing?"

The Chief Justice could see that her lips were moving, but he could hear no sound. It seemed that she was unable to form the words. Then she recovered herself.

"He was leaning on him," she said, "pressing down on him, doing something to his neck. There was a lot of blood on his hands, too." She paused. "He didn't see me at first."

"And then?"

"I screamed. I just stood there and screamed. I couldn't do anything. I could only scream. That was when Mr. Stebbs came in."

"How much later would that be?"

"I don't know. I can't remember."

Her words were suddenly coming faster. She had raised her

voice now; it was the first time the Chief Justice had been able to hear her properly.

"I can't remember anything about that night. It was all too awful. I don't want to remember. I just want to be dead myself so that I can forget about it."

The Attorney General raised his hand and coughed into it.

"Thank you, Lady Anne," he said. "I shall not trouble you any further."

While he was still speaking, Sybil Prosser had gone across to the witness box. She might have been a nurse in attendance. Pushing back Lady Anne's veil, she fed her like a baby with little sips of water from the glass that had been placed on the ledge beside her.

The Chief Justice tapped with his pencil.

"I must ask that the witness should receive no further assistance here in Court," he said. "If Lady Anne's Counsel sees fit to ask for an adjournment, I have already said that I am ready to grant it."

It was Lady Anne who shook her head.

"I'm sorry," she said, faintly. "I am quite ready to go on. It's only that I thought that . . . that it was all over."

The Chief Justice looked hard at her for a moment. He was worried; another outburst like the last one and he would refuse to allow her to go on. But she seemed to be composed enough now. She had lowered her head again, and her hands were back on the rail in front of her.

Reluctantly, the Chief Justice turned and nodded in Mr. Das's direction. Mr. Das rose slowly, far more slowly than he had risen for the other witnesses. He was diffident and apologetic. Even his bow seemed humble.

"Lady Anne," he said, "it grieves me very much that I should have to question you at all. You must believe me when I say that it is deeply painful for me too. I would have wished to spare you anything more. But my duty requires it."

He paused.

"Would you please, Lady Anne, fold back that veil that you are wearing?"

The Attorney General was immediately on his feet.

"M'lud," he began, "I must protest most strongly. Can it really be necessary that . . ."

This was an entirely different Attorney General: a fiery one. His voice had just the right edge on it. He was using his arms very effectively, too.

But he need not have troubled even to rise. Lady Anne had already thrown back her veil. She had thrust her hand under it angrily, as though it were in her way. And she had raised her head again.

Mr. Das bowed back to her.

"Thank you," he said. "That is much better. Now we can see each other."

He paused. It was an even longer pause than last time. He simply stood there, his eyes fixed upon her.

Then his smile returned.

"Lady Anne," he asked, "was it you who murdered your husband?"

Chapter 45

THE COURT was now deserted, except for the cleaners. These were divided into two bands. The first were going round with watering cans and a bowl of canteen tea leaves to lay the dust. Behind them came their superiors with the brooms. They were gathering up the wet sludge that was all that remained of the thin reddish powder from the loose gravel in the entrance drive. The operation was performed daily. If anyone even walked along the drive, he was followed by a cloud of dust that seeped endlessly in under the doors and through the Works Department woodwork of the window frames. The air vents were frequently clogged solid.

It was the jury room that had become the center of things. And that was incommunicado. The last contact with the everyday world had been when the messenger had brought in a tray with the two large jugs of lemonade and the carton of cuplets beside them. He had then turned the key in the door behind him. That was nearly two hours ago.

The time had passed slowly. Already the clock on the wall showed three-fifteen, and every five minutes or so the foreman kept glancing up at it to see if it could have stopped altogether.

The cocoa man had been elected by his fellow jurors as foreman. He was sitting in his shirt sleeves, wiping his forehead with his handkerchief. His tie, crumpled and sodden where the knot had been, hung over the chair back behind him.

For the moment, they were all talking at once.

"I still didn't hear what she said before she fainted."

"If she *did* faint."

"Well, they had to pick her up off the floor, didn't they?"

"Anyhow, he made her repeat it afterwards."

"I didn't hear that time either."

"Does it matter? She isn't the one who's on trial. The judge said so."

"But it still requires an answer, doesn't it?"

The chairman brought his gavel down upon the sounding block; by comparison, West Coast cocoa auctions suddenly seemed so quiet, so orderly.

"Gentlemen, gentlemen," he said. "One at a time, please. Let's clear up the points as we go along. First of all, if she'd said she *had* murdered him, do you imagine they'd have let the trial go on?"

The jurors all turned accusingly toward the one who hadn't heard. He was the new headmaster of the Amimbo High School. A pale, waxen-faced man, as mild-looking as an unlit candle, he had proved to be the one troublemaker in their midst.

"No, I suppose not," he admitted.

"Then she must have denied it, mustn't she?"

The schoolmaster was silent for a moment. He was twisting the cap of his fountain pen as though he were winding the thing.

"All right," he replied at last. "I won't press the point. It's simply that I want to be on record that I didn't hear."

"Okay."

The foreman took out the damp, discolored handkerchief again and began mopping the back of his neck.

"So let's forget about Lady Anne, and all the rest of it, shall we?" he suggested. "Just concentrate on Old Moses. Is that agreed, then?"

He looked round the table as he finished speaking and gave a quick nod for each one of them in turn. Nobody disputed the decision. Mr. Ngono, however, felt rather hurt: the chairman had been so brusque, so rapid, that he hadn't given him enough time to nod back.

"Very well," the foreman resumed. "Now for a look at the facts. It was Old Moses who had his hand on the murder weapon, and there was blood all over him. Right?"

He glanced up for a second, jerking his head back as he did so; it was a habit that he had retained from the old days when it had been part of his business to make sure that there were no late bidders.

One hand went up. It was the bank manager's. He was known to be a steady, reliable sort of man, and the rest were prepared to take notice of him. Up to the present, he had simply sat there, listening.

"That's something we've got to be quite sure about," he said. "Everything else hinges on it."

"Correct," the foreman told him, "and that's where the eye-witnesses come in. Two of them, remember."

"It's the eyewitnesses that I was thinking about," the bank manager replied, speaking slowly, as though he were being asked to arrange an overdraft and was still dubious about the security. "They may have misled us, you know."

"Are you calling Lady Anne a liar?"

This time, it was the superintendent of railways who had spoken. Over the years he had climbed slowly to his present position and was a great respecter of authority.

So was the cocoa man.

"Through the chair, please, if you don't mind," he told him. "Let's try to keep things orderly."

The bank manager folded his hands together.

"It's not a question of calling anyone a liar," he said. "It's merely that they may have been mistaken. I'm bound to say that I was very much impressed by the demonstration. There didn't seem to be any difference in the way he was holding it."

"Nor was there," the schoolmaster added.

"None whatsoever. The judge damn well said so," Mr. Ngono added.

The foreman reached out his hand for his gavel. If he allowed the conversation to become general again, they would be there all night.

"It wasn't the judge," he corrected him. "It was Counsel. That's a very different matter."

The bank manager's hands were still folded.

"Not so far as I'm concerned, it isn't," he said. "I don't mind who said it. I could see for myself."

It seemed to the foreman that this was one of those occasions when it might be wise to play for time.

"You were saying, Mr. Ngono?" he asked.

Mr. Ngono, as it happened, had stopped thinking about the demonstration. His mind was on something else: he was wondering whether, with a word in the right quarter, a hint dropped in someone's ear at a cocktail party, he couldn't interest the authorities in the complete overhaul of all the Court furnishings—chairs, tables, clocks, even quite little things like lemonade jugs and penholders. Handled properly, it would be worth a small fortune.

"I agree with everything that has been said," he replied. "I haven't got so much as one single damn doubt about it."

"About what?"

"About what the gentlemen have just been saying. It is all most extremely clear."

The foreman thanked him and turned away.

"And you, sir?" he asked. "May we have your views?"

This time, it was the head cashier of the European Emporium that he was addressing. A plump, owlish man, caged up during most of his working day behind steel bars somewhere at the back of the shop, he gave the impression of having only just emerged into the daylight. As he spoke, he kept blinking.

"I don't see what it's got to do with it," he said. "The grip, I mean. Just because that's the way you'd hold it if you were pulling it out doesn't prove you weren't doing the other thing. Not if the two grips were the same, if you follow me."

The foreman saw this for his opportunity.

"And there's another aspect we haven't touched on—Old Moses losing his speech like that. I'm not saying it isn't genuine. It may be, for all I know. But it seems very peculiar to me. Very peculiar indeed. It stops him admitting anything."

"That is, if he's got anything to admit," the schoolmaster reminded him.

"Precisely. But look at it this way. Suppose you'd lost your voice, and somebody accused you of committing murder. Wouldn't you find some way of denying it? Even shaking your head, or something?"

"I might. I don't know. It's never happened to me."

The bank manager leaned forward.

"It's a good point," he conceded. "A very good point indeed. I must admit, it hadn't occurred to me."

He was at once supported by the superintendent of railways.

"Quite agree," he said. "Always thought there was something fishy about that voice business."

Even the owner of the Missionary Bookstore, sitting beside him, was impressed.

"You'd have thought he'd have made *some* effort," he said. "Found some means of communicating. Unless, of course, he *is* guilty. In which case, the less said the better from his point of view. It's all very . . ."

He paused long enough to make them think that something new and of importance was coming.

". . . very disturbing," he added. "The uncertainty, you know."

"And what about you, Mr. Ngono?" the chairman asked. "If you were falsely accused, wouldn't you find some way of defending yourself?"

This time Mr. Ngono really had been listening; concentrating hard, in fact.

"You're damn well right, I would," he replied fervently.

The chairman did not attempt to rush them. He gave them all ample time to consider the significance of the last three answers.

"And Old Moses hasn't done so, has he?" he asked at last. "Not once made the slightest attempt to clear himself. I'm afraid that points only one way, in my opinion."

"We still haven't established any motive," the schoolmaster persisted. "You can't have a murder without motive. It doesn't make sense."

Under the stress of argument, his complexion was changing. There were now faint patches of color in the center of his sallow cheeks.

The superintendent of railways ignored the chair altogether.

"If you'd seen what I've seen," he said, "you wouldn't talk like that. Remember that last affair? One of our local controllers slashed to death for absolutely nothing. And who was responsible? His own chief clerk. Someone he'd looked after and promoted."

"They're certainly like that," the shipping-company representative agreed. "It's just the mad streak coming out. All Mimbos have got it. They're just savages."

Mr. Ngono swung round in his chair and faced the man. The foreman noticed the movement and became apprehensive. But he had underrated Mr. Ngono. Mr. Ngono had handled delicate situations before. He was smiling broadly and holding out his monogrammed gold cigarette case with the built-in lighter.

"Smoke?" he asked. "Egyptian, your side. Hand-rolled Virginian, over here."

All in all, a bit of light relief was, the foreman decided, just what had been needed. It helped to keep the rest of it running smoothly. And in any case, things weren't going too badly; already there were the first signs of progress. He was particularly pleased that at last he had got the shipping representative to join in the discussion. Up to that moment, it had seemed that nothing short of a First Class stateroom accommodation could have roused the man.

"I'm afraid he's right," the foreman said slowly. "There isn't a motive every time."

The schoolmaster was fiddling with his fountain pen again.

"Mr. Das suggested a motive," he pointed out.

But this was too much for the foreman. He thrust the pad, with his pencil notes scribbled all over it, away from him and sat back.

"Can't bring that up now," he said. "We agreed to forget all about it. 'Just concentrate on Old Moses' were the words I used."

"You may have agreed it," the schoolmaster came back at him. "I didn't. I never said a word."

"Does the last speaker mean that he thinks that Lady Anne and the Stebbs fellow *were* having an affair together?" the superintendent of railways asked, speaking formally through the chair this time.

"They may have been. I don't know."

"And plotting to murder Sir Gardnor?"

The schoolmaster put down his fountain pen and brought his fingertips together.

"The two things go together," he said. "If they were having an affair . . ."

"But he denied it, didn't he? Or couldn't you hear that bit either?"

Already the chair had been forgotten, and the superintendent and the headmaster were confronting each other.

"I most certainly heard him. And of course he denied it. If he were a guilty party, he could hardly have been expected to do otherwise. And, if they were both guilty partners, there is your motive for wanting to put Sir Gardnor out of the way."

"Like stabbing him to death?"

The schoolmaster looked over the top of his glasses. He was finding it increasingly difficult to talk, quietly and logically, to anyone so obviously undereducated as the railway man.

"The method is entirely immaterial," he said.

"Well, I think you should be bloody well ashamed of yourself," the superintendent shouted back at him. "Filling people's ears up with dirt like that."

He was thumping the table while he was speaking, bringing his closed fist down on it.

"My God," he wound up, "and to think that you're the sort of man we get to look after our children."

The foreman glanced up at the clock again. It showed nearly four o'clock by now. Picking up his gavel he brought it down, viciously this time as if he were trying to crack something. The report startled them.

"Gentlemen, please," he said. "May I just remind you of something. We've been here over two hours, and we are now back where we started. At this rate, we're never even going to reach a verdict."

Now that the foreman had temporarily regained his authority, he was anxious to show them all how alert he was, how smart at picking up any loose ends.

"If there had been any love affair, I feel we'd have heard more about it," he observed. "And there's another thing that weighs with me—the way Old Moses behaved. He'd have been the first to know about it. The suggestion obviously came as a great shock to him."

"I'm inclined to agree," the schoolmaster said quietly. "I was only arguing the point."

"Then you think that Old Moses did it?"

The schoolmaster had brought his fingertips together again.

"I haven't said so," he replied. "Not yet. But if Old Moses *had* just committed a ritual killing, then naturally he wouldn't want the whole thing reduced to the level of sordid domestic tragedy. It could account for his sudden, unexplained anger."

"So you think he's guilty?"

"On balance, yes. It's the logical conclusion. But only on balance, mind you."

He had separated his two hands while he was speaking and was now busily winding up his fountain pen again.

The foreman smiled back at him. And he intended to make the most of his new advantage. This was clearly the moment for going round the table as rapidly as possible.

"You don't have to ask me," the superintendent of railways replied. "You know my views. You could have had them when we sat down. Guilty."

The foreman moved on farther down the table.

"No doubt about it. Guilty Plain as a pikestaff. Afraid so."

The chief cashier hadn't even bothered to look up as he was speaking.

"And you, sir?" the foreman asked, turning toward the bank manager.

"I'm by no means sure he did," the bank manager replied, "and I'm by no means sure he didn't. He had the knife in his hands, that's for certain. And as our friend here"—he indicated the chief cashier as he said it—"explained to us, it doesn't prove anything how he was holding it. If it wasn't him, I don't know who it was. So, I suppose, it's guilty."

The shipping representative did not hesitate: even without any evidence at all, he would have been ready to convict.

"Guilty," he said.

They had come back to the schoolmaster. His fingertips were pressed together in readiness.

"I too say 'guilty,'" he replied, separating his hands for a moment and then bringing them back again. "But only for the time being. I may still change my mind. I don't by any means regard the case as closed, you know."

The chairman thanked him and passed on hurriedly: he felt that a mind like that needed very gentle handling.

"And you, Mr. Ngono?"

Instead of answering immediately, Mr. Ngono tried to light another cigarette. But it was no use. His hands were trembling too much.

"It's up to you," the foreman reminded him. "It's your opinion we're waiting for."

Mr. Ngono was aware that all eyes were turned on him. They were eager, expectant eyes: he knew how warmly they would light up if only he said the right thing. And they were certainly the elite of Amimbo who were sitting there: between them, they could be of immense business assistance. They could make him.

On the other hand, there was Mr. Talefwa: he too cast a long shadow. Mr. Ngono remembered very clearly their last talk in the *War Drum* offices: recalled sentence by sentence what Mr. Talefwa had said about the brief future for White Rule everywhere; about an all-African Government in Amimbo when Independence came; and most of all, about himself installed at the new Ministry of Commerce. Mr. Talefwa had more than half-promised.

Mr. Ngono decided, therefore, that the only thing to do was to keep talking. He spread out his hands, palm upwards.

"Why damn well bother so much about me?" he asked. "Why not rely on these other distinguished gentlemen?"

"Unanimous or nothing," the foreman told him. "That's the law."

Mr. Ngono shifted in his seat.

"Then why not a ballot?" he suggested. "In secret, of course. That would give you our inmost thoughts. And in writing, too."

The foreman shook his head.

"No ballot," he said.

Already the eyes seemed to have hardened: they were glinting at him.

Fortunately, he still had his skill as a debater: it comforted him to remember how many times his speeches at Cambridge had been admired, how often he had been congratulated.

"You really want the goddam truth?" he asked.

"I do."

"Then I say we're barking up the wrong tree," he said. "Being led up the garden path by our bloody noses, in fact. One eminent Counsel says one thing and the other eminent Counsel clouds our minds for us. What do we know about the law in comparison with such clever people?"

"It's got nothing to do with the law."

Mr. Ngono saw this for his opportunity. With his debating experience, he felt sure that he could keep things going indefinitely—simply wear them down until they grew tired of asking him.

He threw up his arms above his head. "Nothing to do with the law if he's guilty?" he demanded. "Then I damn well ask you what is the law there for?"

Mr. Ngono, however, was forgetting that the cocoa man had spent most of his life on the equator: he knew what it was to get caught up in native arguments.

"You're wasting our time," he said bluntly. "I'm asking you a straight question: is Old Moses guilty, or isn't he?"

Mr. Ngono put his hand over his heart this time.

"You are asking me that again?" he replied. "I have only just answered you. My advice is that we keep out of it. Not take sides at all. It is most kindly meant advice, too. Entirely considerate."

" 'Yes' or 'no'?" the foreman repeated.

Mr. Ngono tried again to light his cigarette, but he could not keep the flame steady enough.

"I am prepared to say 'yes,' " he answered. "But only in the sense that it is one of them. Nobody in particular. No hard personal feelings. No grudge. But one of them, definitely 'yes.' Of that you may have no damn doubt whatsoever."

He paused.

"Those are my views. No beating about the bush. No frills, either."

The foreman drew out his wet, sticky handkerchief.

"You're playing the fool with us," he said. "That's what you're doing. Just playing the fool."

It was the schoolmaster who leaned forward.

"Would you mind if I asked our friend a few questions?" he inquired. "I think it may help to clear things up."

"Good luck to you" was all the foreman said.

He was wiping the back of his neck again.

The schoolmaster was all ready. His pen was wound up, and his fingertips were together.

"In your view, is Mr. Stebbs the murderer?" he asked.

Put that way, the question shocked Mr. Ngono. He had always liked Harold Stebbs, and he felt sure that Harold Stebbs liked him too.

He banged on the table.

"That is just the kind of thing I damn well warned you against," he said. "It is jumping to extremely false conclusions. Like some bloody bull in a china shop. Mr. Stebbs is my friend, and I say 'no.' Even if you wish to keep me here all night I shall continue to deny it."

The schoolmaster nodded.

"Then the A.D.C., perhaps?"

This time Mr. Ngono laughed quite openly. He did not even attempt to conceal his feelings. It was a rude, mocking sort of laugh.

"That snob?" he asked. "You are suggesting that he would

harm someone with a title? An H.E. at that! If you think that sort of thing, you damn well don't know human nature. By God, you damn well don't."

He had managed to light his cigarette by now, and he blew the cloud of smoke carelessly into the schoolmaster's face.

"Besides," he added, "he is like so many of his sort. He is just a poof. A harmless, bachelor poof. He wouldn't bloody well kill a mosquito. It would be too damn much like bad manners."

Bringing in the word "bachelor" was very clever: the schoolmaster was unmarried too.

"What about the kitchen boy?" the schoolmaster asked. "He wouldn't mind killing things, would he?"

So it was back to racialism: Mr. Talefwa had warned him from the start that it would go that way. This time Mr. Ngono got really angry.

"If that brave young man himself was in the room," he replied, "you wouldn't damn well dare to utter a word."

His stomach was turning over again, and he had to raise his hand to his mouth to excuse himself.

"Besides," he resumed, smiling quite charmingly, "we are all men of the world, aren't we? I mean, we all have been in some pretty dirty spots in our time. Most disgraceful, in fact. When we were younger, of course. Before we had reached our present high positions. And we damn well know what the kitchen boy was up to that night, don't we? His tribe is renowned for it."

"So you don't think it was the kitchen boy?"

Mr. Ngono winked back at him.

"You know damn well it wasn't."

Even turned as he was full face toward Mr. Ngono, the schoolmaster did not seem to have noticed the wink. He was deep in thought; intense, painful thought. The tips of his fingers were pressed so tightly together that he might have been praying.

"Then are you telling us that it's Lady Anne?" he asked.

He had separated his hands as he was speaking and was holding them out in an open gesture of invitation for Mr. Ngono to come forward.

But Mr. Ngono saw it at once for the trap that it so obviously was. Instinctively, he drew back.

African independence was one thing, and well worth waiting for. But it was still a long way off; no more than a bright gleam in the eye of Mr. Talefwa, in fact. In the meantime, Mr. Ngono had his European business connections to consider. And how could he ever hope to secure another contract within the community if he was known to have gone around suggesting that Governors married the kind of women who might murder them?

Thinking of the terrible position in which he might have found himself, he became indignant.

"Lady Anne is a most pure and virtuous person," he replied. "A saint, in fact. For her of all people, a halo would not be too damn much."

He was aware of the eyes again: the accusing, probing eyes all round him.

He looked hard at the schoolmaster.

"The stink of what you have just said hangs all round you," he told him. "It is most extremely nauseating."

He raised his thumb and forefinger in the air and squeezed both nostrils hard together.

"Then that brings us back to Old Moses, doesn't it?" the schoolmaster asked him.

A fresh stab of pain shot through Mr. Ngono's stomach.

"I have told you before," he shouted back. "Old Moses has damn well nothing to do with it."

"Oh, but he has," the schoolmaster replied in the same quiet classroom voice. "You said it was one of them, and you've ruled out all the others. There's no one left now but Old Moses, is there, Mr. Ngono?"

Mr. Ngono's shoulders were heaving. He was pressing down hard on the buckle of his trouser belt.

"You must excuse me," he said. "I am most extremely unwell. It is my bad digestion."

"Then, as we're all agreed, shall we go through?" the foreman asked.

They had been shut up with each other for nearly three hours, and the prospect of release seemed merciful. There was the immediate scraping of chair legs.

Only Mr. Ngono remained seated. Ever since the schoolmaster's last question, he had been sitting with his hands on his knees, looking downwards at his feet. He was utterly exhausted; too exhausted even to care any longer.

If only Mr. Talefwa had been there in person, he would have seen how courageously he had fought. How stubbornly, too. Even brilliantly, at times. Mr. Ngono could not find it in him to reproach himself: the reason for his defeat was simply that he had been so hideously outnumbered.

The Chief Justice did not prolong things. After the days of heavy strain on the prisoner and remembering his advanced years, it would, he said, be kinder to bring the trial to an end without delay. It had been a fair one, he added, and no exertions had been spared to secure an acquittal. Nevertheless, the evidence had been overwhelming, and the finding of the jury was both just and inevitable. He produced the black cap and passed sentence accordingly.

Mr. Das instantly gave notice of appeal.

That same evening, Mr. Ngono was beaten up on the way back home from his night club.

Public feeling was undoubtedly behind the assault. But the fact that his monogrammed cigarette case, gold pencil, and chiming wristwatch were all missing suggested that common robbery might have figured somewhere in it too.

BOOK IV

Truth and Consequences

Chapter 46

BY NOW they had been three days at sea, and already Amimbo seemed far off and long ago.

Mr. Frith had sent for Harold as soon as the trial was over. It was that eye of his that was worrying them, Mr. Frith had said: he'd had a word with the Governor, and they both agreed that if he didn't want to lose the use of it, he ought to get it properly attended to. Moorfields was what Mr. Frith had in mind, and that meant a trip back home for him. He'd fixed up the bit about sick leave, and there was a boat leaving on Friday. If Harold got to work on it straightaway, he might just be able to make it.

Going away or staying made not the slightest difference, Sybil Prosser told him: so long as she was around, no one was going to see Lady Anne.

It was a miracle that she had survived the trial, Sybil Prosser added; and if Harold was any friend of Lady Anne's, he'd see that the kindest thing that he could do now would be to leave her alone so that she had a chance to recover. Of course, he could write if he wanted to: she couldn't stop him doing that. After all, it was only natural that Lady Anne would like to hear from him. Letters weren't nearly so tiring as visitors.

Joining the ship wasn't quite the everyday affair that Harold had imagined: word had got round, and they were on the lookout for him. He found himself a someone, a celebrity. It wasn't every day that they carried a star witness from a big murder trial, and the Captain was proud to have him on board.

He was popular, too. Everyone liked the decent showing he had made under cross-examination. The whole of the First Class passenger list agreed that after what he had been through, he deserved to be left alone to get a good rest and invited him to join them at little parties specially laid on around the bar on the afterdeck.

But it was no use: he simply wasn't a good mixer; and after one or two disappointments, they began to leave him alone again. Not that it was altogether Harold's fault. There was that everlasting pain that went on underneath the eye patch; and his mind wasn't on what was being said anyhow. It was on Lady Anne mostly.

She kept coming back into his mind, uninvited and unannounced. If he picked up a book and began reading, there she was, in between his eyes and the page, looking up at him. She even spoke sometimes. It was mostly as he was going off to sleep that he heard her. Just his name usually, spoken quite quietly; whispered almost. And with the sound of her voice came that perfume that she always wore; little eddies of it kept drifting across the cabin and then getting lost again as the blades of the endlessly whirring fan began to play on them. Once, during the night, when he was still asleep, he had thrown out his arm in the darkness groping to feel if she was there beside him.

The two letters that he had so far written had both been torn up again. Torn up very small, too. He had stood at the rail tossing the bits over, one by one, so that they could never be pieced together again. He was a rotten, bad letter writer, he decided.

The musical chimes that announced dinner had already sounded, and Harold was in front of the mirror brushing down his hair. The image that stared back from the looking glass rather amused him: it was as though the two of them had never met before. It wasn't simply the grotesque eye patch that made him look a stranger: it was everything about him. The fresh, pink-complexioned young man who had traveled out on the *Ancarses* was no longer there. He'd been replaced. This one was thinner, even sparse-looking. And his face had trimmed down, too: the skin was drawn tight in places, and pitted with tiny scars where the rock splinters had entered. There were two lines that hadn't been there before running beside his mouth and beginning to drag the corners down.

"I'll have another shot at it in the morning," he was telling himself. "Perhaps I can do better after breakfast. In any case, I can always send a cable. Send a cable, and then write properly when I get back home. Really say what I want to."

He reached out for his tie and carefully drew the two ends down to the same length. It was Hong Kong silk, fresh from the European Emporium: one side was fraying open already. He bent forward to make sure that his collar was in place.

But it was not the starched, African-laundered shirt front that the mirror was reflecting. It was Lady Anne's face that confronted him: her face, with the dark hair loose over the temples and those remarkably fine eyes of hers looking back into his. The eyes, however, were scarcely at their brightest. They were sad and anxious-looking; even frightened. In another moment, there might have been tears in them.

But as he stood there she was fading, going away from him again. The Hong Kong tie and the two rolled gold studs were beginning to show through. The portrait frame had become an ordinary dressing-table mirror again, and he was standing in front of it.

In any case, she's bound to have written to me by now, the thought came to him. She'll have got hold of the address somehow. She's probably air-mailed it. It'll be there waiting for me when I get home. I know it will.

That had been nearly a month ago; a month, and still no letter from Lady Anne.

It was because he was in the hospital, he told himself. Somebody hadn't readdressed the envelope; it must simply be lying there at his bank, or at the Colonial Office, or on the tray in his aunt's front hall out at Reading; either that or it had been stuck into the crisscross tapes on the green baize board down below in the entrance hall.

She'd have had his letters by now: that much was certain. They must have been arriving in batches, too, the way the mail in Amimbo always came. He'd been writing every day. Or had been up to the time of his first operation. There'd been a break then; he'd missed five whole days in succession.

And it looked now as though there was going to be another break. It was the big operation that was coming up tomorrow: they warned him that he would have to take things easy after that one. That was why he had spent most of the afternoon writing. She wasn't to write a long letter back, he had ended up by telling her: he didn't want her to go tiring herself, or anything like that. Even a post card would do—just so that he could know that she was all right.

As it was, the only news of Amimbo had come from Mr. Frith. There had been two letters. That in itself was rather disturbing, because it showed that the mail was coming through all right: there wasn't any holdup on the line to Nucca. And Mr. Frith's were the kind of letters that Harold would hardly have missed if they had gone astray somewhere.

The first had been about the reprieve. Mr. Drawbridge had acted promptly; and the act of sparing Old Moses' life had, Mr. Frith said, been well received by all communities, the Asian included.

The second letter dealt mostly with smaller matters. The budget looked like going through pretty much as they had presented it. Harold wasn't to worry about the state of the bungalow garden while he was away, because Public Works would keep an eye on the boys to see that they didn't let up on the watering. Mrs. Drawbridge was expected out there as soon as she had fixed up about the children. And the staff in the Cottage Hospital had successfully reset Mr. Ngono's nose that had been broken in the beating-up affair. There had been a fire in the marshaling yard, where a spark from the Coronation Flyer had landed on a consignment of copra. And Harold wasn't to go using that eye of his too much until he'd heard what the doctors had to say. Mr. Frith hoped that there were some good shows on in town. And if it wasn't too much trouble, he'd be grateful if Harold could bring him back some HB refills for his mechanical pencil.

The letters had been handwritten on his Telegraph Hill notepaper, and there was a lot of smudging and crossing-out toward the bottom of the second page. Harold got the impression that they must have been written late at night; the bit about the refills had been added as a postscript to both of them.

There had been no mention of Lady Anne or Sybil Prosser in either letter.

Now that the operation, the big one, was all over, Harold rather admired himself for having taken the outcome so calmly. Not that it would make much difference to him: he'd been used for so long to going around in an eye patch. And in any case, he'd known what he was in for when the Sister had brought him the hospital form to sign. The only thing that he didn't fancy was going along to the place in Holborn so that they could match up the color with the other one.

For the time being, he was resting. He was back with his aunt in the little villa in Reading, and she was looking after him. Large cups of milky coffee, and soft cakes with icing on them, were put down beside him when he least expected them; and there were fresh flowers in his bedroom. It was all part of the process of building him up again, his aunt kept saying, and she was thoroughly enjoying it.

There was another three weeks of sick leave stretching ahead of him, and he spent the whole of it feeling ungrateful. It had been his idea to get out of England in the first place, he kept reminding himself; and he knew now that the only real life for him was back there in Africa. That was why he kept looking at the calendar, waiting until it could all start up again.

He'd got used to the idea that he might not be hearing from Lady Anne; no longer expected to, in fact. And in a way, he was glad. It showed that she trusted him. Even if she was too ill to write, she knew that he was coming back to her, and on what terms. It had all been there in that long letter that he had sent from the hospital before the big operation. Perhaps the surgery had made him more apprehensive than he realized: whatever it was, he'd found it easier that afternoon to say what he really meant.

The one thing that he wanted her to know was that he really loved her; loved her forever, that was. That it hadn't just been one of those sudden affairs that flare up so often simply because someone is lonely and there doesn't happen to be anybody else around.

If there had been a relapse, if she were really ill again, Mr. Frith would have been sure to mention it: even preoccupied as he was about the refills for his mechanical pencil, he could hardly have overlooked a thing like that.

Chapter 47

It was because he was living for the next meeting with Lady Anne, because he had already rehearsed it in his mind so many times, that he decided, before he went back, to go down and see young Timothy.

The visit wasn't quite so easy to arrange as he had expected. Boys could not be taken out except by their parents or guardians —unless, of course, one of them had written first; and unfortunately, there had been no letter of any kind, the headmaster explained. He was sure all the same, that Timothy would be most interested to talk to someone so recently back from Amimbo, he went on, and perhaps Harold would care to meet him over tea in the house.

The school was set out in the countryside somewhere beyond Devizes. It did not seem to be near to anywhere; and to make it more isolated still, it had its park spread all round it. The taxi took Harold up a long drive alongside rugby fields with half-sized posts, past the swimming pool with its corrugated-iron changing shed, and brought him to the big front portico, with the row of fives courts built up against the side wall. Small boys, heads down, were hurrying from nowhere. Harold told the driver to be back for him at five o'clock.

Tea, despite the trouble that the headmaster's wife had taken, was hardly a success. Young Hackforth was a large, silent boy; so large, indeed, that his resemblance to his father was quite startling. It might have been the Governor himself who was sitting there in those light-looking gray shorts and the blazingly bright pink blazer. He had, too, the same rather condescending manner as he got up to shake hands: Harold felt that he should have apologized for disturbing him.

And either he was concealing his feelings or he really didn't care. He ate his way steadily through the tomato sandwiches while Harold was telling him what a great man his father had been, that he was now a legend in the Service, and how black as well as white had wanted to contribute toward the memorial that was going to be erected to him.

Young Hackforth brightened a little at the story of the buffalo hunt, and even asked the make of gun that his father had been using. Then he turned to the Madeira cake and was silent again. When Harold spoke of Lady Anne, the boy did not seem to know even that she had been ill.

The headmaster kept Harold behind after Timothy had left them. There wasn't a train now until six-fifteen, he said, and it was warmer in his study than waiting about on the platform. He seemed anxious somehow to prolong the conversation.

"I take it you're a friend of the family," he said, answering himself in the same breath. "You must be, or you wouldn't have gone to the trouble of coming down here."

"I thought someone ought to look him up," Harold replied.

"Did . . . did Lady Anne ask you?" he inquired.

"Nobody asked me," Harold told him. "It's just that I was over here, and I thought I would."

He got the feeling that the headmaster was rather relieved that Lady Anne hadn't sent him. The feeling grew stronger with the headmaster's next question.

"You haven't heard if she's thinking of coming back to England, have you?" he asked.

Harold shook his head.

"Not that I know of," he said. "She talked of setting up house out there."

A look of relief passed across the headmaster's face again.

"It would certainly make it easier," he said. "After all, it's the boy's future we've got to think about, isn't it?"

There was a pause while the headmaster blew out the spirit lamp under the teakettle.

"If you do see Lady Anne when you get back, you'll tell her the boy's all right, won't you? He's well up in his form. I'm not at all anxious about Eton entrance."

There was another pause.

"Did Sir Gardnor ever discuss Timothy with you?" he asked.

The question rather amused Harold: it showed that the headmaster didn't know Sir Gardnor.

"He wasn't that sort of man," he said. "He didn't talk about his private affairs. He was just hard at it all the time being Governor."

The headmaster seemed restless: he was now pulling down the loose cover where Timothy had been sitting.

"I gathered you admired him greatly?" he asked, looking up.

"I did," Harold replied.

The answer obviously pleased the headmaster. It made things easier for him. But he was still troubled.

"Pity all the same," he said. "A boy ought to see something of his mother. It's all so difficult having to deal through the solicitors."

"Through the solicitors?"

"Didn't you know?" the headmaster asked, and then stopped

himself. "Then perhaps I shouldn't have mentioned it. But I take it you're on Sir Gardnor's side. You are, aren't you?"

The headmaster tried to draw back. He saw suddenly what a risk he had taken. It wasn't until this moment that he'd realized that the young man with the funny shiny eye might be the one that all the questions had been about. Perhaps Lady Anne had sent him there to spy on them.

"I don't think I'm on anybody's side," he said. "I don't really see where I come into it."

The headmaster had got up and stood with his back to the fireplace. It was his natural position, Harold suspected: the place where he usually stood when he was giving good advice to people.

"No, no, of course," he said, quickly. "I realize that now. It must all have been before your time. It's simply that Sir Gardnor gave instructions that Lady Anne wasn't to be allowed to see the boy."

Harold remembered a conversation that he'd had long ago in the Residency when Lady Anne had first shown him Timothy's photograph; he hadn't believed what she had told him then.

But already the headmaster was glancing down at his watch. It was nearly five-thirty, and he didn't want his visitor to miss his train.

"It's really the future I'm thinking about," he said. "The legal position now that Sir Gardnor's dead, I mean. I suppose the solicitor will tell me."

He broke off and began moving toward the door.

"I had a letter from Sir Gardnor himself just before he went on that safari," he added. "He told me that the solicitors would know exactly what his wishes were. Strange, isn't it, putting it that way? It's almost as if he'd had a premonition or something."

The three weeks had used themselves up at last. Harold's bedroom, with the open suitcases in it, already had the air of departure. Or of return, rather. Stained and battered-looking as they were, no one this time could mistake them for the baggage of a newcomer.

His aunt was against the whole idea of his going back; in his present state, there must be a job for him here in Whitehall, she argued. And it was only natural she should be worried about him: she'd had the feeling ever since he had come back that there was something on his mind. If it was all those horrible things that had been said at the trial, he was simply to forget about it; and if he had any silly ideas that he could somehow have saved Sir Gardnor's life, he must remember that he'd been ill himself at the time, because of that eye of his.

Sooner or later, he'd want to settle down, she kept reminding him. He wouldn't find the right sort of girl, not out there in Africa; and by then someone else would have snapped up all the nice ones that he might have married if he'd been sensible and stayed at home.

He spent the last afternoon buying his aunt a present. She liked little things about the house, and he knew that secretly she must have been disappointed that he hadn't brought her any of those ebony elephants and ivory-tusk gong holders and bits of beadwork that other African travelers usually carry back with them. She was, however, delighted—overawed almost—by the big radio set, with the carved sunset scene in the front of it, and pretended to be cross with him for having spent so much money on her.

And then, on the last morning, the letter came.

The cerise-colored Amimbo stamp, with the impala in the corner, showed up on the breakfast table, long after he had told himself that he would never see it there.

But the letter was not from Lady Anne. It was from Sybil Prosser, and big as her handwriting was, there were under two pages of it.

She hoped that the operation had passed off successfully, she said, and everyone had been asking after him. Anne, she was sorry to say, was still very far from well. The doctor had ordered complete rest and said that she wasn't to be bothered by anything. That's why his letters had only upset her—they kept reminding her of what she'd been through. It would be better, therefore, if he didn't write to her again; not until she was properly better, that was. She was sure that Harold would understand, and he'd know that it was only Anne's health that she was thinking of. The letter was signed, "Hurriedly, Sybil."

His aunt had been watching him carefully while he read the letter.

"Does it make any difference?" she asked. "About going back there, I mean."

He folded up the letter and put it into his wallet. Then he patted his pocket down to make it go flat again.

"Yes, it does," he said. "I've got to go back more than ever now."

Chapter 48

THEY WERE back at the Milner Club together.

Harold had just climbed onto one of the high stools beside the bar; it was the stool specially reserved for Mr. Frith's personal guests. The stools were all entirely backless, and Mr. Frith himself made a point of occupying the corner seat, with the solid brick wall of the clubhouse behind him.

"Thought I'd get you to come along," Mr. Frith explained. "Bound to be feeling a bit down the first night you're back. Change of climate and all that."

While he was speaking, he had been scrutinizing Harold very closely. He had narrowed his eyes up as he did so, and now leaned forward so that he could add something in the strictest confidence.

"Damn good match," he said at last. "Not sure it isn't a better color than the real one."

Harold twisted his head round so that Mr. Frith could not see his eye. He had already decided that he would go back to the pink celluloid patch tomorrow.

But Mr. Frith was still fascinated.

"Can't imagine how they do it," he went on. "Never have told you were wearing one if I hadn't been in the know."

"I think it's bloody awful."

The reply seemed to shock Mr. Frith: he evidently felt strongly about it.

"You're wrong there," he told him. "Quite wrong. I'll show you."

He broke off for a moment and beckoned the bar boy over. The boy had already reached out for the cork of the Johnnie Walker bottle, but Mr. Frith stopped him.

"Come here, boy," he said.

The boy grinned back at him: he liked being obliging to important Club members.

"Yassah," he said.

"Now, put your thinking cap on," Mr. Frith told him. "Take a good look at Mr. Stebbs here, and then tell me if you notice anything different about him."

The grin disappeared. It was all very embarrassing. The first thing that the steward had taught the boy was never to stare at anyone: it was a pronounced Mimbo trait, staring. But Mr. Frith was First Secretary now, and he supposed that it would be all right for him.

"Yassah," he repeated.

The boy took a half pace to one side so that he could get a better view. He rocked back on his heels. He tilted his head a little. Then the grin returned. It widened into a broad, triumphant smile.

"Yassah," he reported. "Fresh eye, sah."

He was secretly very glad of the opportunity to examine the eye at really close quarters. It was the first thing that he had noticed about Harold when he came in, and he had been staring at it ever since. That was because it was so much the brighter of the two. Caught in the proper light, it sparkled. The boy admired it enormously: he envied Harold. Mr. Frith nudged Harold.

"Anyhow, no point in drawing attention to it," he said. "Just go on wearing it, and people'll forget you've got it in. Soon get used to anything here, you know."

Harold was glad when Mr. Frith suggested, at last, that they move over to the table.

On some nights, he left it so late before he asked for the menu that the kitchen side had entirely closed down and the bar boy had to fix some sandwiches. And some nights Mr. Frith simply cut out dinner altogether; those were the occasions when he felt so out of sorts and fidgety next morning and kept complaining about Colonial Office indifference.

Harold waited until they were both seated. There were other things that he wanted to talk about besides his eye: one in particular. But he didn't want to rush it; didn't want Mr. Frith to know how much it mattered.

Mr. Frith was busy shaking out his napkin.

"Remembered to thank you for the refills, didn't I?" he asked.

"You did."

"Can't think where the last lot got to," he said. "Brought back a whole caseful. Stolen probably."

He broke off, because he had run into difficulties. One of the corners of the napkin had been starched down, and he was trying to prize the hem open with his knife.

"Steal anything," he added. "Doesn't matter how useless it is."

The knife slipped suddenly, and Mr. Frith uttered a loud "Damn": he had managed somehow to cut the napkin. There was now a little triangular flap hanging down from it. He ripped it off and let it drop on the floor beside him.

Then he folded the napkin up again and replaced it carefully on the table. He just wasn't feeling like food, he said. But that wasn't to worry Harold: he'd be perfectly happy watching him do the eating while he brought him up to date on what had been happening.

It was a commentary, rather than straight history, that Mr. Frith provided.

"Didn't know he had the guts," he began. "Never thought he'd do it."

"Do what?" Harold asked.

"Ban it," Mr. Frith told him.

Harold had seen a paragraph in one of the London papers about the shutting-down of *War Drum:* it was the side heading, POLICE POUNCE ON PAPER, that had caught his eye. It had been printed as the third item in a 'News in Brief' column, with a double "m" in Amimbo.

"Can't say I'm surprised," Mr. Frith went on. "Fairly been asking for it."

"What's become of Talefwa?" Harold asked.

Mr. Frith took a sip of his whisky. He had brought the glass over to the table with him.

"Gone to ground," he replied. "Hiding somewhere. Heard he's trying to sell off the paper. Germans'll probably be after it."

"And Ngono?"

The question was automatic. After eighteen months out there, Mr. Talefwa and Mr. Ngono were the only two Africans of Harold's acquaintance.

Mr. Frith put his glass down rather carelessly. He spilled a little. A broad smile had spread across his face.

"You should see him," he said. "He's a proper sight, I can tell you. That nose of his."

"What's wrong with it?"

"Gone all sideways."

Mr. Frith put his thumb up against his nose and pressed hard.

"Like that," he said. "Would keep taking the plaster off to see how it was getting on. Drove the nurses nearly mad. Now he's paying for it."

"Did they arrest anyone?"

Mr. Frith shook his head.

"Everybody in bed at the time. Not a soul around. Just happened." He bent forward and beckoned Harold toward him. "Got a boot in his face," he confided. "That's what did it. But wassitmatter?"

His voice, Harold noticed, was beginning to soften and become blurred at the edges. One by one, the consonants were being decapitated: at this rate, later in the evening it would become a massacre.

But for the time being, Mr. Frith was lively enough. Twisted right round in his chair, he was signaling for the drinks boy to come over. There was no point, he told him, in having to interrupt himself every time he needed something: he'd better just bring the bottle and leave it there.

"You've heard about the A.D.C.?" he asked. "Never could stand the fellow. Got it written all over him."

"Bad luck if you're born that way."

"Mind you," Mr. Frith said, "there was another side of him altogether. Behaved like one of us when it came to it. Simply packed his bags and cleared out. No goodbyes. No scenes. No excuses. Just vanished in the night, like that."

He tried to snap his fingers to show the suddenness of it all, but found that he could not produce the click that he had expected.

"Left a pile of letters behind him," he added. "Had 'em sent round by hand next morning. That's what I call good manners. Wanted to spare other people's feelings."

He wiped his eyes for a moment as though moved by the recollection of such thoughtfulness. Then he looked down at his watch. It showed eleven-thirty; and this was remarkable because it seemed that Harold had only just finished dinner: he must be a slow eater, he supposed.

Mr. Frith poured himself another drink. There were lots more pieces of news that he wanted to pass on.

"Wouldn't know him if you saw Old Moses now," he said at last. "Different man. Got his speech back."

It was the first mention there had been of Old Moses all the evening: Harold hadn't even liked to ask after him. He didn't care to think of him now, shut up in a cell somewhere in the prison hospital block.

"Is he . . . is he still on hunger strike?" he asked.

Mr. Frith did not answer immediately. He was preoccupied, looking at the level of the whisky. It was lower than he had expected. Taking hold of the bottle, he began tilting it to make sure that he was reading it correctly.

"What was that you said?"

"I asked if he was still on hunger strike."

"Dead by now if he had been," Mr. Frith replied. "You've been away a long time, remember."

"What made him change his mind?"

Mr. Frith was finding Harold downright obtuse this evening.

"Hungry, I suppose," he answered.

He pushed his chair back from the table as he was speaking. It was clear to him that it was time for Harold to go to bed.

"Gotterbreakitup," he said. "Busy day tomorrow."

Harold saw this for his opportunity.

"How's Lady Anne?" he asked.

Mr. Frith placed his hand on the back of his chair to steady himself.

"Oh, they got away all right," he said. "Quite a crowd to see 'em off. Must have been at least a hundred. No band, though: Lady Anne didn't want one. Governor couldn't go himself. Sent me instead. Got the special coach put on. Special coach and all the trimmings."

Harold was facing Mr. Frith.

"Where . . . where have they gone?" he asked.

"Traveling," Mr. Frith replied. "Just traveling. Couldn't leave any address because they didn't know where they were going."

"Did they say for how long?" he asked.

"How long?" Mr. Frith repeated. "It's final. Moved out for good. Mind you, nothing to keep 'em; not now the trial's over. Better away from the place, I say. Don't think she was ever happy here."

Mr. Frith paused.

"That reminds me," he said. "Nearly forgot all about it. Asked me to give you a message. Just as they were leaving, it was. Stuck her head out of the window. Said she hoped your eye was better, and not to worry about her: she'd be all right."

"I didn't know," Harold heard himself saying. "I just didn't know."

Mr. Frith had just let go of the chair to see how he felt when he was standing up without it.

"But that's erstrornery," he said. "Talked to the Prosser woman on the platform. Said she'd written to you. Must have gone astray somewhere. Said mosterstinkly that she'd written."

Chapter 49

IT WAS becoming increasingly evident that one way or another, they had entirely misread the character of the new Governor.

Perhaps it was the pipe that had deceived them. The spectacle of Mr. Drawbridge working at his desk in his shirt sleeves, and with his tobacco pouch and matches beside him, had led everyone to expect that they were in for a quiet period of retrenchment.

Whereas it was clear now that it would be nothing of the kind. Education estimates had already been practically doubled, and he had killed outright the plans for a ceremonial archway that Sir Gardnor had personally approved.

Nor was this all: Mr. Drawbridge was dabbling in politics. To everyone's dismay, he had suddenly asked for proposals for drawing up a new electoral register; and to show that he meant it, he had called a three-day conference of District Officers and A.D.O.'s to explain what it was all about. The news had at first left Amimbo numb and dumfounded. But by now a vicious two-pronged attack upon the scheme had been organized and was being launched.

One prong represented the Council of Native Chiefs. Membership on the Council totaled eleven. All of them were, in the ordinary way, mutually hostile, even occasionally warring. But on this issue they stood united. Blood feuds were temporarily forgotten, and any raiding parties that happened at the moment to be operating in their neighbors' territory were hastily recalled.

For good reason, too. Being a Chief was already a pretty precarious occupation. Suppression of local slavery and the handing over of taxes to the Government had long since nearly ruined the profession. Even the big ones were feeling the pinch; and at least half of the Council, including some of the oldest and proudest, were undeniably poor.

The whole eleven of them saw the red light simultaneously. Any system based upon owning property and a literacy test would eventually mean handing the country over to the hard-working, the educated, and the intelligent: this was something they were not prepared to tolerate. And as one man, they addressed a powerfully worded petition to their Governor.

The other prong had Mr. Frith for its mouthpiece. While the Chiefs were worrying about their wives, their witch doctors, and the store of ancestral wisdom that they jointly represented, Mr. Frith was preoccupied solely by thoughts of the Service. All in all, despite the lethargy of successive Colonial Secretaries, it was not a bad life. Nor a worthless one. Mr. Frith, and a lot of other frustrated, dedicated people just like him, somehow or other managed to get things done. There were roads, bridges, hospitals to show for it: Amimbo was undeniably a better place since the Service had moved in.

Mr. Frith shuddered to think of the collapse of discipline and public order once the Executive Council was full of black men with black tribal loyalties. Looking into the bleak and impending future, he could only too plainly see a Mimbo warrior in full ceremonial feathers and a row of copper bangles halfway up his shins perched upon the Presidential throne over at the Residency, and the Milner Club so noisy and overcrowded that it would be impossible for a tired administrator to relax there after the day's labors.

What really maddened him, however, was that except for Mr. Talefwa, nobody really seemed to want African rule at all. And here was Mr. Drawbridge, entirely unasked, preparing his own eviction order. Mr. Frith had already had one go at him, warning him of the pitfalls of premature self-government. Not that it seemed to have made much impression. Mr. Drawbridge was notoriously impassive. While Mr. Frith had been reminding him of recent local killings and the Leopard Men, Mr. Drawbridge had gone on smoking his rather objectionable-smelling mixture. Then, right at the end, he had merely remarked that he was sure that there was a great deal of common sense in what Mr. Frith had to say but it was a bit late in the day to start trying to put things into reverse.

And as proof that he hadn't been paying proper attention to what Mr. Frith had been saying, Mr. Drawbridge had even switched the conversation to ask how the new teacher-training courses were coming along.

Toward midnight, when the houseboys had finished their last bottle of native beer and rolled the final crap game of the evening, Harold thrust his feet back into his slippers and strolled out into the garden.

It was Government property, this bit of Africa. While he had been away, the boys had been busy on it, brushing, watering, scratching, tidying up. Between them, they had broken off one of the front legs of the rustic cast-iron seat; tilted sharply forward at one end, the thing now looked as if it were curtseying. But the stones round the circular flower bed were all newly whitewashed, and the wooden post that supported the mailbox had been freshly painted.

She might at least have made the effort, Harold was thinking. She can't have been that ill. Not all the time. She could have written. She could have said *something*.

Here in the garden, the air was close and bathroomy: it clung to him. The big trees, the shrubs, even some of the taller flowers, all had their own festoons of vapor wrapped round them. This was a sure sign: it would not be long now before the next rainy season was on them. And when the rains broke, everything in Amimbo—clothes, food, cigarettes, office stationery—would become limp and squeezable again.

God, don't I know what it'll be like, he reminded himself. Like living in a bloody laundry. And why the hell should I stay on anyway? I don't belong here. Not any longer. There's nothing to keep me. If she'd wanted to, she'd have got word through somehow.

Behind him, the lights in the Residency had all long since gone out, and there in the blue mist-filled saucer below him lay Amimbo. The street lamps were showing down the length of Victoria Avenue, and amid the corrugated-iron roofs and palm trees, odd domestic bulbs were still burning. Over the center of the city, the illuminated clock in the cathedral tower shone like a small captive moon.

Damn waste of time writing all those letters, he reflected. She's older than I am. It would never have worked out. Probably have got sick of me anyway.

Then, simultaneously, the lights went out, came on again faintly, flickered, and were restored. This showed that it must be twelve o'clock. The nightly switch-over always took place around the hour. Sometimes the late-shift supervisor forgot and pulled the switch down too hastily before he had cut off the daytime supply. Then there would be a bright flash over at the substation beside the marshaling yards, and engineers of the Amimbo Generating Corporation would have to go round next day repairing things.

Everything's crazy out here, he reminded himself. The electricity. The people. The things that happen to you. I've had enough of it. I'm clearing out. They can have my resignation. I'm through with Amimbo.

The garden was silent now, except for the cicadas. These were everywhere; the branches overhead were plastered with them. They were of all ages; the lustiest of the youngsters were happily chirruping away astride the burnt-out husks of their ancestors.

I wonder if she's all right, he began thinking. There must be some way of finding out. Oh God, I do love her so. I can't just lose her like this.

Chapter 50

THE POSITION of Mr. Das was certainly unenviable. Through no fault of his own, he had become Amimbo's resident outcast. Nor was there any foreseeable prospect of his ever being able to get away again.

With Mr. Talefwa in hiding, and Mr. Ngono so much embarrassed by his hospital profile that he was avoiding the capital altogether, Mr. Das has been left entirely without sponsors.

So long as Mr. Talefwa was around, there had still been hope. Arguments between them about the fee had proceeded practically without interruption ever since the verdict; often they had gone on late into the night, with the noise of the quarrel drifting out across the sleeping city. Mr. Das did not mind that kind of thing in the least: he was used to bargaining. But the sudden closure of *War Drum* came as nothing less than complete disaster. At one blow it deprived him even of the chance of something on account.

He had, with difficulty, found himself temporary accommodation in a native rooming house over by the marshaling yards. But already there were signs of racial unpleasantness: the large and terrifying landlady would keep on demanding her money. In consequence, Mr. Das, unlaundered and half starved, made a point of slipping out of the house very early in the morning and spent most of the day simply hanging round the law courts, ready to take any brief that might turn up and wondering all the time where his return ticket would be coming from.

Things had eventually reached such a pitch that the Bar Association of Amimbo decided to do something about it. It was not good for their professional standing, they felt, to have one of their number going about with holes in his socks and loitering outside the cheaper eating places in the hope of being invited inside to share a meal. Not that any invitation seemed likely; the very fact that he had failed to get an acquittal for Old Moses had endeared Mr. Das to practically nobody.

In the end, the members of the bar agreed between them to put up the money for the railway fare; and the Clerk of the Court was asked to slip round to the station to buy the ticket. The Attorney General stipulated that it should be put in an envelope, with no covering letter, and placed in the otherwise empty pigeonhole to which Mr. Das went so pathetically every morning to see if there were any messages for him. It was not Mr. Das's thanks they wanted: merely his absence.

The stratagem, however, failed. This was because the Clerk of the Court, in idle conversation with a friend, happened to mention the little trip that he had taken to the railway station. By next morning, the news was all round Amimbo, and people began putting two and two together.

The Coronation Flyer had made two departures since Mr. Das

had collected his envelope. Each time, however, there had been such a posse of eager creditors waiting for Mr. Das at the barrier that he had been afraid to go onto the platform.

Harold did not hand in his resignation. After a night's rest, he felt better about things: quieter in his own mind, and almost reconciled.

She can't just have disappeared, he kept telling himself. I'll catch up with her one day. Before it's too late, I'll catch up with her. I know I will.

And in the meantime, he had been transferred to Treasury. On the whole, he was rather pleased with himself. It wasn't simply the extra grade that counted: it was being on that side of the administration. This was where the brains of the Service were concentrated. He was on the way up, all right.

He had his own square of carpet. Tea in the afternoon was served in thinner china. There was a thermos jug for the iced water. And any day now—even this week perhaps, his clerk told him—they would be installing the new internal telephone. The one that was there now had never worked properly even when it was new.

They were certainly pleased to see him over in his new Department. There were only three weeks to go, and the estimates were still all coming out too high. Also, tempers were somewhat frayed. Public Works had gone over the head of the Finance Secretary to say that if the present lot of cuts were forced on them, there would be no road this year, or next for that matter, leading up to the newly finished bridge over the Omtala River. And Health and Education were fighting it out at first hand—in the office, up at the Milner Club, even at home over the weekends.

Most nights, Harold was at his desk again after dinner. He looked tired, and his houseboys grew worried about him. They left slices of cold chicken covered up in cheesecloth, and pink blancmanges with an upturned plate on top of the dish, on the side table in the dining room in case he fancied anything after they had gone to bed. They agreed that he needed a woman; that much was obvious. But which one? They went over the *bwana* ladies in some detail—age, build, state of the teeth, and so forth—and rejected the lot of them.

They suggested each other's sisters. They discussed their merits. They giggled.

They left it at that and continued to put out the cold chicken and the pink blancmange.

Reports by now had begun to come in that Mr. Talefwa had been seen again in the streets of the capital, and it was only the continued absence of Mr. Ngono that kept people guessing.

Speculation quickened when the police removed the chains from the front door of the *War Drum* offices and the decorators moved in. There was plenty for them to do. While the place had been left deserted, hooligans had smashed all the windows on the street side, and refuse, empty cans, and the bodies of departed cats had been tossed in at random through the broken panes.

It was the relettering of the signboard that aroused the most comment. The words WAR DRUM were laboriously scraped off and new wording, BLACK AND WHITE SUNRISE, was painted in thick capitals over the top of it.

It was not until nearly a fortnight later that the first edition of the paper finally appeared. And when it reached the news stalls, gossip was intensified.

For a start, there had been a significant change in editorial policy. The front page, in addition to announcing a ten per cent all-round reduction in advertising rates, came out wholeheartedly on the side of the Government. "No Progress Without Co-operation" was the new slogan, and readers were pledged, not asked, to give their support to Mr. Drawbridge.

The whole keynote of the article was the future. "Now that petty and undignified racial strife has once and for all been abolished by the recently announced and extremely democratic measures of our most enlightened Governor," it ran, "whom can he turn to in his hour of exceptionally desperate need?"

The answer was given in the very next paragraph.

"Never shall it be said," it continued, "that the Mimbo

people were cowardly, slothful or slow to take advantage. If our genial Governor requires the selected flower of our manhood for official positions, they must be his to command them. It is men of keen insight, top attainments and no disqualifications what-soever that the new Legislative Council will be requiring."

Toward the end of the article, the author issued a particularly carefully worded note of warning.

"While an educational course at an approved University of the utmost top international rank is essential so that Amimbo's many grave and disastrous problems may be coolly judged in world perspective," it cautioned, "it is not necessary for our representa-tives to bear the dubious honour of some high-sounding, foreign degree. What our Governor now searches for is someone between the ages of twenty-eight and thirty, of noble family, highly popular with all sections, exceedingly progressive in outlook and ideas, of good appearance and social manners, and wide practical commercial experience in the difficult import-export business on which our national life depends. Who shall name him? Long live Amimbo."

Putting two and two together, Native Affairs was able to hazard a pretty shrewd guess as to the identity of the new proprietor.

It was impossible, however, to put the question direct to Mr. Ngono. He was still absent from the capital. That was because he wanted to avoid all possibility of coming face to face with Mr. Das. From long experience, Mr. Ngono had learned never to get entangled in arguments with Indians: they were endless, and they got you nowhere.

Not that Mr. Ngono need have worried. If there was one man who desperately wanted to get away from Amimbo, it was Mr. Das; and he had already made his plans.

It was on Wednesdays and Saturdays that the Coronation Flyer steamed out of the Terminus, and after that first ugly threat of violence, Mr. Das had made no further attempt to board it.

But he still went along there. And he deliberately drew atten-tion to himself. He selected the most conspicuous position on the bench in the waiting room exactly facing the doorway. He kept inquiring in a loud voice if the train would be leaving on time. He asked if it would be crowded. And he inquired about obstructions along the line.

The scheme worked perfectly. At first, all his creditors were ranged up once more around the barrier, noisy and threatening. And on the second and third occasions, too. But by the fourth and fifth, they had begun to thin out. Those who were owed least stayed away soonest.

Today, for instance, there were a mere handful—his enormous landlady; the laundress who still had possession of his one washable shirt; the café proprietor from just opposite; and one of the clerks from the Post Office who had already transmitted the first half of a telegram that Mr. Das had handed to him and now refused to let the other half go out until he had received his full money.

And all the time, Mr. Das simply sat on there, asking questions and generally making a nuisance of himself. They were thus entirely unprepared when Mr. Das suddenly made a dash for it, climbed over the wooden gate which had already been closed against latecomers, and sprinted up the platform after the receding train.

He was compelled to wrench open the moving carriage door by sheer force and fight his way like an animal into the already overpacked compartment. And it was not so much death beneath the wheels that he was fearing as loss of face if he had failed to get onto the train. That would have made him cry.

As it was, he was miserable enough. It was the heart-rending nostalgia of it all that affected him. He remembered similar departures from other railway stations—from Calcutta, from Bombay, from Lahore. From Lahore, in particular.

That had been when, just as he had thought that all the formalities were over, one of the creditor ladies who was seeing him off had suddenly pursed up her lips and squirted betel juice over his new white jacket.

Chapter 51

IT HAD happened.

The witch doctors having received their appropriate fees, the rains had come. All in all, they had been good rains, copious and long drawn out. More cattle had been drowned than usual. In places, bridges, railway lines, telegraph poles had been swept away. Whole settlements had vanished.

But these were the short rains. A month later it was all over, and things were back to normal: rebuilding began, and the villagers returned. Victoria Avenue was powdered from end to end with a fine, gritty dust, and the ventilating system in the Law Courts was blocked solid again.

It was during the drying-out period that the budget had finally been approved and Harold was able to get time for rest. Shut up in his new office, with the fan still not working, he had lost nearly seven pounds. Every time Mr. Frith sent for him, he had to hitch his trousers up round his waist before going out into the corridor.

It was now the Political Department that was getting it. The Representation of the People (Voting Qualifications) Bill had them all foxed. The Attorney General was already on his fifth draft, and the proposed amendments were coming in like Christmas cards. For the first time in years, native Chiefs and senior civil servants were standing shoulder to shoulder: they were united in opposing almost everything.

Nevertheless, within the Service, the plain truth had glumly been accepted: sooner or later, black men would be ruling other black men, drawing up impossible budgets, embarking on long-term schemes of infinite forlornness, punishing their brothers for not complying, creating new loyalties, enjoying themselves.

It was, as much as anything else, the domestic atmosphere up at the Residency that helped to keep things running so smoothly. Mrs. Drawbridge, after some trouble over getting her youngest satisfactorily settled in the right prep school, had at last managed to join her husband, and once more the capital had its own first lady.

An unsmart, motherly sort of woman, she set a new fashion by going round without gloves. Usually she simply didn't wear any, and on official occasions, when her lady-in-waiting trailed after her carrying them, she left them about on beds in new hospital wards, on the top of foundation stones, and on the balustrades of public buildings that the Governor had just opened.

With the Drawbridges there, the Residency had assumed a more homely note. The plate was brought out less frequently, and Mrs. Drawbridge insisted on arranging the flowers herself. She even had the disconcerting habit of going to the telephone in person when she heard the bell ringing. And she wore the same jewelry all the time: a small diamond brooch during the day, and a string of imitation pearls in the evening.

But she was undeniably a success. She liked the house, she liked the people, she liked looking after Mr. Drawbridge. In return, everybody liked her. There was a relaxed, easy feeling all round. The wives of senior civil servants stopped drawing comparisons, and Lady Anne's name was hardly ever mentioned.

The same relaxed feeling ran through the whole Colony.

The monument to Sir Gardnor was very nearly ready behind the bamboo screen that had been erected in front of it, but nobody bothered to inquire how it was getting on. Mr. Ngono, rather proud by now of the Wellingtonian profile into which his nose had finally settled, was back in town and had selected a prominent site, two blocks down the road from the Royal Albert, for a new swimming pool. Crown Cottage was occupied by the recently married Finance Secretary, and the young couple—he was just on forty—were planning to convert the garden room into a nursery. Out in the bush, the police had given up and were no longer arresting every tall bronze-colored vagrant on suspicion that he might be the missing kitchen boy. And over in the prison hospital block, Old Moses had been provided with a ground-floor room with French windows as his own private apartment.

As for Harold, one week seemed very like another. They added up into months and went by, placid, uneventful, practically indistinguishable. He had plenty of work to do, and he had given up caring. He was even beginning to wear the same steady-going, composed expression as the rest of the department. Mr. Frith continued to be very pleased with him, and the Governor had already spoken of the next A.D.O. job that might fall vacant.

Then, one afternoon when he got back to the bungalow after the office had closed, he found Sybil Prosser waiting for him.

There she was in the chair he always sat in, over by the window. She had kicked her shoes off, and they were lying higgledy-piggledy on the rug beside her. It had been hot, very hot, all day, and her feet were swollen. Harold could see the pattern of the leather strap embossed across her instep.

It was Sybil Prosser who was the first to speak.

"You can give me another drink if you'd like to," she said. "I had one when I got here."

There was a pause; quite a long pause.

"I needed it," she added.

She was no longer even looking at him. The collar of her blouse was undone, and she was dabbing at herself with her handkerchief. There was the smell of eau de cologne all round her. The top of the bottle was sticking out of her open handbag, and she kept resoaking the handkerchief so that she could apply it farther and farther down. Bending so far forward, she could not breathe properly. She gave a little gasp every time the spirit touched her.

The first drink had brought some color back into her face. But the flush had not spread itself. Sallow-complexioned as always, she had been left with two burning red patches just below her cheekbones.

She lifted her head for a moment.

"It's whisky," she told him. "Just ice. No water."

Then she ignored him altogether and went on dabbing.

"You're still wearing your eye patch," she said. "You can't say I didn't warn you."

"How's Anne?" he asked.

Sybil Prosser was rebuttoning her blouse.

"It's Anne I've come about," she said. "That's why I'm here."

"Then tell me."

He was still standing, facing her. Sybil Prosser stretched herself out. She had got one of Harold's cushions underneath her feet.

"Oh, for heaven's sake, man, sit down, can't you?" she asked him. "Don't hang over me. It's like trying to talk to a waiter."

Harold took the other chair, the one he didn't usually sit in.

"Go on," he said.

Sybil Prosser's eyes were fixed on him now.

"Why don't you go to her?" she asked.

"What makes you think she wants to see me?"

Sybil Prosser shrugged her shoulders.

"Hadn't you better find out?" she asked. "That is, if you still want to."

"Does . . . does she ever talk about me?"

"She used to."

Harold began straightening the corner of the rug with his foot.

"It's been a long time," he said.

The rug still wasn't straight; when she had sat down, Sybil Prosser must simply have collapsed into the chair, dragging the rug along with it.

"Then what are you waiting for?" she demanded. "Is there someone else?"

"There'll never be anybody else."

"Well?"

"She's forgotten about me."

Sybil Prosser's pale, empty-looking eyes were fixed on him again.

"How do you know?"

"If she'd wanted me, she could have answered my letters, couldn't she?"

"Not if she didn't get them, she couldn't."

Sybil Prosser had thrust her hand down into her handbag beside her. She brought out a flat packet and threw it over to him. It was tied up with a length of narrow blue ribbon that might have been round the edge of a nightgown.

"There they are," she said. "Now you've got them back. All of them."

"Did she give them to you?"

Sybil Prosser smiled. It was a thin, rather pitying kind of smile.

"She never had them."

"I don't believe you."

"Look for yourself, then. They're not even opened."

The bundle smelled very strongly of the eau de cologne. He could see the notepaper, the handwriting. The top of one of the envelopes had been slit across with something blunt: a finger, possibly. The emblem of the shipping line had been ripped right through.

"That one's been opened," he said.

"That's the one I answered."

"Then you read it?"

Sybil Prosser's lips were drawn back again.

"That's why I stopped the others."

"D'you mean she doesn't know I ever wrote to her?"

Sybil Prosser nodded.

"She thinks I went off without a word?"

There was the same nod.

"You did this deliberately?"

Sybil Prosser seemed rather surprised at the question.

"Naturally," she said. "I *wanted* her to forget about you."

"And now you expect me to go back?"

"It's entirely up to you." She paused. "But only if you feel you have to. Not if you just feel sorry for her."

"Whose side are you on?" he asked.

The pale eyes were still fixed on him.

"Hers," she said. "I always have been."

There was a movement behind the bead screen in the doorway, and Harold turned. The houseboys had been listening again. He could hear their bare feet padding back along the passage toward the kitchen.

"And what's Anne going to say when I tell her?"

Sybil Prosser's eyes did not flicker.

"I don't know. I shan't be there." She looked down at her

watch for a moment. "Is there going to be anything to eat?" she asked. "I can't have another drink unless you give me something."

Sybil Prosser had crumpled up her napkin and set it down upon her plate.

". . . *and* I'm not so young as I used to be," she was saying. "I'm an old woman now. That's what other people don't seem to realize."

Now that her hat was off, he could see along the line of the parting: there was an half-inch-wide band of white running right across her head. On either side of it, the familiar straw color was still there. Not so bright as it had been, perhaps, but still distinctly straw.

"There's one comfort," she said. "I shan't have to go on taking so much trouble about appearances. I only kept myself looking nice for her sake."

Sybil Prosser had brought her chin down as she said it; the creases in her throat spread out all round. She looked older than ever now. With her hands resting on the table top, he noticed how large the knuckles were.

"Is Anne alone?" he asked.

"She was when I left her." Sybil Prosser ran her tongue across her lips; the lip salve that she had been using came away with it. "How much longer," she added, "I wouldn't like to say. She hasn't changed any. That's what the rows were about. You weren't the first, remember."

Harold said nothing.

"And if no one's around, she'll start drinking too much. She always does when she's miserable. I'm the only one who could ever stop her."

"Then why don't you go back to her?"

"Because I'm no use, that's why. She told me so herself."

She had taken her grimy handkerchief out of her handbag and was crying into it.

"It's got to be a man," she said. "She's made that way."

She was a tall woman: in the ordinary way, she towered. But

crouched forward and with her face buried in her handkerchief, she seemed to have become much smaller. Harold suddenly felt sorry for her.

"You do love her, don't you?" he said.

Sybil Prosser looked up defiantly.

"Love her?" she replied. "If I could have, I'd have married her."

There was the sound of a car approaching; it drew up outside, and the driver turned off the engine.

Sybil Prosser began getting her things together; she took out her pocket mirror and peered into it.

"Not that it matters," she remarked, almost as though talking to herself. "There's no one at the hotel to see me."

She was just about to snap the clasp of the bag together again when she plunged her hand back inside.

"You'd better have that," she told him. "It's the address. I've written it down for you."

He took the piece of paper without glancing at it.

She was standing by now and was pulling on the shapeless white sun hat that she had been wearing.

"Well, there you are," she said. "I've done all I can."

She came nearer, as though she had just remembered something.

"You can kiss me goodbye if you want to," she told him. "Anne did. And you don't have to believe everything she says about me. She's an awful liar. You never know whether it's the truth she's telling you."

Chapter 52

Unless one of the pipes in the boiler were to burst, or the guards' van derail itself again, they looked like being in Nucca by midnight.

All in all, it had been a record run. They had kept up a steady forty-five miles an hour over even the roughest sections, and in the restaurant car the diners had long ago given up any thought

338

of actually eating or drinking anything. The last of the crockery
had gone crashing from the tables as they had gone over the
switch at Tibebwe hours before.

But he was on the train, and he was nearly there; there was all
that mattered. It was the first train, too, out of Amimbo since
Sybil Prosser had called on him. He had spoken to Mr. Frith next
morning, saying as casually as he could manage that he felt that
he could do with a day or two down on the coast, and Mr. Frith
had raised no objections. Sea level and sanity, in his view, was an
essential for anyone who had done more than six uninterrupted
months in the capital.

It was certainly pleasant enough in itself to be going down to
Nucca. The Portuguese had made themselves very comfortable
there.

The railway station, in particular, was a guidebook feature. It
had a broad veranda of ironwork pineapples and acanthus leaves
running right across the front. The metal was painted bright
blue; and the local Nuccaese, waiting for a train to arrive,
waiting for one to leave, or just waiting, could stand on the
veranda drinking an excellent light beer and looking down on
the sunbonnets of the horses in the little courtyard below.

It was twelve midnight exactly when the train finally reached
Nucca, but the hotel was still open. The manager and his wife
were eating a late meal behind the reception desk, and they were
delighted to see him. The manager congratulated him on having
got there before daybreak; assured him that dinner had been
kept waiting for him; and asked his wife to carry up the bags
while he himself made a note of the number on Harold's
passport. Breakfast, he explained, was available in the dining
room from seven A.M. until midday; or, with a small extra charge
for room service, right on through the afternoon and early
evening.

Harold spent longer than usual dressing next morning. He laid
out his gray suit and his white one, sent them both down to be

339

pressed, and then chose the gray. He looked at his ties and wondered why he hadn't bought any new ones. He remembered that his brown shoes were new, but that his black went better with the gray suit.

It was his eye that chiefly worried him. He had got used to wearing it nowadays. He just popped it into place when he went through to the bathroom in the morning and then forgot about it. Everyone knew that he had a glass eye. But not Lady Anne; not if Sybil Prosser had stopped his letters.

And now that he looked at himself in the mirror, he could see that it was a bit of a shiner. It caught the attention. If he went in wearing it, she wouldn't notice anything else about him. He decided on the patch.

Harold took out the piece of paper that Sybil Prosser had given him. The driver recognized the address immediately: it was only the other day that he had driven the tall, agitated foreign lady away from it.

The house stood back from the road, and a semicircular drive led up to it. There was a fountain in the middle of the front lawn, and the house itself was porticoed. It was a big house for two women to live in; ridiculously big for one.

His heart was thumping as he tugged at the bellpull. He could hear the peal echoing into the distance. Inside, everything sounded hollow.

The colored woman who opened the door was suspicious; she left the chain drawn across it. There was nobody in, she said. They had all gone away. She did not know where. She was merely the housekeeper. She had work to do. She was busy.

Harold gave her money.

It was only one of the ladies who had gone away. That had been last week. No one had seen her since. Naturally, they were anxious.

Harold gave her more money.

The other lady had not left the house since the disappearance. She was prostrate. Shut away in her bedroom, she was seeing no one. Only the doctor was allowed to call. Sometimes he too had to be sent away again because she was too ill to see him.

Harold took out his billfold.

The colored woman removed the chain and stood back for him to pass.

A visitor, someone to amuse her mistress and make her laugh, was exactly what the lady needed, she said. She would tell the lady the good news immediately. Even if she had to break down the bedroom door, she would do it. Her hand went wandering out toward the billfold.

The room into which he had been shown was stifling. Behind the drawn curtains, the windows were all closed and the jalousies fastened. The housekeeper gave a little tug to straighten the lace antimacassar on the nearest chair back and said that she would be returning immediately.

He could hear the *slop-slop* of her shoes as she went away down the corridor. Then there was silence. It was broken only by the ticking of the gilt clock on the mantelpiece and the sound of someone sweeping on the balcony outside.

Ten minutes later, when he could not breathe, he got up and opened one of the windows. Then he closed it again to keep out the dust. The sweeper himself was hidden in the midst of it. Harold undid his collar.

Half an hour went by. The housekeeper came back to say that the lady was still sleeping. She slept very badly nowadays. Sometimes she was awake all night. It would not be right to rouse her, even to say that a gentleman was there. But it should not be long now. Any moment, in fact. Who could say? She shrugged her shoulders and left him.

Harold tried opening the window again. The sweeper had moved away, but one of the garden boys had taken over. He was changing the earth in a row of flowerpots along the balcony. Dead petals lay all round him, and the newly sifted soil rose up into the air like smoke. Harold took his coat off.

This time the housekeeper was already shrugging her shoulders as she entered the room. The lady was awake, she said. She could hear her moving about. But she refused to answer. She would try again later. It was all a question of selecting the right moment. She asked if Harold would like coffee.

When she brought the tray to him, she said that it was now only a matter of time. In any case, the lady had not yet had her breakfast. Then there would be the bath, and choosing what she should wear. It could not all happen in an instant. She begged him to be patient.

The delay was even longer now. Harold could hear the dragging feet of the housekeeper as she went back and forth along the corridor, but each time she went straight past his room. He began to wonder if she had forgotten about him.

Then, breathless and excited, the housekeeper burst in. She had delivered the message. Its effect on the lady had been tremendous. She had never seen anyone so deeply moved. There had been both smiles and tears. No doubt, she was dressing at this very moment. The housekeeper could not stay any longer, in case the lady needed her.

There was silence again. He could no longer even hear footsteps. Out in the front of the house, the endless sound of sweeping continued. But that was all. Even the tick of the gilt clock had grown so familiar that he had ceased to be aware of it. Pulling up a stool, he thrust out his legs and lay back. He was wondering if he ought to have brought flowers.

That was how Lady Anne found him, all slumped down in his chair, when she came in. It was the sound of the door opening that woke him. He scrambled to his feet and stood there, staring at her.

He thought that he had never seen her look so beautiful. She was wearing one of those plain schoolgirl dresses that she had used to go about in back in the Residency garden, and her hair was loose over her shoulders, the way she knew he liked it.

Her eyes were on him, and her lips were parted.

"I saw you arrive," she said. "You've waited quite long enough. You can go now."

It was late when the messenger arrived.

In the dining room, the solitary waiter was already going round folding back the corners of the striped tablecloths so that the floor underneath could be scrubbed properly.

It was, the manager and his wife agreed afterwards, almost as though Harold had been reluctant to touch the envelope, let alone open it and read what was inside. He simply sat there, not moving, looking down at the pink notepaper with the big excited handwriting that he knew so well.

The manager's wife had to repeat, quite loudly the second time, that it was for him, that it was urgent, that it had only just arrived, and that the boy who had brought it was even now recovering on the porch so that he could run all the way back with the reply. Then, and only then, did Harold begin to understand.

He reached out for it, and the manager's wife noticed that his hand was shaking. He could hardly insert the knife to slit it open. But she could make out nothing from his expression while he was reading. Pink and scented and obviously feminine as the letter was, it might simply have been a trade circular for all the emotion he was showing.

"There's no answer," he said quietly. "Just no answer at all."

"But it's not exactly the center of the world, remember. I knew that there wasn't another train out of here until tomorrow," Lady Anne was saying. "Otherwise I might have been really worried that you wouldn't come."

She broke off for a moment to stir the ice in the glass that she was holding; in that heat it was necessary to keep adding fresh lumps all the time.

"But I knew you would. I was sure of it. I didn't see how you couldn't."

Harold drew in his lips.

"We've wasted nearly one whole day," he said.

"Whose fault was that? I wrote to you, didn't I? I said I was sorry." She paused. *"And* I sat up all night waiting for the answer. I didn't go to bed at all. I was here in this chair by the window so that I could see you if you did come."

She had left her chair while she was speaking and gone over to the side table where the bottles were. On the way, she paused long enough to stroke the backs of her fingers down along his cheek.

"Just to feel that you're really here," she said.

Behind him, he could hear the sound of the whisky splashing into the glass.

"It's only to make it taste of something," she told him. "I mustn't start stirring this one."

Again there was the feel of her fingers brushing across his cheek as she passed. He tried to catch her hand, but already she had drawn away from him.

"And don't go on sulking because I wouldn't see you," she said as she sat down. "It didn't mean anything."

She was smiling at him. It was an extremely possessive kind of smile.

"Anyhow. None of it matters now. You're back again. That's all that counts."

"And you do believe about the letters?" he asked. "About Sybil Prosser stopping them, I mean?"

Lady Anne shrugged her shoulders.

"It's just the sort of thing she would do," she said.

"She obviously had it on her conscience," Harold replied. "Otherwise she wouldn't have come and told me."

Lady Anne gave a little laugh.

"She's got a lot more than that on her conscience."

There was the little catch in her voice as she said it. Harold wondered how long she had been sitting there drinking before he had arrived; how long she had sat on all those other nights.

"Why don't you get away from here?" he asked. "What's the point of staying on like this?"

"What's the point of doing anything—now?"

He sat back and looked at her. The lines under her eyes were new: they were deep lines. And the corners of her mouth had begun to drag downwards.

"Don't . . . don't you even want to see Timothy?"

"Not any more. He reminds me too much of Gardie."

"I went to see him," he told her. "I wrote all about it in one of those letters."

She did not answer for a moment.

"You're very sweet," she said. "Really you are. But you shouldn't have bothered. I don't want to see him."

"He may want to see you."

"Not Timothy. He's learned to get along without me. He's like Gardie."

He noticed again this mixture of bitterness and the pet name.

"You can't just bury yourself here."

"Why not? I like it here."

He got up and went over to her.

"I'm not going to let it happen."

She moved away from him; drew back in her chair as if she did not want to be touched.

"There isn't anything you can do. Not any longer."

"Everything's going to be all right," he told her.

He tried to put his arms round her, but she pushed him away from her.

"That's what Sybil used to say. And it wasn't all right, was it?"

She lifted her head, and he was looking down into those astonishing, deep eyes again.

"It's no good," she said. "We'd better just give up."

He started to speak, but she stopped him.

"I'm finished. That's what you don't seem to realize. I'm finished. I'm no use to anybody. Not after what happened."

He thought for a moment that she was going to start crying. But instead she reached over and took up one of the photograph frames from the table beside her chair. As she held it in front of her, the lines around her mouth softened.

She passed the photograph to him.

"Look at that, and you'll see what I mean," she said. "That was me at eighteen. I'd only just met Gardie. Don't you wish you'd known me in those days? I was something, I can tell you. That was before I knew how it was all going to turn out. That's the way I like to think of me."

He put the frame back onto the table.

"I'll take you as you are," he said.

Her head was to one side, so that the long curve of her neck was showing.

"I believe you would," she told him.

He glanced down to look at his watch, but Lady Anne put her hand over it.

345

"You're not to look at your watch," she said, "and you're not to go. I've been horrible to you. I've talked about myself all the time. I didn't mean to. Really, I didn't. It's just that I haven't seen anyone."

She was already holding her arms out to him, and he could see that her hands were trembling. It was always the same: the trembling and the catch in her voice went together.

"I don't see why you've got to go at all," she said. "It means that we shall both be alone then. Don't go back to that dreadful hotel. Stay here with me. Tell me you'll stay."

She began to stroke his cheek again, very slowly this time.

"Poor, poor eye," she kept saying. "And I didn't know. It's all my fault. And I didn't know a thing."

"It wasn't your fault it happened."

"Oh, but it was. I should have warned you."

He shrugged his shoulders.

"It was an accident. I moved."

She let her hand rest on his cheek, fondling it.

"You wouldn't have believed me, so I didn't tell you."

"Tell me what?"

"That Gardie meant to kill you. It's what I was afraid of all the time."

Chapter 53

THE HOUSEKEEPER had grown reconciled to the new arrangement; even rather liked it, in fact. Having a man in the house gave a feeling of security and permanence. Admittedly, there was more cooking to be done. But anything, she reflected, would be better than a lifetime spent endlessly waiting on a single lady.

"And they're beautiful letters," Lady Anne was saying to him. "I've never had letters like that before. Gardie was a terrible letter writer. I didn't always finish his."

She was leaning over the back of his chair while she was speaking, and she kept stroking the sleeve of Harold's jacket.

"If I'd ever had them, I don't think I'd have been ill again. I don't see how I could have been. But that's what Sybil wanted. She didn't want me to get well. Then I'd have been independent."

She reached down and put her hand over his.

"I don't know what she told you about me but, whatever it is, it isn't true. She was just a wicked old woman who went round inventing things. You'll always believe me and not Sybil, won't you?"

She turned so that he could kiss her. She was looking down at him, and her face was half hidden by a wing of dark hair that fell across her forehead.

"She didn't tell me anything," he said.

The letters, thrust back into their envelopes, were spread out on the rug in front of them. Lady Anne had gone down on her knees and was gathering them up again.

"I shall keep these for always," she said. "I'll let you look sometimes. Just to remind you when you've got tired of me. But nobody else is ever going to see them."

She was holding them up against her bosom as she said it.

"I'm glad Sybil only opened the first one," she added. "I couldn't bear to think of her touching any of them."

She had put the envelopes very carefully together, smoothing out the crumpled corners as she did so. Then she tied them up again. It was Sybil Prosser's piece of ribbon that she was using.

"They're too precious to get lost," she said.

"I meant what I said in the letters," he reminded her. "I meant every word of it."

"Even the cross, rude ones when you hadn't heard from me?"

"Even the cross, rude ones." He reached out and pulled her closer, so that she was resting up against him. "And are you going to marry me?"

She turned her face toward him. Her eyes seemed larger than ever now.

"You know how much I want to," she said. "I want it more than anything."

"Then . . ."

"But I can't. Not yet. You must see that."

"Why not?"

"It's too soon. Much too soon."

"It's nearly a year."

"People would start talking."

"There isn't very much left for them to say."

"It's you I'm thinking of. They can't say anything new about me."

She gave a little laugh as she said it; her old Residency social laugh that didn't mean anything. And she began pulling his wrists away from her. Then she stood up, running her hands down her dress where it had become crumpled. She was completely composed again.

"We've just got to be sensible," she said. "There's no point in rushing things. I couldn't marry you while Old Moses is still alive. I just couldn't. It wouldn't seem right somehow."

"Old Moses may live for years."

Lady Anne shook her head.

"Not much longer," she said.

"And we can get married then?"

She had her head on one side, smiling at him.

"Haven't I got you into enough trouble already?" she asked.

It was the one train of the day, and at Nucca Terminus the restaurant car was already being loaded up with ice, fresh vegetables, sea food, liquor, hot rolls. By the time the passengers got there, most of the ice would have melted; there would be large pools of steamy water underneath the kitchen coaches.

"I don't see why you've got to catch it at all. Why can't you just stay here with me?"

She stubbed out the cigarette that she was holding. Inside the ash tray, it went on smoldering.

"I've got a job to do," he told her.

"Is it much more important than I am?"

"Not to me it isn't. Only to other people."

"I'm sick of other people."

She pushed the ash tray away from her while she was speaking.

"I didn't want it," she said. "I don't know why I took it. Sybil was the one who smoked, not me. I must have been thinking about something else."

She was smiling again; not directly at him, but quietly, contentedly to herself.

"It was about us. When we're married, we can be together all the time. You won't ever have to go away again. We can just forget about other people. We needn't bother about anything."

"There'll still be my job."

"Not unless you want it. Gardie was awfully rich, really. Timothy gets most of it. But there's still plenty left over. It was the settlement part that Gardie couldn't alter."

She spoke as though she had been at pains to make sure. He suddenly saw her going over the will carefully, clause by clause; with Sybil, possibly.

"But I don't want to live on Gardie's money."

He realized as he said it that it was the first time he had ever called him by that name. It was as though already Harold had become one of the family; but in a strange way, it was still Gardie's family.

"He wouldn't have minded. Gardie liked you."

"Last time you said he tried to kill me."

"So he did. That hasn't got anything to do with it." She paused. "Gardie was quite mad, you know."

She spoke as though it were something which, between friends, she would have expected Harold to realize.

"That's why I was so frightened of him." She broke off to brush away some ash from the cigarette that she hadn't wanted. "He'd killed somebody already, remember. Miles committed suicide. Gardie drove him to it."

Harold was watching her closely now. She seemed unconcerned enough; even not concerned enough, perhaps.

"I don't believe it."

"It was before you came out," she said simply.

She spoke as though that disposed of the whole matter, made it not worth talking about any longer.

"You never had to live with him, did you?" she added. "You never knew what he was really like."

"We got on very well together."

She laughed. It was a quick, unamused sort of laugh.

"Oh, that wouldn't have stopped him killing you."

The traveling clock on the table beside her gave a little *ping*. It was the half-hour. Harold looked down at his watch. The first of the passengers were probably already seated in the train by now.

"He knew all about us," she said. "The A.D.C. told him. That's what he was there for. And Gardie couldn't just let it go on, could he? You must see that."

"I still don't see why he should have wanted to *kill* me."

"Because of India: that's why."

Again she said it as though it were self-apparent; as though anyone who knew Sir Gardnor would have understood straightaway.

"He couldn't go out to India with that hanging over him. They'd never allow a divorce in Government House. A shooting accident beforehand, when it wasn't his fault, would have been quite different. It would have solved everything."

Harold was silent for a moment.

"Did he ever talk about divorce?"

"Not this time. He did at first when it was Miles. That's when he made me give up seeing Timothy."

"What made him change his mind?"

"I've told you: people started tipping Gardie for next Viceroy. That's what altered everything."

"Then why did he bother to save my life the first time?"

"Because he thought you didn't matter. That's when it looked as if he'd been passed over. India was all he cared about."

She glanced again in the direction of the clock and began smoothing down her dress.

"Gardie wasn't that mad," she explained, almost as though defending him. "He wouldn't have killed you unless there'd been a reason for it. He'd rather you'd finished his book for him."

Chapter 54

MR. FRITH could not have been more genuinely glad to have Harold back.

While he had been absent, the work had piled up quite alarmingly. On his own initiative, the native clerk had divided the files into Very Impatient, Overdue, and Extremely Necessary; and what Mr. Frith most wanted was to see some of the paper work beginning to move out again. At the present moment, there was a distinctly disused air to the whole department.

The Drawbridges too were pleased that Harold was around again. By now, Mrs. Drawbridge had put him at the top of her stand-by invitation list. She kept reminding him, rather coyly, that though single men were so useful for dinner parties, he must think about getting married himself one day, mustn't he?

The other person who was happy about Harold's return was Mr. Ngono. His swimming pool, his Lido, had turned out a great disappointment. The stream that should have fed it had run dry, and though the deep end had a good two feet of water in it, the shallow part, which was uncovered, had already cracked and splintered in the sun.

Mr. Ngono was at the moment suing the contractor. It had all been arranged: the contractor would go bankrupt and Mr. Ngono would take over his business. Once he had the truck, there were endless Government projects for which Mr. Ngono would be able to bid, and he was hoping that Harold would be able to put in a word for him.

Even so, they all noticed that it wasn't the same Harold who had gone away. The change was for the worse, too: he had become moody and preoccupied.

351

It was really communications with Nucca that were to blame. The telephone service was notoriously unreliable. Floods, landslides, uprooted trees, termites, absent-mindedly wandering elephants, even high winds, regularly brought the poles crashing down along the route; and particularly in summer, electrical storms put isolated sections of the long circuit temporarily out of commission.

Nor was the Royal Mail any better. Admittedly, there were the two trains each way every week. But the van from the General Post Office at either end did not always manage to connect with them. The mailbags, on those occasions, simply had to be left neatly piled up at the barrier, and chickens, young children, bunches of fruit, hand luggage, and other oddments would be placed carelessly on top of them. The bags themselves would be discovered only when the station staff began clearing up the mess long after the mail train had departed.

It was therefore in batches that the letters always arrived: sometimes in threes and fours, sometimes as many as half a dozen all in one delivery. The blue envelopes, with Lady Anne's big, excited handwriting scrawled across them, used to overlap the brass tray on which the boy brought them to him.

The letters told him everything; and nothing. She loved him, she said. It was like being in prison when he wasn't there. She had reread all his own letters until she knew them by heart. Why didn't he write longer ones? She had practically given up drinking: it was only when she hadn't heard from him that she even thought about it nowadays. When was he coming? Why not next weekend? She had started going to the hairdresser's again; some of her hair had been cut off, but not enough to spoil it for him. He shouldn't have spent all that money on sending her scent, but it was heavenly and she adored it. She was trying to eat more so that she wouldn't get too skinny-looking. Did Harold remember that each night, at eleven o'clock exactly, she stopped whatever she was doing and just thought about him? She could tell immediately when he had forgotten, because everything seemed to go dead inside her. Could he possibly imagine how much she was missing him? Did a man ever really understand that kind of thing?

And back in Nucca, Harold's own letters were arriving just as regularly. The housekeeper herself had to pick them up at the Poste Restante counter. She resented it. As soon as she reached one of the quieter streets on the way back, she would hold them out at arm's length and spit on them.

The telephone rang while Mr. Frith was still at breakfast. It was the Prison Governor. Old Moses had suddenly started giving trouble, he explained: he was demanding to see Mr. Drawbridge. Yes, Mr. Frith had heard him aright: "demanding" was the word Old Moses was using. He wanted him round at the jail for certain before six P.M. that evening; after that, it would apparently be too late.

While Mr. Frith stood there listening, he watched his coffee getting cold; it was his last cup, and he knew that there would be no more left in the coffeepot. That was why he was so rude to the Prison Governor. He reminded him that Council met at ten; that he didn't keep a copy of Mr. Drawbridge's engagement book beside him on the breakfast table. He still thought that the Prison Governor was making altogether too much of it.

Mr. Drawbridge, on the other hand, was ready to take it quite seriously.

"Does he, by Jove?" he said, when Mr. Frith told him.

Mr. Drawbridge very deliberately took his time relighting his pipe.

"I thought he might," he added. "Perhaps we ought to get the C.J. to go round and see him."

"The C.J., sir?"

"He may want to make a statement, you know."

"It was you he was asking for, sir."

"Did he say why?"

"Just said he wanted to see you before six o'clock."

"I wonder what's special about six o'clock."

"Nobody seems to know, sir."

Mr. Drawbridge turned to his A.D.C.

"Put it in the book, will you," he said. "I may be a bit late,

353

but that can't be helped. Say I'll be round as near six as I can manage."

When the Chaplain delivered the message, Old Moses was obviously displeased by it. Six o'clock, he kept repeating; six o'clock.

Carrying on a conversation with Old Moses had become difficult. That was because of some ridiculous bones that he kept playing with. Nobody quite knew where they had come from; one of his visitors had given them to him, most probably. The little pieces of bone, bleached white by the sun, were now ivory-colored in places from constant handling. When not in use, they were kept wrapped in an old newspaper in a pouch that Old Moses wore round his middle.

Most of the time, he kept tossing them up in the air, watching carefully how they fell.

The Chaplain asked if he would like to see the Prison Doctor.

There was nothing that any doctor could do for him, Old Moses replied.

Might there be any special food he fancied?

Not any longer: he had given up eating again.

Was there anything else he wanted?

Only Mr. Drawbridge.

Would Old Moses like him to come back later?

No: it was Mr. Drawbridge he was waiting for.

Did he feel like having a passage from the Bible read out to him, or joining the Chaplain in a prayer?

A prayer preferably, he said. But only after he had seen Mr. Drawbridge.

Up went the bones into the air again as he was speaking, and the Chaplain got up to leave him.

When the Chaplain looked back, Old Moses was crouched forward on the floor studying the pattern into which the bones had fallen. It was evidently highly satisfactory, because he was smiling and rubbing his hands over them.

As six o'clock approached, everyone was becoming a bit edgy. Mr. Drawbridge looked like being late, and the Prison Doctor and the Chaplain were there in the cell to keep Old Moses company.

He was seated cross-legged in the center of the floor, the remains of one of his homemade cigarettes between his lips. His bone toys were spread out on the floor in front of him again. And as they watched, they saw Old Moses stick out a long, spidery thumb and begin poking at the farthest of the vertebrae. He twisted it round until the base was facing him. Then he sat back and waited.

It may have been a trick of the light, or the effect of a draft from the cell door, which the Chaplain had left open, but it appeared that the bone turned itself round again. All by itself, it seemed to give a little wriggle in the dust so that once more it could present the narrow part to him.

Old Moses was obviously delighted. He picked the bones up and cuddled them. Holding his cupped hands up to his mouth, he appeared to be speaking to them. Then he tried again. The bones fell as before. He shifted the end one out of position and sat back and waited. This time, the Chaplain distinctly saw the movement. The bone gave a jerk and reversed itself. The Chaplain remained calm: there must be a hair attached to it, or something, he told himself.

The Doctor dismissed the idea of a hair, because there wasn't one: it was all done by static electricity, in his opinion. Rubbing the bones in the hand first was an essential part of it.

When the Prison Governor joined them, he seemed rather surprised that neither the Chaplain nor the Doctor should have recognized what Old Moses was up to. He was laying a curse, he said; and to judge by the time it was taking, it must be a particularly powerful, long-range one. The upcountry Mimbo were famous throughout Africa for their spells and magic: he'd known some of the spells to cause their victims lasting misery and unhappiness. The bones were probably from the tail of a leopard, he added.

But apparently Old Moses had finished. He gathered up the bones and put them back into the pouch. Then he began to hobble over to the bed. He paused before each step like a clockwork toy with the motor beginning to run down, and when he had crossed the room, he could not raise his leg high enough to clamber up onto the mattress. The Chaplain had to go over to help him.

Not that Old Moses seemed to notice. He had squirmed his way under the strip of prison sheeting, and was now huddled close against the wall. His face was pressed up against it. Outside, the wire of the bell hammer tautened, and the prison clock struck the first stroke of six.

When the doctor bent over him to see if he was all right, Old Moses had already stopped breathing. Five minutes later, there were no heartbeats either. Unfolding the single blanket that had been hanging on the bed rail, the doctor spread it over him and covered up his face.

When Mr. Drawbridge arrived, the mortuary bearers had been over. He stood in the doorway, looking at the empty bed.

"Were you with him all the time?" he asked.

"I was," the governor told him.

"Did he say anything?"

"Not really, sir. It was earlier on he was asking for you."

"Do you know what he wanted?"

"It was a request, sir. He asked me to put it to you. He said he would like to be buried in the Christian cemetery. That's where his wives are all buried. He wanted to be with them."

"And what did you tell him?"

"He didn't expect an immediate answer, sir. Just asked if you'd consider it."

"Well, why not?"

The Governor was pulling at the top button of his tunic. It was a nervous habit he had; the button stuck out noticeably farther than the others.

"He *was* a convicted murderer, sir."

"But doesn't the reprieve make any difference?"

Mr. Drawbridge let go of the button and started reaching in his pocket for his pipe.

"What do you say, Chaplain?" he asked. "More your side of the house than mine."

Chapter 55

"DARLING, IT'S marvelous. I adore it. Simply adore it. Really I do."

Her voice sounded tiny and far away. And every time one of the operators pressed his switch down for another caller, fresh bursts of crackling cut across the line; they drowned the words completely.

"I'm wearing it now. I won't ever take it off again. I always hated the one Gardie gave me. It's only that you shouldn't have . . ."

Somewhere, at one of the exchanges, another operator had joined in: the crackling noises became louder and more incessant. Even if she were still speaking, Harold could not hear her.

But at least the ring had got there; and she was actually wearing it. That was something. She had refused, at first, even to discuss it; wouldn't put it on her finger even if he sent her one, she said. It was *secret,* their engagement: surely he saw how important that was, didn't he? If she went round wearing a new ring, everybody would know about it. They might just as well announce it straightaway; and that's what they didn't want.

She had given in at last only because he had been so persistent; and, even then, she had teased him about it. He was behaving like a little boy, she told him: he seemed to think that the marriage wouldn't be legal, or something, if he didn't buy her an engagement ring first. But it was sweet of him, and if he really wanted to that much, of course she'd love it more than anything. She wouldn't take it off for a moment, not even to wash her hands, once she had it.

The crackling began to die down.

"Darling. Darling. Are you there? I can't hear you." For a moment, at least, the line seemed to be working again. "I'm glad it's come. I want to see you wearing it. But there's something else . . ." he started to say.

"I still can't hear you. You've got to talk louder."

"There's something else I want to talk about."

"That's better. But you sound frightfully serious." She paused. "Has . . . has anything gone wrong?"

"It's Old Moses," he told her. "He died this evening."

"Oh." There was a pause again. "Could he talk?"

"He could talk, all right."

"And did he say anything?"

"What about?"

"Oh, just about anything."

"Not that I know of."

"Who was with him?"

"Only the prison people."

"And he didn't say anything?"

It was Lady Anne who sounded serious now.

"He left a message for Mr. Drawbridge, if that's what you mean."

"Why Mr. Drawbridge?"

The line, at least for the time being, was perfect: it might have been a local call that he was making. He could even hear the catch in her voice as she asked the question.

"Thought he was the only one who could help him, I suppose."

"What was the message?"

"About where he was to be buried."

"Was that all?"

"So far as I know."

"Then everything was quite peaceful, was it?"

"I think so."

"I'm glad." There was the same catch in her voice as she said it. "You don't know how glad. I've been feeling so dreadful about him. Shut up in prison like that."

The line began to crackle, and they were cut off from each other. When it was cleared, Lady Anne was speaking again.

"What did he die of?" she asked.

"Old age, the doctor said. Just that."

"Poor old thing," she said. "He must have had a terrible time of it. Ever since the trial, I mean."

"You're very forgiving."

"Why not be? It's all over now, isn't it?"

Her voice sounded different as she said it.

"What's the matter?" he asked.

"It's nothing," she told him. "Really it isn't. I can't help crying. That's all it is. It's just that it's been a bit too much for me."

"It's what we've been waiting for."

"I know." She paused. "And he didn't say anything else?"

"No."

"Just kept everything to himself, and died."

She said the words slowly and reflectively.

"Poor, bewildered old thing," she added.

"Don't go on thinking about it," he told her. "Say you love me."

"You know I do."

"Then when are we going to get married?"

There was no answer. The line was perfectly silent. Harold was afraid that it had gone dead once more.

She was crying: he could hear it.

Then she spoke to him.

"I don't know. I can't tell you. I'm too tired. I can't think properly."

"Listen," he said. "Don't try to talk: just listen. I'm coming down to you. I'm coming straight away. As soon as I can get there."

He heard a quick intake of her breath as he said it.

"D'you mean it? Really mean it? I'd be all right if you were here. It's only when I'm alone I . . ."

It had been an unusually long call already, and long calls always excited curiosity. Section by section, every one of the operators would be listening in by now.

"I love you," he said. "Love you, love you, love you."

Lady Anne's voice sounded somehow calmer when she answered.

"Oh, I'm happy," she said. "I don't deserve it. I just am."

He heard her draw in her breath.

"Will there have to be an inquest?" she asked. "They won't have to go into it all over again, will they?"

Chapter 56

THE GUARD had rolled up his green flag as though it were an umbrella; those passengers without tickets, and large parties traveling with too few, had finally been ejected; and the Coronation Flyer, its brass alarm bell clanging, had started to pull out of Amimbo.

Harold Stebbs leaned back and undid his collar.

Tomorrow, and I'll be there, he was thinking. Only one more night. Then we'll be together again. I should never have left her. It's being alone so much that's done it. She'll be all right once I'm with her. I know she will.

From his corner seat in the front compartment, he could see down the whole length of the platform. There were the Sleeper Reservation hut; the new concrete lavatory, with the OUT OF ORDER notice hanging on the door; the glasswork and flower baskets of the main ticket office; the parcels office, half hidden behind that day's delivery of miscellaneous, unlabeled rubbish.

Because everyone else was waving, Harold lowered the window and waved too.

I'll get her away from here, he thought. Right away, so that she can forget about all this. England, if she likes. Then she can see Timothy. She ought to see him. After all, she's his mother. But get her away from here: that's what matters. And I don't mind where. Not so long as I'm with her.

The Flyer had cleared the switch by the marshaling yard, and the train was gathering speed. It began to rock; the blind tassels were hitting the windows and bouncing back again.

We'll settle down somewhere. It'll all work out. They'll find a job for me. Not back in Amimbo. Can't go back there. Lots of other colonies. Plenty of places going. We'll fit in, wherever it is. Do her good seeing a different set of people.

The door of the compartment opened; it was the restaurant attendant, with the initials of the railway company embroidered on his jacket, who stood there. He was getting to know Harold.

"Tickets for first and second luncheons, sah," he was saying. "Cold beer, mineral waters, spirits . . ."

Harold took the pink slip of paper with the large figure "2" printed on it.

Make a proper home for her. Start living like normal people. Got it all in front of us. Years and years of it. Just Anne and me. Probably raise a family. Might do.

The train had reached the long, uphill curve toward Burindi. There was a three-mile gradient here, and the driver had given the Coronation Flyer all the steam he had. Wiping his forehead with a handful of cotton waste, he was now looking anxiously at the pressure gauge, wondering whether the ancient engine could take it.

Beyond the embankment to the south, the capital city of Amimbo was spread out beneath them. But already it had grown smaller; much smaller. It wasn't like a real township any more: just a colored page out of the guidebook, with the blue dome of the mosque, the Cathedral tower, the vermilion gas tank, and all the trees. Away over to the left, he could see the outline of the Residency, shining white against the green lawns around it. Then the hump of Telegraph Hill cut it off from him; and a moment later, the train had run into a cutting. Amimbo had disappeared.

And that's forever, he told himself. Nothing to go back for now. Have to get the rest of my things sent on somehow. That is, when I know where. Got to be somewhere she likes, of course. Wouldn't do to finish up in some dump or other. Not with her. But no need to worry. I won't let her down. She knows that.

Even though the window opposite was closed, there must have been a draft somewhere: he shivered.

It had been like that the first time he saw Amimbo.

The Anglican church of St. Mark's, Nucca, stood in one of the side streets off the main square. It was a weatherboard building, scarcely larger than a mission hall. Even so, it seemed too big: the eight rows of highly varnished pews behind them were entirely empty.

That, however, was how Lady Anne wanted it.

"Only the two of us," she had kept saying. "And the parson, of course: he's got to be there. Nobody else: it's not their business. Just you and me. It's our wedding, not other people's."

More than once, he had wondered why she wanted to be married in a church at all: back in Amimbo, it had been only memorials and parades and the children's carol service at Christmas that she had ever attended. But when he asked her, she had become upset.

"Because it's important," she had told him. "Very important. I'm older than I was when I married Gardie. I know what I'm doing now. It's different. I want the service, and the ring, and the blessing; all of it." And after being silent for a moment, she had added, "It means a lot to me. It's all got to be right this time. Really right, I mean. Don't forget: it's forever, darling."

And now the English chaplain had closed his prayer book and put back the embroidered bookmark and was asking them to come through to the vestry to sign the register.

Throughout the ceremony, the chaplain had tried to keep the right note of cordiality in his voice; but at heart, he was a bitterly disappointed man.

From the moment Harold had first come to him, he had been planning great things. There were not many Protestants in Catholic Nucca, and he had allowed his imagination to stray a little. He would whip up a choir somehow, he had told himself: have all the old hymns, and let them try their hand at a simple anthem. A full church at last; and a sermon.

And now, in the makeshift built-on vestry, with only the British Consul and the Portuguese housekeeper as witnesses, this dreadful feeling of flatness. In his eyes, the whole affair seemed somehow strangely furtive and clandestine. Even signing the register was an anticlimax. Here in Nucca, a Protestant clergyman had no real standing: in order to make the marriage legally binding, bride and bridegroom had been required to present themselves at the Town Hall on the way round to him.

But there, at least, it was: all filled in and freshly blotted on the yellow, parchmenty paper. In his upright, rather laborious hand, with the big curving loops to the letters, it showed that on the 14th May, 1933, Harold Edward Stebbs, aged twenty-five, single, had married Lady Anne Victoria Hackforth, aged thirty-one, widow, *née* Bowen.

The difference in their ages was not important, the chaplain supposed; not with anyone so strikingly beautiful as Lady Anne. He had never seen eyes quite like hers. There was an inner radiance about them that amazed him: he had noticed it before in the eyes of people who had emerged from great suffering into eventual happiness. The note of true spirituality was something he felt qualified to recognize.

"But I don't want to go back to see Timothy," Lady Anne told him. "It'll only upset both of us. He's much better as he is. He's settled down now."

They were back in the drawing room of the rented villa; Lady Anne had refused to go away from it.

"Of course I don't like it here," she said. "Nobody could. But we're together. That's all that matters. And I don't want to start meeting a lot of other people. Not yet."

And so they had stayed on there, with the jalousies closed against the sunlight; and the Portuguese housekeeper; and the terra-cotta urns on the terrace outside; and all the dust.

"You'll have to leave here sometime," he reminded her.

"Sometime, yes. But not yet." She paused. "I don't want anyone else. I just want you. After all, this is our honeymoon."

She turned and held out her hand toward him.

"You're not getting bored with me already, are you?"

They had been married for three days by now, and it was the second time that she had asked him that question. The first had been when he had said something about the Service; when he had wondered aloud where in the end they would be sending him.

"You know I'm not."

He had taken her hand and was fondling it.

"I don't know anything of the kind," she replied. "It's like being married to Gardie all over again. He couldn't stand just being alone with me either. You don't really want us to go over and see Timothy: it's simply that you want to be doing *something*."

She drew her hand away from him and reached out for another cigarette. The ash tray at her side had a whole lot of stubbed-out, lipsticky cigarettes in it. Some of them were less than half smoked: just lit, and then put down again.

"And I don't want you to think that I blame you, darling," she said. "Because I don't. I know exactly how you feel: you're a man. You've been doing a job, and going about and seeing people. It's different for me: this is all I've been looking forward to."

She suddenly thrust the cigarette down into the other litter in the ashtray. And she was too abrupt about it: the cigarette broke in half between her fingers.

Then she turned to him again.

"The trouble with me is that, now I've got you, I can't make myself believe it."

His arms were round her, and he was kissing her. They were small, gentle kisses; on her hair, her forehead. It might have been a child that he was comforting.

"It was awfully lonely after Sybil left," she said. "And I kept getting so frightened. That's why I began to drink so much." She paused. "You nearly married an alcoholic."

She gave a little laugh as she said it; there was just the faintest trace of huskiness in her voice already.

"I'd like another drink now," she said. "Only I don't want you to leave go of me."

"I'll get you one if you like."

She pressed herself down closer onto him.

"Later," she said. "I don't want to move. I'm too happy."

He was still kissing her; the same, soft caressing kisses. It was growing late. He had heard the footsteps of the Portuguese housekeeper as she had gone up to bed long ago: soon they would be going through themselves into the bedroom. He began to slide his hand down into the open neck of her housecoat.

As he did so, he felt her draw away from him. It was not his touch that she minded: he was sure of that. It was rather as if somehow he had interrupted her, cut across some private thoughts that had been passing through her mind.

"What was I wearing when you came into Gardie's tent?" she asked. "Was it my housecoat? I can't remember little things like that. I've thought about it so much, it's all muddled up by now."

Chapter 57

OVER THE past week, the wedding presents had started to come in; the postman, sheltered from the sun by the large white umbrella that he always carried about with him, kept arriving at the front door, arms laden, like a black St. Nicholas.

The most imposing of the gifts was the one from Mr. Ngono. It was enormous. A great, shining silver-gilt box, it was too large for cigarettes; too large for cigars, even. It was picnic-size. And was obviously very expensive. But it must have been pure love that had prompted it: the entwined initials "A" and "H," with, for some reason, an embossed coronet over them, had been engraved in the center panel.

"Well, I think it's sweet of him. Absolutely sweet of him even to have thought of it," Lady Anne said. "It must have been for your sake he sent it, because I hardly knew him. I don't think he even particularly liked me."

She was looking down at a telegram that the housekeeper had given her. It must have come the day before; telegrams weren't delivered in Nucca after four o'clock.

"Well, this is funny," she said. "Really funny. It's from Tony. And to think that he's the one Gardie had to spy on me. Now he wishes us every happiness; I wonder if he really means it."

"Where is he?"

"It doesn't say. It never does on a telegram. Somewhere on the Continent probably. London might have been a bit awkward for him. He didn't come out of it awfully well, did he?"

She folded up the telegram again and put it down on the pile of letters, greeting cards, other telegrams, all heaped up there on top of the desk.

"They're more than I expected," she said. "We'll have to answer them some time. It'll be ghastly. But it'd be too rude not to."

She was running her finger over them as she said it; and as she did so, she began smiling. It was a half-hidden, private kind of smile.

"I wonder what Gardie would have made of all this if he could have seen it," she remarked. "I think he'd have been rather pleased. He couldn't have borne it if people hadn't noticed. He'd have thought they'd forgotten about him, or something."

Her glass was empty and she held it out toward him. She had been drinking on and off all the evening; had started before dinner because, after the heat of the day, she was always so tired, so suddenly played-out at sundown.

"It doesn't matter having another one like this when we're together, does it?" she asked. "It's only drinking alone that's bad, isn't it?"

She was speaking very fast by now; the sentences came tumbling out one on top of the other. But the tiredness had all gone. There was color in her cheeks, too; and she was wearing her hair loose over her shoulders.

He kissed her when he brought the glass over to her. Then she settled herself back deeper into the cushions. There was something catlike about the way she made herself so comfortable.

"This is what I always knew it would be like," she said. "Just you and me. I knew it'd be all right from the moment you told that lie about us—about not being lovers, I mean. After all, it wasn't any of his business, was it? And it was better for Gardie that way. It kept him right out of it."

She took another sip of the whisky.

"That was when I felt certain you really loved me," she added. "I can still see you standing up there in that little box place. It can't have been nice for you. Because you're not the sort that tells lies, are you? You're like a Boy Scout: you don't approve of them. But everything was all right once you'd said it. I was quite sure then. I knew you'd be ready to go through with it."

"Go through with it?"

There was the sound of a siren from the direction of the harbor: the two short blasts of a steamer that was leaving.

"I don't know why it makes me so sad when I hear it," she said. "But it does. It means the ending of things. It was worse hearing it in the night when I was all alone. That's when I always thought about killing myself."

She was smiling again.

"I suppose I was lucky Gardie didn't kill me first. But that wasn't the way his mind worked. He was always so careful. He liked planning everything. That was his trouble. He planned once too often."

She had leaned back, and her hands were clasped behind her head, rumpling up her hair. She was staring up at the ceiling.

"Gardie wasn't all that bad, though," she said quietly. "Not right through and through. There were *some* nice things about him. It's just that we weren't right for each other. And that's what is so strange. Because he rather liked women: they always made such a fuss over him."

She had dropped her voice while she was speaking; it was so low that he could scarcely hear her. And when he looked across at her, he could see that her eyes were closed. She seemed to have forgotten about him; seemed simply to be thinking a whole lot of her thoughts out loud.

"But I don't think he was ever once unfaithful. It would have taken up too much of his time. And he'd never have let that happen. He was always working. That was half the trouble. He hardly came near me again after Timothy was born. He'd got what he wanted."

Her eyes were open again; she had turned her head slightly and was watching him.

"D'you realize that we probably wouldn't be here, not like this, if he'd needed me even a little bit more."

"I need you."

She did not seem to have heard him.

"After all, I was only eighteen when I had Timothy. That wasn't exactly ancient. I didn't even want a baby; not particularly, that is. I just wanted to be loved. There's nothing unnatural in that, is there? So I had to find somebody when Gardie wouldn't. Only they weren't always awfully nice people. I wish now I hadn't."

She sat up and was facing him.

"Miles wasn't the first, I mean. That's what I'm trying to say. You don't think I'm wicked, do you? Not *really* wicked, I mean?"

The words had come all in a rush as though it were something that had been in her mind for a long time, the one question that she had to ask.

Harold sat there, staring past her.

"I don't think about it at all," he said. "I don't want to."

There was a rustle from the couch, and she came over to him.

"I didn't have to tell you, did I? I only did it because I love you so much. It just wouldn't have been right to have any secrets between us."

She was standing in front of him, smoothing back her hair. He noticed that she was swaying slightly.

"But all that's over. I shall be as good as gold from now on. We won't ever talk about it again. There's no need to."

The gilt clock on the mantlepiece struck one: they'd sat up a long time talking.

Lady Anne pushed her foot up against his.

"Give me another drink," she said. "And then we'll go to bed. I feel all at peace inside me. That's because I've told you everything."

He was careful about the drink that he poured her. There was not much whisky in it; just enough for her to feel that she hadn't actually been refused it. And she didn't seem to notice the pale straw color when he gave it to her.

She was smiling to herself again.

"It might quite easily have been the other way round," she said. "If he'd had his way, all those presents would have been for Gardie and his new wife. He was still frightfully attractive, you know. He'd have got married again for certain, if I hadn't killed him."

The hands of the clock showed two-fifteen.

She got up and went over to the window, standing there with her back against the closed shutters. It was as far away from him as possible.

"Well, what are you going to do?" she asked. "Hand me over to the police, or something?"

She was calm now; perfectly calm. Only the catch in her voice showed that she had been drinking; but that had been earlier, much earlier.

"Don't," he told her. "You can't know what you're saying."

She laughed; it was a hard, unpleasant little laugh.

"That's what Sybil was always telling me," she said. "That's why she wouldn't let me see anyone."

"She was only trying to protect you."

There was that same high-pitched laugh.

"No, she wasn't. She didn't want other people to know about *her*." She paused. "Sybil was in this too, you know. She was just longing for something to happen to Gardie. She used to keep on about it all the time. Then we could go away together, she said: that's what she was waiting for. She prayed something would happen."

"That didn't mean she wanted anyone to kill Gardie."

Lady Anne raised her eyebrows.

"He's dead, isn't he? Somebody must have killed him."

She was still standing there, pressed up against the shutters; the whole length of the room was between them.

"It was Old Moses who killed him," Harold said.

He spoke very slowly so that she could hear every word he was saying: so that she could remember every word.

"They arrested him. They tried him. There was a jury. They found him guilty. Old Moses didn't even appeal when the judge sentenced him."

Lady Anne did not laugh this time; she just spread her hands wide open to show the sheer hopelessness of trying to convince him.

"How could he? It was all over by then. It was all over for him as soon as it happened."

"He could have denied it."

"And let me be hanged?"

She gave that little laugh again.

"You didn't know Old Moses like I did. He could never have let that happen. He loved Gardie too much: Gardie was Master. Besides, he was afraid of Gardie's spirit. He knew if he said anything it would come back and haunt him."

"Not if he was innocent."

Her hands were still spread out. She was speaking quite quietly now; reasoning with him.

"Gardie wouldn't have wanted everyone to know that his own wife had murdered him, would he?" she said. "People would have started talking: they'd have said that there must be a reason. Dying in the course of duty was quite different. Gardie wouldn't have minded it that way."

"Old Moses couldn't have known that."

Lady Anne was silent for a moment.

"I think he did," she said.

Harold passed his handkerchief across his forehead. Even though in Nucca it got quite cool, chilly even, after nightfall, he was sweating.

"Old Moses is dead," he told her. "And Gardie's dead, too. They're both dead."

There was a sudden movement from the window where Lady Anne was standing.

"But Sybil isn't."

She started to come forward as she said it.

"Ask her. She knows. She saw it all happen. I was still standing right behind Gardie when she came in. That's when I got all that blood on me. She had to burn the housecoat. She told me so."

She had come close to him now; he was looking full into those fine, dark eyes of hers. Only they weren't particularly fine to-night: the whites were all bloodshot from the crying, or the tobacco smoke, or the whisky, or whatever it was.

"And I thought you knew all the time," she said. "That's what makes it so funny." She gave that little laugh again. "After all, I only did it for your sake. I had to stop him sending that letter."

"What letter?"

For a moment she stood there, not answering. Her hand was up to her forehead and she was frowning.

"Then that's something else you don't know," she said. "You'd better read it. I've kept it just as it was when he was writing it. I don't need it any more. It's all yours now."

EPILOGUE, PART TWO

Absolution, Almost

THE CHIEF Magistrate took out his spectacle case, opened it, and began wiping the lenses; in that heat, they had steamed up in his pocket while he had been sitting there talking.

"You still think it's necessary?"

The man opposite nodded. He didn't say anything; just pushed the envelope closer and sat back in his chair again, waiting. He seemed composed enough.

Ever since he had asked the question, the C.M. had been staring at him across the table. But he could not see his expression. All that he could make out in the semidarkness was the black triangle of the eye patch and the white, neatly clipped moustache.

The pressure lamp made a shrill, hissing sound as the C.M. turned it up. The Governor had shifted himself round a little, sheltering his good eye from the sudden brightness.

"It's sealed down, y'know. I'll have to break it," the C.M. said.

As he inserted his finger, pieces of the red wax went scattering over the bare table top. He brushed the larger fragments aside. It was a single sheet of paper that the envelope contained: a single sheet, folded over and discolored.

The C.M. spread it out in front of him, smoothing down the ridges with his finger tips.

"It's badly stained," he said.

"He was still writing the letter when it happened," the Governor told him.

The C.M. drew his hand away rather hurriedly; he was, however, by nature difficult to convince.

"It doesn't look like blood."

The Governor gave a rather weary little sigh.

"It's been a long time drying."

The C.M. was peering down at the paper again.

"Some of the words are quite blotted out," he observed. "They're indecipherable."

"Hold it up to the lamp. It's easier that way."

With the light coming through the paper, the words showed up plainly enough; it might have been only yesterday that Sir Gardnor had written them. There was no mistaking the handwriting; it was a distinctly elegant script, with something of a flourish to it. In his heyday, Sir Gardnor's penmanship had been very much admired. The date at the top of the Government House notepaper was 14th May, 1931.

"Read it out loud," Harold told him.

"Dear Mr. Raymond," the C.M. began.

"That was Raymond of Raymond and Walsh," Harold said quietly. "They were his solicitors."

The C.M. was tilting the notepaper a trifle, so that the light could penetrate into the creases.

He pursed his lips and went on reading; to himself, this time.

"So he wanted a divorce; was that it?"

"That's what it says."

The C.M. screwed up his eyes and bent his head down lower over the paper.

"And you were the one he was going to cite."

Harold nodded.

"But I thought you said he didn't want a scandal."

374

"Not while India was still on, he didn't. That's what I was explaining. It was different when he knew he'd lost. He didn't mind after that."

The C.M. was reading to himself again. He did not look up until he had reached the end of the sentence.

"Then Lady Anne was right about the A.D.C. He *had* been spying on you."

"All the time. He couldn't very well have refused. H.E. knew too much about him."

There was still a little gin left in the bottle. The C.M. poured it out for both of them.

Then he went on reading.

"There's something about no marital relations," he said at last. "I can't really make it out: it's all smudged. It appears to suggest Miss Prosser as a witness." He paused. "That might have been a mistake, mightn't it? I understood she was on Lady Anne's side."

"It would have come to the same thing. She wanted the marriage broken up. She was jealous."

The C.M. did not seem even to have heard the reply. He was frowning slightly.

"If the letter had gone off, it would have ruined you, wouldn't it?" he asked. "Ruined your career, that is. You'd have had to leave the Service."

"Yes: I'd have been thrown out."

The C.M. was still frowning.

"There is, of course, the other side. This letter would have affected Lady Anne as well. There'd have been a new will. And fresh provisions for the child, no doubt. Lady Anne would have been left far worse off. She had a powerful motive."

Harold started forward.

"That wasn't why she did it."

The C.M. did not reply immediately; he was brushing the smaller fragments of sealing wax into a little heap.

"Have you shown this to anyone else?" he asked at last.

"You're the first person to have seen it."

"Then why show me *now?*"

"I couldn't any earlier. Not while my wife was still alive."

The answer was clearly unsatisfactory. The C.M. began tapping the table with his forefinger.

"But your wife's been dead for a long time, hasn't she? Ten, twelve years it must be."

"There was Timothy," Harold reminded him. "It wouldn't have been very nice for him if all this had come out."

"And now it doesn't matter?"

"Not any longer. It was there when I got back. My *Times,* I mean. I saw it in the Deaths. That's why I came over."

He broke off and seemed to be working out some sort of calculation in his mind.

"Forty-six, it said. That makes it about right. He was still at prep school last time I saw him."

He passed his hand across his face as though wiping something invisible away.

"There's no one else left to worry about."

The C.M. seemed rather quick to fasten on the point.

"That's what I was thinking," he said. "They're *all* dead now."

"There's one that isn't."

The C.M. raised his eyebrows.

"And what can he do?"

He studied Harold very carefully as he asked the question. There was a sense of urgency about him, an eagerness almost, which was unusual.

"Make a statement," he replied. "On oath. Put it right for the record."

"To what purpose?"

"Clear Old Moses. That's one thing."

"And the other?"

"My own conscience," he said. "I've had to live with this."

There was silence again. They remained there, not speaking, with the lamp and the letter and the Gordon's gin bottle between them.

Then the C.M. gave a little cough.

"You retire some time next year, don't you?" he asked.

"First of September." He paused. "I feel about ready for it."

The C.M. had pulled his pencil out of his pocket and thrust it sideways into his mouth with the point sticking out on one side and the stub end on the other. It was a gesture with which counsel were familiar when the C.M. was pondering.

Then he flicked his nail across the letter.

"Will you leave this with me?" he asked.

The sigh that Harold gave was a long one; there was sheer relief, almost contentment, in it.

"It's all in your hands now," he said. "I've done my bit."

He got up from the table as he was speaking and laid his hand on the Chief Magistrate's arm. The C.M. was rather surprised how firmly he was gripping it.

"You don't blame me, do you?" he asked. "Clearing out like that, I mean. But I couldn't have gone on, could I? Not living with her on Gardie's money. That's why I never saw her again. I left her that same night. And that's why I can't forgive myself. Just when she needed me most, I walked out on her. I let her down, didn't I? That's what you must be thinking."

The C.M. did not go to bed when Harold had left him. He lowered the flame in the pressure lamp and sat on there, with the letter still open on the table in front of him and his pencil stuck between his lips again.

He was getting on toward retirement age himself; had a whole lifetime's experience of the law behind him. He had long ago ceased to be surprised by anything that was told him, in court or out of it; so long as there were human beings around, the most unexpected things were bound to go on happening.

By the time the C.M. heard about them, it was always too late to do anything; what was left was to assess the consequences. On the bench there were, of course, the rules to help him: his task was not too difficult. The system worked. It was only when moral judgments were called for that he realized how hopeless, how impossible, it all was. That was why he wished that Harold had never asked him that final question.

What else was there that Harold could have done? he asked himself. It was sheer common sense to have left her. On any showing, he was far better shut of the woman: she had been too much mixed up with Fate already.

Not that he was necessarily condemning Lady Anne. There

had been pressures on her too. In a sense, she had been driven to it. Indeed, in their separate ways, every one of them had been driven: that was what made it so difficult to disentangle.

And come to think of it, they were all much nicer people than Harold made them sound; Harold himself included. The C.M. saw quite clearly that he could make out a case for every one of them. A good case, too. And the underlying motive, even though they would have been unaware of it, was an uncommon one: it was loyalty.

Take Sir Gardnor, for instance. His loyalty had been to the Crown. Rather than allow any scandal, he had been prepared to see his wife sleeping around with anyone she could get hold of. And what had he done about it? Nothing at first; simply closed his bedroom door on her.

Admittedly, it was a rather ugly sort of ambition that had driven him: nothing less than sheer greed to reach the top. And India *was* the top. That was why he had stuck it out so long, with the knowledge that his whole household staff was laughing at him behind his back. To a man who, over the years, had been prepared to endure all that, even the thought of murder—and the C.M. was inclined to accept Lady Anne's version of the shooting accident that had cost Harold his eye—was quite understandable. Sir Gardnor would simply have told himself that he was doing the right thing: defeating the gossipmongers.

And Lady Anne. She was by no means the first frustrated, highly sexed young woman whose affairs had, in the end, come up to him. The courts were full of her sort all the time. And they were not necessarily unpleasant females. When they found someone to satisfy them, they were ready to go to any lengths to protect him. Poison was the method they usually employed; but with the hysterical type, stabbing—or shooting—fell recognizably within the pattern. Harold would have been quite right: when she killed her husband, Lady Anne would not have been thinking about herself for a single moment.

The C.M. stretched out his legs and found himself wondering what, in her prime, Lady Anne had really been like. There must have been something rather remarkable about her. Otherwise, why should anyone as solid and dependable as Harold have been ready to betray his own employer, and then ruin the rest of his life by covering up for her afterwards?

The C.M. only dimly remembered the pictures of Lady Anne at the time; what was far clearer was the one they had printed with the obituary. He recalled quite plainly the large, rather startling eyes and all that carefully waved white hair.

About Sybil Prosser he was not so sure: she sounded like a singularly unprepossessing sort of person. Not nice, in any sense. But certainly loyal. Even ready to make the sacrifice of giving up what she had fought so hard to get; she couldn't have liked doing it, even though she knew she'd lost.

Best of the whole lot, of course, was Old Moses. The C.M. dismissed out of hand the idea of fear of Gardie's spirit. After all, there were plenty of ways of fooling and defeating disgruntled spirits; for a fee, any good witch doctor could have seen to that.

No: there was much more to it than fear. Old Moses had really loved Sir Gardnor; had loved everything that belonged to him. Those belongings included Lady Anne, and the memory that Sir Gardnor was leaving behind him. Rather than see anything go wrong with either of them, Old Moses had been prepared to offer up himself.

Admittedly, he had been well over eighty at the time; nobody knew quite how old. But those last few years had presumably been precious; nobody, black or white, really likes bringing the shutters down.

Then there was Harold himself. He had been, the C.M. would have thought, exactly cut out for an even, uneventful sort of life. The C.M. doubted very much whether he had really wanted to get mixed up with Lady Anne in the first place: it had been merely one of those things that happen. And, with a foot-loose, good-looking woman a little older than himself, he'd probably never stood a chance; wouldn't even have suspected at first what forces he was really up against.

But it had lasted a long time. There must have been moments—in between seeing her, for instance—when he could have seen the way things were going; the kind of chances he was taking with his life. It would have been perfectly in character if he had simply decided to cut his losses and drop out. He hadn't done so, however. Not that there was anything particularly loyal about that; sheer weakness, rather.

The loyalty had come right at the end, when it was all over; that was what made it so extraordinary. And he had certainly paid the price for it. No family; no home life; no love even. Just going on, solitary and uncaring, through all those years in the Service, being shifted from one post to another until he had finished up at last in Kubanda.

It was down somewhere at the bottom of the list of British colonial possessions, Kubanda: a second-rate, down-at-heel protectorate really, with one silted-up harbor and no hinterland. But if it had been any bigger, the C.M. reflected, Harold Stebbs would probably never have got his Governorship.

As it was, he had been left there, only halfway up the ladder, waiting; waiting, watching himself grow old, and turning eagerly to the Deaths column whenever a fresh batch of *The Times* arrived from home. With what object? Simply in order to make this futile, uncalled-for statement that he had set his heart on: to tell a policeman, as it were, and put his mind at rest.

The C.M. got to his feet and winced as he began to straighten himself. Flexing the toes upwards was the only cure he knew when cramp caught him; it quite often came on when he had been sitting for too long in one position. He was still hobbling when he went through to the sideboard in the dining room and came back with the big brass tray that the boy used for bringing round the drinks.

The tray was so large that he had to move the Gordon's bottle and the water jug and the empty glasses before there was room for it on the table top. And even then, it half covered up Sir Gardnor's letter and the long, official-looking envelope.

He pulled the letter out, holding it between his thumb and forefinger, and with the light of the pressure lamp shining down on him, he proceeded to tear the Government House notepaper into long, narrow strips. The paper was so old it was quite brittle; little pieces, the black ones particularly, broke off as he tore at it. Then he shredded down the envelope and dropped the remains of it on top. It looked as if a wastepaper basket had been emptied there.

He was prepared to burn the bits one by one, holding them out taper fashion. But when he struck a match and tried it, the whole pile ignited; dry like that, it kindled immediately. The paper bonfire blazed up, darkening one side of the porcelain lamp shade with its smoke, and died down again. All that was now left on the tray was a charred and fragile skeleton, the kind of relic that a bush fire leaves behind it.

He went through to the veranda, down the steps, and out onto the lawn of the small garden. In the small hours, there was always a wind blowing off the sea in Kubanda; and when he lifted the tray and shook it, a dense, sooty dust cloud blew past him. It was gone; all gone. Nothing now remained on which to base any reasonable confession.

The C.M. felt rather pleased with himself. What he had just done was clearly so sensible. Suppressing that last piece of evidence had not worried him in the slightest. Not now that it was all over. It would have been awkward, of course, if the Governor had brought it to him while Lady Anne was still alive. Then he would have had to consider it. As it was, he had saved everyone a great deal of unnecessary trouble. And above all, he had prevented people from talking. A Colony was a terrible place for malicious, ill-informed tittle-tattle. Once started, it would go through the place like an epidemic.

Besides, after all those years in Africa, the Governor deserved a decent retirement: some proper rest and quiet when he got back to England; even a little happiness and contentment if he could find it.

The C.M. himself still had some time to go before retirement. He was comfortable enough as things were. And there was always the chance that the next train from Motamba would bring the new fan that Stores had ordered. Or, if not the next train, the one after; or the one after that.